PRAYING FOR WAR

The Collin War Chronicles Book One
By
W.C. Hoffman and Tim Moon

HAGS 4 LiFE !

W C Hoffman

This is a work of fiction. All of the characters, organizations, products, and events are either products of the author's imagination or are used fictitiously. Any similarity to real persons, living or dead, is purely coincidental and not intended by the authors.

ISBN-10:1533548056
ISBN-13:978-1533548054

DEDICATION

To our families.
Thank you for always believing in us.

Praying for War is proudly brought to you by,
HAGS
For Life

CHAPTER 1

Collin War was still, but the bed he lay in shook violently.

At the furthest reaches of his awareness, Collin felt the movement rattle through his spine. His teeth chattered gently behind his lips.

A rhythmic beeping sounded lightly in the distance. As he listened, the sound grew nearer and nearer. He felt like he was lying in a boat, being thrown about by waves.

Collin's eyes fluttered briefly and dull light glanced through his lashes. The beeping sound continued buzzing loudly nearby. He turned slowly to the left and looked at the source of the noise.

On a thin, metal pole hung a machine glowing faintly with green light. A bright dot raced across the screen, occasionally jumping up and down, leaving a trail of fading light behind it. He couldn't remember what the machine was, but he had a vague understanding it was a good sign. Normal.

He scowled at the machine then glanced down at his chest. His body was covered in thin sheets and a ratty, old blanket. He was wearing an unfamiliar, blue garment that was too thin for the cool air. A pair of wires were attached to his left arm and he felt something attached to his chest. He struggled as he looked around at his surroundings. Collin pushed himself up to his elbows to get a better look.

The room was dark and barren. He couldn't see much beyond the immediate area around his bed, other than a dull, yellow light that gleamed through a small window set into the door to his room. It cast a diseased, amber glow in the room.

A scream. Piercing and mixed with pain.

Collin shot up in bed. His movement pulled the cords connecting him to the machine. Instinctively, Collin jerked away from the sensation, his heart raced with a shot of adrenaline. The green light accelerated, beeping in time with the thumping in his chest as the metal pole was yanked, tipping and crashing to the ground.

Another scream echoed through the room, but this time it was joined by others. A chorus of tortured souls calling out for relief.

Collin feverishly pulled the wires off of his chest and arms. He started to tug at one on the back of his hand and realized it was an IV. He slowed down briefly, extracting the needle with care. He pressed down on the tape that held the needle in place to slow blood from the hole in his vein from welling up.

With a quick look around the large, dingy room, Collin swung his legs out of the bed. They ached with disuse. He ran a hand over one of his

1

thighs. It felt thinner than he was used to. But he felt no pain and couldn't find any injuries.

There was a loud boom. A rumble sounded through the building and everything shook. The windows rattled lightly in their frames. The metal bed shifted against the floor, squeaking loudly against the tile floor, making Collin cringe. Dust dislodged and rained down on him as he slid off the mattress and ducked beside it. Dust tickled his nose and throat. He buried his face in his elbow in an attempt to muffle any coughing or sneezing that would give away his position.

The building rollicked for several long seconds.

Earthquake? He wondered. Collin glanced over the edge of the bed, waving his hand to clear the air and watching the window in the door. Suddenly, all the lights snapped off, leaving Collin enveloped in darkness.

His eyes strained to pull in enough light to make out his surroundings.

Nothing.

In his mind, Collin had fixed the location of the door. This place was clearly not safe. He knew he had to leave, but had no idea where he was or where to go.

His legs quivered slightly as he stood. Collin steadied himself and took a moment to test his muscles and take stock of his physical condition. He was in no immediate danger, so he channeled his experience from years of exercise and physical activity where he learned to isolate and flex most muscles like a bodybuilder, but without striking goofy poses.

Collin started by wiggling his toes before moving up to his calves. So far, so good. He moved on to his quadriceps. Flex and release. Then his hamstrings. Flex and release.

After a few seconds of this routine, Collin quickly determined he was indeed weaker than he remembered, but not dangerously so. He wasn't injured in any obvious way, despite being in some sort of hospital; he felt fine, if a bit weak. He knew he'd be able to run, dodge, and jump, or defend himself should the need arise. His senses were on high alert and he felt a tiny swirl of panic in the back of his chest, but he held it at bay and channeled his focus. The way he was…trained to? He wasn't sure.

Focus, he told himself.

The door.

Collin heard noises outside as he felt his way around the bed and slowly walked, slightly crouched, toward the door of the room. He held a hand out in front of him searching for obstacles. He found none.

Another blood-curdling scream pierced the air. Collin winced. It tugged at fuzzy, half-forgotten memories at the edge of his consciousness.

Collin counted eight steps before his fingers bumped into something hard. Collin stopped walking and carefully felt the object. It was the wall. He felt around quietly for the door frame. The wall was mostly smooth, but he could feel dust accumulating on his palm and fingers.

Unusual for a hospital, if that is in fact where I am, he thought.

A moment later, Collin felt the edge of the door frame to his right. He slid over and found the door handle. He rested his hand on the handle, but didn't turn it. Collin's instincts told him to check the hallway first.

The only remaining light was a small splash of orange light on the wall. It flickered and partially illuminated the hallway, but he could not make out the source of it. All he could see was a barren hallway. At some point, an overhead light popped out of place and hung at an angle in the middle of the hallway. Farther down the hall, debris was scattered across the black and white tiled floor.

It looked clear.

Time to go, he thought.

Glass shattered behind Collin, tinkling on the hard tile floor.

He whirled around in a defensive crouch that came to him instinctively, leaving the door closed behind him.

Two people, large men judging by their bulk, smashed through the windows from ropes. A wave of cold night air flooded the dark room. Collin's flimsy nightgown fluttered in the breeze and his skin tingled as goose bumps raced across his arms.

The men lazily swept the room with flashlights that appeared to be attached to their rifles, but neither of them spotted Collin because their lights were obscured by the bed and their own carelessness. Collin scowled in disgust. He hated sloppy work.

Apparently satisfied there was no immediate threat, the two men focused on steadying themselves on the glass-strewn floor while disconnecting from their ropes.

Collin didn't wait for them to find him. Better to take advantage of the few precious seconds of surprise he had left.

He rushed forward in a crouch.

As he closed the short distance, Collin began to make out details. They wore dark military or police-style clothing and motorcycle helmets. Each man carried a rifle, from what he could see they looked like M4 carbines.

One man had detached from the rope, but he was two strides beyond the other man. Collin sprinted, dipping his shoulder as he plowed into the closest man, who dropped his rifle and tumbled to the ground in a tangle of rope and limbs. Collin continued with the forward momentum and kicked the second man in the knee, just as he was raising his rifle.

The weak joint sounded off with a satisfying crunch as tendons snapped and the patella was driven into the joint. A howl erupted from within the man's helmet. Collin dipped his head to the side and swept the rifle barrel aside with his right forearm to avoid getting shot, while grabbing the stock with his left hand. Collin's large hand clamped down over the other man's hand pinning it to the rifle. Collin gave a short jerk toward himself and then shoved the rifle hard at the man. The force of the blow shattered the visor of the helmet, opening a hole and exposing half of the man's bearded face.

It did no damage to the man, but it stunned him and freed the rifle from his grip. Shock and pain were evident on the man's face. A foul odor filled the air and Collin realized that his foe might have pissed his pants. Collin glanced over and saw the man he knocked over untangling himself from the rope.

A dark scowl creased Collin's face. These were no professionals. Only an amateur would drop his rifle and fumble like an idiot for so long.

Collin kicked the injured man hard in the chest. His bare foot tingled with the shock, but it didn't hurt him nearly as much as it did the other guy. Then, he took two short steps and swung the rifle like a baseball bat right into the man's lower back.

He groaned, clutching at his back, as if that would help him, and crumbled to his knees. Collin kicked him so he sprawled on the floor, helpless and vulnerable. Then he stomped hard on the man's ankle to disable him. Another crunch reached Collin's ears. He felt strangely satisfied at his handy work, despite not knowing how or why he was doing it. Instinct was carrying him through the motions.

Holding one rifle already, Collin picked up the other one and carefully made his way to the broken windows, dodging most of the broken glass along the way. Collin swung the rifles and flung them out the window.

Whatever was going down, he'd be better off fighting silently than shooting his way out of a building filled with an unknown number of hostiles. And he sure as hell wasn't going to leave the weapons with the two guys writhing on the floor - disabled or not.

A sharp pain suddenly pierced the back of his head and radiated behind his ears. Collin held the back of his head; his eyes squeezed shut, as he gasped at the pain. Moments later, as Collin settled his racing heartbeat, the pain was gone just as quick as it came on. His breaths came in heavy pants. He slowly ran his hands through his hair, rubbing his scalp, and wondered what was wrong with him.

Collin looked down at the men moaning on the floor. He walked over and bent down cautiously near the guy with the broken leg. Collin noticed a knife earlier and decided he wanted it.

Thankfully, the man had forgotten to use the blade himself. Definitely not professional. Collin wasn't sure how he knew that, but he was as certain of it as he was about his own name.

Collin grabbed the handle of the knife and pulled it out. The man stammered inside his helmet. His one exposed eye was wide with fear. But Collin didn't kill him.

Instead, he stood up and quickly walked over to the door. He peered out the small window in the door, double-checking that the way was still clear. Everything looked the same, so he pulled the door open and crept out into the hallway. Collin held onto the door with one hand, and slowly eased it shut behind him.

He crouched and turned sideways to make himself a small target, holding the knife in a strong hammer grip by his side, ready to strike.

He moved down the darkened hallway, staying to the right of center.

An open doorway off to his right caught his attention. Collin slowed, peeked around the corner, saw it was an empty room and kept moving. There was a faint orange glow, also on his right, down a connecting hallway. Collin glanced around but couldn't see an exit sign or stairwell. He'd have to find his way out the hard way, like a rat in a maze.

A door slammed open. Shoes slapped against the floor; someone was running. Collin froze where he was.

"Run," a woman's voice yelled. The pace of the running increased noticeably as they obeyed the command.

"Come here, bitch," a man's voice said.

Then a short squeal echoed off the walls. Grunting and dull thumps followed it.

"Oh, God," another woman groaned. Her voice sounded choked up with tears.

Collin stayed crouched, but continued forward to get eyes on the situation.

Shadows danced on the wall to Collin's left, backlit by the orange glow. He could now make out the scent of burning wood, but it didn't seem like the whole building was burning, because the flames hadn't grown since he entered the hallway.

Collin stayed at an arm's reach from the wall and leaned his head out to see what was happening. He was mildly surprised to see another pair of men in black uniforms with matching helmets. One woman was on the floor with a man straddling her. The man hunched over, leaning on his left hand, which clamped firmly on her throat. His other hand moved in short, fast strokes as he stabbed her in the side.

A half-second later, the second man caught the other woman and flung her to the floor, next to her friend. The nurse recoiled from the pool of blood, but it was everywhere. The two women's eyes met. She screamed.

Her fellow nurse was already dead.

Collin took a step forward to help the woman.

"Why? I didn't do anything," she pleaded with her attacker. "Please, n-"

The man plunged the knife into her throat and tore viciously to the side. The nurse gurgled as her blood rushed out onto the floor, mixing with that of her co-worker.

Collin cursed and quickly retreated to his hiding spot.

It wasn't that he had never seen such things happen before, he knew he had. Yet, he was still shocked at the situation. His heart ached at the pain he'd seen etched into the face of the women.

What was happening? Who were these men in black? Where the hell was he?

Since he was too late to help the women, Collin opted to continue down the hallway. Both men were so engrossed in the revelry of their murder that they wouldn't notice him.

He heard the noise behind him a split-second too late. A well-muscled arm snaked around his neck, jerked his head back, and the cool metal of a knife blade pressed against his windpipe.

"Drop the knife," a man's voice whispered in his ear.

Collin reluctantly complied.

Slowly, the man forced Collin around so he was pressed up against the wall. The two men were face to face.

"What's your name?" asked the man. His voice was rough and his breath was hot against Collin's neck. A disturbing sensation.

Collin knew he could refuse to answer the man, but that would probably enrage him. An angry man with a knife to his throat didn't bode well for his future.

A voice in Collin's head told him to do whatever it took to survive; make it to the next second and see what happens.

Collin asked, "What's *your* name, asshole?"

The man shoved Collin against the wall, as some sort of retribution.

"What's your name?" the man yelled. "Tell me your name."

Collin heard footsteps and could make out the forms of the two men he assumed had been stabbing the nurses walk over to investigate.

Caught off guard, the man holding Collin flinched in surprise. He whirled to the left with Collin held in front of him like a human shield. Big mistake.

As he did so, the man lowered the knife from Collin's neck and held it out to ward off the newcomers. That was his second mistake.

Collin twisted violently against the momentum and grasped the knife hand with both of his. He griped the wrist as hard as he could. Then Collin pivoted left, thrust his hips out and flung the man over his back, snapping the arm and freeing the knife in the process.

The two newcomers backed up as the body flew in their direction.

Collin now had control of the knife. He charged the closer of the two men, the one on his left.

His enemy held up his hands in a weak attempt to fend off the sudden charge. Collin batted the man's arms aside with his forearm. With the same arm, he launched a palm strike that pushed the enemy's head back, exposing his neck, where the knife sunk deep until Collin felt the blade of the knife grind against the man's spine. He withdrew the knife without hesitating and pivoted on the ball of his bare foot to face the last attacker.

Behind Collin, his enemy slumped to the floor choking to death on his own blood.

The other man was slow to react but he was still holding his knife, which he raised in front of him. The blade quivered with fear, flicking droplets of the nurse's blood on the floor.

Collin feinted right. The lone man thrust out wildly with his knife hand to block a strike that never materialized. Instead, he gasped in pain as his knife clattered to the ground.

Collin slashed the man's forearm deep across the muscle and tendons, disabling his hand. Collin followed through with his attack, stepping forward, throwing an arm around his enemy's shoulders and stabbing him quickly in the side, just under his ribs. The blade penetrated deep into the man's body in rapid succession, slicing tissue, severing veins and puncturing both the kidney and liver. Dark blood poured out of the wounds and splashed on the tile.

Collin followed the man, as he collapsed to the floor, into a pool of his own blood. He knelt on the man's back as an unearthly groan escaped his throat. He clutched at his side in a feverish attempt to plug all of the holes in his body.

Too much noise, Collin thought.

Collin set his slippery, blood-drenched knife behind the man where he couldn't reach it, and pulled off his helmet. Collin pulled the man's head up so his back was arched, grasped it firmly, and twisted hard until he heard the crack of the cervical vertebrae. Then he twisted again for good measure.

Collin picked up the knife, wiped it off on the man's shirt and stood up.

Realizing the first guy hadn't been neutralized, Collin looked around for him, but he was gone. Collin stood and looked down the hallway that came in from the right, the one with the orange glow.

Around the corner was the nurses' station. Two bodies lay splayed out on the floor. The women he'd seen these bastards murder.

Holding his broken arm close to his chest, the man seemed to be staring at something in the nurses' station. Collin couldn't see what it was, because it was behind the counter. Not that it really mattered.

Suddenly, the man reached in and grabbed something with his good hand.

"No," a woman shouted.

Collin's eyes grew wide. A survivor.

Collin padded down the hall, then sprinted the last few feet. He dropped into a baseball slide and slashed across the back of the man's ankle, severing his Achilles' tendon, just above the edge of his shoe.

The man screamed in shock and pain. His leg drooped at an odd angle, freed from its anchoring foot.

Collin stood up and looked down at himself. He was soaked from sliding through the nurses' blood that covered the mess from his own victims. He staggered back against the wall, breathing heavy. He just killed two men and debilitated two others. All without thought. Or hesitation.

Somehow, he knew that it was not the first time he'd fought...and killed. However, he had no memory of learning the techniques he used to take their lives.

He needed to get out of this place. He needed to escape. Collin's eyes darted around, seeking an exit.

His eyes caught movement. Frightened eyes peered over the edge of the nurses' station, staring at him. Collin stared back. Seeing the fear he felt reflected in another's eyes was oddly calming.

Collin took a deep breath and pushed off the wall. He looked down at the man wailing on the floor. Then Collin noticed the orange light he noticed earlier was from a small barrel fire at the end of the hall, where the nurses came from.

Collin cocked an eyebrow at the oddity. It was so out of place, but then again, he'd been attacked in a mysterious hospital-like facility, making his frame of reference wildly skewed.

He looked back at the woman. She was beautiful. Young and sweet looking.

"You're lucky. You know that, right?" he asked softly, looking at the woman after glancing at the two nurses on the floor.

The woman stood up, but didn't look down at her friends. Tears glistened in her eyes.

"They would have killed you too, you know," Collin said. "Or worse."

She looked at him and glanced down pointedly at the knife in his hand. She still hadn't spoken.

"How do I get out of here?" Collin stepped toward the woman. He stepped over the man still groaning on the floor.

She backed up.

"It's okay. I won't hurt you," he said. He moved his knife hand behind his back and she seemed to relax a little. "I just need to get out of here. Can you help me?"

"You'll need some clothes," she said, glancing down at his blood-stained blue gown. "It's cold outside."

"What're you my doctor?"

"I'm a nurse," she said, shaking her head. "My name's Anna. Anna Horner."

She held out her small hand. Collin ignored it.

"There are more of them," Anna said, gesturing toward the man on the floor.

Collin scowled. That wasn't what he wanted to hear.

"You know this building, which means you know how to get out of here and how to avoid them. Help me get out of here and you can go your own way," said Collin. He didn't care where he was, he just wanted out. And he didn't care where she went.

"What about him?"

Collin shrugged. He didn't care about the fate of the man either. "Show me how to get the hell out of here. That's all I want. I'm not going to hurt you."

The woman nodded.

"We should move him before we leave," Collin said, pointing with his knife at the last remaining attacker.

"Why?"

"Just grab him." Collin cupped a hand under his armpit and stared at her. She caught the hint.

Together, they dragged him into a small room beside the nurses' station. It looked like a converted utility closet to Collin. Now it functioned as an office of sorts.

"Anna, no. Please, help me," the man said, panic overtaking him. He flailed as if they were dragging him into a torture chamber. He tried to grab the doorjamb, but Collin kicked his hand away.

"Anna, c'mon. Please Anna, don't kill me!"

The pitch of his voice rose into a painful shriek.

Collin stopped pulling him into the room, knelt down, clamped a hand down over the man's mouth, and plunged his knife into the crook of the man's neck just behind the collar bone. It slid in smooth and easy, almost as if the skin, muscle, tendon and subclavian artery parted to make way for it voluntarily. The tip of the blade bumped into bone, so Collin eased it back slightly and twisted the blade to widen the puncture. Blood pulsed out of the wound, hot and fast, coating Collin's hand with warm, sticky fluid.

With one swift motion, he withdrew the blade, and held the bloodied knife at Anna's throat.

"How the hell did he know your name?" said Collin through clenched teeth, his hand as steady as his voice. Blood dripped off his hand, splatting softly on the floor.

Anna cringed a little and looked disgusted as the man's blood ran off the blade and trickled down her throat into the depression of her collarbone.

She gulped.

"There's a lot going on here that you don't know about," she said, regaining her composure and glaring at him.

Collin was mildly impressed at her fortitude. She was a strong woman.

But she dodged the question. He leaned in close, spoke calmly and enunciated his words, "How did he know your name?"

She made a disapproving sound and furrowed her brow.

"I knew him a long time ago, in a past life."

"And now?"

"Now there's nothing," she said, looking down at the man's body. His face was frozen in a grimace. Flecks of blood covered the side of his face where it was exhaled with his dying breaths. His entire neck was crimson. "You didn't have to kill him," she added softly.

"They tried to kill me. He would have tried to kill me and you."

No excuses, just simple facts. The men killed the nurses and tried to kill Collin, but he wouldn't permit that to happen. Considering the body count, it was clear his instincts agreed.

Collin thought for a second. "Why *do* they want to kill me? What's going on here?"

None of it made sense.

"There's too much to tell you here. It's not safe," she said. "For either of us. I'll lead you out."

"Why do they want me dead?" he said.

"There's a lot you don't understand, Collin."

He was mildly surprised she knew his name, but presumably he had ID on him at some point, and after all, she was his nurse. At least she claimed to be.

"The world is different from what you remember," she said. In the orange glow, he could tell she was serious, but there was a hint of compassion in there too.

What a strange thing to say, he thought. His curiosity was piqued. "Like what?"

"For starters, you've been in a coma for sixteen years." She met his eyes for a moment, then looked away. It was almost as if she was ashamed.

Silence.

Collin didn't know how to respond to that. Sixteen years in a coma? A flurry of questions clouded his mind. What? How? Even if that was true, however improbable it seemed now, what did that have to do with people trying to kill him?

He took a deep breath and released it like a gust of wind. Finally, he shrugged. "A lot to catch up on then."

She nodded.

"But I have one thing to attend to first," he said.

Collin stood up and wiped the blade of the knife on his blue gown, careful not to expose his body to Anna, since he was nude underneath the thin material, even though he realized she'd probably already seen everything he had to offer.

"Come on." He gestured at Anna to follow him, then turned and walked away. Bloody footprints marred the tile floor.

Collin strode back to the room he woke up in. There was one attacker left, and if Collin judged his size accurately, his clothes should fit reasonably well.

He pushed open the door and could just make out the outline of the man in the room. He had pushed himself over to the broken windows. He was leaning against the wall, fumbling with the rope, trying to reattach it to his harness.

Without a word, Collin walked over and severed the rope at eye level. It swung outside the window, swaying back and forth uselessly, while the rest dropped to the floor, taunting the man.

"Please don't kill me," he wept.

Collin stood with his hand on his hip and pointed at him with the knife. "Take off your uniform. Now."

The man stared at him blankly for a moment.

Collin stared back. He jerked the knife blade in a hurry-the-hell-up motion.

The crippled man removed his uniform jacket and tossed it to Collin. He slid into it and tested the fit. It was slightly baggy, but fit reasonably well. He took it off and laid it on the bed.

Then the man undid his rappelling harness and struggled to pull it off without moving his injured leg too much.

Anna stood quietly in the doorway watching, one arm crossed over her chest, the other hand covering her mouth.

It was taking far too long for Collin's taste. He knelt down beside the man's destroyed knee and set the knife down by his foot. Then Collin began unlacing the boots. Pulling them off elicited agonizing groans of pain from the man, but eventually Collin had a pair of boots waiting for him.

"Take off your pants," Collin said, picking up his knife and standing.

"Please don't kill me."

"Shut up and move."

Once the man's pants were undone, Collin set the knife on the bed, grabbed the pants by the ankle cuffs, and yanked until they came free. It wasn't a graceful move; the man's renewed wailing proved that.

Collin saw Anna out of the corner of his eye, as he took off his gown, and dressed in his new clothes. She smiled slightly, but looked away politely.

He smiled to himself, then looked at the man on the floor. A cold mask replaced the smile as he calculated his options. The man was useless. He sat in his underclothes holding his leg, leaning against the wall beneath the windows, breathing hard.

Collin picked up the man's helmet, while he thought about his next moves, and used the knife to smash out the other half of the visor.

"What should we do with him?" he said, tucking the helmet under his arm.

"Leave him?" Anna said tentatively, walking over to stand beside him.

"Don't leave me," said the man. "Please. Please, help me."

"You tried to kill me," Collin said evenly. He couldn't believe this entitled prick expected help from them.

"Help me, please. You're a doctor, right?"

"We could take him with us and use him as leverage," Anna suggested.

"He's a liability. Slow and noisy."

A distant thump caught their attention. Something about the sound was familiar to Collin, although he couldn't quite place it.

Then the room rumbled as something exploded beneath them. The building shook and bucked, throwing Collin and Anna to the floor as fixtures crashed down around them. His knife slid off the bed and clanked to the floor. They scrambled away toward the door while the injured man eyed the knife and attempted to crawl toward it. Dust billowed in from the broken window.

Collin covered his face, waiting for the initial rush of dust to flow over and past him. When he looked up, he saw the floor was cracked and tilting perilously at a downward angle. Several of the other windows had shattered. The injured man had his fingers dug into a crack, keeping himself from sliding away on the canted floor. He held on with wide eyes, alternately glancing behind him, and staring at Collin. His eyes pleaded for help.

Another thump sounded.

"Move," Collin said, turning away from the man and shoving Anna along the floor. They crawled toward the door, as another explosion hit behind them. Concrete split, shattered, and crumbled. Debris hit his leg and his foot went numb. The building bucked violently for a moment.

When things stopped moving, Collin turned to look behind him. He let out a sigh of relief to see his leg was still intact. It hurt something awful, but he could begin to feel a tingling sensation in his toes as feeling returned.

He was shocked to see a dark void where the room had been a moment before. The injured man was no longer there. In fact, very little remained. The entire side of the building on their floor, and the floor above, collapsed in a cloud of dust. It was a miracle they had survived.

Then - another thump.

Mortars? He thought. Collin wasn't sure but he knew one thing for certain: "Run," he shouted. "Get out. Go, go, go."

He scrambled to his feet. As he stood up, he threw an arm around Anna's waist to help her along.

Another explosion. This one was farther away, possibly a miss. The floor barely trembled.

Guns began cracking and booming, the noise coming in through the gaping hole in the building.

Collin led her straight down the hall, away from the nurses' station.

They rounded a bend, but Anna pulled on his arm.

"Wait," she said, pointing to an unmarked door.

"Go." He ran toward the door and shoved it open. Anna went through first.

He entered behind her, and saw what turned out to be a stairwell, rather than the hallway he expected. Without hesitating, they took the stairs two at a time, bounding down toward the lower floors - toward freedom.

Downstairs, they heard a door creak open and pounding footsteps echoed up the concrete stairwell.

Collin grabbed Anna's arm, pulled open the door on the next landing, and they exited onto a darkened floor, similar to the one they'd left. He hadn't noticed which floor they'd ended up on, but he suspected it wouldn't matter that much.

Another set of footsteps thumped rhythmically in a nearby hallway.

Collin cursed. People seemed to be everywhere, trying to corner them.

It was difficult to see because it was so dark inside; this floor had no lighting or burn barrel. Thankfully, Anna seemed to know her way around, because she gestured for him to follow. He fell into step and quietly stalked behind her.

She led him part way down the hall, tested a door handle, and pulled it open.

"Here," she said.

Collin took the door from her and eased it closed behind him. The click of the door mechanism was barely audible.

He ducked down to stay below the large window set into the door. Made of security glass with wire mesh embedded into it, the window was lightly frosted, but not entirely opaque. Anna also stayed low and duck-walked over to him.

"We're almost out," she whispered close to his ear.

Her breath was warm and tickled his ear. His neck tingled, but he forced himself not to laugh or cringe away from her. He bit his cheek and focused on their escape.

The footsteps grew louder.

At least three or four people, Collin thought. He squeezed the knife in his hand firm, ready to go.

Dark shapes moved past their door, flashlights sweeping the hallway and the door windows. Collin held still.

He counted four people in the group. From what he could see, they were dressed differently from the people he fought upstairs.

Anna let out a big breath as they passed by without incident. Collin glanced at her.

"Who were the guys upstairs?" Collin asked softly when he felt sure they wouldn't be discovered.

"They're known as Vipers. It's an unruly group of survivors," she said.

"Why didn't they all carry guns? Other than the two guys on the ropes, all they had were knives." He held up the one he held as a demonstration.

"The Vipers prefer knives and bows. Plus, ammunition is hard to come by these days."

"Bows?"

Collin saw her shrug her narrow shoulders. "Yeah, they almost never carry guns."

"Are these guys Vipers?" Collin gestured at the door.

"No. These guys are known as Eagles."

"Are we in a goddamn zoo?" Collin asked.

She stifled a laugh. "They're Eagles, so they prey on Vipers."

"So we're in Mexico?"

Anna gave him a quizzical look.

"Eagle and viper, just like the Mexican flag."

"No," Anna said with a smile, slightly embarrassed she didn't get the reference right away.

Gunshots rang out and they heard footsteps pounding in the stairwell again. No one passed by their room.

"So, who are the good guys?" Collin watched Anna closely to gauge her reaction.

"I suppose that depends on how you define 'good'," she said. "You killed those men upstairs. Are you good?"

Collin frowned. Then he grunted. "I'd like to think so."

Before he could add anything else, they heard a crash like breaking glass. An orange burst cast shadows at weird angles.

Anna gasped. Collin turned back to the door, expecting it to burst open at any moment.

When nothing happened, he crawled forward within arm's reach of the door and peered over the edge of the windowsill.

"Fire," Collin said with a curse.

"We need to get out of here now," said Anna.

"Lead the way."

"We need to find my mother. She's the only one who can help you."

That struck Collin as odd, but no more so than anything else since he woke up.

Collin pulled the door open and cleared the hall - no one.

He waved Anna out. She followed him into the hallway, stepped past him and led the way out.

The two of them ran down a hallway, turned right, passed through a large set of double doors, down another stairwell, and out a side door.

As soon as they emerged from the door, lights blinded them.

Collin held up his free hand to block the light, but it seemed to come from every direction.

Two men approached him with rifles raised; one on either side of him in an amateurish flanking maneuver. Big mistake.

Collin launched into an attack. In the back of his mind, he heard a voice, "Strike first, strike hard. No mercy."

He grabbed the rifle barrel of the man on his left and yanked it up as he sidestepped to avoid being shot by his teammate. His next step led him into a short kick to the side of the man's leg. Collin heard a pop as tendons and ligaments snapped apart.

With a grunt of pain, the man collapsed to his good knee.

The other man held his fire for fear of shooting his buddy. He was frozen in place just like Collin expected, as worthless as a crumbling statue.

Collin kept moving. He pivoted behind the man, pulling the rifle out of his loosened grip, tossing it aside, and drawing out the man's pistol from its thigh holster.

Anna rushed to stand in front of the frozen gunman. She held her hands out to keep him at bay.

"Collin, please stop," she said. The concern in her eyes looked genuine.

With the first man down and Anna blocking his way, Collin stood exposed to the second gunman. He also had to consider who might be behind the blinding lights.

Only one option left.

He lunged forward and wrapped an arm around Anna. His pistol aimed at her head.

"Wha- What the…" she sputtered, slapping at his arm in a weak attempt to free herself. "What are you doing? Let go of me."

"Drop it!" unseen men yelled in unison.

One shouted, "Let her go!"

"Drop the gun," another said.

Several soldiers advanced into the light, so Collin could see them. They all had rifles trained in his direction, though he doubted any of them had enough skill to shoot him without hitting Anna. He hoped she was too valuable to sacrifice.

Collin kept his head low to reduce his profile. He ignored their commands and backed up a few steps, pulling Anna along with him.

"Gentlemen, please," a smooth voice said.

Collin lifted his head slightly to look over Anna's shoulder, as a man moved into the light with his hands raised. They were empty.

The man motioned the others to lower their rifles and step back. They obeyed without a word.

He looked directly at Collin with a piercing gaze and strode forward another step.

"Mr. Collin War, my name is Pastor Paul Pendell, and if you ever want to see your family again you will drop that weapon."

Chapter Two

A man in black attire, wearing a small white band where a tie would normally go, stood before Collin with his hands outstretched.

Collin looked him up and down. Then he studied the man's dark, weathered face. Freckles dotted his cheeks, a feature he hadn't seen before on a black man. His dark curls were cut short, and featured a healthy mix of gray hair that was also reflected in his well-trimmed goatee.

Their eyes locked.

"Please, Mr. War," said Pastor Pendell. "There's no need for you to hold the good lady hostage. Please put the gun down and walk with me. We have a lot to discuss."

The pastor continued forward. Collin narrowed his eyes.

Everyone else backed away, fading into the darkness behind the lights, but Collin knew a dozen or more men stood nearby, ready to kill him.

"Can we talk, Mr. War?" He took another slow step toward Collin.

"Please, Collin. Just talk to him," said Anna, struggling under the pressure of Collin's forearm on her slender neck.

"Quiet," he told her.

Pastor Pendell held a hand out toward Anna. "Can we let the lady go? Hold on to your gun if you must. But let's be civil, shall we?"

Collin could see what the pastor was doing. It only took a moment for him to calculate his odds.

Collin dropped his arm from Anna's neck. In a brief flurry of motion, he locked the slide back, ejected the chambered bullet from his pistol, and squatted down behind Anna to set the gun down to his right. Collin stood back up with his hands raised before the bullet stopped rolling on the pavement.

Pastor Pendell's face lit up with the most grandfatherly smile imaginable. Anna took the pastor's outstretched hand and he guided her gently past him. Two armed men rushed out to escort her to safety. Pastor Pendell never took his eyes off Collin, a fact that didn't go unnoticed.

Collin stood relaxed. He lowered his arms to his sides and looked curiously at the man before him. Something about Pendell didn't sit right with him. But he couldn't quite figure out what it was.

"Like I said, I'm Pastor Pendell. Nice to meet you, Mr. War," he said as he extended his hand.

Collin didn't like the formal use of his name. After a brief hesitation he reached out and took the Pastor's hand in a firm but brief shake.

"You have a lot of catching up to do. I'm sure this," he said with a gesture to the surroundings, "is all a bit new to you."

Collin said nothing.

"Well, my son. You have nothing to worry about." The pastor smiled, patted Collin on the shoulder, and gave it a squeeze.

Collin's hand flew up and crushed the pastor's hand. Collin twisted it off of his shoulder, locking the wrist and forcing the pastor to the ground. As the two men went to the ground, Collin snatched his pistol from where he'd set it down, clicked the slide forward and held the gun to the Pastor's head.

"Where is my family?" Collin growled.

Shadows flitted over them and a chorus of shouts rose as the armed men stepped forward with their rifles aimed at Collin.

"No," shouted the Pastor.

A man strode out in front of the others. Collin briefly glanced up at him. The glint of light on metal caught his eye - a major's oak leaf cluster. Something in the back of his mind told him the rank insignia should have been a subdued, non-metallic brown to eliminate light reflection.

Collin pressed the gun hard into the back of the pastor's head.

"Don't shoot. Stand down," said Pastor Pendell. He waved his free hand to urge his men back.

No one moved. The man with the major's insignia looked down his gun's barrel at Collin, then lowered his arm. The others stepped back and lowered their weapons uneasily. Obviously, the pastor led an obedient group.

"Where are they?" Collin said. Then it dawned on him that the situation may not be so straightforward. "Do you have them? If you hurt them, I swear-"

"To God?" the pastor asked. He turned his head sideways and looked at Collin with one eye. "Were you going to swear to God?"

"Where is my family?" Collin said slowly. He enunciated each word clearly, remembering that doing so often helped people in stressful situations comprehend his questions.

"You should turn to God in times like these," Pendell said, his tone serious.

Collin squeezed the back of the pastor's neck causing him to wince.

Pendell shook his head as best as he could.

"I don't have your family. If I did, they would be here to greet you."

"Where are they," Collin shouted with a snarl.

"I don't know where they are exactly," Pendell said, maintaining his composure. "But I can help you find them."

Collin didn't respond. He didn't move. His breathing was heavy with anger and confusion.

Pastor Pendell moved his head and looked at his captor.

"Mr. War, are you prepared to die?" His voice was calm, serious, and

18

thoughtful. "You see, I am. If the good Lord chose you to deliver me unto Him, then I am prepared to go. I have to say, it would be a tragedy for you to die so soon after waking up. A lot has changed since you fell asleep all those years ago. Sixteen years to be exact, Collin. Nearly two decades."

Collin's gut told him there was truth in the man's words. His mind told him he couldn't survive if he shot the pastor; the odds just weren't with him, and his heart yearned for his family. Familiar faces in an unfamiliar time.

He looked around. Not much to see other than men waiting for the opportunity to end his life. And Anna. She stepped into the light. Her hands were clasped in front of her, a sympathetic look in her eyes, and a slight smile on her lips.

"Please, Collin," she said. "Listen to him. We can help."

Anna's sincerity struck a chord with him.

Survive to see what the next minute brings, the voice in his head told him.

Collin eased his grip on Pastor Pendell, slid off of his back, and squatted on the ground. He dropped the magazine from his pistol, cleared it, then he set it down on the pavement.

"Okay," he said with a nod.

Men rushed in to help the pastor up. Three ran over to apprehend Collin. One man started to secure his hands while the other two covered him with their rifles aimed at Collin's broad chest.

Pastor Pendell ran his hands down his chest and thighs, dusting himself off. Before the soldier could zip-tie Collin's hands, the pastor said, "Gentlemen, that's quite unnecessary. Mr. Collin War is our honored guest. He's no threat to our safety. Isn't that right, Collin?"

The fatherly smile was back on the pastor's face. He walked over to where Collin was still crouched on the ground, and offered his hand again.

Collin nodded his thanks. "That's correct."

He reached up, took Pastor Pendell's hand, and stood up.

Glancing around at the Eagles, Collin noted they were still very skeptical of him.

Fair enough, he thought.

The blinding lights dimmed, and the soldiers parted before Collin as he followed Pastor Pendell out of the alley.

Chapter Three

Pastor Pendell smiled at Collin and gestured down the alley.

"Shall we walk?" asked Pendell. It didn't sound much like a question and he didn't wait for a response, he just started walking.

Collin looked after him then glanced at Anna.

"Don't be scared." She smirked at him.

He found himself grinning at her. Something about her made him vulnerable. He knew next to nothing about her, yet trust came easy. Too easy.

Collin made a mental note to keep that in check. He couldn't afford to have a blind spot.

Together, the two of them followed the pastor.

The Eagles formed a protective half-circle around them. All of the soldiers, not exclusively male Collin noticed, wore a uniform that looked slightly less sinister and more militaristic than the Vipers. The Eagles were alert and operated with practiced movements. They had discipline, training, and carried guns, three notable differences between the two groups.

"This hospital has taken a quite a beating over the years," Pastor Pendell said, pointing out areas of damage. "Nothing like tonight though."

Some of the damage was severe, like the blown out floors where Collin and Anna had previously been. On this side of the building, most of the damage was less extreme, like the dozens of pockmarks that dotted the hospital's facade from a hail of bullets. While the hospital looked worn, the sidewalk and driveway were clear, suggesting a semi-effective cleanup crew of some sort and a certain level of pride in the appearance of their town. Piles of rubble filled space where plants would have grown long ago.

No light emanated from the building. It appeared that the external lights were busted out, likely from whatever battles marred the façade, and the large front doors were missing glass. In fact, Collin noticed that none of the buildings he could see was lit up.

"For the last few weeks, you've been my only patient," Anna said.

"I hope I wasn't too much trouble," Collin said.

"Not at all. Well…if you don't count tonight," she said, looking a little shy. She cleared her throat before continuing. "For the most part, I was able to get a lot of reading and research completed."

Collin raised his eyebrows and nodded, hoping he looked interested. In reality, the only thing on his mind was his family and the apparent loss of sixteen years from his consciousness. He knew in his heart he had a wife and a kid, or maybe even several kids, although he couldn't quite make out their faces or names in his mind.

"Where are we going?" he asked. "I'd like to find my family - ASAP."

"Of course you would. Right now though we are headed to the church to get you cleaned up and in some, shall we say, better attire." Pastor Pendell looked Collin over with a critical eye and gestured to the street ahead of them. "We must cross town to get to the church. It won't take long and I believe you may find it informative. Consider it an opportunity to get a feel for where you are."

Naturally, Collin had been taking mental notes the whole time. He had taken forty-nine steps since he stood up and accepted Pendell's peace offering. So far, he noticed an open space directly across from the hospital, possibly a parking lot or a park.

A narrow green sign told him they were walking down the middle of Park haven Street. The crossroad was called 14th Ave and the only notable feature of the streets was their lack of asphalt. As far as Collin could see, the roads were gravel. Collin didn't realize America still had towns with no paved roads.

"Where are we?" Collin asked.

"You, sir, are in the beautiful Big Sky State of Montana," said Pastor Pendell. He waved a hand across the space in front of him, like he was presenting a tantalizing game show prize.

"And this place is called...?"

"Goshen," said Anna.

Collin nodded in satisfaction. He'd never heard of the town, but he knew Montana fairly well from road trips he took as a kid, and a short stint living in Kalispell back in high school.

"Who were those people back at the hospital?" he asked. Anna already told him, but he wanted to see what the pastor would say.

"Godless souls," said Pastor Pendell. "We don't have much and what we do have, we share. Now look here. Every Sunday, after service of course, we open up these buildings and have a big block party. I suppose you could call it a Goshen social. It's a chance for everyone to come together to enjoy the Lord's bounty. You will, of course, be joining us this week."

Collin pretended not to notice how the pastor dodged the question and instead considered the man's request; after all, attending the social was a great chance to gather intelligence. He could also read between the lines. He understood that it wasn't actually a request at all. It was a commandment delivered to him by a man of the cloth.

Pendell led them through the intersection. On either side, sat the low buildings he mentioned. Small shops and restaurants back in the day, by the look of it. Now they looked abandoned. There were still no lights in the windows and no one peered out at them from inside.

Vehicles were conspicuously absent from the roads. Not a single car or truck was parked along the sidewalks, which were paved. Collin glanced down at the gravel road - no ruts or tire tracks. Just the vague outline of shoe prints.

"We are a relatively large community nowadays," the pastor said, continuing his introduction. "Back before the fever, we were a small town. A small community where most people knew each other."

Pastor Pendell chuckled. "We know each other much more intimately now though. Yes, indeed. The good Lord has seen fit to bring together the faithful in our little town. We have been blessed by His grace. In fact, you, sir, are something of a miracle. Did you know that?"

Collin was thoroughly confused. Lots of people, a fever, small community, and some religious mumbo jumbo. He certainly didn't feel like a miracle. He felt rather normal, and somewhat uncomfortable with the new situation he found himself in.

"If you say so, pastor," Collin said, skepticism thick in his voice. His stomach felt hollow. He needed food, and soon.

"I do."

"Why did those men at the hospital attack me?" Collin stopped walking and looked pointedly at the pastor.

Pastor Pendell made a face and waved his hand like he was batting away a mosquito.

"You're not appreciating the gravity of the situation, Mr. War. You are a unique soul. Not just here, but from as far away as we get news, you're the first person to ever wake up from the fever." Pastor Pendell spoke with such excitement it was hard not to get swept away by it.

"I have no idea what you're talking about," said Collin. "And you still haven't answered my question about the attackers."

Anna didn't say anything. She just watched Pendell, with a curious look on her face.

Pastor Pendell put a hand on Collin's shoulder to urge him on down the road, but paused a moment, looked down at his hand and let go. He smiled somewhat sheepishly.

Collin turned and continued walking slowly.

"We are all quite surprised you woke up. You certainly lasted the longest after coming down with the fever. Then several days ago, your vitals were improving and we put a twenty-four hour watch on you to see what might happen. And here you are walking around after all those years in a bed." Pastor Pendell looked at him with wide eyes, as if he expected Collin to sprout angel wings and a halo.

Or maybe he just wanted Collin to feel the amazement he did.

Collin did feel something. Hunger.

Sixteen years? he thought. He was surprised it was possible to live that long without moving or eating real food.

"How am I able to walk after sleeping for so long?" he asked.

Pendell gestured to Anna.

"Electric stimulation combined with muscle manipulation and massage therapy. The other nurses and I would come in a couple of times a day to hook you up to a machine that would send little electrical pulses to stimulate your muscles and simulate real exercise," she said. "You still lost some body mass and a lot of your strength, but you seem to have fared amazingly well."

"Thank you," Collin said simply.

Anna blushed a little. "It's what we do. Take care of the sick and heal the living."

"I mean it. Thank you."

"You're welcome."

They walked another quarter mile before they were firmly in residential territory. The moon glowed brightly above them and he could see fairly well.

Goshen sat among low hills and flat river land, at the feet of a towering dam and rugged mountains. Details were impossible to see at night, but he got a good sense of the terrain. As for the neighborhood, most of the houses he saw were ranch-style homes on large lots with fenced yards. In some places, Collin could see slivers of light peeking out from behind window coverings. Livestock seemed to fill the yards, from cattle to goats and sheep to pigs. A few houses even had large chicken coups and wire mesh on the fences.

A dog barked up the street. Collin couldn't help but smile. The sound reminded him of his dog; he knew he had one, but the name was slow to materialize in his mind.

"We have been able to survive because we were more livestock focused than most areas of the country, which relied heavily on produce." The pastor pointed out a few of the animals. They apparently had alpacas and llamas too. A few lay on the ground huddle close together along the fence line. One lifted its head and stared at them as they passed by, its large eyes twinkled in the moonlight.

"If you look over here, this bridge is the only one in the valley that connects the two banks of the river," said Pastor Pendell. "Our farmers tend fields on the other bank. Mostly feed for the livestock, but we also have some produce."

"You've emphasized the livestock twice now. Why don't you grow much produce?"

"Mr. War-"

"Please call me Collin," he said, cringing at the formal use of his name.

"As you wish, Collin. How much do you remember prior to succumbing to the fever?" asked Pendell.

"Yes, what are your last memories," Anna chimed in eagerly. "My mom, Dr. Horner, will want to know."

Collin thought for several long seconds. He knew he had a family, a dog, a house, and presumably a job. No names came to him, and the image in his mind of his family was blurred beyond recognition. Although he'd been to Montana in the past, he had no recollection of how he ended up here.

"Enough to question why I'm in Montana." Collin felt he shouldn't offer too much information. He didn't know these people. He had no idea if he could trust them. Sure they kept him alive, but to what ends?

"That is a mystery isn't it? All we know is you ended up in our care and we've extended that care to you for nearly two decades." Pendell smiled.

"I appreciate that."

"Do you remember anything specific?" said Anna.

"No, not really," Collin said. Control the flow of information; don't reveal more than you have to, a voice in his head warned. "I do appreciate your hospitality though."

"The bridge is our connection to the outside world. It is also our weak point." Pastor Pendell look at the structure with a mixed expression.

"Against the Vipers?" Collin said.

Pendell nodded after a brief flicker of shock passed over his face.

Then a man started across the bridge toward their group. One of the soldiers flanking Anna stepped forward and shouted a challenge to him. The man must have responded appropriately because he was allowed to approach their group.

Everyone turned toward him, waiting to discover what brought him over.

"Good evening Pastor. Major," he said nodding at the officer without saluting.

Maybe they don't do that anymore, Collin thought.

"The perimeter is secure," he said. "We sent out canine patrols, and we should know shortly how the intruders penetrated our security."

"Very well," said the Major. "Bring me your report as soon as you have anything. Wake me up if you have to."

"Yes, sir." The soldier hustled off back to his post.

When the man was out of earshot, Collin turned and asked, "Was it the Vipers who attacked me?"

Pendell nodded again.

"What do they want?"

"What do lawless heathens always want?" Pastor Pendell asked. A rhetorical question. "Influence, power, and especially these days - resources."

"No chance of converting them?" Collin smirked.

"We've tried various methods, but the devil has his talons sunk deep into those tortured souls."

Collin saw Anna clench her jaw. She caught him looking at her and turned away.

"Hmm…well, any chance I could trouble you for some food? I'm starving," Collin said with a chuckle.

Pendell smiled. "We'd never let you starve. Follow me, we'll stop by the cafeteria."

They continued walking down the gravel street.

Anna trailed behind the Pastor and Collin.

"What kind of defenses do you have out there?"

"The Eagles are our soldiers," the pastor said, gesturing at the men with guns. "High up in the trees along the river bank, we have trimmed back branches and installed old hunting tripods that serve as fighting positions. Eagle's nests, as we call them."

Pendell sounded proud of those. Maybe they were his idea?

"Any defenses on the ground? At night, those watch towers are much less effective since you don't have lights. Unless you've equipped them with night-vision goggles that is," said Collin without much thought. He paused, surprising himself with the knowledge.

Collin heard a snort behind him. He glanced back and saw the Major sneering at him.

"We have some," said Pastor Pendell dismissively. "But let's focus on getting you some food."

It wasn't long before Collin made out the hulking form of the church in the darkness. Even in the darkness, he could tell the building was painted white, like most churches. It practically glowed in the moonlight. The building itself was medium sized with two short wings and a tall steeple, which almost certainly housed a bell to summon the faithful on Sunday mornings.

Pastor Pendell looked ready to invite Collin in, but a ringing sound filled the air, near the church but not from the church. High pitched and melodic, it sounded like wind chimes or a triangle.

"What's that?" Collin asked.

"Ah, it's supper time," said Pendell. "I told you we'd get you taken care of."

Collin chuckled.

"What's funny?"

"I remember my grandparents called it supper, too." He chuckled again. "I always thought it was odd and old fashioned."

"Well I'm certainly not your grandparents," Pastor Pendell said with a smile.

"Probably old enough though."

"Hey now," Pendell said with a laugh. "But you're right we are old fashioned here."

"You don't say."

They both chuckled.

Their laughter trailed off and silence filled the air. The mood was right for his inquisitive mind.

"Pastor, I noticed there are no lights around town. But the equipment at the hospital had electricity. Did you guys lose power in the attack?" Collin said, glancing at Pendell before continuing his assessment of the town. He knew intuitively any information he gathered now, would come in handy at some point in the future.

"No." Pendell shook his head. "We have a steady power supply thanks to our hydroelectric dam. Years ago, Major Logan recommended better light discipline. It was a prudent recommendation and easy enough to implement."

"Hydro, huh?" Collin noticed the looming form of the dam earlier. Instead of letting on what he figured out on his own, it was interesting to see what the pastor would divulge on his own.

"We are lucky. Truly blessed. We get it from the dam on the river. It was completed before..." He went silent.

Awkward silence.

"Before what?" Collin asked.

Pastor Pendell turned and look Collin in the eyes. His gaze was serious.

"Before the Rapture."

Collin suppressed a laugh. Was this guy serious?

"The what?"

"The Rapture. They finished the dam many years before the start of the Rapture, when the whole world was consumed by hell, God took his chosen." His voice was reverent, soft yet firm in his conviction.

"You mean the fever you and Anna talked about?"

"It was the Rapture, my son."

"Forgive my ignorance, Pastor, but if it was the rapture, why are you still here?" Collin was truly confused by the divine attribution to this fever they kept mentioning.

Pendell nodded solemnly. "The Lord works in mysterious ways. For a long time, I pondered that question and then it came to me during prayer. I realized I needed to stop feeling sorry for myself. The Lord doesn't give up on us - any of us - and there are still people to bring into the flock. I am his shepherd."

"I see." Collin didn't, but he played the role of sympathetic outsider. No sense in stirring up trouble over ideological differences.

Another silence settled over them, so he turned toward the church. "Nice place you have here, Pastor."

"Like I said, we have been blessed. There will be time for a tour, and prayer if you'd like, but first let's enjoy the Lord's bounty." Pastor Pendell looked Collin over again and made a tsk, tsk sound. "This will not do. If I bring you to the table looking like that it may be the end of me."

He waved over one of the Eagle's, a man roughly the same size. "We can't have our guest showing up to supper looking like this. Give him your uniform shirt, please."

The man hesitated, shot Collin a dirty look, then pulled the uniform shirt over his head and tossed it carelessly at Collin.

"Perhaps we can discuss my family's location and this…fever," said Collin, as he took off his own shirt. He balled it up and handed it to the soldier before he put on the clean uniform. Collin was eager to learn as much as possible about these questions.

"Much better," Pastor Pendell said.

"How about my family and the fever?"

"All in good time, Collin." Pastor Pendell turned and spoke in a low voice to Major Logan.

Evasive and preachy, Collin thought. But he would get his answers. Eventually.

Major Logan turned and barked a few orders. His soldiers rushed off in different directions to follow his commands. Only a few remained to join them for supper.

Collin watched them go, evaluating. He looked around and was surprised to see that Anna had wandered off.

"Good, good. We're all set. Let's go inside," Pastor Pendell said.

They made their way to a low, medium-sized building that vaguely resembled the outside of a school administration building Collin had seen at some point in his life. Inside the cafeteria, dozens of families sitting at long tables. The kind of tables where the seats are attached and the surface is little more than laminated particleboard. Everything was clean and organized, which was a drastic change from the poor condition of the hospital.

Conversation tapered off and everyone turned to stare at the newcomer. People here weren't shy at all about staring at him.

A plump woman with golden hair overgrown with gray, rushed over. Her round cheeks flushed pink from the exertion while she nervously smoothed out her purple dress.

"Greetings Pastor," she said. Then she looked at Collin with a playful smile. "Hello, my name is Doris."

She offered her soft hand.

"I'm Collin. Nice to meet you Doris." Collin took her hand in his and gave it a courteous shake.

"Doris is our kitchen manager," said Pastor Pendell. "She does a fantastic job keeping our stomachs filled with delicious food. Not to mention, keeping the dining facility running smoothly."

"Thank you, Pastor," Doris said shyly. She looked back at Collin. "Welcome back from the sleep. Please come eat, you must be famished."

"You have no idea." Collin smiled wide and followed her to a table.

Chapter Four

Everyone held hands, heads bowed, as Pastor Pendell said grace.

Collin peeked around, taking advantage of the distraction to scan the room unobserved. It was a large room, with white walls and fluorescent ceiling lights that they had replaced with something more efficient. Shutters covered the windows, likely part of the light discipline Major Logan recommended.

His face tingled. Collin glanced over and saw Major Logan staring hard at him, lips curled into some kind of snarl or sneer. Collin wasn't sure, but no matter how he cut it, the guy had a problem. And he had no idea why.

"In the Lord's name we pray," Pendell said, finishing his prayer. Collin dipped his head back down.

"Amen."

The response reverberated in the room filling it with a sense of unity.

When Collin looked up, Major Logan was all smiles and bright eyes.

Silverware clanked, glasses clinked, and the solemn mood gave way to conversation and the laughter of children. For some reason, Collin was caught off guard by the sounds of children. Their voices were a welcome addition to the evening. He watched them for a moment before turning his attention to the meal before him.

Collin looked down at the lunch tray, so typical of public schools and other institutions. He'd been served a baked chicken leg, two meatballs, a large scoop of mashed potatoes with a generous wedge of bread atop it, and a mix of grilled vegetables.

"Don't be shy Collin," said the Pastor. "Dig in, and if you want more, just take your tray to the window over there." He pointed over Collin's shoulder where a middle-aged man and woman stood waiting to dish up more food.

Collin took a bite of the mashed potatoes. When he looked up, he realized dozens of people were watching him.

He smiled and raised his fork in a small informal salute. They smiled back, a few saluted, and everyone went back to eating, apparently satisfied.

Through a mouthful of food, a cheerful looking Asian man asked, "So tell us, was it really Anna's kiss that woke you up?" His eyes crinkled slightly at the edges as he smiled brightly. Laughter came from all the tables around theirs.

A woman gasped, her cheeks turning a rosy pink. "Koby!"

Collin couldn't help but chuckle. He looked at the woman who scolded the man, a woman he assumed was Anna's mom, Doctor Horner. "Anna is too professional for that."

"Thank you," she said, stabbing at the meat on her plate while shooting an evil look at the man.

"Koby, maybe you should introduce yourself," said Pastor Pendell.

"Sorry, my name is Gary Kobyashi," he said with a beaming grin. "Most people call me Koby."

"Nice to meet you, Koby," Collin said. "What do you do here?"

"Other than harass the rest of us?" Major Logan grumbled.

Dr. Horner and the pastor smiled.

"I run the hydro plant, which provides all of this glorious electricity we are now enjoying." Koby gestured up at the lights and looked pointedly at his detractors. "I also manage the irrigation system for the crops, among various other tasks the Council assigns me."

Collin nodded his head and cleaned the meat off his chicken leg. He wiped his mouth on his cloth napkin, it looked slightly worn and faded along the edge, but not bad all things considered.

"I'm sure you've guessed by now, this is Anna's mother, Doctor Julie Horner," said Pendell.

Collin smiled and nodded at Dr. Horner. "I figured that. Nice to meet you, doc."

"You too, Collin."

Kobyashi made loud kissing sounds setting off another wave of laughter from the surrounding tables.

Pendell gestured at the next man. "This is Major Logan," he said loud enough to be heard over the laughter.

"What do you do?" Collin asked Major Logan, knowing full well, but enjoying a chance to needle him. He had a feeling it would be important to understand how this man would respond to him.

"I'm sure you gathered that I'm in charge of security, law enforcement, and military operations," Logan said evenly although his eyes narrowed slightly.

"Like at the hospital?"

Silence fell across the room. Some might say he took it too far considering they'd just met, but Collin felt he had some leeway, being the new guy.

Major Logan tightened his grip on his silverware and cleared his throat. When he spoke, it was slow and tempered, "Even the best defenses can be breached. The fact that you're here, after all this time, I think, is testament to our effectiveness. Wouldn't you say?" He cocked he eyebrow at Collin.

Pastor Pendell glanced between the two men but didn't interrupt.

Collin shrugged and took a big bite of the mixed vegetables. He grunted in pleasure. "These are great."

After finishing his bite Collin said, "During our walk, you mentioned you guys mostly raised feed crops across the river, right?"

"This is true," said Pastor Pendell.

"So are these veggies canned or packaged military food? They taste so fresh. Please tell me my physical state hasn't declined that much?"

Kobyashi smiled. "Fresh as can be, my friend."

"Indeed. We operate several greenhouses and indoor gardening systems. Setup with Koby's expertise," said Pastor Pendell.

Kobyashi raised his hand and nodded several times, as if he was accepting accolades from a large audience.

"How does that work?" Collin asked, genuinely curious.

"Have you ever heard of hydroponics or aquaponics?" Kobyashi said.

"Perhaps in school," Collin said with caution. He had a vague sense that his roommate in college had been quite the hydroponics enthusiast.

Kobyashi chuckled. "Well, it's not all about growing weed. No sir, we have a very efficient and productive system that allows us to grow a safe, secure, and reliable supply of food. We actually run a surplus so we do a lot of canning. Some of the excess goes to the livestock. They're quite spoiled compared to…you know, before."

Kobyashi went back to his food. Any time the past was brought up people seemed to fade away, unable or unwilling to talk about it.

"I hate to bring the conversation around to business, but when you're all filled up, I'd like to invite you to our Council meeting. We already had one planned for this evening and I think I can speak for everyone when I say we are hoping you'd like to be our guest of honor," said Pastor Pendell.

Just then, the lights flickered. They cut out for a moment and then came back on. No one appeared to be startled or concerned.

"You still haven't resolved that issue?" said Logan, staring hard at Kobyashi.

"I've been too busy with your mom," Koby shot back.

Seeing the confusion on Collin's face, Dr. Horner said, "That was a power bump, nothing too serious. But they've been occurring more often and should be taken care of." She glanced at Koby.

"Power bump? Not sure I've ever heard that before," Collin said.

"It's basically a temporary power outage. I need to re-optimize the system," said Kobyashi.

"I'm sure Koby will deal with this right away," Pastor Pendell said. "Now, back to the Council meeting. Would you consider being our guest of honor?"

Dr. Horner cut in and leaned forward over the table. "How are you feeling?"

Collin thought for a moment. "I feel a little weak and there's some soreness, but other than that I feel good. I'm actually not sure I'll be able to get to bed on time tonight." He smiled.

"A sixteen year-long nap will do that to a guy," said Major Logan.

"Yeah, about that…" Collin said, turning to the doctor. "How is it I was out for so long?"

"We don't know too much about it," Dr. Horner said. "Think of it like you were in a coma, even though it wasn't the same thing exactly. Your body was still functioning, but your brain kind of switched off, much like a coma. We fed and watered you with an IV and used electric therapy to help you retain muscle mass," she said. "Luckily, you could breathe on your own which made things easier. Actually, you've been lucky. From what I heard, you retained an exceptional level of motor skill."

"Everyone keeps telling me I'm lucky." He supposed he felt lucky, if uneasy. Less than an hour ago, men tried to kill him, only to lose their lives. Their blood still stained his pants and boots. "What happened...to the world?"

"Clearly it went to shit," said Major Logan with a frown.

"We can discuss that later," Pastor Pendell said, cutting in. "As you can imagine, it's quite a long story with a lot of moving pieces. At the Council meeting tonight, you'll get a good overview of where we are as a community though."

"Okay," said Collin. Someone at another table laughed, triggering a flash of memory. Trees, a small wooden table, a young boy running by. It faded away as fast as it had come. He grasped at it in his mind, willing the memory to come back, to unfold itself in detail. But it was gone.

"Collin?" said Dr. Horner.

He looked up at her.

"Doris asked you a question," she said.

He turned the other way and saw Doris leaning over his shoulder. She had a concerned look on his face.

"I'm sorry, Doris. What did you say?"

"It's nothing really. I just asked if you enjoyed dinner?" Her eyes grew wide with anticipation.

Collin smiled and leaned back, gesturing at his tray, which was empty.

"It was lovely, Doris. Thank you very much."

She blushed and smiled. "I'm happy you enjoyed it."

"In fact, if it's possible, I wouldn't mind some more of those vegetables."

"Of course, of course, right this way."

Collin picked up his tray and followed her over to the serving station.

Chapter Five

In a spare bedroom being used as a hydroponic garden, Gary Kobyashi tended to his produce. Despite being low-maintenance, it was part of his early morning routine. And being that it was Sunday, he wanted to get some of his chores done before church.

In this particular room, he grew a several types of lettuce and a large row of spinach. Koby bobbed his head as music played in the background. Everything looked to be in order as usual. His system had been refined over the long years since the fever outbreak.

Journey's hit song, "Don't Stop Believing," started blaring from his living room record player, just one of the many vinyl albums in his collection. They were the last remnants of his high school and college years, and he still loved them. Perhaps now more than ever.

"Just a city boy," he sang. "Born and raised in south Detroit."

He danced a little as he sang.

"He took the midnight train going-"

The music stopped.

He stopped dancing. "What the shit?"

He listened carefully for anyone in his house who may have turned off the tunes.

"Hello?" he asked as he strolled over to the door and peeked his head into the hallway, half-expecting to see someone.

He didn't see anyone. Koby felt relieved no one heard him singing; he wasn't a big believer in torture, but he felt slightly deflated that apparently no one had come to visit him.

He ducked back into the gardening room, looked around, and realized the water pumps in the room, which kept the hydroponic system circulating, had also stopped. Hence the silence. He groaned in frustration.

"Goddamn dam," he muttered.

The town had been suffering from power bumps, or brief outages, for a couple of weeks. Koby was the most technically knowledgeable person in town, so the dam fell under his management. He'd read a multitude of massive, painfully boring manuals to learn more about how the dam worked. It helped, but like all quality leaders, Koby relied heavily on his crew to fill in his knowledge gaps. His crew consisted of a pair of technicians from the original crew who worked at the dam before the fever. Between the three of them, maintenance was straight forward, but none of them had been able to nail down the root cause of the power bumps.

It wasn't a water flow or generator issue, so they worked their way down the line and narrowed it down to the electrical systems. Currently, Koby and his crew were slowly working their way through, searching for the problem. It was tedious work.

Koby walked down the hall to check on the record and make sure it hadn't been scratched when the power died. He noticed the lights on his digital clock had gone out, so he'd have to reset that. Doris, the cafeteria manager and his close friend, told him more than once over the years to get something old fashioned. It wasn't his style so he'd resisted, but he couldn't help but think she was on to something.

He groaned. "Well, I guess I know what I'm doing today," he grumbled.

The record was still unscathed. He pulled it off the spindle and carefully slid it into its paper sleeve before tucking it back into the large album cover. He smiled at his collection of records, which filled an oak shelf he built specifically to hold his collection of more than two hundred albums.

"Possibly the finest collection left in the world," he said, as he replaced the Journey album back in its place.

Koby went to the kitchen to fill a thermos with coffee. It was likely to be a long day at the Goshen dam, so he started a fresh brew. His kitchen featured a large gas stove, so he could light it without needing electricity. While the water heated up, he walked into what would normally be the front room. In Koby's house, it was equal parts workroom and parts collection.

Some townsfolk thought it was chaotic, but to Koby it was glorious.

He picked up his bag of tools and went back to the kitchen to wait for the water to finish.

Once the kettle started its slow build to a piercing whistle, he turned off the heat and poured the water slowly through the coffee filter on top of the thermos.

"Ready to rock hard," Koby muttered.

If he was lucky, his technicians Mark and Paul would already be fixing whatever problem was ailing the aging dam. He'd feel much better when they finally found the main problem and fixed it. The dam had begun to consume a lot of his work time. With managing the town's gardens and other projects, he was a busy man.

Koby shouldered his tool bag and walked out of his house, heading toward the dam. He briefly thought about the new guy, Collin, and wondered what he was doing. Most newcomers found the interior of the dam to be mesmerizing; he would have to show Collin the inner workings one day. Koby enjoyed giving people a firsthand look at the things he managed; it gave him a sense of pride. He pushed those thoughts aside and mulled over possible solutions for the dam's current problem.

Since the dam could easily produce more electricity than the town needed, they only needed to keep one of its five generators in operation. Most of the problems cropped up in the summer or during extremely cold winters. Naturally, on hot summer days, people turned on their air conditioning and in the winter, heaters ran around the clock.

Age had been kind to the dam and Goshen as a whole. Thankfully, the electrical and water management systems didn't rely on a computer to control them. All of that was pleasantly old-school. Switches, wires, levers, cranks, gears, and pulleys held tight and functioned without the need for fragile and temperamental hardware or software controls. Nevertheless, as the dam neared its centennial birthday, it seemed to need more attention.

Coming out of the Great Depression, Goshen had commissioned the dam's construction with the assistance of the state and federal governments. Most of the funding came from President Roosevelt's "New Deal" legislation. The dam was large enough to be able to provide electricity for most of Montana and parts of north Idaho. Koby had seen construction and dedication photos.

It was a big deal back in the day, providing thousands of jobs, and hope for people living in a small out-of-the-way community. He was always impressed by what people had done in the first half of the twentieth century, when America was building its infrastructure. The ambition, the national pride, the dedication, and the sense of working together to improve everyone's lives were inspiring.

Decades before the fever brought the world to its knees, people had sounded the warning bells about the deteriorating state of the country's infrastructure. They were lucky Goshen dedicated money to maintaining the dam as well as they had, because it still ran, and didn't seem to require the kind of major construction they were wholly unprepared to provide.

It's a fussy child, Koby thought. *But it's my fussy child.*

He was startled when Pastor Pendell fell into step beside him and said, "Good afternoon!"

"Fuck me sideways!"

"I beg your pardon," Pastor Pendell said sternly.

"You startled me, pastor." Koby patted his chest to calm his racing heart.

"My apologies. You did appear to be deep in thought." Pastor Pendell rubbed his chin as he followed Koby. "It appears you're headed to the dam. Am I right?"

"Do dogs piss on brick walls?" Koby said, not expecting an answer.

Pastor Pendell looked at him sideways, refusing to partake in the current tone of the conversation.

"Well, I wanted to give you these," he said, removing a set of keys from his front pocket. He held them up and looked at them, dangling from his crooked old fingers. "I've held on to these for far too long. I know you and your technicians only have one set between the three of you. So these should come in handy."

Koby glanced at the keys. They appeared to be a set of keys for the dam.

They were identical to the set his team already had. But this was only a partial set. Koby had seen Pastor Pendell's keys for the dam, and looking at what was before him, he realized there was at least one key missing.

"Why now, after all this time?" Koby asked, suspicious.

"When you first came to us, I wasn't sure we could trust you. Then it was my own sins which led me to cling to them." Pastor Pendell began walking slowly in the direction Koby had been heading.

"Your sins?"

Pastor Pendell rubbed his chin. "Lord knows I've spent many an hour asking for forgiveness for my sins," he said with a sigh. "I like to help people, to feel needed. And my own pride and need for attention kept these in my possession longer than necessary, rather than giving them to their rightful caretaker - you."

"I see…" Koby said, although he wasn't really sure if he did.

Did micro-managing qualify as a sin?

In either case, he was happy to receive another set of keys. If anything happened to the originals, it'd be less of a crisis.

The pastor still hadn't handed them over.

Pastor Pendell didn't say anything for a minute or two as they continued walking towards the dam.

"It's beautiful in its inanimate strength isn't it?" he said finally.

Koby followed the pastor's gaze up to the dam. It towered before them, straddling the riverbanks; water churning at its base threw up a large cloud of mist that rained down on the rocks and vegetation lining both sides. Several large rocks jutted out from the riverbank on Goshen's side.

During the summer, they were popular with rebellious youth who loved to jump off of them into the water below. It was dangerous because the water was so rough, especially if the spillway was active. Goshen had already lost a young couple, years ago; who drowned after the water pressure wedged them under the edge of a boulder deep underwater.

"Yes, it is."

"Living near the dam is what I imagine it would be like to live near Mount Rushmore," Pastor Pendell said.

"She's an oldie, but a goodie." Koby looked at the man beside him. The pastor was acting strange.

"We're lucky to have her. And grateful too," Pastor Pendell said. "Grateful for her and you too."

"Me?"

"Of course. Without you, our gardening program wouldn't have turned out to be a smashing success. And you keep her running," Pastor Pendell said, gesturing at the dam. He slowed his pace.

Koby liked feeling appreciated, but he didn't see the things he'd done as special or remarkable. Most of the time, he felt like he was winging it. It was luck, more than anything that not everything he worked on failed.

"Will you be joining me and the boys at the dam?" Koby asked.

No response.

Koby turned and saw Pastor Pendell about fifteen feet behind him, just staring at the dam. The look on the man's face was unusual.

"Pastor?" Koby waited for him to catch up but he didn't move. "Hello?"

The man stood staring at the dam. It was an unsettling sight.

"Earth to Pastor Pendell. Do you copy?" Koby asked loudly, hoping to get the man's attention.

Pastor Pendell blinked a few times and looked at Koby.

"Yes?"

"Um…Are you coming with me?"

"I've been thinking-"

"A dangerous past time," Koby said with a smirk.

"Indeed."

They both chuckled. Pastor Pendell approached Koby, who waited politely for him to catch up.

"I trust you," Pastor Pendell said, placing his hand on Koby's shoulder.

"Okay?"

"I'm going to be honest with you. When it comes to the dam, I'm about as useful a four-cornered triangle."

Koby smiled.

"There's no reason for me to go there with you. Now or ever," Pastor Pendell said. "Plus, I have to go prepare for today's service."

"Okay?" Koby repeated. He had no idea where the pastor was going with this, but he was starting to feel uncomfortable, especially with the man's hand on his shoulder.

Pastor Pendell pulled the keys from his pocket again. Koby hadn't seen him slip them back in his pocket. It was as if the pastor was still struggling with whatever personal demons made him unwilling to part with the small pieces of metal. They tinkled lightly in the breeze, like a miniature set of chimes.

Koby held his hand out to help the pastor. The man's eyes flicked from the keys to Koby's hand and back.

With seemingly great effort, Pastor Pendell placed the keys in Koby's hand. "What I'm saying is…"

Koby quickly closed his hand around the keys and shoved them in his pocket.

"We've been blessed with power, in the literal sense. I don't know what has happened the world over, but I imagine most do not have electricity the way we do. I was protective of it and didn't fully trust you. Now I do. You have earned the trust and respect of not just me, but the whole of Goshen."

Koby wasn't sure to say to that.

"You'll find the yellow key will open up more doors than the others. Your team's current set of keys does not include a yellow one. You may find additional supplies or parts to assist your repairs." He took a deep breath again. "Koby, I need to say this one more time. Forgive me."

"No problem at all, Pastor," Koby said uneasily. He wasn't used to seeing Pastor Pendell this way. "Honestly, I'd rather not go back inside the old girl either."

The pastor's head snapped over to him, his eyes wide and surprised.

"But someone has to babysit this giant beast, right?" he said, gesturing at the dam.

A smile slowly spread on the pastor's face. "Right," he said in a low voice.

Then Pastor Pendell straightened up, stretching himself up to his full height, a good six inches over Koby. "Right. And that someone is you, of course. Please carry on and restore the power," he said with a smile. "I'm sure the kitchen staff would appreciate it."

"Will do."

Pastor Pendell gave him a brief wave and turned to leave. He walked away briskly.

Koby stood and watched him go for a few moments. He realized the pastor had indeed watched over them quite often while they worked. It had always been a slight distraction. Now they were free of that. He felt relieved. Something about the encounter didn't sit right with him though.

Pastor Pendell mentioned that the yellow key opened doors that his team's set couldn't open. He was curious and as soon as he had free time, he could go exploring.

Something to look forward to, he thought as he made his way around the building that had served as a combination Public Works Department and Mayor's Office. Across the road was the old fire hall.

While Goshen still had a functioning fire department, with a horse drawn carriage as their fire truck, they had no Mayor. Pastor Pendell led the town council, and for more than a decade the town ran smoothly using this system. Koby realized the old Mayor's office wasn't currently in use. He filed it away in the back of his mind as a potential space for future projects or an expansion of his indoor gardening project.

Koby hustled around the last block to the overgrown chain-link fence that wrapped around a squat concrete building. The building provided access to the dam's interior, including a series of stairs that zig-zagged in tight switchbacks, reaching the top of the dam. It was the route used by the Eagle's sniper teams when they kept watch from the dam. Walking up the steps was long and tiring but it was actually quicker than walking through the interior to the service elevator.

Koby took out the keys Pastor Pendell had given him and prepared to open the lock on the gate. The red key was for exterior doors, the blue key was for interior doors, and then there was the yellow key. The yellow key was the one the pastor said would open up new areas of the dam.

A key was missing from the usual four that Pastor Pendell carried on this keychain. For the life of him, Koby couldn't recall what color the other key was, but he was sure that the Pastor's set included four keys.

He used the red key to open the lock. The metal clanked and squeaked as he pushed open the door and entered the restricted area.

Cracks in the concrete steps that led up to the small building sprouted weeds. The rusted and worn handrail was rough under Koby's hand. Both were a testament to the age of the structure and of times gone by. He looked up at the dam, smirking at graffiti teens had painted on part of the dam, before moving to unlock the door.

Of course, Goshen's high school mascot was the Fighting Beavers. A distinction that always made Koby giggle inappropriately. After all, beavers do build dams, so in a way, it made perfect sense. It also inspired crude jokes, which Koby loved, and ridicule as evidenced by the graffiti.

Water roared in the background as it left the outflow and crashed back into the river. Climbing along the cliff and jumping into the deep pool below was almost a rite of passage for the young people. The ledge was a landmark of its own. He knew several proposals that had taken place there, and rumors swirled about babies conceived there. He was thankful for the old beast that gave life, a small sense of meaning, and unity to Goshen.

He smiled as he slid the key into the keyhole. In contrast to the aging structure around it, the lock functioned smoothly from frequent use and thoughtful care. With a screeching grind and thunk, the deadbolt slid back and released the huge metal door which Koby pushed open.

The door swung easily on its greased hinges. Light lanced in while Koby fumbled to turn on the lights that operated on a different circuit than the town itself. The dam generated its own power, thanks to a relatively small water wheel generator, making the structure self-sufficient. Inside, it was cool and musty smelling. Humid air filled the concrete structure, which felt surprisingly refreshing.

His practiced hand found the light switch. The lights snapped on, illuminating the large room. A small desk sat in the corner where Mark or Paul, his technicians, sometimes left things while they worked. Today there was nothing on the desk. He wondered if either of the guys were on station.

Koby turned and pushed the door closed, turning the lock to secure it.

To the left of the desk was a long dark hallway. The ceiling was high, so light filled the hall for quite some distance. He could see the stairwell that climbed up to the summit of the dam. From the top of the dam, the view of the town and the valley that contained it was virtually unparalleled.

Beyond the stairs was the door Koby wanted. It was identical to the door he just entered with the exception of the color. Instead of red, the interior door was painted blue.

Leaving the roaring water outside, he was quickly greeted by the muted roar of water inside the dam. Behind the blue door was a metal catwalk that led down to a concrete walkway that ringed, and looked down on, the five generators and lone water wheel that took up the space below. The metal catwalk Koby stood on was rickety. Each time he traversed it he did so with bated breath. It clearly was not built with the same care as the rest of the structure. It wobbled slightly as he walked over rusted and broken floor panels. He maintained a kung-fu grip on the railings, just in case. If he fell through the floor, he'd plummet a good thirty feet onto the concrete walkway below.

Generator One, or Alpha as Koby liked to call it, was running nicely, churning at a steady pace. Likewise, the water wheel that powered the dam itself looked like it was working. Not surprising since he turned on all of the lights. Koby liked to point out to visitors that the same waterwheel design powered Hoover Dam, which started construction just a few short years after the Goshen Dam was constructed.

Koby carefully made his way across the catwalk, down to the walkway overlooking the generators. He looked down at the electrical console mounted on the wall near Alpha. A red light was flashing, indicating a problem. Experience told him that he probably just needed to replace a small part or flip a switch.

Shouldn't be too much trouble, he thought.

The generator room was huge. The ceiling rose about sixty feet from the generator floor to its max height. Rushing water filled the room with noise. In a way, Koby enjoyed the noise. Its steady, powerful rumble was oddly comforting and relaxing.

He made his way to the small stairwell that took him down to the bottom floor. He emerged near the Alpha Generator and opened up the control panel. One of the safety switches had flipped. When they started working together, Mark tried to explain the details of how these things worked, but a lot of it simply went in one ear and out the other.

Koby wasn't very interested in the technology of the dam. It was old school and he preferred the circuit boards of computers and the electrical systems that had made his gardening initiative such a massive success. He learned enough to keep things running and left the detailed stuff to the other guys.

Koby retained a mental set of instructions to correct this particular problem. He only had to flip a couple of switches and press a large green button. A bright yellow light flashed as the system checked itself. If all was well, the green light would come on, and it did.

He let out a sigh of relief.

Then it hit him.

The key missing from the pastor's keychain was a green key. And there was only one green door that he'd seen before. He saw it just once when was with the pastor in a section of the dam that rarely required their attention. They never gave it much thought before.

A green key for a green door. A key that wasn't with the others he was given.

Suddenly he had the urge to investigate. Pastor Pendell had acted so strange, how could he not look into it? It was his duty as a responsible resident of Goshen and a member of the Council.

Most of the rooms that weren't used directly for producing electricity, or maintaining the structure, were relegated to storage. Koby knew of several rooms that still held military style MREs, or Meals-Ready-to-Eat. He had no idea if the food was still good or not but the damp air wasn't conducive to storing other types of food. The MREs, sealed in thick plastic bags, were kept for extreme emergency use only and had been collected from FEMA supply drops not long after the fever hit. After almost a year of consistent delivery, the supply drops had tapered off and then quit all together.

Koby still remembered the tough situation Goshen was in when he arrived. The residents were surviving primarily on the MREs. Koby wasn't thrilled about being reliant on someone else for food. So, after a couple of months, with a dwindling supply of MREs, he'd been able to construct gardens and grow enough produce to supplement the town's food supply. Two years later, the town was completely self-sufficient, with the MREs hidden away like a bad memory.

Another room held spare parts for repair work and a small room held tools and cleaning supplies, like brooms and mops. Koby wondered what could be in the green room.

Normally, he wouldn't care. He'd ignore it even. Now that he was aware he didn't have a key for it, he wanted to know why. He needed to know why.

Church would be starting in a couple of hours and he didn't have time to go exploring now. Plus, he needed to check in on Collin and see how his first night being conscious and mobile in Goshen went.

Koby planned to return later in the day to satisfy his craving for the dam's secrets. If there was something that Pastor Pendell was hiding, or keeping secret, it wouldn't be easy to get to. He couldn't simply ask for the key, and acquiring it without the pastor's knowledge was sure to be a challenge.

A challenge he was willing to accept.

Chapter Six

Collin woke and sat up in bed. The delicious aroma of bacon filled his room. How long had it been since he smelled bacon? At least sixteen years, but the comforting smell felt like yesterday. He savored the scent as he arched his back, stretching in bed.

A smile was glued to his face as he clung to the fading memory of his dreams. There was a family with a young child playing Frisbee in a large, grassy yard. His gut told him that it was his family, although he still couldn't recall their faces.

A blue and yellow Frisbee flew through the air. It skimmed the top of the grass and came to a rest underneath a rose bush with bursts of red petals boldly punctuating the green shrubbery. A woman who must have been his wife, found the Frisbee and threw it back toward him and the child. Her laughter filled his ears with cheer. He tried hard to see her face, but the harder he looked the blurrier her visage became. Seeing a glimpse of their faces would give him so much hope, but there was nothing there. The way it made him feel was so real, so tangible, that it seemed more like a memory than a dream. Either way, Collin wished he could hold onto that dream forever.

Collin stood up and pulled his shirt on, sturdy old beige long sleeve t-shirt. It dawned on him that he hadn't looked at his own face since he woke up from the fever. He wasn't even sure what he would see when he found a mirror.

The home he was assigned to was a generous two-story home just a couple of blocks East of the church, close to the foot of the mountains. He liked the house despite being excessively large for just one person. Pastor Pendell insisted he take one of the few remaining unoccupied homes for himself. They had set houses aside for any newcomers to Goshen but no one had wandered into town in years and since the town lacked apartments, he didn't have much choice. Once he found his family, it would be perfect.

His house was fully furnished and the townsfolk had even donated clothing that would fit him. It was starting to get warm outside. When she delivered the clothing, Julie told him not to worry; there was plenty of clothing to fit him when the weather heated up in a couple of months. Doris promised to knit him a sweater in time for fall.

Collin walked down the hall to the only bathroom on the second floor. The previous owners painted it a pastel yellow with white stripes. Too bright for his taste but he wasn't about to complain.

Had Pendell been right? Collin thought. *Was Goshen really a blessed town?* Sometimes it certainly seemed like it. They still had running water, electricity, and a stable food supply. From the way things were described to him those were all luxuries that most of America had been without since the fever struck.

Collin leaned on the sink and stared into the mirror. His long brown hair looked unkempt. He'd have to ask about the town barber.

Wait, he thought, peering closely at his reflection. He didn't remember those streaks of gray that had snuck in near his temples. He chuckled at the realization. Other than that, there was nothing surprising. He looked the same as he remembered. The same lines, familiar eyes, and the same strong chin.

He turned the knob for cold water and washed his face.

Water streamed down and dripped off of his nose and chin. He smiled into the mirror and examined his teeth. They were all there and seemed to be in good working order.

Collin raised his shirt and looked at himself. His muscles lacked the fullness he was used to. He looked like a starving person, but he guessed that was to be expected after surviving so long on a liquid based diet. There was no doubt that Doris would enjoy putting some meat on his bones. He had to watch out for that one, he thought with a smile.

Collin caught another whiff of bacon and remembered hearing a sound in the kitchen. Someone was in his house. He was presented with the house after the Council meeting, but he didn't remember anyone coming in with him that night.

Satisfied with his appearance, Collin found the stairs and quickly descended to the first floor. He padded quietly across the floor, following his nose in the direction of the kitchen. He pushed open the swinging kitchen door, ready for anything, and was mildly surprised to see Kobyashi in his kitchen.

Collin took in the room, squinting against the bright sunlight reflecting off the white subway tile. The kitchen was setup farmhouse style, very comfortable and welcoming. On the counter next to the stove, was a plate piled high with a small mountain of bacon.

"Good morning, Koby," he said, quickly stepping around his friend to snatch a piece of bacon before he could be denied.

"Hey!" said Koby, swatting at his hand like a mother hen. "Good morning Sleeping Beauty."

Collin rolled his eyes and quickly stuffed the bacon in his mouth. It was the best thing he'd eaten since waking up in the hospital.

"Are you ready?" Koby asked, frowning at Collin.

"Yes, I'm starving."

"For church. I meant, are you ready for church?"

Collin looked down at himself and gestured with his hands. "It's breakfast time, man. Stop joking around."

Koby folded his skinny arms over his tiny chest in his best tough guy stance and stared at Collin.

"Why the hell did you cook bacon, in my house I might add, only to try and whisk me away to church of all things?" Collin was genuinely disappointed.

"You don't remember Pastor Pendell asking you last night? And then you agreed to attend church. All of this was after the Council meeting. Ringing a bell yet?"

Collin's head and shoulders slumped in defeat. "Damn. That's right. Do I really have to go?"

Pastor Pendell had indeed "asked" him to attend church. Collin knew damn well that church attendance was essentially mandatory in Goshen. So of course, he had agreed.

Koby shot him a look.

"Fine. I'll go get ready," said Collin with a groan. He pushed his chair back and stood up.

"Sit down and eat first. I was just messing with you." Kobyashi laughed, waving his hand to stop Collin. "You should have seen your face, man. Like I just dick punched you. Priceless."

"Idiot." Collin sat down.

Koby brought out a pan from the oven with hash browns and set it on the counter. He piled some on a plate, with a stack of bacon and a pair of fried eggs.

"Toast is on the way," Koby said as he put the plate in front of Collin.

His eyes grew wide at the feast. "This is amazing, man. Thanks."

Conversation was sparse as both men ate quickly, enjoying the small feast.

Collin looked up at Koby, who was shoveling food into his mouth.

"Did you know Pastor Pendell before the fever?" he asked.

Koby shook his head. "Never knew him or the town until I showed up. I was a wanderer that they took in. Thankfully, I had useful skills to offer in return."

"Did you come alone?"

"No. There were others. The fever is a cruel bitch. Most of them were consumed by it before we started receiving BT76. A few died from Viper attacks," said Koby. He looked at Collin and said, "Technically, you've been in Goshen longer than I have."

Collin grunted. "What the hell is BT76?"

"Basically, it's a vaccine of sorts. It temporarily protects us from the fever. I'm not up on all the medical lingo, but we have Dr. Horner for that," Koby replied.

Collin chewed his last mouthful of eggs and hash browns and made a mental note to talk to the doctor about the fever.

After breakfast, Collin dashed upstairs to shower and change. Before

Koby finished washing the dishes, he was dashing down the stairs ready to go.

"That was quicker than losing my virginity," Koby said when he appeared downstairs.

Collin shrugged. "Scrub and go. No need to dawdle."

Koby gave the frying pan a quick scrub, rinse, and set it on top of the stove to dry.

"Let's go then."

They exited the house. Collin pulled the door closed behind them and followed Koby down the stairs to the sidewalk. He was surprised to see the streets dotted by hundreds of people making their way toward the church.

"Wow. That's a unique sight," said Collin. "It's like a mass migration. I had no idea there were so many people here."

"Oh?" Kobyashi smiled. "Yeah. Well, I guess I've gotten used to it."

"Everybody goes?"

"Except for the Eagles, yes." Koby nodded. "When the fever unraveled our lives and caused civil society to crumble, people turned to the government and the church for help and protection from criminals and the fever. Government is made of normal people who have their own lives to worry about, while the bond among the faithful proved to be stronger. So I guess that lesson stuck with people."

Collin paused a moment before saying, "Why not the Eagles? Busy with guard duty?"

"Pretty much," Koby said. "Pastor Pendell meets with them separately. Guard duty is heavier during service just because the town is so vulnerable, while some of the guys get to sleep in."

"That must be nice," said Collin. He returned a wave from his neighbors.

"Yet another perk afforded to the alpha males of society."

Collin laughed.

"So if the Eagles are for defense, who polices the streets?"

"In town there's not much crime. The Eagles take care of police work when it's needed. Outside in the woods it's another story. That's where the Vipers lurk," said Koby.

He met the Vipers in the hospital and could understand Koby's ominous tone.

Pastor Pendell stood outside the church greeting people as they made their way up the steps. Collin thought he looked an awful lot like a politician working the rope lines.

"Good morning, Pastor," said Collin with a wave as they made eye contact.

"Good morning to you," said Pastor Pendell grinning widely. "We've been blessed with more beautiful weather. Please go in and have a seat."

Pastor nodded at Koby, thanking him for restoring the power earlier that morning.

Collin and Koby each shook hands with Pastor Pendell before entering the church.

"I'm sitting in the back. You mind?" said Collin. He pointed to a pair of chairs at the end of a row.

"I don't mind at all," said Koby. He lowered his voice. "To be honest, most of the time, I sleep or daydream about work stuff. Or hot women."

Collin chuckled.

Doris spotted them before they could sit down and blend in with the crowd. She waved a hand at them and hurried over politely. She wore a pastel yellow dress with little white flowers, which made her stand out in the crowd like a beacon. As soon as she reached Collin, she wove her hand through his arm, linking them together.

"Collin, would you like to join us up front?" Doris said.

"That's sweet but I was actually hoping you'd like to join us back here. I'm trying to avoid too much attention," said Collin. He tried pulling away gently so he could sit down, but the old lady had a firm grip. He looked at Koby for help.

"The ladies from the women's auxiliary would love to meet you," Doris added.

"Yeah, go meet the ladies, Collin," said Koby with a huge grin. "It'll be fun."

Doris must have taken that as consent.

"Great, right this way," she said, pulling Collin along with her.

He waved at Collin and said, "See ya later buddy."

Collin turned and shook his fist at Koby, which just made him laugh.

As Doris led him slowly down the aisle, clutching his arm as if she knew he was a flight risk, he became aware of the quiet stares, whispers, and buzz that his presence was generating. It was exactly why he wanted to stay in the back. She was probably eating this up.

Collin felt bad for thinking that. He didn't know her that well, so he shouldn't judge her. All the attention did give him pause. He looked around at the people watching him. He nodded and waved at a few people. One woman blushed and waved back. He realized that he was the closest thing these good folks had to a celebrity in their broken world. Pastor Pendell called him a miracle. Others told him privately that he gave them hope. Should he deny them that hope?

Doris stopped at the front of the church. Collin half expected her to introduce him to the entire congregation. Thankfully, she simply gestured for him to take a seat in a row full of middle-aged and older ladies in the first two rows on the left side of the church. He couldn't have imagined a less desirable place to sit.

A couple dozen women looked at him with beaming smiles. Collin looked back, smiled awkwardly, and gave a brief wave. He sat down as quick as he could and Doris squeezed in beside him, trapping him there.

Almost on cue, music started playing, and a choir filed out of a hidden door. They stood on a small raised platform in matching black and red robes and began to sing. Everyone reached forward to pull out a small blue book, turning dutifully to the recommended page on a black and white board at the front of the church. Sensing his confusion, Doris helpfully pointed it out to him. He nodded and smiled.

On some subtle cue that completely escaped Collin, the entire congregation stood up. He was caught off guard and remained seated until Doris poked him for being too slow to join in. He smiled again, hating himself for not running away from this town and taking his chances in the woods.

He played the part though, even attempting to lip sync the song.

They sang several more lines before the song mercifully came to an end. On another cue everyone but Collin sat. Doris tugged on his shirt and he quickly sat down. Women giggled behind him.

"Thank you," he said quietly, feeling his face redden. "I'm completely lost without you."

"My pleasure, dear," she said proudly. She smiled and sat a little more straight.

Pastor Pendell strode out of a door hidden in an alcove behind the podium opposite where the choir had emerged.

Now that the process no longer required his participation, Collin's mind wandered elsewhere.

His thoughts immediately went to his dream and how it related to other dreams and flashbacks he'd experienced. For some reason, he could never see people's faces. He'd get a sense of their form and personality but he could never truly see them. It was as if someone went in and intentionally blurred every memory he had.

He was vaguely aware of Pastor Pendell making references to him. Doris nudged him a few times and he looked up and smiled. It seemed to be sufficient.

One reference did catch his ear though. Pastor Pendell compared Collin's awakening to Jesus rising on Easter Sunday and ascending into heaven. The comparison to Jesus made him uncomfortable, but he wasn't about to interrupt the Pastor. Much better to leave him to the business he knew best.

Distracted from his thoughts, Collin took some time to look around the church and satisfy his curiosity. He felt like he'd sat in churches like this before. As usual, he couldn't pinpoint any references from his past, but it felt like a good mental exercise to compare what he saw to the impressions hiding in the shadows of his mind. If he was lucky, something he saw might unlock a memory.

Behind the podium where Pendell spoke, stood a massive white cross carved with a depiction of crucified Jesus. Collin never understood the fixation with the mechanism of Christ's death, but so many churches featured his crucifixion, that it was an expected feature. Just behind the cross was a large, ornately carved wooden dresser, with decorative backing that reached up to the ceiling. It's top edge was punctuated by miniature spires of varying height. Set in the wood, above the dresser, was a tall, ancient looking painting of Jesus looking regal and holy in a white robe.

Given the intense social pressure to attend church, he wondered what happened to those who failed to conform. Were any of those people still around? Collin got the impression they would be made to feel most unwelcome.

The church was packed to beyond capacity. If there were still Fire Marshals around, one would shut this place down. With all of the seats taken, people were standing along the sides and in the back. He even noticed a few sitting cross-legged in the aisle.

He sighed. Nothing so far brought forth a memory.

Then he noticed some of the people staring at him. Some smiled, some looked neutral, but he could suddenly feel dozens of pairs of eyes laser-focused on him. It made Collin want to melt in place and puddle underneath the pew. But he also couldn't help wondering how many of the people had really come to church that morning to see him. The survivor.

Being the new guy in a small town drew attention. Being the new guy in a small town, and the first to awaken from a catastrophic disease that had supposedly wiped out society, was on a whole other level.

Collin sighed and focused on the sermon.

It was incredible the influence that Pastor Pendell wielded in Goshen, especially for an African-American man. Montana wasn't exactly a racially diverse state. When Collin lived in Kalispell during his sophomore year of high school, his friend Joel was the only black kid in the whole town. A fact made slightly more difficult since he was also adopted. They had played on the football team together.

The vivid recollection surprised Collin.

Did the Fighting Beavers of Goshen still play football? He was dying to ask. Collin glanced at Doris and realized that she was deeply entranced by Pastor Pendell.

Best not to interrupt, he thought but made a mental note to ask about football at lunch.

Collin leaned back and sat politely through the rest of Pastor Pendell's service.

Several times, Collin found himself drawn into parts of Pendell's sermon by his deep voice and rhythmic speech pattern. There was no question that Pendell was charismatic when he was preaching. You could see his passion for the material burning in his eyes.

That didn't stop Collin from being among the first to exit the church once the sermon concluded. After a brief thank you and goodbye to Doris and her friends, he swiftly dodged through the crowd to the fresh air outside. He'd done the same thing after the Council meeting the night before too.

On his way out of the church, several people stopped him to congratulate him and welcome him "back." Collin shook their hands politely but hustled away as fast as he could.

He made his way down the steps to the gravel road without waiting for Kobyashi.

Chapter Seven

Collin walked home thinking about how last night the town seemed so mysterious, while daylight revealed it as a rather generic looking American town. The kind you'd drive through without stopping but still remark on its quaint, small town charm.

The quick flowing river was the soundtrack of Goshen that could be heard almost everywhere. The soothing splash and burble of the water pulled him toward the riverbank as he walked down the street. Snow was still melting off the peaks from the surrounding mountains and working its way down their slopes, filling the river with spring runoff.

On the way to church, he noticed there was a tiny park not far from the bridge where he could sit. The park was little more than a large, abstract shape of grass with a bench, a garbage can, some trees and a paved path running around it all.

There was also a small playground for children. Collin had observed a decent number of kids in the food hall and at church service. He sighed to himself and wondered how different life in this new world would be for a child who knew nothing of what had come before.

No one else was around which fulfilled the key points for Collin, that it was empty and quiet.

Collin sat down on the bench and leaned back. A soldier crossing the bridge gave him a short wave. Collin waved back. Then he turned his attention to the water, watching it ripple and curl around rocks before it slowed into a calm pool under the bridge before continuing into the distant mountains, which hugged the town on three sides.

Truly, it was a spectacular area, full of beauty and a sense of calm.

Collin watched the water and tried to clear his mind. He hoped relaxing might trigger memory flashes. So far nothing else he tried had worked. The flashbacks seemed to be random, not necessarily set off by a sound or smell like he originally guessed. Dr. Horner told him that his memories would probably return slowly over time, of their own accord. He didn't want to wait. He wanted to remember everything now.

Collin took a deep breath, enjoying the cool spring air. He stood up and stretched and slowly meandered along the shore of the river.

One-hundred twenty-seven steps was all he'd taken when he heard crunching gravel behind him. Glancing over his shoulder, Collin saw Julie and Koby heading toward him. He stopped to let them catch up.

"Hey guys, how's it going?" Collin asked.

"Better now that I'm away from Logan," said Kobyashi.

"We just wanted to catch you up on everything, and give you a chance to ask us questions. Pastor wanted to do it himself but you know, running a town is demanding work," said Julie. "So he sent us instead."

"No patients today?" asked Collin.

"Nothing until after lunch. It's usually slow around the hospital, unless there's an attack and we take casualties," she said. "And now that you're not there, we have a lot less work to do."

"Do you have a staff at the hospital?" Collin asked. He almost slapped himself in the face when he realized he had witnessed the murder of two nurses. "I'm sorry. Those two women. I'm sorry for your loss."

"Janet and Mia were both great nurses. It's going to be tough now that they're gone." Her voice trailed off.

Kobyashi took up the slack. "I suppose we should start at the beginning, right? The fever and all that preceded it."

Collin nodded, not that he had much choice. He already knew Koby well enough to know that his new friend was about to drop a knowledge bomb on him.

Koby thought for a moment, tapping a finger against his chin.

"What do you know about bees and agriculture?" he finally said.

Collin snorted. "The basics that everyone learns - they make honey and pollinate plants."

"Not just any plants," said Kobyashi. "They pollinated many of the major crops that people around the world relied on. For many years prior to the fever, the bee population was suffering from colony collapse disorder caused by pesticides and other things such as mites, climate change, and habitat loss."

"And this caused people to go into comas?" Collin said, confused.

"Not directly," Koby said. "So, bee populations were collapsing, and it affected agriculture and how much food was available. People grew irate at the lack of food, starvation was on the rise, and that sparked a lot of crime. Desperate people will do anything to survive. The streets filled with protesters, people fought over food, and the cost of produce and, well, most food skyrocketed. Eventually recognizing that they ignored the root causes for too long, governments and businesses scrambled to do whatever they could to fix the problem. Sadly, it was too little, too late."

Julie cut in. "One solution they explored was a line of genetically modified crops that would produce more pollen, deter pests, and be safer for bees than the previous pesticides."

"Yeah, that was the problem there," said Kobyashi. "I mean, how is it going to help the bees if the plants produce more pollen? It was a strange approach in my opinion, but they were clutching at anything. The company that developed the GMO crops was able to get them to the market quickly, like within months. It was almost like they had them ready for years just sitting there waiting to be used. And then the law of unintended consequences kicked in."

"What does that mean?" Collin asked. "And what are GMO crops?"

"GMO is an acronym that stands for genetically modified organism. Normally it's a safe process by which agricultural companies try to improve crops. In fact, before the fever, all major crops were genetically modified in some way, either through selective breeding or through more specific alterations in a lab. The problem was that the pollen produced by this new line of crops had a serious flaw which was overlooked in the rush to market," said Kobyashi.

Doctor Horner nodded and said, "The alterations and the pollen were flawed, deeply flawed. It not only accelerated the loss of bee populations, but it also made people sick. The infected get terrible fevers and fall into a coma caused by an imbalance of chemicals in the brain. It's actually quite fascinating how it happens."

She glanced up at the two men when no one responded. Collin and Koby both gaped at her.

"Um...from a medical science perspective. Of course, it's been a terrible tragedy," she quickly added.

Koby shot Collin a look.

Collin raised his eyebrows, but didn't say anything.

Their meandering walk brought them near the bridge. Collin slowly started across the bridge.

"People all around the world were falling into these fevered comas which were labor intensive to maintain. Mind you, this was happening by the thousands, maybe by the millions. Many died after just a few days because the hospitals were full; the rest didn't receive adequate care. More died as resources began to diminish, which of course, made things worse. A vicious circle." Julie sighed as she brushed a piece of hair behind her ear. "Essentially, cities filled with people slowly wasting away."

"With no one left to keep things running, things spiraled out of control," Collin said. He let out a low whistle as he contemplated what that must have looked like.

"Basically, yeah," said Kobyashi. "It turned into a big cluster. Basic services began to fail and things went from bad to worse. Border skirmishes erupted as people migrated in search of food and medicine. Basically anything they could find – dogs, cats, and rats become common meals."

Silence.

"How many people did we lose?" Collin asked. He wondered what chance, if any, his family actually had, if it was as bad as Koby and Dr. Horner made it out to be. Was Pastor Pendell just toying with him?

Koby glanced at Dr. Horner. His hands were fidgeting with the buttons on his jacket.

"From what we could tell before broadcasting failed, it was around eighty percent of the population," she said. "But that's just the US, of course in less developed countries the casualty rate would be higher, due to lack of medical care."

"Without BT76, most of the initial survivors likely contracted the fever," Julie added.

Collin stopped walking. He could barely breathe - eighty percent? At least. A tragic disaster of epic proportions. He could hardly believe it. What had become of his parents? Friends, neighbors, and distant relatives? Probably all dead.

"How did you guys survive such terrible odds?" Collin said gasping for air.

"We got lucky here because we are relatively isolated. Traditionally, this region favors livestock over agriculture, which helped," Kobyashi said. He kicked at the gravel. "After an attack by the Vipers that burned a bunch of our food crops, I realized we'd need a safer way to grow produce. That's when we started the indoor gardening systems in everyone's basements and spare bedrooms."

"Sometimes the best things happen when you least expect them," said Dr. Horner.

"Like a finger in the butt," Koby proudly said, laughing at his own joke. He stopped fidgeting.

The doctor made a vomiting sound.

Collin cracked a faint smile. It quickly faded. His mind was still reeling at the thought of what happened. With so many people gone, what would the world look like, how would it function, was it possible that humanity would go extinct?

"Do people still come down with the fever?" said Collin.

"Rarely these days. We have a treatment called BT76, which protects us but we have to take it consistently, every month," said Julie. "Sometimes supplies aren't always consistent."

Collin glanced at her. "Where does this treatment come from? Do you know if my family has access to it?"

Julie raised her hands. "I really don't know anything about your family. The treatment comes from a company called Hathaway Agricultural Genetic Sciences, who air drops it periodically."

"They know about the town?" asked Collin. "Why don't they send help?"

Kobyashi shook his head.

Julie shrugged. "Who could they send?"

"Thing is," Kobyashi said. "HAGS is also the bad guy. I mean, they're the whole reason we're in this mess. They created the crops that ended up infecting everyone." He took a deep breath. "They destroyed the world."

Collin didn't say anything.

Julie touched his arm and it sent a shockwave of emotion through him.

"That's why I would like to ask you to help me with something critically important."

He looked at her, curious about how he could help. He was no scientist that much he knew for sure. However, he had a feeling that he would do whatever she asked of him.

"Since you're the first to wake up from the fever, that means your body must have some mechanism for beating the infection. I would like to take periodic blood samples in order to synthesize a vaccine. This way we can wean the town off BT76 and free ourselves from reliance on HAGS." She looked hopefully at him.

"If my blood is able to help people, I'm honestly surprised you didn't already take it while I was in the hospital," he said with a crooked smile. "It's not like I could have objected."

Koby snorted. "That's what we told her!"

"There was no way to know he wouldn't succumb eventually, and until he woke up we had no idea how special he was," Julie said to Koby, slapping his shoulder. "Besides, unlike some people, I have ethics. I wasn't going to take and use blood samples without consent."

"I'm special too right?" Koby joked, causing the doctor to roll her eyes.

Collin pushed Koby playfully and said, "I appreciate the consideration, Doctor."

Just then, he felt something splatter on his ear and trickle down his neck. It was too sunny to be rain. He touched his ear and felt something sticky. Looking at his fingers, he realized it was blood.

During their walk, the group had wandered underneath one of the Eagle's Nests, the security posts the town installed high up in trees. Collin looked up just as another droplet splashed down the side of his neck.

Koby saw the blood on Collin's hand. "Hey, you okay?"

"Yeah but whoever is up there isn't," Collin said pointing up the tree.

Rustling. Thumping. A body dropped between the branches.

Collin launched himself at Julie, pushing her out of the way.

The body slammed into the ground behind him with an audible crunch.

Collin turned to look at the body. The man landed on his side but twisted so his torso faced the sky. His head arched back unnaturally from a ragged, sloppy gash low across his throat. It gaped at him like a demonic grin.

Julie gasped. She quickly looked him over then said, "I'll tell the guards." She ran off in the direction of a nearby patrol.

"Christ!" said Koby. He slowly backed away from the body until he bumped into the tree. Startled, he ran a few dozen feet away from the tree. Once he realized he just bumped into the tree, he stopped and stared at the body.

Collin was looking at the tree figuring out how to get up to the nest. The

Eagles operated in pairs and whoever did this might still be up there. Or the other soldier may need his help.

He rushed around to the far side of the huge tree, the side facing the town, and found a ladder.

Twin lengths of thick rope hung down from branches high up in the tree supporting solid wooden rungs. Wood spacers attached to the back of each rung pressed against the tree trunk for stability, yet left ample space for hands and feet. Collin also saw several places where rope was looped around the tree to provide lateral support.

Collin grabbed the ladder and started up.

Koby's panicked voice yelled at him from behind. "What are you doing?"

"I'm going to see if the other Eagle needs help," Collin said.

"Are you sure that's a good idea?"

Collin ignored him and kept climbing.

The strong, sappy scent of pine surrounded Collin as he pushed and pulled himself higher through the branches to reach the Eagle's Nest. His shoulders and forearms burned with the effort, but he kept going.

Another odor mixed with the pine. One he'd smelled in the hospital after the attack.

Death.

Finally, Collin reached the bottom of the nest.

The structure was just above him. Entry would be through a big cutout in the camouflage-painted, wooden floor. Not ideal. He'd be exposed. Of course, he was exposed the entire time he was on the ladder.

Collin stopped below it, pulling his feet under him so he had to bend over to not bump his head against the edge and settled his breathing. He didn't sense anyone inside. That didn't bode well for the other soldier.

Straining his ears for any sound, he plotted his entry strategy. Coming up through the hole would be awkward, and anyone inside would have an easy shot at him. Speed was the key and he hoped he could muster enough strength to move quickly.

With his strategy decided, Collin held onto the rungs just below the opening. He moved his legs up underneath him as close as he could, so he was effectively squatting down like a frog. He took a deep breath and sprang.

He launched up, caught the edges of the hole with his hands, and held his weight as he moved his legs up. He flung a knee on the floor and crouched. There wasn't much room to move and it was readily apparent that no attacker was inside. Where had they gone?

Collin was impressed with the Eagle's Nest.

What started out as a simple tree stand had been heavily modified. A necessity given the amount of time Goshen needed to defend itself.

There were two hunting-style tree stands securely lashed to the tree trunk, facing roughly thirty degrees apart, giving the two soldiers overlapping fields of fire and a full view of the valley and farmland below. The wooden structure was like a small tree fort. It was minimal but would provide cover from the elements and incoming arrows. It consisted of a simple slanted roof and a low wall with a wide windowsill to accommodate sandbags for the soldiers' rifles.

Slumped sideways, dead in the second seat was another Eagle. A long knife protruded from his chest. It pinned a note to the man's body.

Collin snatched the note away and read it to himself. He shook his head in disbelief.

Before heading back down, Collin looked around for any clues, but he saw nothing of interest. So he climbed back down.

As he neared the halfway point and was partially visible below, Kobyashi yelled, "Anything?"

"We need Major Logan and Pastor Pendell right away," he replied.

Julie came jogging back with a half-dozen Eagles before Collin reached the ground. He looked down and saw them covering the body with a sheet, and preparing a body bag.

"What were you thinking?" Dr. Horner said, wagging a finger at him like an angry mother as soon as his feet hit the ground.

Collin scowled and stepped back from the ladder. "I was thinking the other guy might need help."

Her eyes grew wide and she looked up, then back at Collin.

He shook his head.

"This was stuck to his chest," he said pulling the note out of his pocket. He cleared his throat and read it to them. "The next drop of BT76 is ours. Leave it be. Try and die."

Everyone was quiet.

Chapter Eight

"You two go," Julie said. "I'll stay here and do what I can."

A couple of Eagles were already climbing up the rope ladder to retrieve their friend's body.

Collin nodded and glanced at Koby. "How fast can you run?"

"Faster than you, Sleeping Beauty." Koby took off at a fast jog toward the bridge.

Collin quickly rolled the note and held it in one hand, like a relay baton. Then he took off after Koby.

By the time he neared the bridge they were neck and neck. Koby bumped him with an elbow, which he returned.

Kobyashi lost half a step trying to dodge the elbow bump and failed.

Collin estimated the distance to the church, where they were most likely to find Pastor Pendell, at about three-fourths of a mile.

He shook his head at the realization that it'd been at least sixteen years since he ran that far. It still blew his mind. Even after just two days, he was feeling stronger. Strength was returning at a much faster rate than his memories were, which was frustrating.

Koby and Collin jogged along together, feet crunching gravel, rushing to pass the news on.

"You're fast," said Kobyashi between breaths.

"Thanks. You too," said Collin.

With a single block remaining until they reached the sidewalk in front of the church steps, Koby sped up. Collin said, "Aw, hell no."

The two men sprinted down the street like kids during summer vacation. Arms pumping, legs churning, and lungs processing oxygen at a magnificent rate, they reached the massive white building.

Koby had him by half of a step.

Huffing loudly he said, "Great run, sir."

"Thanks." Collin wiped his arm across his sweaty forehead. He felt fantastic — so alive — as the energy buzzed through his body. "Okay, okay. You ready to do this?"

Koby nodded and motioned for a him to follow.

The pair made their way through the center aisle of the church while they tried to catch their breath from the sprint. They would need to do so prior to reaching the staircase to Pendell's office.

Koby slowed until they were shoulder-to-shoulder. Then he started humming, "Here Comes The Bride."

Collin chuckled, but elbowed his friend. "Not the best time for jokes."

"You're probably right."

The alcove containing the cross and carved wooden display was much larger up close than it had seemed earlier. Ten feet past the podium where Pastor Pendell had given his speech, Koby motioned to the right. Through an oversized door was a winding staircase. Collin followed Koby up the staircase to the second floor. A short hallway led to the office.

Koby knocked hard three times and waited to be summoned inside.

Muffled from behind the thick doorway, they heard Pastor Pendell say, "Please come in."

Koby opened the door and held it open for Collin.

Pastor Pendell was sitting behind his desk. To their surprise, Major Logan was seated across from the Pastor. Collin ignored Major Logan's skeptical glare.

"Pastor, there's been an attack on the Eagles. This note was left behind," Collin said, leaning forward to hand him the note.

Major Logan's hand shot up and snatched it from Collin. He stood up and read it. His jaw clenched, tightening the skin on his reddening face.

Lowering the note slightly, Major Logan looked at Pastor Pendell and said, "I told you this day would come." Then he slammed the note down on the Pastor's desk and began to pace the room.

Pastor Pendell stood up calmly and fixed a hard stare on the man. "Major, I would remind you to address me with the respect I am due."

Major Logan stopped pacing and stared back. "Of course," he said slowly. "My apologies."

The major went back to pacing. Pastor Pendell sat down and looked at Koby and Collin in turn.

"Please sit." He waved a hand at the two empty chairs across from him. "Tell me what happened."

Kobyashi looked at Collin and motioned for him to go ahead and explain. So Collin told him everything, that they were walking and discussing things when the body suddenly fell out of the tree. He told them how Julie ran for help and how he climbed up to try and help the second Eagle or stop the attacker, but there was no attacker and the second Eagle was already dead. No one spoke when Collin finished.

"What does the letter mean?" Collin finally asked.

Pastor Pendell flattened the paper down on his desk. He stared at it for several seconds before pushing it to the side.

"Nothing you need to concern yourself with," said Pendell. He folded his hands calmly on the desk in front of him and leaned forward. "It's no trouble at all. Just more of the usual boasting. The Lord is watching over us, and we shall be thankful for his blessings."

Collin couldn't believe Pastor Pendell. He turned in his chair and glanced at Major Logan pacing.

"You've gotta be kidding me. Two men, who should have been safe, just died gruesome deaths. Gauging by Major Logan's reaction this isn't exactly a normal situation. It's not just the 'usual boasting.' I'm tired of getting evasive answers to things," said Collin. "What's really going on here, Pastor?"

"I don't believe I need to explain myself to you." Pastor Pendell watched him sternly over his folded hands.

"You've been teasing me along since I woke up. I have yet to hear an explanation about my family's whereabouts. I have no tangible evidence that you have any clue about them at all," said Collin. "When I was asleep, I had no choice about where I was. Now I do. If you can't back up your claims, then it's time for me to move on."

Pendell continued staring at him. Kobyashi didn't say anything. Major Logan stopped pacing.

Pastor Pendell shifted slightly in his chair. Collin didn't budge.

"Perhaps you're right-"

"Perhaps?" Collin said.

"No. You're right. I haven't been entirely forthcoming with you." He took a deep breath before continuing. "The Vipers are becoming more bold and ambitious in their attacks. A few months ago, an assault like the one they perpetrated on the hospital would have been unthinkable. They're clearly growing desperate."

"Desperate for what? The BT76 treatment?" said Collin.

"Exactly. They want to steal what isn't theirs and deny our peaceful citizens their treatments. We can't allow that. The Vipers will feel the Lord's wrath." Pastor Pendell slammed his fist on the desk.

No one said anything.

Then Collin leaned back in his chair. If his family was still alive, they would need BT76. Helping the town protect their supply would help his family. He sighed.

"What can I do?"

Pastor Pendell guffawed. "Not fight. The fight with the Vipers is our fight. Besides, you're far too valuable to risk on the battlefield."

"Have you already forgotten?" Collin said looking at Pendell like he was crazy. "That was me in the hospital. Taking out Vipers. Alone. I'm sure I can handle myself out there."

"Too true. I remember all too well," Pendell said. He rubbed his wrist, looking uncomfortable with the memory. "Very well, but we need you to stay off the front lines. Can you do that for me, please?"

"I suppose," Collin said grudgingly. "Then what can I do?"

"Stay back with us and help guard the town in case any of those bastards slip through."

"Babysit you mean?"

"There's no shame in safeguarding the weak, Collin. We have many families who lack your particular set of skills. They could use your help. Kobyashi and Dr. Horner could use your help. Major Logan has sufficient manpower within his Eagles to handle these Godless scoundrels."

"Sorry to interrupt," said Kobyashi. He stood up and cupped his ear. "Do you guys hear that?"

"Is this another stupid joke?" said Major Logan.

"I hear it too." Collin jumped up from his chair and rushed for the door.

Kobyashi followed him.

Collin looked over his shoulder and yelled at the others, "Come on."

A steady thumping grew louder and louder. Something was coming closer to the church.

Collin and Koby burst out of the church just as two Apache helicopters escorting a Blackhawk flew by overhead. The Blackhawk broke off from the other two, diving toward the farmer's fields. Both Apaches flew in slow circles overhead, while the Blackhawk slowed and flared some thirty feet off the ground. Two olive drab supply crates painted with bright white HAGS logos popped out of the side door. The chopper immediately began to rise and turn away from the town before the tubs even hit the ground. As the Blackhawk gained elevation, the Apaches circled around and took up their flanking positions.

Both tubs landed along the edge of the field to minimize crop damage, placing the tubs near the tree line.

"Well, I wasn't expecting that," said Collin, who thought there was going to be an attack. He watched the helicopters until they disappeared from view.

Collin looked over at the tubs in the field and caught Major Logan's eye.

Major Logan said in an annoyed tone, "Well, Mr. War, in case you were wondering when the message on this note would come into play, the time has come."

Chapter Nine

Major Logan strode down the road, heading toward a building called The Eagle's Bar. Prior to the outbreak of the fever, the private club served drinks and fellowship for its members, but had since been re-purposed as the central precinct for Logan's Goshen Eagles.

Collin volunteered to tag along with Major Logan and offer any assistance he could, since anything was better than babysitting civilians. Even if Logan was a dick.

The town was bustling with activity as citizens prepared for an assault that everyone knew instinctively was incoming. Collin understood the stakes; the medicine was vital according to Dr. Horner, but would the Vipers really attempt to destroy the entire town?

Not likely, he thought.

They pounded up the steps to the bar and a soldier opened the door for them. The basement was still dedicated to entertainment, while the ground floor was strictly business. All four walls were lined with lockers, shutters covered windows like they did in all the buildings, and benches gave soldiers a place to sit and tie their boots. Each soldier kept their weapon with them at all times, eliminating the need for a weapons locker.

Most of the men were geared up and awaiting orders.

"Eagles, attention!" shouted one soldier. Everyone snapped to attention as Major Logan and Collin entered the room.

As Major Logan began talking to his men, Collin experienced another flashback.

He saw himself standing at attention in Boot Camp, listening to a tough looking leatherneck Drill Instructor chewing them out. Then he flashed to weapons training. He was lying prone on the rifle range, clearing his jammed rifle while the DI yelled at him for moving like a pile of shit in a snowstorm.

When Collin's experience ended, Major Logan was already tasking squads with orders.

"Wilson, Turnbull, you guys are up on the dam. Wilson, your team's on the farm side watching the mountains. Turnbull, your team's in the middle of the dam. Copy?" said Major Logan.

"Copy, sir," Wilson, Turnbull, and their spotters said. They were the Eagle's best sniper teams and each was assigned a Barrett 82A1 .50 caliber rifle. Beast rifles.

Awesome bullet slingers, but overkill versus people armed with arrows and knives, Collin thought.

All the other sniper teams were dispatched to the Eagle's Nests. The rest of the soldiers were distributed among other key locations. Collin learned they had prepared fighting positions near the river, the bridge, and the near side of the fields.

"Remember Eagles, we are strong and prepared, but do not get overconfident nor underestimate our foe, for these are the seeds of doom. We are seventy-five against roughly three hundred Vipers. What they lack in firepower, they can make up for in cunning and sheer numbers. We will not go the way of General Custer," Major Logan said. "Keep your head on a swivel and stay alert."

He looked at each of the soldiers - men, women, young and old.

"We aren't just fighting for medicine. BT76 is vital, but we are also fighting for all of Goshen. Our town. Our homes. Our families," Major Logan said raising his voice. "The ruthless murders at the hospital the other night are but a small reminder of what these heathens will do if they prevail."

He let that sink in for a moment.

"Will we allow the Vipers to rape and pillage Goshen?"

"No, sir!"

Collin shot a questioning look at Major Logan.

"We have the training. We have the firepower. We have the good Lord on our side." Major Logan straightened up and shouted, "Stay alert!"

"Stay alive!" Everyone shouted in unison.

Collin felt goose bumps. He wanted to grab a rifle and defend Goshen too.

"Fly, Eagles," Major Logan said.

"Fly!" shouted the soldiers.

So corny, Collin thought.

Major Logan turned to Collin and motioned for him to follow.

They walked past the soldiers as they hustled out of the building to their positions. In the back corner was a door that led to a small room.

In the middle of the room was a large rectangle table containing a map of the town and surrounding area. A roster list hung on the front wall. The roster listed each Eagle's name, age, gender, and a box listing two and three letter codes.

"What are these codes?" Collin said.

"They represent various skill qualifications the soldier has passed," said Major Logan. "We have three broad categories of Eagles - assault, defense, and special skills. Special skills are snipers, demolitions, comms, et cetera."

Collin nodded his approval.

"Come look at this." Major Logan motioned for Collin to join him in looking over the map.

"I'm surprised you're showing me this," Collin admitted.

"Pastor Pendell wanted me to show you how we pull this off," Major Logan said. "I follow orders."

"Fair enough."

Everything was laid out on the map - the town, the river, the dam, the fields - and some detail in the surrounding forest. Major Logan pulled open a drawer under the table and started placing chess pieces on the map to indicate his soldiers' disposition.

"These here are our snipers on top of the dam. Of course, we have other sniper teams in the nests that ring the fields. Here we have Alpha Team." He pointed near the town-side of the bridge. "Along our side of the river is Bravo Team to provide covering fire. Bravo can also move out with Alpha if needed. These two positions here are our heavy weapons bunkers. Here and here we have mortars, although we rarely use them because ammo is running low."

"Impressive firepower."

"Indeed. Now then, a flare will be the signal for Alpha Team to move out and secure the supply crates with grappling hooks. We have horses positioned on our side to pull the crates to safety, while Alpha Team covers the extraction. Once the crates reach the bridge, Bravo team will secure them in this position by the bridge, open the crate, and manually transport the packaged medication to the hospital."

"You guys have done this before?"

"Many times. Why?"

"If the Vipers are out there, then they've seen this before," Collin said. "It's predictable, which makes us vulnerable."

"They'd be fools to try anything." He waited for any other questions. "If there's nothing else then let's head outside. We will watch the extraction from the church."

"I'll follow you, Major," said Collin.

The Eagle's Bar was only a block away from the church, which made their trip brief. Soldiers were buzzing about all over. Collin spotted Dr. Horner walking toward the bridge, presumably to observe the handling of the crates. Up ahead, on the stairs of the church, stood Kobyashi. He gave them a short wave as a greeting.

"Hey, Koby," Collin said. "You joining us?"

"If you don't mind, Major?" Koby said.

"If you must." Major Logan pushed past him and into the church.

Koby rolled his eyes. "He's still mad that I spend so much time with his mom," He whispered to Collin. "But I'm cool. I told him he doesn't need to call me daddy or anything."

Collin smiled.

They went back to the staircase that led to Pastor Pendell's office, but instead of stopping at the second floor they followed Major Logan up the spiraling staircase.

Pastor Pendell must have noticed them passing by because he called out for Koby. Collin looked back at his friend.

Koby rolled his eyes and said, "Damn. See ya later."

"See ya." Collin continued upstairs.

Major Logan was waiting for him at the top of the staircase, holding open a faded green door that led to an attic space in the bell tower.

"Where's Koby?" asked Major Logan.

"Pastor Pendell called him into his office."

Major Logan shrugged. "This way."

A wooden walkway crossed over rafters stuffed with insulation. There was another door and more stairs. These stairs were dusty and obviously rarely used. Each step creaked out a unique tune, bowing ever so slightly under their weight. Major Logan pushed open a hatch and climbed out into the open space above.

"Here we are," said Major Logan.

In the center of the square tower was a massive bell hanging from the pointed roof above them. A short railing kept people from wandering into the path of the swinging bell, even though they would have to be well over six feet tall to get hit. A walking space about four feet wide surrounding the bell took up the rest of the floor space. A waist high wall ran around the perimeter with a gap between the wall and the roof open to the outside world so people could hear the ringing bell.

The view was fantastic. From this height, they could see most of the town and nearly all of the farmland. They could see across to the dam where they saw the snipers, moving along the top to man their position. From this distance, they were little more than dark spots against the gray concrete but Collin could imagine their rifle barrels protruding over the edge; even though it'd be against sniping doctrine under normal circumstances. The Eagles had no fear of return fire since the Vipers only used primitive weapons.

"Why don't you position snipers here? This is a great location," said Collin.

"Pastor Pendell won't allow it. He doesn't want to make the church a target of retribution, plus he says the Lord's house shouldn't be used to take lives, even Vipers' lives." Major Logan lifted a pair of binoculars to his eyes and looked across to the medical supply crates.

"How does it look?" Collin asked.

"It's quiet, but my guess is Vipers are already out there watching our movements. We need to get those tubs secured," said Major Logan. He pointed under the railing on the far wall, where a set a hand-held flags hung. "Wave the green flag in the direction of the dam."

Collin stepped over and pulled the flag from its hook. He leaned over the short wall and waved the flag back and forth.

"That's good," said Major Logan.

They stood for a while just watching the fields waiting for the snipers on the dam to give the signal.

"So what's your story?" said Collin. He leaned against the wall enjoying the afternoon breeze that came down off the mountains.

Major Logan looked at him for a moment.

"My father served in the Air Force, so I grew up on air bases around the world. Went to university in Washington, D.C. I like the color green and have a German Shepherd named Chewy."

"That's sweet." Collin chuckled. "And how did you come to lead the Eagles? What are your qualifications?"

Major Logan's eyes narrowed briefly. Then he tilted his head and said, "I was a U.S. Army Ranger with the 2nd Ranger Battalion at Joint Base Lewis-McChord in Washington State, with two tours in Iraq. Later, I served in the 7th Special Forces Group out of Eglin Air Force Base in Florida although I spent much of my time in Afghanistan."

Major Logan turned back to survey the fields.

"Nice. What was your MOS?" Collin knew that some guys would boast to civilians about their military career and this simple question about their Military Occupational Specialty — or job — was a simple way to weed out most fakers.

Major Logan cocked his eyebrow at Collin. He looked surprised. "My last primary MOS was 18-Alpha, detachment commander. But I was 13-Foxtrot when I was enlisted with the Rangers before going to Officer Candidate School at Fort Benning, Georgia."

Collin nodded. "What about the Eagles? Any vets among them?"

It was Major Logan's turn to chuckle. "Many of them are experienced. They're a mix of military and law enforcement. It's work they already know and enjoy doing. Of course, the town recognizes their hardships so we reward them with the recreation room in the basement of the Eagle's Bar and a special selection of fine liquors. Eagles also receive special hunting permits that civilians don't, as well as a higher fishing limit. They can keep what they kill without having to share, although most of them do."

"Sounds fair."

Major Logan turned to look at Collin. "What about you? What's your real story?"

Collin should have expected the question considering he asked first. He opened his mouth but stopped. He shrugged.

"It's frustrating. I feel like I should know my own life story but I don't remember that much," he said. "Just a few bits and pieces and a vague sense that I've been to places like Washington, D.C., but nothing that connects them. They're just random blobs in my mind."

"That's it, huh? You don't know who you are, or why they kept you alive so long?"

"That's all I remember. Insignificant flashes of the past."

Major Logan grunted.

Still no signal from the snipers. Collin wondered what was taking so long but Major Logan didn't look concerned so he relaxed.

"You handled those Vipers at the hospital with impressive skill, according to Anna. Plus, what I saw with my own eyes in the alley," Major Logan said. "That tells us something."

"I guess. It all just flowed without thinking. It was like instinct. I'm kind of nervous to find out who I was before the fever. Maybe I was a bad person?" Collin said.

"You're kidding, right?" Major Logan said.

"I don't feel regret for killing those guys."

"They were murderers, why would you?"

Collin shrugged.

"C'mon, seriously. You really don't know who you were?" said Major Logan with a laugh.

"No. I don't know." Collin frowned. "Do you?"

"You have no clue why you're important?" Major Logan laughed again. "Why do you think they kept your sleepy ass alive?"

"Dr. Horner seems to think she can use my blood to help the people of Goshen fight the fever without BT76."

"Hmm, so I've heard. I wouldn't put too much stock in that," Major Logan said. "I would be surprised if we had the equipment needed to analyze and synthesize a vaccine. But she seems confident."

"Do you know who I was? Why they kept me alive?"

A bright red flare shot through the air from the dam and drifted down through the air on a parachute, glowing brightly even in the daylight.

"Ah, here we go. Showtime," said Major Logan. "We'll have to save the soul searching for later, sir."

Sir? Collin thought the formality sounded odd, considering the source.

Alpha team rushed over the bridge in two staggered columns. The last man in each column held the grappling hooks. Ropes trailed behind to a pair of draft horses that stood ready to pull the supply crates to safety.

The columns of soldiers leap-frogged across the fields, their guns trained toward the tree line. It only took a minute or two before they were halfway across the fields.

Three shrill tweets from atop the dam broke the silence.

Alpha team stopped advancing and knelt in the tilled soil.

"What's that?" said Collin.

"Vipers have been spotted."

"Why are those snipers revealing their position?"

"They're far out of the Viper's range, and they're in the best position to see the enemy and alert everyone else. Unconventional for sure, but it works."

Nothing happened. No attack. No movement.

Alpha team leader stood and motioned for his men to follow. They were on the move again.

Collin felt more nervous watching these soldiers risk themselves, than he felt that night in the hospital.

More whistle blasts from atop the dam.

"What's that one mean?"

"No idea," said Major Logan. He raised his binoculars and looked up at the dam then swung them across to the tree line.

Suddenly, a buzzing filled the air. Collin saw what could only be a massive cloud of arrows buzzing in a large arc toward Alpha team. Without thinking, he leaned over the wall and screamed, "Take cover."

If Alpha team heard him, they didn't react in time. They couldn't have anyway. Hundreds of arrows rained down all around them. All over them. No cover in the fields and plenty of cover in the tree line. Bodies full of arrows slumped to the ground. Legs kicked, arms twitched, and a few cries could be heard.

"Christ," whispered Major Logan.

Classic tactic, thought Collin. He shook his head, saddened by the team's loss.

Booming shots rang out from atop the dam. Then shots cracked from the Eagle's Nests too. A steady, methodical rhythm as the snipers picked away at the Viper's numbers.

Bravo team rallied on the bridge. One squad fanned out and took a knee while the other squad rushed out to help Alpha team. It was futile but understandable.

Another volley of arrows whistled through the air. This round was less effective because most of the remaining squad wasn't in range.

To the left of the bridge, on the farm side of the river, a heavy weapons position opened fire with a machine gun.

"Pound 'em," Collin said to himself.

The right side heavy weapons position also opened fire. Their fields of fire would criss-cross each other, converging at different angles on the Vipers shooting position. Sniper fire continued at random intervals.

A loud blast rocked the edge of the farmland, as if a bomb detonated. Trees shivered from the blast wave as it dissipated against their trunks. The smaller trees toppled over. Another boom echoed across the valley and two massive pine trees leaned toward the fields, falling slowly then speeding up as they gained momentum. The Vipers must have used a line of detonation cord, wrapped around the trunks of the big pines, to bring them down.

Bravo team soldiers in the field scrambled back toward the bridge. The massive trees landed with ground-trembling thumps, kicking up dust and dirt that mixed with the cloud of debris from the explosives.

Through the smoke, Collin could make out something moving.

He pointed. "Do you see that?"

Major Logan looked through his binoculars.

"I see something moving but it's too...wait. What the hell?"

Wind coming down off the mountains cleared out the smoke and unveiled the Viper's secret weapon.

Shaped like a massive turtle shell was a metallic structure. It rolled along slowly, moving along the improvised path. The two tree trunks they had felled flanked it, providing cover.

For a brief moment, none of the Eagles fired their weapons. Everyone had to be thinking the same thing - what the fuck?

Then an eruption of firepower exploded through the air. Even from the bell tower, Collin could tell the rounds weren't doing anything to the shell. How could it? The damn thing seemed to be made of steel plate.

"Christ, that thing must weigh nearly a ton," Major Logan said through clenched teeth.

The shell stopped rolling, tilted back and settled against the ground.

Sensing their ineffective shots, or perhaps on order, most of the shooting ceased. However, the two snipers on top of the dam continued firing. They had the benefit of .50 caliber rounds. Massive rounds that couldn't be stopped by such simple armor.

"The .50's are punching through," Major Logan said. "Atta boys!"

The shell levered up and began rolling forward again. It was close to the medical crates. Very close.

"Damn." Major Logan slammed his hand against the wall. "We can't lose that medicine."

Another shot by the .50s and the shell stuttered to a stop again. Unexpectedly, a few men sprinted out of the woods toward the shell. Two barely made it before the Eagle's Nests opened up on them. The third man wasn't so lucky. His body slumped face down in the dirt, and didn't move.

"I'd kill for a radio system."

Collin grunted.

The structure moved forward again to cover the last few feet to the crate full of BT76. Now they knew it was man powered, and given the way it levered up before moving, it must be working like a giant wheelbarrow. That would certainly make it easier to move all that weight.

It stopped again and didn't move. Nothing happened for a few minutes. Then another volley of arrows filled the sky at the same time as four men ran out to grab a supply crate. One was shot as they dragged it back under the cover of their turtle shell.

"No," shouted Major Logan. "We can lose men, we can lose medication, but we can't lose the medication to them."

He grabbed a purple flag from the rack and waved it.

"What does purple mean?" said Collin.

"The end of that damned contraption they built," said Major Logan.

A minute passed.

Major Logan was fidgeting. "C'mon, damnit."

Another minute.

Then a loud thunk sounded, something streaked through the air from one of the Eagle's Nests and slammed into the side of the steel-plate turtle shell in a loud explosion. Sparks and smoke shot up into the air. Another thunk from the other side of the field. This one hit low, throwing up dirt and hurling the remains of the turtle shell against the fallen tree trunk. Metal plates blown off from the explosions flipped through the air like falling playing cards.

"Holy shit, Major. You have AT4s?"

Major Logan smirked at him. "Man portable glory."

The few surviving Vipers broke for the woods. Collin was surprised any had survived. Sniper fire chased them the whole way, and only a few made it to the tree line. Collin watched, as the fleeing Vipers were dropped mid-step. He was truly impressed by the marksmanship skills of the men on the dam.

When the smoke cleared, they could see that half the panels on the left side had blown off. Body parts were strewn about, and a large hole was notched in the ground where the turtle shell used to sit. The remains of the armored shell lay crumpled against the tree. They could see the abandoned crate of medical supplies. It was damaged, but it was still on the field.

The Eagle's succeeded in keeping the BT76 out of Viper's control.

Sensing the enemy was fleeing, Bravo team moved forward and secured the hooks to the crates. The horses pulled them across the field, while Bravo turned its attention to recovering Alpha team's bodies.

"Let's head down there and check out the packages," said Major Logan.

Collin headed down the hatch and ran into Koby.

"I missed all the action?" Koby said.

"Yup, we're going out to check on the medical supplies, c'mon," said Collin.

Koby turned around and led the way out of the church.

Once in the street, they jogged the rest of the way to the bridge. Two soldiers were unhooking the crates, which up close, Collin saw were large plastic military supply crates, the kind he'd seen during his service.

Collin concluded that he definitely served in the military at some point before the fever hit. Too much of it was familiar to him. With his fighting skills on display in the hospital combined with his knowledge of weapons and the rank structure, it only made sense. He wasn't sure of much these days but that was one he would bet on.

Kobyashi looked at all the damage and shrieked. "Ohhh! Look at that mess."

"It was quite a battle," Collin said in a low voice. They lost Eagles, good people he was sure, and that was always tough even if he didn't know them. He honored their sacrifice.

"A real ball buster," said Koby. He held a hand on his forehead.

Collin could see his new friend going over the work in his head - logging the trees, cleaning up debris, removing body parts, and preparing the soil. He was thankful it wasn't his job.

Soldiers crowded around the crates.

"I can't believe those heathens attacked us with shovels and pitchforks. Did they really think they could win?" said one of the soldiers, laughing.

Collin gave the idiot a stern look. It was hard to believe he'd just heard such a remark.

Major Logan's fist shot out and flattened the nose of the inconsiderate bastard. There was an audible crunch and the man groaned, stumbling backward. He tripped and fell on his ass.

"We lost seventeen good soldiers to the Viper's arrows." Major Logan kept pounding away at the soldier who held his free hand up in a weak defense. "That's more than shovels and pitchforks you dumb sonofabitch," Major Logan shouted with a snarl. Logan punched him again before Collin caught his arm.

"Major, maintain your professional decorum for Christ's sake," said Collin. "He may have a big, dumb mouth but he's an Eagle too."

Major Logan shot him a sharp look and jerked his arm out of Collin's grip. He turned to face Collin. Leaning in close, he said, "If you ever lay a hand on me again in front of my men, it will be your blood on my hands, not some loudmouth private's."

Major Logan wiped his bloodied hand off on Collin's shirt and stalked away to attend to his other soldiers.

"What an asshole," said Kobyashi when the Major was out of earshot.

Collin and another soldier helped the loudmouth off the ground. "Get yourself to the hospital. Dr. Horner will fix you up."

He nodded and walked away, cupping his nose tenderly.

Chapter Ten

Collin followed Major Logan into the Eagle's Bar for the second time that day.

Walking down stairs to the rec room, they entered into an entirely different type of room. From the neat and orderly first floor to the dim, bar room was quite a change.

One side of the room had three pool tables with low-hanging lights and hanging on the wall behind them was a faded, battle damaged American flag in a large, oak frame. Collin made a mental note to ask about the flag's history when the time was right.

On the opposite side of the room, a bar took up the entire wall. Behind the bar were mirrors and glowing lights to show off the various bottles of liquor. Clinging to the corner edge of the bar was a giant golden statue of a bald eagle with its wings spread and beak open in the middle of an ear-splitting screech. A middle-aged man stood behind the bar, near the eagle, drying glasses and watching the two men. He gave a brief nod to the Major. He eyed Collin with curiosity. There was a dartboard in one corner and an odd assortment of posters covering the wall featuring sexy women striking alluring poses with bottles of various brands of beer. Tables and chairs filled the room with several padded booths along the third wall.

"Double whiskey," Major Logan said, rapping his knuckles twice on the bar for emphasis. Then he jerked his thumb at Collin. "And whatever he wants."

Collin looked at his options. He shrugged. "Same thing. Double whiskey neat, please."

The bartender nodded and pulled down a large bottle and two old fashioned glasses. He filled them with an expert pour, not a drop wasted, and then set each cup before them.

Major Logan raised his at Collin. "To the Eagles."

"To the Eagles," said Collin. He had no problem drinking to fallen soldiers. They had a rough day out there. He took a drink and savored the smoky flavor as it warmed him up inside.

Major Logan emptied his drink.

"Fill me up," he said to the bartender. The liquor flowed. Major Logan motioned for Collin to drink more.

Collin finished his double and set his glass down. The bartender topped him up with another.

Collin sniffed the whiskey, enjoying the smell. He saw a younger version of himself at a party of some sort, probably in university. Collin took a gulp of the whiskey, and as it ran down his throat, he remembered that he didn't actually like whiskey.

Turning to Major Logan, Collin set his glass down and said, "You know what the difference between you and me is?"

"What's that, sir." Major Logan looked at him.

Collin finished his whiskey and held up the glass, once again ignoring the use of sir when being addressed. "You drink to forget, I drink to remember."

Major Logan gulped his whiskey and set the glass down with a thud. "Come on."

Collin glanced at the bartender who just smirked at him.

"Thanks," Collin said to the bartender. The man gave him a little salute with a tip of his head. Then Collin stood and followed Major Logan back upstairs.

Major Logan led him back to the planning room. As soon as they entered, Major Logan stormed over to the table and swept his arm across the map, knocking all the pieces over. He roared with anger and flipped the table over. It clattered to the floor.

"Sonofabitch!" he yelled.

Collin stood in the doorway and waited for Major Logan to cool down.

Behind Collin in the main room, the Eagles were quiet. They continued dressing down, removing their dirty gear and prepping it for cleaning. Frustration, anger, and sadness were palpable in the air.

Major Logan pointed out the door. Collin stepped aside and let Major Logan pass. He walked into the main room and looked around at the soldiers; the men and women who fought and defended Goshen.

He stood with his hands on his hips and his head bowed.

"Good job today, Eagles," he said slowly. He raised his head. "We faced a unique threat today and you did your jobs well. We will remember those we lost today, they'll live on in our hearts and minds. We will honor them and their sacrifices. Let's take a moment of silence for the fallen."

Everyone around the room stood with their hands held in front, head bowed.

Major Logan said, "Amen." Which was echoed around the room.

"Carry on," he said.

The Eagles went back to cleaning up.

"Bring in the crates," Major Logan said to an Eagle. He had sergeant stripes on his arms.

"Yes, sir." He rounded up four guys, went outside, and carried in the large plastic tubs.

Up close, they were even bigger than Collin estimated. Each one was roughly six feet long by three feet wide and about three feet tall. The Eagles carried each of them in and set them in the middle of the floor. The second container was damaged. Some of the plastic had melted and chunks of metal were stuck where fragments of the steel plate had peppered them.

Each container had a thick padlock on it.

"Why do they have locks?" asked Collin.

"To keep the Vipers out of them," said Major Logan. "The first time we received BT76 from HAGS, the combination was painted right on the container. But since then, the number hasn't changed."

"Seems like a lot of effort if the Vipers can't get them open."

"No lock is impervious to destruction. It just makes it more difficult for them." Major Logan smiled like a shark. "One time they stole a box and it proved to be such a nuisance that the Vipers came back to kidnap our unit administrator - or secretary, if you will."

"No shit?"

"Poor girl was tortured because they believed she knew the combination."

"How do you know she was tortured?" said Collin.

"We mounted a rescue mission and were able to retrieve her from those bastards." Major Logan frowned. "This is the first time in more than a year that the Vipers have tried to steal a crate."

"Where is the girl now?"

"She won't come near this place. It makes her too anxious," Major Logan said. "Now she's a nurse and works for her mommy."

Collin realized he was referring to Anna, Dr. Horner's daughter. He thought back to that first night in the hospital when he'd rescued her from the Vipers. She seemed level headed to him, especially considering she had been under attack from the Vipers yet again.

Major Logan still hadn't opened the cases. Collin wasn't sure what he was waiting for.

"Are we waiting for something?" said Collin. "Who knows the combination?"

"Can you keep a secret?" asked Major Logan waving Collin closer.

When Collin got close enough, Major Logan threw his arm over Collin's shoulders, and pulled him even closer.

Collin turned his ear to listen to the secret code.

"So can I," said Logan with a chuckle.

Shaking his head, Collin stepped away. It wasn't critical that he know the number and in fact hadn't expected the Major to trust him with it. His little game was still annoying.

"How often does HAGS make a supply drop?" said Collin.

Major Logan stopped and looked up at Collin. "How do you know about HAGS?"

"You guys told me about them. First, at the Council meeting. Then later, when Kobyashi and Dr. Horner were briefing me about the town's background." Collin didn't see what the big deal was.

"I see," Major Logan said. "I wouldn't have told you. I don't trust you and never did."

Odd change in direction, Collin thought.

"Never did?"

"I didn't trust you when you were asleep, and I don't trust you now," said Major Logan.

"Why did you share your battle plans with me then?" Collin gestured at the room behind them. "Why am I even here now?"

"You're here with me only because Pastor Pendell wants you to be here," he said. "I only agreed because of what I saw you do at the hospital. You're a capable fighter and I need all the help I can get. Especially now."

Major Logan knelt down and turned the dial. He didn't try to hide it. If anything, he left it uncovered so Collin could see it. He turned the dial, entering the combination of 01-15-16. The lock clicked open.

Pulling off the lock and sliding out a metal rod that helped secure the edges, Major Logan lifted off the lid. Inside the thick padded case were shrink-wrapped blue and white boxes. On each box was printed the same HAGS logo that Collin recognized as the one from the sides of the choppers that had made the drop. Two neat rows of six small boxes sat in a cardboard tray, packaged together into bricks of twelve. Dozens of bricks were stacked neatly in the container.

"This is what my men died for." Major Logan tore a box out of the pack and tossed it to Collin.

Collin looked at it with interest. "How many doses are in one box?"

"Three doses per box in pre-filled injectors. Each box is enough for one person for three months. You just stick yourself in the thigh with an injector every month and you're all set. We like to give each person two boxes in case a shipment comes late," said Major Logan. "It's happened before and it creates a lot of tension in town."

"So everyone just gets two boxes?"

"Everyone but my Eagles. Each of them receive three boxes plus the standard two boxes for each of their family members."

"Understandable," said Collin. "Is there any stored up for emergencies?"

"Dr. Horner keeps a stash locked away somewhere for emergencies and critical personnel. Whatever the hell that means." Major Logan stood up.

"What happens if someone misses a dose?" Collin opened the box and looked inside. A foam block had cutouts for three injectors, as described. The liquid was in a tiny clear tube. It was bright blue like candy.

Major Logan handed Collin another box. His rations apparently. "If someone misses a dose, they get the fever. Right away or in a month, it's hard to say. But they will get the fever, they will fall asleep, and unlike you, they won't wake up. Then they'll spend several days or months slowly wasting away until their organs fail and they die."

Collin didn't like the way he framed the explanation but he wasn't in the mood to argue.

The Major went to the other case and unlocked it.

An Eagle came inside. "Major Logan, Pastor Pendell is outside and would like to speak with you, sir."

The Major sighed but stood up and started to head outside. "C'mon Collin, I'm sure whatever he has to say you'll need to hear it too."

"Shouldn't we just invite him inside? I'm sure he'll want his ration."

Several Eagles chuckled.

Major Logan smiled at him. "The good pastor won't set foot in here because we serve alcohol downstairs. He thinks it's a sin." The Major rolled his eyes.

"Ah, I see. Never mind that Jesus drank wine." Collin smiled.

The Major held his hands up in mock surrender. "We've had that conversation." Then he turned to the sergeant from earlier. "Sergeant, you're in charge of distribution. When you're done, get these cases over to the hospital. If Dr. Horner wants help unloading them, please oblige her."

"Yes, sir."

Collin followed Major Logan outside.

Pastor Pendell was standing in the middle of the gravel road, hands behind his back, waiting for them. "Good afternoon, gentlemen. Major Logan, could you please bring me a roster with the names of your fallen Eagles for the memorial tomorrow?"

Collin stood beside the Pastor.

Major Logan sighed. "You could have told my soldier to tell me that." But he turned around to fetch the requested information from inside the Eagle's Bar.

The Major strode quickly back toward the building that served as their military headquarters, when a massive explosion slammed into them.

Collin and Pastor Pendell were thrown back several feet, as the blast wave pummeled them. Their momentum ground them along the gravel road like a cheese grater, before they skidded to a stop. A dust cloud blew over them. Collin raised his head a little but couldn't see Major Logan.

Uninjured, but rattled, Collin was slow to stand up. His ears rang from the blast. Pastor Pendell appeared to be uninjured, but he wasn't conscious. Collin dragged him across the street in case there was a secondary explosion, and propped him gently against a tall oak tree. He placed his cheek near the Pendell's nose to feel for breath, found he was breathing fine, and went back for Major Logan.

It was difficult to see with all the smoke and dust. Collin covered his nose and mouth with his hands and pressed on. The mountain breeze was slowly clearing the view and he found Major Logan after only a minute of searching. Collin could hear commotion and yelling, but it was muted by the ringing in his ears. A terrible gift from the percussive blast wave.

The Major was closer to the blast. His face was peppered by fragments of glass and wood. One splinter caught him just underneath his left eye. If he was lucky, it wouldn't affect his vision. Blood trickled from the various small cuts but he didn't appear to have any major external injuries. Only the doctor could determine if he suffered any internal blast injuries. Collin carefully dragged him across the road and propped him up beside the pastor. The two men lay there slumped together like over-sized rag dolls.

He couldn't see clearly with all the smoke billowing from the building. So he jogged across the road and looked at the Eagle's Bar.

Or where it had been.

The explosion littered the area with splintered wood and bodies - whole or in pieces. The building itself was blown apart. Whatever was left had collapsed in on itself. Smoke curled out of the wreckage where small fires started burning.

Collin gasped and covered his mouth in shock. Just moments before the blast, he was inside. The soldiers had laughed at his naive question about Pastor Pendell coming inside. Now they were gone, all of them.

Realization of what happened slowly dawned on him. The Viper's hadn't just tried to take the medication. Instead, they had somehow booby-trapped it to deny Goshen the vital medication and kill, or injure, the Eagles.

Ruthless, thought Collin. He was furious and sickened at the loss of life.

Townspeople began arriving at the Eagle's Bar. Some collapsed, sobbing, as they realized their loved ones were likely inside. Proactive people went up to the building and began moving debris, hoping to find survivors.

Collin joined them, both anger and agony burning his eyes, as sweat streaked his soot covered face.

Chapter Eleven

When Pastor Pendell came to and saw the devastation, he immediately ordered them to open the basement of the church as an emergency medical unit.

The hospital had sustained substantial damage in the previous attack, and even after Koby's hard work, electricity was spotty. Pastor Pendell said even heathens like the Vipers wouldn't dare strike the church for fear of God's wrath. Collin wasn't so sure the Vipers were worried about anyone's wrath considering the low they had just stooped to.

Anna treated Major Logan first, at Pastor Pendell's insistence, plucking out the bits of glass and wood. He was indeed lucky and didn't sustain any permanent damage to his eye from the wood splinter. But his face was puffy and wrapped with bandages, like a mummy.

The pastor had a small cut along his freckled cheek where a piece of wood had embedded itself in his ebony skin. It didn't bleed at all until Anna pulled the splinter out. The pastor didn't require any stitches, just a thick bandage. Collin had made it out virtually unscathed. Just a few minor scratches on his hands where he'd been scraped while clearing debris off the Eagle's Bar looking for survivors.

Pastor Pendell walked with Collin and Major Logan through the makeshift hospital, ensuring everything was in order. Major Logan was limping slightly.

From their initial estimates, the Eagle's lost an additional fifteen soldiers in the blast. If that number stood, it would bring the day's casualty count to thirty-two killed in action. A staggering total for such a small community. Virtually a deathblow to a defense force that was comprised of a mere seventy-five soldiers just hours before.

On one stretcher was a critically injured private. He was maybe in his early-thirties. He was impaled by a massive piece of shrapnel. Just surviving this long was a miracle of its own. It was clear that he wouldn't make it. Doctor Horner just didn't have the trained personnel or equipment available that she'd need to repair his organs and replace the blood he'd lost.

Major Logan stopped and knelt beside the man's cot. He took the private's hand and squeezed it. "You did well today, private. I'm really proud of you."

The man gasped but was unable to form words.

"Shhh. You rest now private," said Major Logan. "You've done enough today. Fine, fine work."

The man settled back in his cot. His eyes fluttered.

"Rest easy, Eagle. Your watch is over." Major Logan held the hand a moment longer. Then he checked the man's pulse and shook his head. He closed the man's eyes and stood up.

"Thirty-three dead." Major Logan rubbed a hand through his hair in disbelief.

"What was his name?" Collin asked.

"Peter Woolworth," said Major Logan.

Collin stood at attention and saluted the man. "Rest easy, Private Woolworth."

Pastor Pendell made the sign of the cross and placed a finger in between Woolworth's eyes. He whispered a short prayer, stood up, and moved on.

Collin pulled the sheet up over his face.

Nurses rushed past them. Soldiers were carrying in another body scavenged from the remains of the Eagle's Bar. Considering the size of the blast, the resulting building collapse, and the fires, Collin was amazed to see dozens of Eagle's in the makeshift hospital. He was grateful so many survived.

Pastor Pendell stumbled. Collin caught his arm.

"Are you okay, Pastor?" he said.

Pendell smiled and nodded although he was obviously in pain. Collin guided him over to a chair nevertheless. He waved over Anna, hoping that she could take another look at his injury.

Anna hurried over, looking concerned. "What's the matter, Pastor?"

"Seems like he's light headed. He just stumbled and almost fell," said Collin.

"Where's the doctor?" asked Pastor Pendell.

Anna looked hurt but she answered. "She's gathering supplies from the hospital. Seems like half the town is helping her."

Pastor Pendell nodded and eased back in the chair. It didn't look like he wanted to move. He closed his eyes for a moment then sat up.

"Major Logan, I'd like you and Collin to go investigate the Eagle's Bar and see if you can figure out what happened. And if any of the BT76 survived. We need that medicine," Pastor Pendell said.

"What about helping here?" Collin said.

"My Eagle's need help," Major Logan said.

The two men looked at each other. Major Logan nodded his thanks.

"Everyone here needs that medicine," said Pastor Pendell. "Even if they survive their injuries, they won't survive the fever until the next supply drop. We have to put the town's well-being first. Goshen must survive. Right now, you two are the shepherds guarding my - our flock."

Collin looked satisfied by the explanation. It was true the citizens of Goshen needed BT76 more than the small amount of help they could offer here in the temporary trauma ward.

"Very well," said Major Logan.

They turned to leave.

"Bring me good news," Pastor Pendell said behind them.

Major Logan started up the stairs. He grunted and leaned against the wall, after just one step. He put a hand on his lower back and winced.

"Are you okay?" Collin stepped up to catch Major Logan.

"Yes, sir. I'm fine. Just a little sore."

Collin looked concerned. Before he could suggest the Major stay behind, he started up the stairs with a grunt.

This wasn't the first time Major Logan called him sir, and it was becoming more concerning each time. He was in no position of authority over Major Logan.

"Why do you-"

"Major Logan!"

It was Dr. Horner. She came stomping down the stairs toward them. She was carrying two bags of supplies. "What's the situation?"

"Sixteen KIA from the blast, possibly more, we haven't fully cleared the building yet. Another thirty or so wounded," Major Logan said. He sucked in a breath and continued up the stairs. "The remaining soldiers were dispatched to their posts to watch for any further aggression by the Vipers."

"Very good." Dr. Horner scurried past them. "Where are you going?"

"Pastor Pendell asked us to recover whatever medicine we can," said Collin. "And investigate the cause of the explosion."

"Good luck," she said.

"You too, doctor," said Major Logan.

Collin watched Major Logan carefully as they finished the flight of stairs and started down the gravel road.

"I think we both have a pretty good idea of what caused the explosion, right?" Major Logan said. He glanced sideways at Collin.

"Some sort of explosive," said Collin. "Attached to the crates somehow. But by whom?"

Major Logan frowned at the obvious implication. "It wasn't HAGS. It was the Vipers."

Collin cocked an eyebrow at Major Logan. "You seem rather certain of that."

"If HAGS had a problem and wanted to eliminate us, all they would have to do is withhold the shipment," said Major Logan. "It doesn't make sense to go through the trouble of booby trapping their own product."

"Would they have any reason to make it look like the Vipers? Or cooperate with them?"

"Doubtful. The Vipers haven't been any more kind to HAGS than they have with us."

Smoke curled through the air. The flames were put out by the firefighting volunteers, but some of the debris still smoldered. The smell of the fire permeated the air.

A man ran up to them. He was breathing hard, but managed to get out his message. He looked at Collin and said, "Sir, Dr. Horner wants you back at the medical clinic right away."

"First, don't call me sir. Second, what does Julie want me for?" Collin stood with his hands on his hips.

"Well, um, she said you have 'O' negative blood and needs you for donations right away. She was very insistent that you come back immediately." The man's eyes pleaded with him not to argue.

Collin looked at Major Logan.

"Fine with me." Major Logan waved his hand.

"Okay. See you soon." Collin turned toward the man. "Lead the way."

They ran back to the church. As soon as he cleared the last step, one of the nurses pulled him into a chair, and began wiping his arm down with an alcohol swab. It was a flurry of activity that Collin tuned out from. He hated giving blood because it always made him feel lightheaded and sick even if he drank juice right after. And from the looks of it there was no juice available.

Collin leaned back and closed his eyes. He understood the need, and was willing to help, but that didn't mean he had to like it.

Suddenly the lights flickered and went out.

"God damn it."

Collin smiled, he could tell it was Julie.

"We're in the Lord's house, doctor." Pastor Pendell reminded her gently as he recognized the woman's voice just as Collin had.

A few seconds later, the lights came back on. An audible sigh of relief filled the room and then the bustling activity picked back up.

Collin resumed his slouch and hoped to mine some more memories while they drained his blood like greedy vampires.

Dr. Horner walked over and patted Collin on the shoulder. He opened his eyes, interrupted yet again.

"How are you doing?"

"I'll be better when you stop siphoning off my body fluids."

Julie smiled. "Don't be such a baby. We're almost done."

"How much longer?"

"Maybe two minutes. And then you can run outside and play with your friends," Julie said.

"Sarcasm. It's one of your better features, doc." Collin closed his eyes and smirked. "And I'm not sure the Major would consider me a friend."

She checked his arm and fussed with something else. Collin didn't want to watch.

When she didn't respond, he said, "How are the men?"

"We stabilized a few, lost a few; it's basically a shit show," said Dr.

Horner. "The bastards really crippled my hospital in the last attack. It's all I can do to keep these brave souls alive. Now with the supply lost, we're in a real bad spot."

"I know." Collin shifted on the hard chair. "Who pulled through?"

"Paul is stable, Andy lost his arm, but he'll live, and Deedra needed stitches on her artery, but she's tough. Leroy is a coin-toss at this point. Roger, Ronnie, and Li passed on. So did Peter Woolworth but I'm told you were there. The rest are critical."

"So many casualties." Collin grunted. "There has to be a way to get more medicine."

"No, not really. HAGS chose the time interval of the drops. We don't even have contact with them."

"I hate this."

"Me too. It's why your blood is so important to creating a vaccine. It removes our dependency on HAGS and frees us from their control," said Dr. Horner. She sighed. "I should get back to the others. I'll send over a nurse."

"You're a good doctor, Julie. Thank you."

She patted him on the shoulder and walked away.

One of the nurses he hadn't spoken to yet came over to remove his IV.

He was about to introduce himself, when he saw Doris come down the stairs. He groaned softly.

The nurse pulled the IV out and pressed a cotton ball to his arm. A strange sensation ran through him, sending a chill across his skin. He'd never given so much blood before. He tried to sit up straight, but immediately slouched down again. The room spun. He gripped the sides of his chair for support but the nurse pried his hand free and bandaged his arm where the IV had been.

"You'll be fine," she said to Collin with a wink.

Doris was weeping. She dabbed at her eyes with a handkerchief. When she saw Collin slumped over in the chair, she ran over and took his hand.

"Good heavens, dear. Are you okay?" Her eyes were glassy with tears.

"It's sweet of you to ask, Doris." Collin sat up a little, to look less desperate. "I'm fine. Please, the others need much more help than me. I just donated...all of my blood, it feels like."

"I came over just as soon as I heard you were by the Eagle's Bar when it blew up." She dabbed her eyes. "I pray every night for the good Lord to smite the Vipers. He does work in mysterious ways. That they're allowed to continue harassing our town, killing our people, is incredible."

Suddenly Doris leaned over and kissed Collin on the cheek.

He froze. Unsure what to do, he simply shifted his position in the chair. She was heavily scented with old lady perfume. White Diamonds by Elizabeth Taylor came to Collin's mind. He was afraid the smell would stick to him and he tried his best not to cough. She meant well, even if she was overly affectionate.

"I'm so thankful you survived," Doris said.

"We lost a lot of good people today."

Kobyashi walked in and came over to Collin.

"Hey," Collin said with a nod.

Doris looked at Koby and rolled her eyes.

"A hospital is a strange place for love birds. Don't you think?" Koby said with a smirk. He raised his eyebrows at Doris.

Doris shook her head in disgust. "You should find better friends, Collin."

Collin smiled.

"Don't be fooled, Collin. She secretly loves me," said Koby.

"You're a disgusting little China man," Doris said, tucking her handkerchief into her purse.

Collin's eyes popped open wide.

"That's not what you said a few summers ago."

"Good heavens." Doris looked at Koby in mock surprise. Collin could see guilt all over her face. He fought to stifle a laugh.

Koby didn't, he just laughed.

"Good day to you," she said and stormed off.

"Doris!" Koby shouted causing her to turn around and look at him.

"Yes?"

"I'm Japanese," he reminded her with a proud smile that quickly melted into a suggestive grin. His eyebrows danced.

Doris didn't respond as she turned and walked away.

When she'd gone back upstairs, Collin sat up slowly and high-fived Koby. "Thanks for saving me, man."

"She's a nice old lady, but a little over eager." Koby fanned the air with both of his hands. "I hope that smell comes out."

"That makes two of us." Collin laughed, covering his mouth with one hand and waving the air with the other. It felt wrong to laugh here, with the specter of death hanging over the survivors, but neither of them could help it.

"The doctor's done with me," he said. "Let's get out of here."

"Good timing," said Koby. "Pastor Pendell is ready for you."

"Where is he?"

"Outside."

Koby helped Collin stand up. Collin got his balance, then turned and caught Dr. Horner's eye. He waved and she nodded back at him.

"Let's go, doc. The pastor wants to see us," he said.

Dr. Horner nodded again. "On my way."

Collin and Koby turned and started up the stairs, Dr. Horner trailing slightly.

When the pastor calls, you come running, Collin thought.

The three of them went to see what Pastor Pendell wanted this time.

Chapter Twelve

Pastor Pendell told the group to enter after only one knock.

Collin, Kobyashi, and Dr. Julie Horner all walked into the Pastor's office to see Major Logan and Pastor Pendell bent over a desk full of paperwork. The two men stopped talking and looked up. The Pastor motioned for them to take a seat, indicating to the three chairs placed in front of his desk.

"Looks like Anna got you fixed up nicely, Pastor," said Collin. "Are you feeling better?"

"Yes, thank you. Anna had to go ahead and stitch it up." Pastor Pendell gently patted the gauze bandage covering the stitches.

"Facial wounds always bleed a lot and often look worse than they are," said Major Logan. He had a large bandage covering a hole under his eye from a giant splinter. Collin remembered how awful it had looked.

"I'm just thankful the Lord was shielding us," said Pastor Pendell. "We're grateful that He watches over us."

Collin cocked his head slightly. So God watched over them but not the Eagles who didn't survive? That didn't make much sense to him.

"Please take a seat," said Pendell. He pointed at the chairs.

Everyone sat down except for Major Logan, who stood off to the side of the desk with his arms behind his back.

Beside Collin, Kobyashi groaned and muttered, "Feels like I'm in the principal's office." Collin bit back a smile as he sat.

"Major Logan, please explain to us what the hell happened," Pastor Pendell said. He scowled at his head of security.

Collin had to cough to cover up a laugh. He'd never heard Pendell curse and at Major Logan no less. It was all he could do not to laugh aloud. He fought the urge to glance at Koby, knowing that if he did he would definitely crack up.

Instead, Collin focused on the problem at hand. Death and destruction sobered him up real quick.

Major Logan looked at each of them in turn.

"We could not have foreseen the tactics the Vipers would use to attempt recovery of the medical crates. Given the circumstances, we responded quickly to the situation. As for the crates themselves, and the incident at the Eagle's Bar, I found some intriguing anomalies," Major Logan said. He shifted his stance and continued. "When I arrived at the building, the firefighters had already put out the fire and the civilians had moved a good deal of the debris."

"With the recovery effort already well under way, I was able to enter the building. The flooring was rickety from the blast, and in fact, much of the flooring collapsed into the basement. Looking around, I found finger-size holes punched through walls and what remained of the ceiling. Whatever they used gave off a lot of fragmentation."

Major Logan bowed his head. His voice took on a distant tone. "It was awful. The level of devastation inside was…staggering. Walking through the building was a challenge, because it was difficult to avoid stepping on body parts. Pieces of flesh were flung about and blood coated many of the surfaces, especially the floor. The steps heading downstairs were puddled with blood."

"That's enough, Major," Pastor Pendell said. He frowned at the graphic description.

Major Logan looked up, blinked a few times, then nodded. "Right."

The Major paused for a moment as if he was trying to remember where he left off.

"Right," he said again. "So, the case I opened to show Collin was largely undamaged but the lid had been removed so the medicine inside was almost entirely destroyed by the blast. However unlikely, some random vials may have survived. I have several Eagles combing through the debris just in case we can salvage some."

"What I found of the second crate was curious though." Major Logan shifted again and tapped his chin. He didn't say anything else.

Finally, Pastor Pendell leaned forward on his desk and said, "What did you find?"

Major Logan grunted thoughtfully. "For the relatively good condition of the first crate, I found almost nothing of the second one. Just a few fragments here and there. Keep in mind these are blast-resistant containers. So it's unlikely the damaged was caused externally."

"What does that mean?" asked Dr. Horner.

"The explosive was inside the container," said Collin. "Ohhh, wow. That changes things."

"Exactly," Major Logan said. "If Pastor Pendell hadn't come along to talk, Collin and I would be dead as well."

"So, what you're saying is, HAGS placed a bomb inside the crate?" Koby asked. He looked skeptically at Collin and Major Logan. "Why would they do that?"

Collin looked up at Major Logan. Earlier, Major Logan said with some conviction that he believed it was the work of the Vipers, not HAGS. Would he stick with that now?

"The explosive was inside the crate. The evidence bears that out," said Major Logan. "However, I don't believe HAGS is responsible. What would be their motivation? All they would have to do to eliminate us would be to withhold medical shipments."

"Much easier that way." Pastor Pendell nodded. "No mess. No mistakes. No survivors."

"Right. So that means it was the Vipers. The only question is how did they open the crate and place the bomb?" Major Logan said.

"They didn't have control of it for more than a few minutes," said Collin.

"True. If they don't know the combination, then it'd be near impossible. But if they know the combo, then the impossible becomes possible." Major Logan stepped closer to the desk and leaned forward a little.

No one spoke.

Collin raised his hand a little. "Who knows the combination?"

"As far as I know, Major Logan and I are the only two people who know the combination," said Pastor Pendell.

"But you said the combination was written on the outside of the first case you received, right?" asked Collin.

Major Logan stood up straight.

"So anyone who saw that first case could have remembered the password and passed on the information. Or waited until they knew it would be vital for the Vipers." Collin jabbed his finger on the desk. "Or they've known the whole time."

Pastor Pendell leaned back in his chair. His fingers pressed together, forming a steeple that he tapped against his lips as he thought.

Dr. Horner sat forward and put a hand on Collin's arm. "This is another reason for you to help me find a cure."

"Was the blood you took today for your experiments?" Collin studied her eyes for signs of deception.

She rolled her eyes and sighed. "If I didn't take your blood against your will while you slept, I'm not going to do it with a cheap misdirection ploy when you're awake."

He sensed she was telling the truth.

"Of course I'll help," he said. "The town needs this. Perhaps now, more than ever."

Dr. Horner beamed a smile at him and squeezed his arm. Kobyashi and Pastor Pendell both sighed in relief.

"You can't keep me locked up in a lab though. I want to be free to come and go so I can help rebuild, and if he'll let me, assist Major Logan with training new Eagles." Collin felt like those were reasonable concessions.

"That works for me," said Dr. Horner.

"Like I said before, Collin. I need all the help I can get." Major Logan smiled a little. It looked more like a smirk, but Collin took it. "Especially once we make the announcement."

Collin glanced at Koby, but he looked just as confused.

"Announcement?" asked Collin.

The lights flickered, then went out again.

"Sonofa-" Major Logan growled.

Pastor Pendell cut him off. "Major."

The lights snapped back on. Everyone looked at Kobyashi.

He threw his hands in the air.

"I was going to work on it today, but then we had the stupid medical drop."

"Don't worry, Koby. With so many Eagles out of commission our number one priority is security," Pastor Pendell said. "Power bumps have been bumped, if you will, to number two."

"What's number three?" Collin said with a smirk.

Pastor Pendell looked straight at him. "Number three is the announcement."

Right, thought Collin. *The "announcement."*

The pastor shuffled papers on his desk. He consulted a spreadsheet and then flipped through some other papers.

"What's this announcement?" said Collin.

"Many more people are about to die, Collin. It's the Council's job to decide who they are," Pastor Pendell said.

"What?" Collin bolted upright in his seat. He looked around at the others. None of them looked surprised by this.

Pastor Pendell stopped shifting the papers and looked at him as if he had to explain himself to a slow child.

"Collin, do you know how many residents Goshen has?"

"Not exact numbers, no," Collin admitted.

"According to our records, minus the ones who have passed on today, the population of Goshen stands at five hundred fourteen souls. Yet, with the total loss of the new shipment we only have enough BT76 in reserve for four hundred and six souls," said Pastor Pendell. "Leaving us with one hundred and eight residents who we cannot possibly treat. They will not survive until the next shipment arrives."

"Given the number of Eagles that remain, we may not be able to secure that next shipment," said Major Logan.

More than one hundred people would die slow deaths because of this situation. Collin's head spun. He felt so helpless.

"When do people need their next dose?" said Collin.

"We make sure everyone in town gets their doses on the same day, so no one comes up short," said Dr. Horner.

"So when does that happen?" Collin looked at Julie.

"Actually, they should have taken it three days ago," said Dr. Horner.

His eyes nearly bulged out of his head.

"What the hell were you all waiting for?"

"We couldn't risk using the reserves," said Pastor Pendell. "We anticipated a drop yesterday, but they were late and came today."

"The weather has cooperated too. It hasn't been windy and pollen count is low right now. So the risk of infection was low," said Dr. Horner. "It was a calculated risk."

"Calculated risk?" Collin shouted. "You're gambling with people's lives."

Dr. Horner nodded in resigned agreement. Koby looked away.

Major Logan pulled out an injector from his coat pocket and set it on the desk in front of Collin.

Collin stared at it for a moment, then sat back in his chair, and crossed his arms.

"I'm not going to take the medicine," he said.

"The Council has already received their meds," Pastor Pendell said, waving a hand at the others. "But I respect your wishes if you decide to opt out."

He picked up the injector and handed it back to Major Logan. "This will go to a resident."

"It's not right that you guys have all taken meds already. Especially when there's a shortage. How do you guys decide who gets BT76 and who is sentenced to death?"

"Last time we did a lottery," said Koby.

"Last time? This has happened before?" Collin couldn't believe it. This whole town barely held together and now what remained was crumbling apart.

"This is the Viper's fault," Major Logan shouted, slamming his fist on the pastor's desk. His eyes were burning. "If they hadn't attacked, if they hadn't planted a goddamn bomb, then we wouldn't be in this fix."

"No, this was a shit show before that. All these years and you only have a reserve of four hundred?" Collin glared right back. "You have to do the right thing."

Pastor Pendell stood and leaned toward Collin. "When will you realize we are at war?" He slammed his hand down, papers fluttered off the desk.

Major Logan turned away and walked toward the window. Collin bit his tongue.

Pastor Pendell stood. He smoothed his black shirt then sat back down.

"Gentlemen, I would remind you that we are in the house of the Lord," said Pastor Pendell in a firm voice. "You will refrain from cursing under His roof."

Collin sighed. "My apologies, pastor."

"Sorry about that, pastor," Major Logan said from the window.

Dr. Horner picked up the papers that fell and placed them on the pastor's desk. She looked at the spreadsheet and a couple other papers.

"There will be no lottery this time," said Pastor Pendell. "This time, only the saved will be saved."

Collin had no idea what he meant, but he was sure he wouldn't like it.

Chapter Thirteen

Collin waved goodbye to Doris as he left the dining hall. As he walked outside, he noticed a group of people bunched together reading something on the wall.

"What's going on?" Collin said to an attractive young lady standing at the back of the group.

"There's an announcement from Pastor Pendell," she said. Her smile lit up her face. She had light blonde hair that curled slightly around her shoulders.

"Thank you," Collin said.

"Anytime," she said, still smiling.

Collin wanted to talk more, but Kobyashi walked up. There was no way Collin was going to hit on a woman with that guy around.

"Have you read it yet?" asked Koby.

"Nope. I just finished eating. I just found out what it was, thanks to this young lady," he said. The woman smiled again, glanced at Koby, and turned away.

He leaned in like he was about to tell a secret and said, "You're not going to like it."

"Why do you say that?"

"Have a look for yourself, Sleeping Beauty." Koby smiled and walked inside.

Collin sighed and stepped closer to the sign. He could barely make it out over people's heads.

It read:

ATTENTION RESIDENTS OF GOSHEN

Due to the recent terrorist attacks by the godless Vipers, there is a shortage of BT76 at this time. Rest assured the Council is working on a solution, and we thank you for your patience. The following names listed were chosen in a random lottery draw and should respond to the church for BT76 inoculation immediately. Those on the list may give up their inoculation to anyone not listed, at their choosing.

It should be noted that all able-bodied men, women, and teens of fighting age will be diverted from their current work assignment and begin defense training under the guidance of Major Logan and the Eagles.

God Be With Us,

Pastor Pendell

"Random lottery draw," Collin muttered to himself. Such bullshit, he wanted to scream. He was tempted to rip the notice off the wall, not that it would help any.

Skimming over the list of names, most of whom were unknown to him, he noticed someone he did care about was missing - Doris. His heart sank at the thought of having to break the news to her. Better to hear it from a friend than the rumor mill or worse yet, walk up to the list only to have her heart crushed by the absence of her name. Collin read through the list one more time but nothing else caught his attention. The only other people he considered friends - Koby and Julie - were part of the Council and had already received their doses of BT76.

Collin walked back inside and caught Koby watching him. He made a face at Koby and walked over to Doris.

"Back so soon? Are you still hungry, dear?" Doris said.

"It was great, but I'm stuffed. Actually, I was hoping we could talk somewhere private for a second."

Doris was already shaking her head. She put her hand on his arm and patted his bicep like she was the one doing the consoling.

"I already know," she said.

"How? I haven't seen you leave the room," said Collin.

"Ever since news of the lottery spread, I knew there was no point checking."

"How could you be so sure without looking?"

"Goshen has been on the verge of shortages ever since they started dropping BT76. This isn't the first time a lottery has been used either," Doris said.

Collin didn't say anything.

"I can talk to Pastor Pendell and see-"

Doris shook her head again.

"No, no, don't you bother yourself or the good pastor with that," she said.

They were silent.

"Look around you, Collin. What do you see?"

He looked around the room. The somber mood was palpable. With the loss of so many Eagles, and then this medicine shortage, it was hard to avoid feeling down.

"I see a room full of people who still don't know if they will be saved or not."

Doris tilted her head. "They all know about the lottery. There's no rush to read the list."

Then it dawned on Collin. Until they actually checked the list to find out the news, there was still a sense of hope. Survival through procrastination.

"I'll be honest. It wouldn't have surprised me if people rioted over the results," said Collin.

She laughed.

"Has everyone simply resigned themselves to this fate? Or is their faith in the pastor and the Lord just that strong?" Colin shrugged.

"Oh sweetie, this is the world we live in now. I know it's new to you, but we've lived like this for a long time," said Doris. She patted his arm. "Death is a blessing. A release from the constant struggle and fear."

Collin couldn't believe it.

"Think back to the world you knew before," she said placing her hands on his shoulders. "What was everyone's preferred way to die, if given a choice?"

Collin's shoulders fell. His head bowed. Then he looked into her eyes. "Peacefully, in their sleep."

"Exactly." She patted his cheek. Then she turned and put an arm around his waist. Collin followed her slowly to the window.

"You know, our men and women died from arrows and bombs," Doris said softly. "Falling asleep doesn't sound like such a bad option. Whether it's old age or the fever matters not. The Lord will bring me home when He's ready for me."

Collin pulled her into a hug.

She giggled and squeezed him. "It was very sweet of you to try to tell me."

Collin smiled. "Why did you assume you weren't on the list?"

Doris sighed.

"I'm old, dear. I can't fight, and I don't go to church as often as I should. Either of which is cause enough to keep me out of the 'lottery.'" Doris made air quotes around the word lottery. "This isn't the first time either."

"You didn't make the lottery before? How did you survive?"

"The first time, Pastor Pendell and the Council managed to get more medicine. Another time it was winter."

"In winter?" Collin thought surviving during winter would be more difficult.

"Well, there's no pollen during the winter, silly." Doris nudged him with her elbow. "So the chances of getting the fever during winter are almost zero. But the snow doesn't last forever and spring brings death. Time is never on our side."

Collin thought about that. Winter was a sort of safe zone. Winter is when he would leave Goshen to search for his family. If they survived this long without him, they could survive until winter.

"Winter. At least we have something to look forward to," said Collin.

Doris looked skeptical.

"Don't forget you woke up just before Easter, and winter is a long way off. If we last that long," she said with a shiver. "And while the river doesn't always freeze over, if it does the Vipers will sneak across and steal our food. With so few Eagles left to defend us, I fear there will be little we can do. Yesterday's attack may have been the beginning of the end for our little town."

"Don't say that, Doris. We will figure something out," Collin said. He felt the conviction in his voice and realized he meant it.

"We'll see." She turned away from the window and faced the room. She looked at the people eating quietly. "You're a good man, Collin. We did the right thing praying for you all those years, we are lucky to have you with us. But in this case, the people who fall asleep may just end up being the lucky ones."

Chapter Fourteen

Collin leaned back in the padded wood chair and kicked his feet up on the railing. In his hands, he held a mason jar of steaming black coffee. After the last few days, he came to enjoy drinking his coffee out of a glass mason jar. The strong, earthy scent drifted up while he enjoyed the quiet morning.

When Koby showed him the coffee orchard he had raised inside one of the greenhouses, Collin actually whooped with joy.

Three weeks had passed since the lottery notices were posted. Goshen had turned into a virtual ghost town. No longer was it the thriving dystopian capital it had seemed to be when Collin first woke up. Residents feared another attack by the Vipers, and they went about their daily activities with less vigor. Many of the residents simply opted to stay home as much as possible.

Collin attended church every Sunday and attendance dropped noticeably every week. It was unsettling to know people were slipping into fever-induced comas. Yet, even some of those who received inoculations stopped showing up for service. Sometimes Collin questioned why he bothered going. For the town, it felt like there was a real shift in attitudes and Collin wasn't sure what that meant for the future of Goshen.

Worrying to say the least, he thought.

He pushed those thoughts aside to watch the sunrise, a new habit he picked up over the last few weeks.

Sunlight lanced through the spaces between mountain peaks, casting beams of light down into the valley. Like spotlights moving slowly across the valley floor, as birds arose and began to sing, the light grew in intensity as the sun rose. Halos of orange and yellow light back lit the mountain peaks. A cool breeze carried the scent of damp soil, half-composted leaves, and pine trees. Collin called it forest cologne. He took a big breath enjoying the freshness that calmed his soul.

Although Collin couldn't see the river, he could hear the water rushing through the hydroelectric dam that kept their town powered. Collin sipped his coffee and watched fog running down the mountainsides, desperate to escape the sun's rays.

He thought he heard a turkey gobble behind his house. It would be fun to go hunting. Right now thought, he was too content to move. Besides, Collin was an Eagle now. Given his unique skill set, it was clearly the most suitable job for him. He could leave the hunting and trapping to the capable citizens assigned to those tasks.

Their skills at harvesting the bounty of the river, and surrounding woodlands, were evident in the number of fur hats and coats among the townsfolk, a necessity as their manufactured nylon, fleece, and Gore-Tex jackets wore out from years of hard use.

Collin stood up and took a big gulp of coffee. It warmed his belly and satisfied his reacquired caffeine addiction. He leaned on the railing and smiled at the beauty laid out before him. He had an amazingly good view from his home. For the first time since his awakening, he felt blessed.

Buzzing drew his attention away from the splendor of nature. A bee zipped by Collin, dipping and swerving through the air. It was the first bee Collin had seen, supposedly a rare sight these days. Collin walked down his front steps as the bee flew along the tops of the bushes that lined his porch, then it reversed course, and dipped down by the sidewalk. The small honeysuckle plant that had sprouted up from a crack in the sidewalk made a perfect landing pad for Collin's insect visitor.

Collin crouched down and watched the bee at work on the fresh blooms.

"Hey there," he said. "I thought you guys were all gone?"

The bee hopped and buzzed from one flower to the next, extracting the minute yellow powder that was the cause of so many problems.

"I'll have to tell my friend, Koby, about you," Collin said with a smile. He stood as the bee flew away seeking more flowers to pollinate.

How could a world so beautiful and peaceful be so deadly? he thought.

Collin stretched and finished his coffee. He then turned to make his way back inside the house for another cup of Koby's greenhouse arabica. His mind kept working through the questions that remained. How did this all get so out of hand? Why weren't people more responsive to the plight of bees, and nature as a whole, before it became a critical problem?

His family was always in the back of his mind. Over the weeks, Collin had experienced more memories resurfacing. He still had the problem where faces were blurred out. None of his family members would be recognizable to him. They could walk right past and he'd never know them from the next person.

Collin started up the stairs and gripped the rail for support. It felt wobbly. He stopped and examined it.

I'll have to fix that, he thought. Then he laughed.

It was the first time he thought of the gifted house as his own. The blue house at the end of the street was his and it truly felt like home. Goshen felt like home too. He cared about what happened to the town and the people in it. He hoped his family would feel the same when he found them.

He rushed up the stairs to refill his coffee jar. He couldn't spend the entire morning sitting around. There was serious work to do around town.

After he got ready, and finished his second jar of coffee, Collin went outside and started down the stairs.

One of the steps creaked. It was the first time he noticed it. He stepped back and tested the wood stairs. It creaked again, revealing its location.

"You're next after I fix the railing," he said. Noting the location of the creak, he left his house, crunching his way down the gravel road toward the Goshen High School gymnasium. He had some training to attend to with Major Logan.

The day after the lottery notices went out; they began training the new Eagle recruits. Collin enjoyed the work. It gave him something productive to focus on. A great side benefit was his rapidly improving strength and endurance. He'd felt soft when he woke up in the hospital. Now his muscles were already rebuilding, growing full and powerful.

He strode down the street looking around, hoping to see another bee or some other surprise. Collin waved at the people he passed in the road. It was a typical morning. Nothing exciting happened along the way. When the school was in sight, Collin felt a burst of energy and decided to jog the last block.

When he reached the building, his breathing was still light. It felt great to stride down the road like a kid just having fun. Collin pulled the old metal door open. It creaked loudly, announcing his presence.

Inside, Major Logan was pumping out push-ups. Collin smiled. Major Logan must be feeling energetic today too.

"Up and at it early, eh Major?"

Major Logan paused briefly between push-ups and said, "We have to train harder than the Vipers if we want to win."

"In this situation, define winning," Collin said. "I was under the impression we were defending and surviving. We aren't going out after the Vipers. And what good is winning if there's nothing left in the end?"

Major Logan hopped up, wiping sweat from his brow. He walked over, scowling, and stopped right in front of Collin.

"I'm a winner," Major Logan said.

Collin wasn't impressed. He looked at the major for a moment before turning away. It was too early for that kind of bullshit, as far as Collin was concerned. Thankfully, Major Logan didn't pursue it any further.

Collin walked a few paces away and started stretching out.

Major Logan began a set of bodyweight squats.

The door creaked open and a pair of recruits entered the gym.

Not wanting to leave any tension between him and the major, Collin glanced at him and said, "I don't know about you, but I'm sure glad Koby had the foresight and resources to grow coffee."

The major grunted.

"While I was drinking my first cup this morning, I saw a bee. It buzzed past me and landed on a flower growing out of my sidewalk," he said.

Major Logan stopped his squats and laughed at him. "Did you spike your coffee? There hasn't been a bee in Montana for at least nine years." He shook his head and began doing walking lunges across the gym.

Collin made a face. Then he got down and started his own set of push-ups. He didn't need to prove himself to the major. He knew he wasn't imagining things; his encounter with the bee was as real and beautiful as the sunrise.

Nine years? Collin thought as he barely finished twenty-five push-ups. That surprising nugget of information made him feel even more excited to tell Koby.

He stood and stretched out his chest and arms. Collin shook his head. He might feel stronger, but twenty-five push-ups — pshhh — he still had a long way to go.

Once all the recruits arrived, Major Logan formed them up. They took a quick roll call, started with some warm-ups and stretches, before beginning a tough physical training session. Soon everyone was sweating, huffing and puffing, and looking forward to skill classes.

By 10:00AM, they had broken into two groups. Major Logan took his group to the far side of the gym and worked on basic hand-to-hand combat techniques. Collin taught a basic knife fighting class.

He reviewed the warrior stance with the recruits since it was basis of the techniques he was about to teach them. Collin had no recollection of learning it himself. Again, he only knew for certain that he knew the techniques backwards and forwards.

Once the review was complete, he passed out rubber training knives from the police station. Training aids from the old days.

"Okay so from the warrior stance, we'll call this 'home'. You hold the knife in your strong hand. Use the same kind of grip you would use to hold a hammer," Collin said. "Glen, what the hell kind of hammer have you been holding?"

Collin corrected his form. The students chuckled.

"Hold up your knife hand, at the ready, just like a normal fighting stance. Keep your empty hand up. It's your guard hand, use it to protect your neck. Good." Collin walked around checking everyone. "Pretty simple, right?"

"The training manuals will tell you that your primary goal is to strike your enemy's vital areas - face, the front and side of the neck, or abdomen." Collin swiped his finger at each area so the recruits could visualize it. "In real life, take any strike you can get. His palm, forearm, thigh, hell - even his foot. A cut will distract, demoralize, and weaken your enemy. If you're lucky, you'll get a good strike, cause massive trauma and then you can bide your time, or move on to the next enemy while the first guy bleeds out."

"That's awful," one lady muttered.

"It is awful, Sandy. But they want to do worse to you. This is war. We are fighting for survival. When you're at the point where you're using knives, there is no room for hesitation. No room for mercy," Collin said, clapping his hands for emphasis. "Strike first. Strike hard. Put them down."

Carrying the momentum, Collin shouted his favorite new cadence call. "Eagles strike!"

"Vipers die!" shouted the recruits in response.

"Goddamn right." Collin smiled at them. "You carry the fight to the enemy. Right, Sandy?"

"Yes, sir," she said.

"We step toward the enemy. Never back." He jogged to the front of their formation, so everyone could see him. "This is your basic knife attack. A simple thrust."

He demonstrated the stabbing move several times. Then he turned toward the formation.

"Home position everyone, basic warrior stance. When I say strike, you stab forward with your knife. Twist your hip like I showed you to put power into the move," he said. "Strike."

"Kill," they said in unison as they practiced the move.

"Strike."

"Kill."

He repeated it several more times, then had them stand easy while he demonstrated a basic slashing move. After a few more revolutions, the recruits were familiar with several thrusting and slashing attacks.

Just before it was time to break for lunch, Major Logan called for everyone to form up. At some point, a large wrestling mat was placed in the center of the gym. Collin had been so focused on knife training that he didn't even notice. He wasn't sure what was happening, but the look on Major Logan's face and the faces of the existing Eagles made him feel uneasy.

Major Logan stepped onto the mat, looking around at all the recruits.

"Learning the moves of basic self-defense is not enough. You must learn to use the moves like a gladiator in a ring. You must practice them, execute them. They must become a part of you, they must become your natural, instinctive reaction to aggression." He clasped his hands behind his back and stood straight. "Sean, Cali to the center of the mat."

The two recruits stepped out onto the mat, uncertain why they were called on. Major Logan turned to them and smiled like a fox in a hen house.

"You two will demonstrate your proficiency," Major Logan said looking at each recruit. "You will fight until knock out or tap out."

Sean smiled and eyed Cali as if she was a steak at dinnertime. Cali looked unsure, but quickly put on a tough face. Collin knew she wanted to be an Eagle and that she worked hard to prove she deserved it. That kind of bravado was admirable but had to be tempered to avoid unnecessary casualties.

Collin couldn't believe Major Logan would do this. There was little practical value in pitting a small, young woman against a much larger, young man. Neither of them were proficient enough to do more than spar with someone their own size. One or both of them would end up seriously injured.

Collin felt a pang of guilt for assuming that Cali would lose. In actuality, either recruit was just as likely to win. Size didn't always count for much when it came to combat. Despite his reservations, he decided to stand back and see how it unfolded. If things got out of control, he had no problem stepping in to break them up.

Even if it meant contradicting Major Logan.

An Eagle stepped onto the mat, holding a whistle in his mouth. The two recruits faced each other. The Eagle held out his hand with three fingers held up. He counted down — three, two, one — then blew the whistle.

Both of the recruits stood still for a moment. Then Cali began to circle. Sean followed her movements.

The crowd was murmuring, but no one was cheering for either side. Collin felt like they were waiting, unsure who to root for, or perhaps unsure who it was safe to root for. Sean was a big, muscular, young man. He'd been working in the fields as a farm hand before this. Collin remembered hearing someone say that he also helped the logging crew when they needed to process downed trees. Sean was also known for having a short temper.

Unwilling to wait any longer, Sean lunged forward and jabbed at Cali. She dipped sideways to avoid any contact and stepped sideways. Sean smirked.

He readjusted his position and faced Cali again. Sean jabbed again but this was a feint. He lashed out with a vicious low kick that nearly caught Cali on the shin. Had it connected, Sean would have snapped her leg.

Either Sean had poor control, or he meant to try maiming his fellow recruit. That was over the line.

Collin stepped forward onto the mat with his arms out to separate the two recruits.

"That's enough, recruits. Back in formation," Collin said.

Before either recruit stepped off the mat, Major Logan rushed over. He stopped inches from Collin's face, eyes burning. Major Logan's whole body quivered with fury.

Collin met his glare. He wasn't easily intimated, even by a man like Major Logan.

"Do you remember what I said last time you disrespected me in front of my Eagles?" Major Logan spoke in a low, tight voice. His teeth clenched and his jaw muscles rippled.

"I vaguely remember some kind of threat," Collin said. "But these aren't your Eagles, they're our Eagles."

As Collin's statement of ownership ended, Major Logan's fist connected with his jaw, sending Collin to his knees.

The recruits gasped in surprise.

I must be getting old, Collin thought. He brought one leg up so he was kneeling and rubbed his cheek, honestly surprised he'd just been knocked down. The inside of his cheek had a small cut. Blood coated his tongue, and his lips felt puffy but there was no serious damage. His jaw seemed to move fine.

Collin looked up. Major Logan was still standing close.

Meeting Collin's eye, Major Logan pointed to the crowd and shouted, "Fall in line."

That's the way he wants to play it, eh, he thought. Collin smiled. He spit blood out and looked right into Major Logan's eyes.

"I'm prepared to bleed for Goshen. Are you?"

The Major's face turned tomato red.

Collin pivoted on his foot, throwing his elbow into Major Logan's stomach. Collin stood up behind the major grabbed him around the waist, pinning his left arm to his side. In the same movement, Collin stepped behind Major Logan's left heel and threw him to the ground, hard.

The major took the toss full on his shoulder, unable to break his fall. He was a tough man and didn't let the attack unsettle him. Major Logan elbowed Collin in the ribs with his free arm. Then he stepped out with his right foot, pivoted left to face Collin, who still had him by the waist.

Collin moved his forehead to the center of Major Logan's chest and tightened his grip around the man's waist intending to bear hug him back to the mat. Major Logan had already grabbed Collin's right elbow, threw up his pinned left arm and twisted Collin sharply off balance.

Collin fell to his back. Major Logan followed him to the floor and began to pound on Collin.

He'd always hated fighting from the guard position. So Collin covered his head and sat up as best as he could. He threw his arms around Major Logan again, dug his thumb knuckle into the Major's spine, pulling him close. Major Logan arched his back and grunted in pain, as the hard knuckle dug in roughly. Collin planted his foot, pushed hard with his leg and twisted to roll him over. Now Collin was on top.

Shoving aside Major Logan's arms, Collin dropped his elbow right across the major's cheek bone. Once. Then twice. The skin over the bone split. Collin threw another elbow, aiming the bony point at the bridge of the nose. He connected and Major Logan's nose snapped. Blood rushed out, rivulets streaming down the sides of Major Logan's face.

The man reached for Collin's face, maybe to gouge his eyes. Collin sat up, squeezed with his knees, and punched Major Logan in the ribs. When his arms came down instinctively to block, Collin swept a hook at the major's head, connecting with his cheek. The cut widened. Sheets of blood were covering Major Logan's face. There was no way he could see what he was doing, so Collin eased off.

As much as he disliked Major Logan, he didn't want to kill him.

Collin rolled Major Logan over onto his stomach, while straddling him. He grabbed the Major's hair and wrapped an arm around his throat. Major Logan clawed at Collin's arm once he realized what was happening.

Major Logan tried to head-butt him, but Collin had his head safely out of the way. He hooked his feet together around Logan's waist. Collin tightened his arm and legs, rolled Major Logan back onto his back so he was lying on top of Collin. Major Logan slapped wildly at his arm.

It was too late to tap out. Major Logan crossed too many lines.

Collin began to arch his back, flexing his arm to cut off the blood flow to the major's head, while squeezing his legs just below the major's ribs. He stretched the Major out as far as he could, rendering the man completely helpless. Major Logan made a gagging sound and slapped Collin's arm with an urgency he knew came just before the lights started to go out.

Collin squeezed harder.

Major Logan's attempts to tap out slowed. His body went limp.

Satisfied that he knocked the major out, Collin immediately released his hold and pushed Major Logan off him. He rolled to the side and stood up slowly. Collin sucked in air, exhausted from the brawl. He leaned forward, hands on his knees, and realized that everyone was staring at him. Some with open mouths.

On the floor, Major Logan stirred as he began to regain consciousness.

Collin looked at the stunned crowd. He stood up straight, wiping the Major's blood off his hands onto his pants.

"Class dismissed."

Chapter Fifteen

d away the remaining blood on Collin's hands as he

thes were in a pile on the bathroom floor. He'd deal
ater. Collin wanted to get cleaned up before heading to
, daily routine with Dr. Horner and her staff. It was
1em, even if he had long ago grown tired of the routine.
ut of the shower and dried off. He could already feel the
harass him for the next week or so. He wondered if
pital would even notice his minor injuries. They would
.ajor Logan's, if he went in for help.
:lean clothes, Collin readied himself for a couple of hours
: grabbed his jacket off its hook and left the house.
ickly down the center of the street, hoping to avoid further
h Collin didn't expect another attack, he was unsure how
ght in front of the Eagles might provoke Logan into doing
d. So he checked all directions every once in a while, to
ibushed.
na, he thought.
y sigh, Collin tried to recapture the joy of his morning. He
other bee and he still didn't have a chance to tell Koby the
news.

The hospital was still as drab as ever. He went in through the busted
front doors and made his way upstairs to begin the monitoring and testing
regime Dr. Horner had ordered.

Due to all the damage from the night of the attack, when he'd woken
up, most of the upper floors had been closed off. So Collin only had to go
up to the second floor. He exited the stairwell, walked down the dim
hallway, and turned right. He pushed through a frosted glass door into what
used to be an outpatient clinic.

Anna sat at the front desk, which was unusual. She was usually busy
prepping things, or doing other medical stuff, Collin wasn't exactly sure
what.

"You get demoted?" Collin said with a brief smile. His fat lip was still
tender.

She looked at him. Something looked a little off with her. Anna gave
him a half smile in return and shook her head.

Collin leaned against the counter and peered through the little glass
window at her.

"Anything new today?" Collin said softly.

Anna shook her head. "Same as yesterday. Fifty-seven with the fever, forty-nine of which are asleep."

"Ugh," he grunted with the emotional weight of it. "So many. It gets me every time."

He thought about the eleven people who chose to end their suffering early. Rather than wither away in their sleep, some opted for the self-imposed route. Collin couldn't blame them. It was quick, and gave them a sense of being in control when so many things leading to that point were out of their control. Still, it wasn't the option that he would go with.

Collin hadn't realized the untreated lottery losers would drop at such a rapid rate. After all, spring was just beginning. He thought of his insect visitor that morning and wondered if the fever would be worse now that bees were back in the mix? He needed to talk to Koby.

"Any casualties today?" he said.

Anna shook her head again.

He sighed in relief but he knew that if they didn't get another shipment of BT76 soon, all of those fifty-nine plus others would die. More than one hundred residents were left out of the latest round of inoculations because of the Viper attack. Collin wished Goshen had the facilities available to keep them all alive, but the small hospital just didn't have enough capacity. Too much was lost over the years.

He rubbed his forehead and asked the question he dreaded to ask, "How's Doris?"

Anna dreaded answering the question as much as Collin hated asking it, he could tell by the sadness in her eyes.

"Still asleep in room two," she said softly.

Collin was still bitter about how the shortage of BT76 was handled. Even though Doris had been content with the result, he knew it was unfair and just plain wrong. At least she was going the way she wanted to — peacefully in her sleep. He requested to carry Doris to her house, so she could sleep in her own bed. He thought she would like that. But Dr. Horner denied the request because of the logistics involved, and the proximity of the morgue.

Anna still seemed off. Something other than work was bothering her, Collin could feel it.

"Come on. I can tell something is bothering you. What's up?" he said.

She looked over her shoulder, then down the hall. Finally, she stood up and came out from behind the desk. She walked over to the frosted glass door and looked out into the hallway. Anna glanced back and motioned for Collin to follow her into the hall.

He raised his eyebrow. "What's with all the secrecy?"

Anna looked down the hall again and confident that no one was around said, "Major Logan just left my mom's office."

"Don't worry about that. We just had to work out a disagreement.

These things happen," said Collin.

"No, no. I get it. Boys will be boys or whatever," said Anna. "But that's not what concerns me."

A nurse came around the corner.

Suddenly Anna nodded and said, "Yes, Doris is still sleeping in room two."

The nurse walked toward them. She was holding linens in her hands and walking fairly quick. Collin didn't recognize her, but she smiled briefly at him.

"Okay," said Collin, playing along and returning the nurse's smile. "Can I go see her?"

"Of course," said Anna.

The nurse passed them and went into a door farther down the hall.

Anna let out a small sigh.

"You can't trust them, Collin," she said.

"Don't you think I know that Logan and I have trust issues?" He pointed to his fat lip.

"No, it's not him," Anna said. "Well, it's not just him."

"What do you mean?"

Anna glanced around again. Her mother, Dr. Horner, came around the same corner the nurse came from just a moment ago. Anna's eyes widened and she leaned forward slightly.

"Not everything in Goshen is what it seems," Anna said quickly in a low voice. "I heard my mom tell Major Logan that if you knew who you really were, you'd be a threat."

Confusion etched itself on Collin's face.

"That's all I know," she added.

Dr. Horner was walking toward them, reviewing a clipboard in her hands. She wasn't moving with the same sense of urgency the nurse had.

He looked deep into Anna's eyes, searching for the truth.

"Who am I?"

She looked sad and nervous. A tear slipped from her eye.

"I don't know," she said with a shrug.

Dr. Horner looked up from her clipboard and smiled. Then she noticed Anna's tears and looked concerned at both of them. Julie put a hand on her daughter's shoulder.

"What's the matter, dear?"

Collin cut in. "Doris," he said, channeling the very real sadness he felt.

Dr. Horner nodded knowingly. She slipped her arm around Anna's shoulders and kissed her forehead. Doris was close with Anna, often watching her when she was younger and Julie was working.

"I know, baby. I know," she said to Anna. Then stepping back and looking at Collin she said, "Are you ready? I believe we have an appointment."

Collin nodded and started to follow her down the hall. He glanced back at Anna.

She mouthed, "Thank you." She waved a little and then went back inside the office to her desk.

Collin turned back around and glanced sideways at the doctor. You can't trust them, Anna told him. It's not all what it seems. Collin got the feeling things in Goshen were about to get interesting.

"I figured you would be down here," Dr. Horner said. "You and Doris became close didn't you?"

Collin shrugged. Given what Anna had told him, he didn't want to share any information that he didn't have to.

"Well, I don't blame you for feeling down. She was a lovely woman. Very kind," she said, her voice trailing off. She pushed open the door to office. Collin followed her inside.

"She is a lovely woman. She's not gone yet," Collin said defensively.

"Of course." Dr. Horner led him through the office to the examination room. Not that Collin didn't know exactly where it was. He'd been there nearly every day since he agreed to help her find a vaccine for the fever.

The examination room looked typical. A small counter and a sink with locked cabinets on one side. Posters on the wall displayed an anatomical view of the human in the traditional DaVinci pose. A cheap, metal wire chair with black padding, sat in the corner for companions. There was also a short rolling chair for the doctor to sit in. In place of the normal metal bed, there was a chair that more closely resembled a dentist's chair.

Collin sat down in the dentist-like chair, ready for Dr. Horner or one of the nurses, to drain him of yet more blood. He folded up his sleeve for the doctor. Glancing down he saw a bunch of little marks where medical staff had stuck him with needles. Both of his arms looked like that now. He shook his head, then sat back, and mulled over what Anna had said to him.

Dr. Horner interrupted his thoughts. "There's no need for that today."

"Why not?" Collin asked suddenly suspicious to the change of routine.

"You've given so much blood at a fairly rapid pace. It wouldn't be safe to take anymore right now," Dr. Horner said. She smiled at him. "I've been monitoring your platelet count. Your white blood cell count is low. I don't want to compromise your immune system any more. We don't want you to get sick."

"Well that's a relief," he said. "I hate giving blood."

Dr. Horner chuckled and pointed at his face. "It looks like you already made a donation today."

"You should see the other guy," Collin said. He watched for her reaction. But she gave no indication how she felt about it. No smile, no disapproving look.

"If the other guy comes in for treatment, I'll get a very good look," Dr. Horner said. "Who was it, if I may ask?"

Collin wasn't sure if she was messing with him or just flat out lying. He hadn't seen Major Logan since he'd left him crumpled on the floor at the gym, and it was possible Anna was the one lying to him. He hesitated, then decided to play along with the doctor.

"Actually, Major Logan did this to my face," Collin said. He gestured to his fat lip. There was a small bruise on his cheek, but it wasn't very obvious. His lip had changed color and stuck out like he was trying to hitch a ride.

Dr. Horner feigned surprise, overacting. Collin knew right away that Anna had told him the truth.

Two taps on the door interrupted them. Dr. Horner pushed her chair over to the door and opened it. It was Pastor Pendell. He smiled and walked inside.

Other than seeing Pastor Pendell at church, this was the first time since the lottery conversation in the Council meeting that they met face to face. They hadn't spoken in the three weeks since. Tension filled the air.

Pastor Pendell smiled at the doctor. Then he sat in the guest chair and looked at Collin.

Both of them were smiling at him, which was weird. Collin felt like a young child about to find out that his parents were divorcing.

Pastor Pendell sat forward with his hands on his knees. He glanced at the doctor, then back at Collin. The smile was still plastered on his face.

"Have you told him yet?" he asked.

Chapter Sixteen

"Told me what?" Collin asked.

Pastor Pendell jumped up, startling him.

"We have a cure!" he shouted. "Praise the Lord, we have a cure."

The pastor stood and smiled.

Collin looked at the doctor. She rolled her eyes.

"We might have a cure," Dr. Horner said, with measured enthusiasm.

Pastor Pendell sat down and put his arm around her shoulder.

"Come on, doctor. The good Lord has blessed us with this miracle. Don't be so skeptical." He gave her a squeeze.

"It could be an effective treatment or it could be a deadly weapon. At this point, we don't really know," Dr. Horner said. She looked at the pastor. "It will take more testing before we know for sure, pastor. Please leave the medical determination to me."

"It's progress, is it not?"

"It is-"

"Yes, it's a huge step forward for Goshen." Pastor Pendell looked at Collin. "I told you our town was blessed."

"Progress doesn't mean cure. And several positive test results do not make it a miracle. We can't make such sweeping statements based on preliminary results. I don't come into your church and give sermons on a whim, do I?" Dr. Horner said.

The doctor and pastor continued going back and forth. Collin tuned them out, stared at his folded hands, and thought about what Anna told him. He wondered if she knew about this. Was this what she meant by everything not being what it seemed? It was hard to say. Had there always been a cure? Was a cure even possible? Had he really been asleep for years? Then thoughts of his family filled his heart and mind.

When Collin looked up he realized that Pastor Pendell and Dr. Horner were staring at him.

A half-smile played across his lips. "So, um, what's next? How can we turn this into an effective treatment as you said, doctor?"

Pastor Pendell shook his head.

"Never mind all that. You should just be grateful that you alone have given hope to all mankind."

"Alone?" Dr. Horner asked, looking sideways at the pastor.

"My apologies, doctor. Of course your lab work has been vital. But without the raw materials from Collin, and divine insight from the Lord, the lab would sit idle." Pastor Pendell smiled at Collin again.

Not wanting to hear them bicker, Collin cut in. "Doctor, can you explain how this potential treatment works?"

"Certainly," she said. She thought for a moment before speaking. "Normally, when an allergen such as pollen enters the body, it is attacked by our immune system, which sends out antibodies to fight the allergens. The antibodies fight off the foreign object, in this case pollen, and the body learns from this encounter and is better able to fight it in the future. Or you develop an immunity. If the body overreacts, then you get symptoms such as itchy eyes, a runny nose, a rash or other more deadly symptoms like anaphylactic shock."

Pastor Pendell waved his hand like he was shooing a fly. "We should give thanks to the Lord."

"If you interrupt me again, you can thank him in person, pastor," Dr. Horner said. She smiled, but Collin didn't doubt her words.

"Very well." Pastor Pendell chuckled. He motioned for her to continue.

"Histamines facilitate the body's defenses against foreign objects, but in the case of allergies they're helping to attack something that's not dangerous to us. It's this overreaction that people associate with 'having allergies' and taking an antihistamine can reduce the body's attack on foreign bodies that aren't a true threat," Dr. Horner said.

"So why don't antihistamines help against pollen now?" Collin asked.

"The pollen produced by HAGS' plants isn't destroyed by white blood cells because they don't recognize it until it's already latched onto cells and the reaction it incites can't be managed by antihistamine. It still kicks the body's immune system into overdrive. It's like the pollen mimics or possibly creates a serious infection so the response is way stronger than it needs to be and that leads to-"

"The fever," Collin said.

"Exactly," Dr. Horner said. "The fever continues to climb until it renders the victim unconscious, sending them into a coma, or sleep as some people politely refer to it. Since we lack a lot of basic equipment, we can't sustain everyone that lapses into a coma. Some people's fever gets so high that they end up dying from that. Others dehydrate or just starve."

"Why doesn't the body destroy the pollen before it infects them?" Collin sat forward in his chair.

"There is still a lot we don't know about how all this happened due to limited resources and facilities. But basically, the white blood cells just don't recognize the pollen as a threat. Almost as if the pollen molecules are shielded until they infect the body." Dr. Horner shrugged. She was obviously frustrated by the lack of specifics. The inability to research the issue effectively had to be wearing on her.

"What does BT76 do that other medicines can't?" Collin asked.

"Good question," Dr. Horner said. "From what we've been able to observe, BT76 attaches to the pollen spores and breaks down their cellular membrane. Once it bypasses the 'shield,' for lack of a better description, then the body's natural response kicks in and it's dealt with like any other minor problem."

"How do I factor into this? What's unique about my blood?"

"Your white blood cells are able to defeat the 'shield' without BT76 and defeat the pollen before it triggers a response. Or at least that's how it developed slowly over time. We think that's why your fever only reached a certain point and then you stabilized. Eventually your immune system was able to defeat the infection without any BT76." Dr. Horner shrugged again. "I'm limited in what I can verify so a lot of this is hypothetical or guessing, really. It took sixteen years, but my guess is that your body evolved, shall we say."

Collin let out a big sigh and leaned back. He thought about what she said. "What are your thoughts?" he asked the pastor.

"The Lord works in mysterious ways, my son."

"Great, I've evolved, but how does that help? We can't keep Doris and all these other folks alive until their bodies figure out how to fight," said Collin.

"Too true," said Pastor Pendell. "Here's the good part. Doctor." He motioned again for her to continue.

Dr. Horner pursed her lips into a frown. Then she continued. "Your white blood cells are special, like I mentioned, they can recognize and defeat the HAGS infection without any assistance from BT76. Thankfully, your blood type is universal so we are trying to use the cells as a treatment."

"So if you give people my blood then they can fight the infection?"

"Yes! A blessing from God," Pastor Pendell said.

His enthusiasm was contagious, Collin thought. He couldn't help smiling, even if it sounded too good to be true.

"Maybe," said Dr. Horner. "We still need to test the procedure and it may not work with everyone. In the lab, our success rate is roughly seventeen percent."

"That's it?" Collin's heart sank. "And the rest of the time?"

"When it doesn't work, it accelerates the overreaction of the defense response. I believe it would lead to a severe case of anaphylaxis and would cause death in a very short period of time," Dr. Horner said. "In a normal case of anaphylaxis, it can cause death in as little as five minutes for contrast media and medication, and as slow as thirty minutes for food ingestion. We don't have enough epinephrine to treat more than a few people, if it even works at all."

"Doc, I have to be honest. It sounds like you're going in the right direction, but those are unacceptable odds. We'd be killing nearly everyone to only save a few," Collin said. He whistled like "whoa" and raised his hands in the air.

"Even if we moved forward and started using the treatment as is, which we are not, it could only be done on people already developing the fever," Dr. Horner said.

"How can we improve the odds?"

"I'd like to attempt to modify your red blood cells to carry antibodies that recognize the pollen and allow the body to destroy it before it causes an infection," said Dr. Horner. "Since you're a universal donor, it seems like our best option. This way, people develop the ability to produce their own antibodies and improved white blood cells that should be like yours and able to defeat the infection. I know you turned down the BT76 from Major Logan and at this point, I've come to the conclusion that you should be immune to the HAGS fever. If I can modify the blood cells, we could effectively immunize everyone."

"What do you need from me, doctor?" Collin liked the doctor's alternative.

"More blood. Not today though. I have enough to attempt the modification. We'll draw some more tomorrow," Dr. Horner said. "Other than that I need some time to try the procedure. I haven't done serious lab work like this in quite some time. If this works we should come close to a perfect solution and even be able to treat the people that have already slipped into a coma. All we have to do is keep them alive while I modify your cells."

Collin nodded. "Excellent."

Pastor Pendell looked deflated.

"But we have a treatment available now," said Pastor Pendell. "If the Lord is with them, people will be saved."

Collin couldn't believe he was pushing the issue. "Pastor, considering our recent losses, we can't afford to lose anyone in town and there's no point accelerating the deaths of the-"

"If they volunteer and I bless them, then it's perfectly ethical," Pastor Pendell said.

"I won't have my blood used on a treatment that has more than an eighty-percent chance of failure," Collin said. He leaned back in his chair and crossed his arms. "We can wait for the new procedure."

"You would deny the people of Goshen the hope of a cure?" Pastor Pendell stood up and glared down at Collin. "Who are you to decide what's good for them?"

"You want to give them false hope, pastor," Collin said. "All we have to do is wait a while longer and let Dr. Horner test her blood cell modification theory."

"This is my town, Collin. You will not dictate to me-"

"I'm not dictating anything." Collin stood and met the pastor's glare. "I'm trying to help you see reason."

"Gentlemen, please. Sit down. Our energy is better focused on solving the problem," Dr. Horner said.

Collin sat down, his gaze never wavering from Pastor Pendell's. The pastor waited until Collin sat before sitting down.

The doctor looked at them both then said, "I should be able to show you preliminary results on the gene modification in a few days."

"Can you accept that, pastor?" Collin said. "A few days to drastically improve people's odds."

Pastor Pendell thought for a moment, tapping his chin.

Finally he spoke. "Fine. Three days," he said. "If you don't have results for me on the morning of the fourth day, I make the announcement, and we go with the treatment we have now, and place our fate in the Lord's hands."

Collin looked at the doctor.

She nodded her acceptance.

The pastor looked at Collin.

"Fine," Collin said. "Let's do this for the people of Goshen."

"Amen," Pastor Pendell said. "The saved will be saved."

After a quick pounding on the door, Anna burst in without waiting. Her face was flush and she was breathing heavily. In her hand, she clutched a wrinkled handful of paper. She thrust them out with a pained look on her face.

Chapter Seventeen

Doctor Julie Horner faced her daughter with concern plain on her face. "Anna, what's the meaning of this?" she said.

"An airplane flew by and dropped these over the town. They've spread everywhere," Anna said, shaking her fistful of papers. "After it dropped the pamphlets, it turned and swooped down, spraying a foggy substance over the crops."

"What the hell?" Collin said.

"Then it just flew away over the mountains," Anna said.

"Let me see," Pastor Pendell said. He reached over and grabbed a paper from Anna.

"Mom, um, Dr. Horner, I haven't see an airplane like that since I was a kid," Anna said. Her eyes were wide and her face was still flushed. "It had the same logo on it that the helicopters have."

Another knock on the door.

"Come in," Pastor Pendell said.

Kobyashi burst into the room. "Hey guys, the nurses said you were in here. Guess what?"

"HAGS just flew over and crop dusted the field," Collin said.

"Good guess, sleeping beauty," Koby said. He looked at Anna and his enthusiasm faded. "She ruined the surprise, huh?"

"Actually, while you came empty handed, Anna brought us this," Pastor Pendell said. He waved the flyer in the air.

"Ouch," Koby said, making a face as he placed a hand over his heart.

"Here," Anna said. She handed everyone a copy of the flyer.

Collin read the paper.

Goshen Residents:

Due to unforeseen complications, Hathaway Agricultural Genetic Sciences is unable to continue providing BT76 at previously supplied quantities. Expect a reduction of 40% (minimum), effective immediately. Plan accordingly.

Where possible, we have fertilized farmland to boost crop yield.

Respectfully,

H.A.G.S.

Sustainable For Life

Collin felt sick to his stomach. For the people of Goshen, in the midst of a massive BT76 shortage due to the Viper attack, and the pending loss of fifty-seven residents currently suffering down the hall, this was the worst possible timing. He sat down heavily and groaned.

Would the residents take this in stride like the "lottery?" Or would this be the straw that broke Goshen's back?

Thankfully, Dr. Horner had a viable plan for dealing with the infection.

So Collin wasn't worried about the long-term plan. He was worried about the immediate state of the town.

Pastor Pendell looked rather furious. Collin suspected it was because HAGS told the entire town instead of going through the leadership.

"Doctor, we'll leave you now. I expect you have a lot of work to do," Pastor Pendell said. "Remember, three days. Let's go folks." He waved his hand to shoo them out of the room.

"What's Julie working on?" Koby asked, looking around confused.

"I'm sure Collin can fill you in." Pastor Pendell glanced at Collin and then walked out of the room.

They filed out of the room, through the office, and walked down the hallway to the staircase. As they walked downstairs Koby asked, "What are you going to tell people outside?"

Collin was thinking the same thing.

Pastor Pendell didn't respond.

As they approached the front doors, Collin could see people standing around outside holding the flyers. He looked at Koby and raised his eyebrows. There was no telling how things were going to go.

"Oh wow," Collin said. Anna wasn't joking about all the flyers the plane dropped. It seemed like they were everywhere. One fluttered through the air and stuck to the trunk of a tree, like a medieval wanted poster.

"Pastor," a woman shouted, pointing at the group exiting the hospital. She ran over waving one of the pink fliers in the air.

The groups of people who were standing around converged on the pastor, their voices rising as they began talking.

"Sonofabitch," Collin muttered, as he looked around at all the people.

What had seemed like a ghost town earlier that morning now resembled the first day Collin went to church. People were in the streets as far as he could see. It was as if everyone in Goshen had decided to come outside to investigate HAGS' message. Nervous energy filled the air.

Pastor Pendell stopped on the sidewalk and held up his hands for silence. The crowd settled down a little, but continued talking.

"Quiet," Collin shouted. Silence fell over the crowd. Fear was etched on the residents' faces.

Pastor Pendell nodded his thanks towards Collin.

"My friends, we are aware of this new development. But fear not, the Lord is with us. We are a blessed town," Pastor Pendell said. "The Council will be meeting soon to discuss our options. We will make an announcement tomorrow morning. If you have questions, please put them in writing, and give them to your neighborhood representative. Representatives, bring those questions to my office before dinner this evening, so the council can review them before we make our decision. There will be an announcement tomorrow."

Pastor Pendell looked around at everyone. "Take heart, my friends. Isaiah tells us, "For I Lord thy God will hold thy right hand, saying unto thee, Fear not; I will help thee.""

Without waiting for a reaction, Pastor Pendell stepped forward to leave. The crowd parted before him. Collin and Koby followed in his wake.

When they were out of earshot of the crowd, Pastor Pendell said, "Council meeting at Kobyashi's house, right now."

Collin glanced at Koby, who looked mildly surprised.

"Um, okay," Koby said.

"Should I go back and get the doctor?" Collin asked.

"No, this is more of a military matter," Pastor Pendell said. "Besides, she has her hands full enough as it is. Right?"

Collin conceded the point with a nod.

They walked the short distance across town to Koby's house in an awkward silence Koby finally broke the tension.

"Here we are," he said, pointing at the house in front of them.

Collin looked over Koby's house. It had a neatly tended yard with shrubs similar to his own lining the large porch. The house was painted forest green with white trim. Koby's front porch wrapped around the side of the house and he had two big trees in his front yard. It was nice. Classic Americana.

Then they saw Major Logan already standing on Koby's porch. He was holding a green tube.

"Awkward," Koby said to Collin. He nudged him with his elbow.

Collin grunted and watched Major Logan.

"You two play nice," Pastor Pendell said loud enough for everyone to hear.

Neither man said anything.

"How'd you know we would be here?" Koby said. "We didn't even know until we left the hospital."

Major Logan looked at Pastor Pendell. Then he said, "I was told to meet you guys here. I've been waiting about twenty minutes. Now that you're finally here can we go inside and get started?"

Logan's face was puffy and slightly discolored, especially his nose, and he had bandages on his cheekbones, covering the cuts. Major Logan looked much worse off than Collin.

"Sure," Koby said, drawing out the word. He looked over his shoulder and mouthed, "What the fuck?" to Collin.

Collin fought back a smile and followed everyone inside Koby's house.

"We can use the kitchen table. Please have a seat," Koby said. "Anyone want a drink?"

"I'll take tea if you have it," Pastor Pendell said.

"Coffee, please," Collin said.

"Make that two coffees," Major Logan said.

"Do you have the maps and documents?" Pastor Pendell asked Major Logan.

"Yes, of course." He opened the green tube and pulled out rolled papers. One was a large map, it nearly covered Koby's entire table.

"Before we get started, can we clear the air please?" said Pastor Pendell.

Major Logan and Collin looked directly at each other for the first time since the fight. Anger brewed in Major Logan's face, mixed with a little fear and perhaps some respect.

Collin spoke first. "I apologize for fighting you in front of the soldiers, Major Logan. It was unprofessional. Let's not let our differences divide the town."

He meant the last bit more than the rest. Right now, the town had to be united.

"I agree and I apologize for my behavior as well."

They each put out their hands and shook on it.

Koby came over with the drinks on a tray. "Good we're all copacetic. Now, can we get to the point of this little meeting."

Everyone sat at the table; Koby handed out drinks and then joined them at the table. He held the largest coffee mug that Collin had ever seen.

"Are you sure that's big enough," Collin said, grinning.

"Pretty sweet, right?" Koby grinned. "I made this bad boy at the high school. They have a pottery kiln."

"Let's focus, please," Pastor Pendell said. "Major Logan, please walk us through your proposal."

Major Logan pointed at the map.

"As you can see, this is the town, here is the dam, the river, and this area is now our farmland," Major Logan said. He gestured to each location as he spoke. "Our weak points are here, the perimeter of the farmland, and here, the river. Of course, the bridge and the dam can be considered weak points too because they're vital infrastructure."

"What I would like to do is build a wall along the bank of the river with sharpened logs, as a way to shore up that weak point and free up some of the Eagles for patrol in other areas." Major Logan looked at each of them.

"Medieval style defense," Koby said. "I like it."

Collin nodded. "It makes sense to me; we use the river as a moat."

"We need to fortify the entire town," Major Logan said. "Given the change HAGS has implemented, the Vipers will be more desperate than ever to get their hands on a med drop. With the weather warming up, the water will be safer to cross. We now know they have access to explosives and the knowledge to use them. Combined with their overwhelming number of fighters, I fear they may launch an all-out assault on Goshen. If nothing else, I believe they will attempt to blow up the church."

"Those heathens wouldn't dare," Pastor Pendell said. He scoffed at the thought.

"Wouldn't they? It's a symbol for our residents," Collin said. "It would be a huge psychological win for them."

"The Vipers will not destroy Goshen," Pastor Pendell said vehemently. "God won't allow it."

"That may be, pastor," Collin said, glancing at Koby and Major Logan. "But I agree we should prepare fortifications for the town. What kind of time frame are we looking at on the wall?"

Koby leaned back in his chair and said, "You know, the logging mill has dozens, maybe hundreds, of logs already cut and ready to go. Actually, I'm surprised we didn't do this a long time ago. As far as a time frame, between the logging team, carpenters, and maybe others to help, we can probably get the wall up in four or five days, assuming the weather cooperates, and there are no major setbacks."

"That's a good time line," Collin said. "We should plan some improvements around the farmland and maybe traps in the wood line. They used the forest to great effect during last time. We should take away that advantage."

"We can worry about that stuff later, after we fortify the town which is more critical," Major Logan said.

"Fair enough," Collin said. "What about the bridge? Any plan to improve the security of the bridge?"

"Good point," Koby said. He took a noisy slurp from his giant mug.

Major Logan glared at Koby. "With the wall up, it will free up Eagles from having to patrol it. We can have more soldiers stationed on and around the bridge."

"If the Vipers ever take the bridge, we can just blow it," Koby said.

Pastor Pendell scoffed.

Collin was surprised he'd suggest such a thing. "Then we'd be trapped."

"The bridge isn't as vital for us as we may think," said Kobyashi. "It'd be slower to cross the river, sure. But we wouldn't be trapped per se. We have more than enough boats for the hunters and trappers and we could ferry across the farmers."

"How would you do it?" Major Logan said.

"With the boats, I just said that." Koby rolled his eyes.

"Destroy the bridge, dumbass," Major Logan said. "How do propose to blow it up?"

"Let's go upstairs to my office." Koby stood up and motioned for them to follow.

"I'll wait here," Pastor Pendell said.

Collin and Major Logan followed Koby through his living room.

"Good God, man," Major Logan said, eying a sea of junk strewn about the room.

"Watch your step. Don't mess up anything," Koby said over his shoulder.

Collin looked around and instantly understood why Koby told them to go into the kitchen. It was probably the only clean room in his house. The living room? It was like a mad man's workshop.

The living room was filled with a variety of electronics, cords, old television sets, vacuums, tools, pipes, wires, and something that resembled a work bench, overflowing with small electronics and toys. Some of the items were opened and appeared to be missing pieces. A small trail to the staircase was the only clear space in the entire room. How Koby could possibly notice if they moved something confounded Collin.

Upstairs they turned right and went into the first room. It was an extension of the living room, but there was a rack of firearms, and a shelf that held military-looking crates. In the center of the room was a table, conspicuously free of clutter. Koby went over to the shelf and pulled off a crate. He grunted with the weight, then turned and placed it on the table.

Major Logan excused himself to use the bathroom.

The box was stenciled with "Property of U.S. Army" and "Live Explosives." Collin was curious what kind of explosives it held.

Koby pulled a crow bar off another shelf. He undid the latches and pried open the lid.

The front door, and then the screen door, slammed shut. Collin looked out the window and saw Major Logan walking away from the house.

"He just left," Collin said.

"Maybe he likes to shit at home?"

"I don't know, but he's full of shit." Collin smiled.

"Anyway, take a look at these bad boys." Koby pointed into the box.

Collin looked and saw four cloth bandoleers and somehow knew right away what they were. "Claymores?"

"That's right," Koby said, pulling one of the bandoleers out. He took the claymore out and set it on the table.

It lay on the table with "Front Toward Enemy" pointing at the ceiling.

"There are only four. Where are the rest?" Collin asked.

"I have no idea." Koby shrugged. "I've never opened this before. I was waiting until we needed them. Kind of like a bottle of fine wine. You know?"

Collin grunted his agreement. He believed Koby. His mind was racing, and he started to form a theory about why Major Logan had left like he did. Collin thought back to the report about the Eagle's Bar explosion and how there'd been holes blown in some of the wood in the ceiling and walls. Collin realized that multiple claymores could have been used in the medical crate. Possibly, the four that just happen to be missing from Koby's Army crate.

Or maybe the Vipers still held a couple of claymores because four in one container would be overkill, he thought.

"These are great," Collin said. He didn't want to mention his theory to Kobyashi just yet.

"They're perfect. Anyway, we should put them away. I just wanted to show you guys - or you I guess, since Major Dipshit ran off - how we can blow up the bridge," Koby said. "In any case, there's no need to rig the bridge up until they get the wall built. We don't want to accidentally blow our load early."

"Good stuff, Koby. You're full of surprises." Collin helped him secure the lid on the crate.

"Let's go check on the pastor."

Collin followed Koby out of the room. Then something on one of the shelves caught his eye.

"Whoa, man." Collin picked up one of the walkie-talkies. He turned it on and was surprised to find that it had power. "These things work?"

Koby turned to look. "Oh yeah, that one does. I didn't know the battery still had juice though. The other one got wet and the circuit board rusted."

"These would be a big help, especially during battles. You should really try to get these working," Collin said.

"Sir, yes, sir," Koby said in a faux military voice.

Collin smiled, turned the radio off, and put it back on the shelf.

When they reached the bottom of the stairs, Collin tapped Koby on the shoulder.

"You have fun with the pastor. I'm going to head home." Collin started toward the door.

"You're gonna leave me with him. C'mon, man."

"See ya later, Koby."

Koby made a face for a second then gave a quick wave.

Collin walked out and strolled down the gravel road thinking everything over.

The sun was beginning to set and it cast a beautiful glow over the entire valley. Collin stopped on his sidewalk and turned to enjoy the view, the way he had that morning.

"Hell of a day," he muttered.

Collin turned to go inside. He glanced down at the cracked sidewalk and the flower growing out of it. He started to look away and noticed his friend, the bee, dead on the sidewalk in front of him.

Crouching down to look at the bee, Collin got a sick feeling in his gut. The return of bees suggested that the pollen was safe. New bees and new pollen could mean no fever and no infection. That would take HAGS out of the equation.

What if HAGS wasn't actually fertilizing the crops? What if they were really spraying insecticide to kill the bees? Collin frowned. But why would they do that? It couldn't be a profit motive, because there was no evidence of payment for BT76.

Nothing is as it seems, Anna said, Collin thought.

Looking around, he spotted a leaf in the dirt near the bushes. Ever so carefully, not wanting to crush it, or remove any residue from the spray, Collin scooped up the bee with the leaf. He thought he could pass the bee off to Koby or the doctor to test.

He lifted the bee up close to his face but couldn't spot anything unusual. Collin looked out at the fields.

Then he turned and walked into his house.

Chapter Eighteen

So many things were on Collin's mind that he was finding it impossible to sleep. He rolled onto his side and stared out his window. A long time ago, before the fever, Collin tended to keep curtains closed. He never liked the idea of people looking inside his house.

Now, with so few people left, and his home's position on a small rise, his window was above where other houses could see inside. So he looked through the window at the beautiful night sky. Free of light pollution, the heavens glistened with a view of the stars that he never knew was possible.

The Big Sky State, indeed, Collin thought. He sighed. It was a remarkable sight, but his mind kept wandering back to all the drama swirling around Goshen.

Collin smiled and wondered if he led a quieter life before the fever. Although with his vast knowledge of combat techniques, he thought perhaps he never knew what a normal life actually was. Now he was helping to keep a town safe from itself and its enemies, not exactly what he envisioned for himself.

He wondered if the town would be able to construct the wall along the river without any setbacks. Koby seemed quite confident even though nothing was going smooth lately. Would Julie be able to modify his blood cells so they could deliver life-saving antibodies to victims of the fever? What if the Vipers attacked again? Who am I? All of these mysteries swirled in his mind.

Then, he thought about HAGS cutting the supply of BT76 by forty percent. It seemed so random. Collin still had no idea why the company would bother making any BT76 in the first place, or why they would transport it around to small towns like Goshen. It was strange that the company behind the downfall of society was also behind sustaining the last remaining survivors.

Could HAGS have been behind the death of the bee, or was he just being paranoid? Certainly they had no proof the airplane had fertilized the field other than what the flyer said. People saw the airplane spray mist over the fields and until they tested it, there was no telling what the content of the spray was.

Collin rolled onto his back, and thought about the claymores and what four missing explosives could mean. Why had Major Logan really left Kobyashi's house? For a brief second Collin thought, he might have to worry about Major Logan seeking revenge for the beating, but he dismissed that. He didn't seem like the vengeful type. If Major Logan was going to get payback, he'd be more likely to do it in front of a crowd of Eagles.

So many questions, he thought. *So much uncertainty.*

Eventually Collin did drift off to sleep. Exhaustion enveloped him and dragged him down into a deep slumber.

For the first time in almost a week, Collin had dreams. Clear, vivid dreams.

He was back in the same large green lawn as before. This time he saw trees along one edge and a tall black decorative, yet secure, iron fence surrounding the property. It was a beautiful day.

The woman and the boy were there again. Collin was playing catch with the boy, but it wasn't Frisbee. This time he had on a leather outfielder's glove. The pop of the ball smacking into the palm of the mitt was unmistakable. The scent of the worn leather and lush, green grass filled his nose. This was baseball. This was America.

The woman wore a wide-brimmed hat and a pair of sunglasses. She was still laughing and even though her face was blurred, she looked beautiful. He still didn't recognize her by voice, rather his instincts told him who she was. His wife. She sat on the grass to the side of him and the boy. Across from Collin, waving his own baseball mitt was a young boy around eight years old.

Unlike his mother, the boy's face was as clear as a picture. He smiled wide and laughed. He had a smattering of freckles across his face and the same shaggy, sun-bleached hair Collin remembered. He felt certain, deep down to his core, that the boy was his son. Collin could easily have been looking at a younger version of himself.

Collin concentrated hard, scrunching his face in concentration as he tried to recall his son's name. Frustrated by the effort of it, Collin instead focused on enjoying the dream. He wanted to soak up as much of the memory as he could.

Collin smiled at his wife and son. He walked over to embrace the boy.

His son ran toward him, arms outstretched. He dropped the baseball mitt.

When it struck the grass, the ground rumbled. A slow ripple welled up like water on a pond and raced away from the impact. Each ripple shook the ground a little harder than the last.

Earthquake, Collin thought. He looked down as his son embraced him and saw fear — no, terror — in his eyes.

Collin looked around for his wife. She was still; trapped in place with her hand reaching for them, as the last wisps of flame went out, leaving behind the charred remains of the woman he loved. Her charred body cracked and crumbled. When the next ripple struck her body, she exploded into a cloud of dust. Collin and his son were coated in the dust. He choked and gagged on it. The burning smell filled his nose.

Flames were everywhere. Collin's heart raced as he squinted his eyes against the heat and curled against his son, trying his best to shield him from the heat. Collin looked for an exit. Any kind of escape.

Between the flickers of raging fire, he saw there was nothing.

Where lush green grass had covered the ground just moments ago, there was now charred earth. Where there had been trees there were now smoldering stumps. Waves of scorched earth radiated from where the mitt had dropped. The mitt itself had burned up and blown away long ago, like his wife. The waves crumbled and crashed, tossing up pieces of smoking dirt. Collin looked to the dark sky and saw a lone American flag, on fire, drifting towards the ground.

They were surrounded. Trapped.

Hell, Collin thought.

Horrendous, painful waves of heat beat on them. His son's knees gave out and his bodyweight pulled down on Collin.

"Hold on," he yelled. He couldn't lose his son again. He didn't even know his name.

When Collin looked down, his son's body burst into a ball of flame.

A scream tore through his chest, but was drowned by the roar of the wildfire. His son's body cracked, crumbled, and blew away.

Collin slumped to the ground.

The pain he felt wasn't physical. It was far worse. His very soul was being wrung between the cruel, thorny hands of fate.

He closed his eyes and let himself be consumed by the fire. Collin willed it to turn him to ash so he could be reunited with his family.

But he didn't burn up.

When Collin opened his eyes, he looked down to see that he was holding a large piece of foam covered in a cheap looking cloth. It was worn and tattered. Enough of the general shape remained that he thought it looked like a seat cushion of some sort. Everything was still shaking, just not as violently as before.

A surge of hope coursed through Collin. Maybe his son was still alive? He just had to call out to him. No, he couldn't, he realized. He still didn't know his own son's name. Panic twisted Collin's gut and he sat up, breathing hard, hoping to see the boy. His boy.

He heard something. It was faint but growing louder.

Collin looked around, searching. Everything was dark. His eyes were closed.

When he opened them he saw Pastor Pendell and Kobyashi staring down at him.

"We've been trying to wake you up for like five minutes, dude," Koby said. For a second, he looked a little concerned but played it off with a smirk. "The Sleeping Beauty act is getting old."

Collin sat up and rubbed his face.

"You were talking in your sleep," Pastor Pendell said.

"Talking? More like yelling," Koby added.

"Oh?" Collin looked up at them, sheepishly. Why did everyone feel they could just waltz into his house?

"Yes. Do you pray before bed?" Pastor Pendell asked.

"Um, no. I guess not." Collin shook his head.

"You should try that. A prayer before bed soothes the soul and settles the mind." Pastor Pendell said it like a doctor prescribing medication.

"Okay, thanks, pastor." Collin was disappointed. He remembered enough of his dream to know that he still didn't know the boy's name. A fact he knew would haunt him until he figured it out. "That was one hell of a dream," he said. His forehead was damp and he felt a trickle of sweat run down his back.

"The last dream I remember, I woke up very happy," Koby said with a sly grin and a wiggle of his eyebrows.

Collin smirked at Koby.

Pastor Pendell scoffed. "Enough."

Looking at the two men in his room, Collin said, "Hold on. What are you two doing in my house?"

"You didn't hear the choppers?" Koby said, surprised.

"No. Clearly, I was very much asleep." Looking out his window, he saw that it was dusky; the sun still hid behind the mountains.

"About fifteen minutes ago, they dropped a case in the field. It's less than two hundred yards from the bridge, I think," Pastor Pendell said. "This time the case has a bright yellow strobe on it, constantly blinking."

"BT76?" Collin said. He felt his heart jump. Considering it was so close to the last drop this might save lives. It wouldn't save Doris but it could save others.

"There's another case," Koby said. "Not in the field though. They dropped it about five miles or so away, to the south."

"For the Vipers?" Collin said.

Koby and Pastor Pendell shrugged.

"Anyway, I watched it fall to the ground and was able to get a bearing on it," Koby said.

"You have Eagle vision?" Collin smiled.

"Funny. No, I was upstairs at home, heard the choppers fly in, and grabbed my binoculars," Koby said. "I was hoping to see something useful or interesting. And what do ya know, mission accomplished. Anyway, my reading put it at two hundred seventy degrees to the southwest of my house."

"I'm glad you thought to take a reading," Collin said. "Reminds me of my days as a Boy Scout."

"Why don't you get ready so you can join the Eagles," Pastor Pendell said.

"Yeah, if you guys don't mind waiting downstairs in the kitchen while I do so," Collin said.

The men walked out of his bedroom.

"Don't dawdle," Koby yelled.

Collin smiled and went to the bathroom to brush his teeth.

Once he'd gotten ready and dressed, Collin jogged down the stairs. He was met by Pastor Pendell and Koby, who held up a big mason jar of coffee for him.

"You're my hero," Collin said, taking a sip. He looked at the jar and nodded.

"Don't forget it," Koby said.

"Let's go," Pastor Pendell said. "We need to get this case secured."

It was maybe ten minutes since Collin woke up, so it was still possible that the Vipers hadn't responded to the unexpected drop. If they were lucky, Collin thought they could retrieve the case before the Vipers had a chance to attack. No telling if they could get to the one dropped in the forest though.

Collin opened the front door for Pastor Pendell and Koby. He noticed two Eagles standing on the path to his porch.

One was a Staff Sergeant, named Jeremy Raiford and a Private, named David Berry. The two men stood patiently waiting for them.

"What's the status of the case?" Collin said over the rim of his mason jar as he took another drink of coffee. He pushed the lingering remnants of his dream to the back of his mind and focused on the situation.

"Sir, Major Logan deployed the sniper teams, and last we heard, there was no movement along the tree line," Staff Sergeant Raiford said.

"No Vipers in sight, sir," Private Berry added.

SSGT Raiford glanced sideways at him for restating what he just said.

"The case in the field hasn't been recovered yet?" Pastor Pendell asked.

"Not that I know of, Pastor," SSGT Raiford said.

PVT Berry shrugged.

"You two go with Kobyashi to retrieve a couple of those explosives you showed me," Collin said, looking at the Eagles and then Koby. "Meet us near the bridge."

"Indeed," Pastor Pendell said. "We need to meet with Major Logan. I want to know what's happening."

They left for the bridge, while the other three walked toward Koby's house.

After the others were out of earshot, Pastor Pendell looked at Collin. He could feel the pastor's eyes on him but he kept staring down the road, waiting for him to speak first.

"Tell me about your dream," Pastor Pendell said. "I have a feeling it is still on your mind."

Collin shook his head slightly. "Not really," he said. "All I remember is playing baseball with my son."

Pastor Pendell's eyebrows shot up. "You remember your son?"

"I recognized a boy and got a strong feeling that he was my son."

"Where were you in the dream?"

"We were playing in a big green fenced-in yard," Collin said.

"Dreams can be echoes of the Lord or the handiwork of the devil," Pastor Pendell said. "Remember the Book of David, chapter four, verse five, which tells us, 'I saw a dream and it made me fearful; and these fantasies as I lay on my bed and the visions in my mind kept alarming me.' He's talking about fear of the unknown. There is much of life that is unknown, but we shouldn't fear it."

Collin didn't say anything, he just looked at the pastor.

"God is with you, and each dream you have may reveal more details about your past." Pastor Pendell looked at him hopefully like he expected a response.

Collin glanced away for a moment. He couldn't believe what he'd just heard.

"You know, pastor, I'm starting to think you don't know jack shit about my past." Collin looked at Pastor Pendell with a mix of suspicion and anger. "I'm just here doing your bidding. Meanwhile, you string me along, right?"

For a split-second, Pastor Pendell looked offended. Then he smirked.

"You may very well be a workhorse, Collin. But I am not the one taunting you with a carrot above your head," he said. He motioned like he was dangling the vegetable from a stick, taunting him. "No. The Lord will enlighten you when you are ready."

"Ready for what?" Major Logan asked.

Collin looked up and realized they made it to the bridge, the whole walk over he was distracted with the pastor and his dream.

"Ready to find out what the plan is," Collin said motioning beyond the bridge to the field.

Collin glanced at Logan and then looked at the field. He could see a yellow blinking light flashing against the trees and reflecting off the water. Although he couldn't directly see the source.

"Earlier, we had an unexpected drop from Hathaway choppers, like before. They dropped a crate in our field, nearly two hundred meters from the bridge. They continued down the valley and dropped a second crate roughly two hundred seventy degrees southwest of us," Major Logan said. "The case here has a blinking yellow light that hasn't shut off. We're not certain if the second crate does as well. I'd like to see if we can retrieve the second crate, just in case it's BT76."

Collin thought it was odd that the major never mentioned Koby to credit him for the information.

"Our new Alpha team has already gone out to secure the crate and should be back with it any minute now," Major Logan said.

"That's great," Collin said. "No Vipers?"

Major Logan shook his head.

"I'm thankful we haven't heard any shots fired yet," Pastor Pendell said.

Koby and the two Eagles approached the group. Collin saw the Eagles had the claymores that he'd requested. A wide grin spread across his face.

"Look," PVT Berry said.

The blinking light was approaching the bridge. They could see Eagles carrying it while the others conducted a tactical retreat to cover their buddies. Everything was going smoothly. No shots fired, no arrows, and, thankfully, no deaths.

Major Logan looked at Raiford and said, "Why do you have claymores, sergeant?"

"Uh, General War ordered it," PVT Berry said, cutting in.

Major Logan glowered at the private for a moment before turning to Collin. "So you're a General now, eh?"

Collin held his hands up in mock defense.

They both looked at SSGT Raiford.

"Private, give those to Major Logan." SSGT Raiford pointed to the claymores.

PVT Berry did as he was told.

"Let's take a walk, private," SSGT Raiford said.

The two Eagles turned and walked away.

Major Logan narrowed his eyes at Collin.

Collin chuckled and raised his right hand. "I swear to God; I didn't tell him to say that."

"But I'm sure glad he did," Koby said, laughing.

Pastor Pendell shook his head and looked down at the ground.

"So, what exactly are the claymores for...General?" Major Logan asked sarcastically. He stood with his hands on his hips, looking skeptical.

Collin sighed.

"If it's okay with you, I thought we could remove the BT76, rig the crate with the claymores, and leave it out. See if we can bag some Vipers. It's possible that they haven't seen us," Collin said. "If they try to steal it, they'll get a taste of their own medicine."

Alpha team set the case on the town side of the bridge, off to the side behind a tree. The soldiers stood around double-checking the tree line and catching their breath.

Major Logan looked deep in thought.

"Major?" Collin said. Should be any easy decision, he thought.

Major Logan nodded slowly and said, "Okay, it couldn't hurt to try, and it would be nice to get them back if they fall for it." He waved over one of the soldiers and told him to bring the crate over.

Within a minute, the case was in front of them. The blinking light was annoying. Collin fought the urge to smash it. Since they were using the crate for Viper-bait then it should remain intact.

Not even hesitating, Major Logan walked up to the crate, knelt down, and grabbed the padlock. Collin saw Koby and Pastor Pendell begin to back away. He grinned despite their valid concern.

"Are you sure you want to open that?" Collin said.

"It's safe," Major Logan said. His voice was tight and harsh. Major Logan's bruised face twisted into a frown. "Stand back if you're worried. Go hide with them." He waved his hand toward Koby and the pastor.

"What if HAGS rigged it with a bomb?"

"HAGS doesn't use bombs. Vipers do and no Vipers have touched this crate," Major Logan snapped. He looked confident in his words.

Collin shrugged.

Major Logan rolled his eyes and began to turn the combination lock. He spun the dial, then he turned it the other direction, and finally he twisted it back again. One, fifteen, sixteen, just like last time. Collin saw it clear as day. For being a "secret," the major didn't do much to hide the numbers from anyone.

The lock's mechanism snapped. Major Logan turned the lock and pulled it off of the crate.

He glanced up at Collin and smirked.

Major Logan flipped the lid up and stood up. Gesturing inside with his hand. Nothing happened.

Collin walked around the end of the crate so he could see inside. On top of the shrink-wrapped boxes of BT76 were a few of the pink flyers they saw before. Supposedly, the supply was only dropping by forty-percent. Yet, they only had one crate. It looked like a fifty-percent cut to him.

Major Logan had already knelt back down to pull out the medication. He didn't even look for a pressure switch. Collin gaped at the man. Surely, he should be exercising more caution considering the explosive properties of their last drop.

Major Logan is either the bravest, dumbest, or most traitorous bastard that he'd ever known, Collin thought.

After pulling out a few of the bricks of medication, Major Logan stood up and yelled for the soldiers to line up and grab the BT76 from him. They began passing the bricks down a line of soldiers. One by one, the soldiers filled their arms and walked away carrying the precious boxes of vials toward the hospital.

Emptying the crate only took a couple of minutes. When it was empty, he pushed the crate toward SSGT Raiford who had returned without PVT Berry.

"Have you used claymores before, sergeant?" he said.

"Yes, sir."

"You sure?"

"Yes, sir. I used plenty of them during Operation Iraqi Freedom," SSGT Raiford said. "We're basically old friends, sir."

"Very well. Alpha team will carry the case out to the field and provide security for you. You setup the claymores to cover the crate and the nearest wood line," Major Logan said.

SSGT Raiford's eyebrow twitched. "Yes, sir."

Collin was surprised that he wanted them setup outside the case and not inside the way the Viper's had done it. Even if both explosives went off, they were unlikely to kill many Vipers. Maybe half a dozen Vipers at most since the thick tree trunks would block most of the blast wave and absorb the thousands of small metal pellets embedded in the plastic explosive.

"We won't get many Vipers if the claymores are outside of the crate," Collin said. "Shouldn't we put them inside so they take it away?"

SSGT Raiford shook his head. "If they don't take the bait, then it would nearly impossible for us to recover the explosives without casualties."

Collin grunted. "Fair enough."

"Sergeant, you have your orders. Carry on," Major Logan said.

"Yes, sir." SSGT Raiford turned and jogged over to the Alpha team leader and relayed the major's orders. They returned with the whole team, picked up the case, and moved out across the bridge.

Once they reached a suitable place to drop the crate, Alpha team lowered it and moved behind in into a right echelon formation to watch the wood line. SSGT Raiford moved up next to the crate and began to place the claymores. Without binoculars, it was difficult to see exactly what was happening.

"How's he setting those up, Major?" Collin said.

"Trip wires."

"Good choice," Collin said. With two claymores, Raiford would have great options for placement. Ideally, their fields of fire would overlap and the trip wires wouldn't be visible until it was too late, if at all. The Vipers were in for a terrible surprise.

Pastor Pendell yawned behind Collin. The sound startled Collin. He hadn't realized that the pastor was still there.

"I'm heading back to the church. I need to get some more sleep before service," he said, yawning again. "Good hunting, gentlemen. May the Lord be with you in your endeavor."

Koby watched the pastor leave and shook his head.

Collin chuckled. "You can go too, Koby."

"Thanks, but I'm fine."

"Who's on over watch," Collin asked Major Logan. Koby watching the pastor leave reminded him to ask.

"Well, General-" Major Logan said, sarcasm thick in his voice.

"See what you started," Collin said to Koby, cutting off the major.

"Whoa dude, that was Private Berry. Not me," Koby said looking surprised.

"Like I was saying," Major Logan continued. "The usual teams are up in the Eagle's Nests, and my best sniper team is up on the dam. They've been there since 1900 hours yesterday." Major Logan didn't look happy about that. "You feel like watching the bait pile?"

"Sure. Who's my spotter?" Collin asked.

Major Logan shook his head. "You'll be mine."

Koby laughed.

Chapter Nineteen

Sunrise from the top of dam was even more impressive than from his front porch. Golden spears of light began to lance down from the dips between mountain peaks. The valley glowed as nature began to wake up. Bird songs began to fill the air, while Collin adjusted his position on the re-purposed yoga mat that provided a minimal amount of comfort on the hard, concrete dam.

This morning though, Collin wouldn't be able to enjoy its beauty. He had a job to do and it required his total focus. It was his first time on the dam and he was impressed with its size, relative to the size of the river. Collin couldn't understand why it was so tall and just assumed it was because it needed space to house all the equipment needed to generate electricity. His knowledge of such things was minimal at best.

The rush of water exiting the dam below them would normally be enjoyable. Considering they were in a tactical situation, Collin couldn't help feeling a little uneasy, since it would be easy for someone to sneak up on them. Major Logan assured Collin that the top of the dam was one of the safest places in Goshen.

Looking around at the mountains surrounding the dam, Collin believed him too. The two sides of the dam sat in stark contrast of each other. Whereas the valley held the town and prosperous farmland, like something out of a story book, the other side looked wild and rugged. Goshen's dam sat between steep mountains and stood over three hundred fifty feet high. The dam itself stretched straight across the canyon, roughly four hundred feet across anchoring into a cliff on the far side, and a steep mountainside behind the town. The road leading to the dam was steep and winding.

Behind the dam, was a gorgeous blue lake stretching into the distance and disappearing around a curve behind a mountain. Major Logan mentioned that a treacherous river and waterfalls coming down off the mountains fed the lake. Collin could see one of the magnificent waterfalls cascading down the side of the mountain, crashing against a huge ledge, before falling further until it finally splashed into the lake. Spray from the waterfall twinkled in the rising sun. Collin imagined the rainbows you could see if you got closer.

"How far is the farmland from here?" Collin asked.

"We had a range finder, before some dumbass broke it," Major Logan said. "According to the measurements we took, the near side of the field is six hundred meters and the far side is just over two thousand meters away. We're looking at a range of roughly seven hundred fifty meters for the crate. Which is why I deploy the Barrett up here."

Collin grunted. He didn't think it was likely that Major Logan could shoot two thousand meters accurately, but less than a thousand meters shouldn't be too difficult. Collin wondered if he was still proficient. Considering he hadn't fired a rifle in almost two decades, if not longer, it was unlikely. Marksmanship, especially for snipers, required consistent training to maintain proficiency.

Probably why Major Logan made me spotter, Collin thought.

The two men lay on their respective shooting mats and scanned the valley below for Vipers. Given the dam's height and the wider valley before them, the view was incredible. Having the dam was a major tactical advantage.

Collin clearly understood why the Vipers had felled the trees before rolling out their armored contraption to hijack the previous medical crate. Quite ingenious really.

After a scan of the tree line around the fields, Collin noticed people making their way toward the church for Sunday service. He had no reason to keep track of days but it was obvious when it was Sunday. Nothing of interest there, so Collin moved on to check out the Eagle's positions. He saw the Eagle's Nests sitting high in the trees. People were working on the wall along the river, carving sharp points, transporting the logs, digging postholes, and placing the sharpened posts. The logs were about twenty feet long, which even after lowering them into the postholes formed a formidable defensive barrier.

He couldn't lay there and watch the construction of the wall though. He had to keep an eye out for the deadly Vipers, a group of killers who had apparently harassed Goshen for years. Collin had never heard a valid reason for why the Eagles didn't go on the offensive and wipe them out. It seemed foolish to sit back and let your soldiers get picked off by a technologically inferior enemy.

Collin sighed. He wasn't finding anything in the forest. He looked up from his binoculars to give his eyes a rest and looked at the valley. If he was going to approach Goshen to investigate a supply drop, how would he do it?

Clearly, the Vipers had the cover of the forest beyond Goshen's border. There was a road leading out of town but it was overgrown by weeds, grass, and bushes. The only way to tell it had even been there was the obviously younger growth. The trees were smaller than the surrounding forest.

The mountains provided good elevation. He doubted the Vipers had a communication system, even Goshen lacked radios. They could signal with whistles, physical messengers running back and forth, or the way Major Logan had during the battle, using flags and flares.

Collin settled back down and began to scan the ridgelines and breaks in the forest for Vipers observing Goshen. After about half an hour, the only thing he saw moving around was a black bear with a pair of cubs and a few birds. No humans.

"Major, how long has it been since you shot the fifty-cal?" he said.

"Not long enough." He adjusted his position and looked up briefly to rest his eyes.

When it became obvious that Major Logan wasn't interested in talking, Collin went back to scanning for Vipers. The two of them had never been friends and probably never would be, especially after the fight in the gym. However, they were the two best warriors in Goshen and each of them knew it.

The sniper team they relieved had passed on a watch to Collin. He looked down and saw that it was almost time for the next team to relieve them. With only thirty minutes to spare, he went back to watching the tree line but he allowed his mind to wander.

Time was running out for the BT76 replacement that Dr. Horner was working on; Collin hoped that Pastor Pendell would reconsider his three-day time limit. He wasn't sure it would even be possible for her to do what she said in only three days. Maybe if the procedures weren't too difficult and she was familiar with doing it but how many family practitioners were? Collin stopped and realized that he had only assumed Julie was a general family doctor. He had no clue about exactly what her specialty was before the fever. Hell, she may have been a dentist for all he knew. Or she could be a top notch geneticist, the fact was, he didn't know and that needed to change. At that very moment, lying atop the of the dam, Collin decided it was time to start getting some answers.

Geneticist or not, he hoped she could make enough modified blood cells to treat the people currently affected. He tried to imagine how such a thing worked, and came up blank. Although he couldn't remember the training, Collin was certain he had combat medical training. His training didn't rely on technical equipment, it consisted of the basics to keep a soldier alive until real doctors were available. So his base of knowledge was limited when it came to lab work.

Collin made a mental note to check in with Dr. Horner and see how she was doing when he finished his stint as Major Logan's spotter. If he was lucky, she'd show him how the process worked.

He glanced at his watch. The second hand ticked rhythmically in its infinite journey, while the minute hand revealed that they only had ten minutes left.

Major Logan was so quiet that Collin wouldn't have been surprised to find him asleep but when he looked over, the major was still alert and scanning for activity. He was vigilant. Collin was impressed.

Collin focused on the crate. It was still there. The yellow light continued blinking, illuminating every second or so. The flashing was annoying but it helped Alpha team locate it when it was dusky outside earlier that morning.

The crate appeared undisturbed and nothing had set off the claymores. He checked the forested area around the case and satisfied that no one was there, he switched to checking the mountainsides for spotters.

"I've got movement sixty-five meters from the crate on the edge of the forest," Major Logan said.

Collin glanced at Major Logan to see if he was messing with him but the major was focused. He went back to his binoculars and checked the entire area Major Logan indicated. He scanned near the tree trunks, the bushes, the dark spots, the light areas, and even the ground with little to no cover. No movement.

"Where?" Collin asked. "I've got nothing."

"Follow the path at the end of the soybeans they planted last week. When you get to the tree line, you should see it."

Collin quickly followed the path with his binoculars and then slowed down in the space between the edge of the field, where the trail stopped and the brush started until he hit the trees. Still seeing nothing he started looking in a zig-zag pattern ten yards to either side of where Major Logan said he spotted the movement. He continued the search pattern until he made his way back to the edge of the crops.

"Closing in on fifty-five meters."

"I still don't see anything." Collin felt frustrated. Then, he looked at the major to see if the guy was messing with him, but Major Logan was laser focused. His finger was near the trigger, relaxed and ready.

"Forty meters from the crate," Major Logan said.

He looked roughly forty meters from the case and all around. Then he stopped and watched one spot, relaxing his eyes and hoping to spot the movement. Nothing.

Logan must be screwin' with me, he thought.

"Okay man, good one." Collin fake-chuckled. He nudged Logan's arm.

Major Logan frowned, but didn't look away, not wanting to lose sight of his target. Instead, he flicked the safety off on the Barrett M82 and began to steady his breathing. "Thirty meters."

"Damn it. Seriously, I can't see shit." Collin glared through his binoculars focusing completely on the area near the crate. Considering the rate of speed, it should be easy to spot whoever was down there.

"It's a small person crawling through the meadow grass," Major Logan said.

Looking at the meadow grass, he saw a few pieces stir. Then a ripple in the grass.

"Ghillie suit?" Collin said, almost whispering.

"Exactly."

Impressive tactical skills.

It took him forever to notice anything. If it was just one person though, they couldn't take the crate. So what was going on? One thing Collin had learned from the last encounter with the Vipers was that they could be very tricky and unpredictable.

"Twenty meters." Major Logan sounded calm and ready.

The infiltrator wouldn't need to crawl much further before the claymores gave them their last greeting.

"I don't see any others," Collin said.

"You didn't see this one," Major Logan said. "I did."

The snide remark stung because it was true. Collin didn't say anything. He knew that this was validation of Logan's decision to designate him as the spotter.

Considering the skill of the Viper crawling toward the crate, Collin began to wonder where he might have started. It must have taken almost the whole time they were on the dam to crawl so far. He watched carefully through his binoculars and realized the reason it was so difficult to see them.

A ghillie suit typically consisted of a jacked or more often, a full outfit like coveralls. This person appeared to be hiding under a makeshift blanket of grass and moss. Since they were so small, if they stopped moving it was impossible to tell them apart from the surrounding foliage. Even when they moved, it was near impossible to spot them.

"Time to go boom," Major Logan said.

The person closed in enough that the claymores could go off at any point. Just one person wasn't really worth the use of the explosives, but it would send a message to the Vipers.

Better than nothing, Collin thought.

No movement after several minutes had Collin wondering if he was looking in the wrong spot. He blinked a few times to clear his straining eyes. The edge of the camouflage lifted just a few inches. He watched closely, hoping to see who was underneath.

The infiltrator was only a foot or two away from where SSGT Raiford had set the tripwire.

"He must have seen the trip wire," Collin said.

"No shit," Major Logan said in a tight voice.

After another moment, the movement of the infiltrator switched directions. They were following the tripwire to the explosive. Once they reached the end of the trip wire all they had to do was sever the firing line, or disconnect the firing line from the power source, then remove the blasting cap from the mine, and it was as safe as a walk in a park.

Were they simply hoping to circumnavigate the explosive to get at the crate?

After a few tense minutes, hoping for the mine to detonate, it was clear the person knew what they were doing.

"Damn it," Collin muttered.

They stopped near the power source. The blanket of camo lifted up and the head and arms of a dirty, camouflaged young boy was visible. Collin sucked in a breath. A kid?

"Jesus," Major Logan hissed.

"They sent a kid." Collin was stunned. "We have to stop him."

Major Logan turned his head and looked at Collin. "What? You want me to shoot him?"

Out of the corner of his eye, Collin saw Major Logan lower his head to the riflescope.

Collin frowned. He didn't want the kid to get shot or blown up. If he was being sent out on missions like this, then he needed to be rescued.

"The crate is too heavy for one man, much less a kid," Major Logan said. "Let's just see what happens."

His stomach knotted up as he watched the boy handle the firing line. He disconnected the power source then pulled the blanket up over him. He moved toward the mine.

"Damn it. Don't do it, kid. Don't you fucking do it," Collin said under his breath.

He inched closer to the mine.

"Turn around and go home. Just leave them." Collin felt his hands grow damp with sweat. "Shoot near him as a warning."

"This is just getting interesting," Major Logan said.

The last thing Collin wanted was to see the boy torn apart by the explosion and small ball bearings ripping into him. He winced as the kid removed the blasting cap from the top of the mine. The boy set it carefully off to the side and pulled up the mine. He set it face down in the dirt and looked at the other mine.

"I can't believe those bastards are using children like this! So wrong," Major Logan said, his voice rumbled with anger. "So wrong. But at the same time, so smart."

"Unforgivable," Collin said in agreement. His mind was a whirlwind of confusion. How could they stop the kid without killing him?

"If he disarms the second one, he's going down. I'm not losing two mines to that kid," Major Logan said, with a hard voice.

Collin sucked in a breath. He understood not wanting to lose the mines and it had been the Vipers choice to send him. *Damn it.*

"Put a round in the crate as a warning," Collin said. "Hopefully, he'll leave the mines and run."

They watched as the boy disconnected the power source.

Major Logan reached up and adjusted the windage on his riflescope three clicks.

The boy pulled out the blasting cap.

"Aiming at the medical crate," Major Logan said. He let out a breath and aimed. "On target."

The boy picked up the second mine.

"Send it," Collin said. The rifle boomed before he finished his command. Collin felt the shot as much as he heard it but he stayed focused on the boy and the crate. A split second later, a hole punched through the crate, sending it tumbling away from its resting spot.

The boy flinched away from the impact as the booming shot echoed down the valley.

Instead of dropping the mines and running for the forest, the young boy inexplicably stood up in full view and turned to face the distant hydro dam where they were perched. A camouflaged hunting mask covered his head and face. It detracted from his humanity but there was no doubt that the boy was closer to ten years old than eighteen. Too young.

Collin thought it unlikely the boy could have located them by the sound of the shot because the sound didn't reach the boy until after the impact. The acoustics of the valley sent the blast rebounding off the mountains in an echo of death.

Despite that, the boy was obviously staring directly at the dam, holding a mine in each hand. The only way he could have known where to turn was to have knowledge that they would be up there watching the entire time.

"C'mon kid. Drop them, goddamnit," Collin muttered through clenched teeth. "Drop them and run away."

Major Logan racked a second round into the chamber, ejecting the large, empty brass shell onto the concrete. It clinked loud and melodic. It bounced and rolled to a stop against Collin's elbow. He flinched away from the hot brass and adjusted his position.

"Put another one in the ground," Collin said. He didn't want to see the kid die for his mistake. If this went bad and Collin ever got his hands on the Vipers' leader, he was going to wring his neck for this tragedy.

"Can't. Ammo is too precious. He takes another step and he dies."

"I know, I know. But at least give him a chance to reconsider," Collin said watching the kid staring up toward them. "If he tries to escape, then take him down."

"Very well."

Shifting the mines to one hand, the boy reached up with the other hand, and peeled off the hunting mask.

Collin gasped.

The boy was the same one from his dream. The very child he had played baseball and Frisbee with in his dreams. The boy he watched burn away into a pile of ash. His son.

"It can't be," he said.

His cheeks were smudged with dirt but even through the binoculars,

Collin could make out the freckles that covered his cheeks and nose. The light sandy hair and the eyes. Last time he'd seen them in his dream, they'd reflected in the flames that were consuming his body.

Did the flames represent the mines exploding? Were Collin's dreams coming to life?

As Collin watched, dumbfounded by what he saw before him, the boy raised his hand, and flipped them the bird with a big smirk on his precious face.

"A friend of yours?" Major Logan said.

"Christ! That's my son," Collin said.

Major Logan scoffed. "Impossible. He's far too young."

"I can't explain it, damn it, Major," Collin growled. He glared at Major Logan, who ignored him. "I know him. That's my son."

"Negative, judging by his age, he was born while your dumbass was still sleeping in the hospital." Major Logan didn't even look up at Collin. "And he ain't from Goshen. If he runs, I'm putting a round right through him."

Major Logan was telling the truth; Collin could feel it, but he also felt the urge to hold the child close and protect him from the exploding and burning world around them. It was overwhelming, vibrating through every cell in his body.

Collin looked through the binoculars and saw the boy drop his hand. At the same time, he turned and began to run through the field, with the awkward gait young boys have on uneven ground.

Without even thinking, Collin threw his hand out and smacked the big rifle as hard as he could. The rifle tilted, shifting the aim of the barrel, just as the major fired.

The Major missed. Collin let out a breath he didn't even realize he was holding, thankful he wouldn't have to watch the boy die again.

Logan ejected the hot brass from the rifle. It struck Collin's arm, searing the skin again. He ignored the pain and looked through the binoculars.

"You sonofabitch," Major Logan yelled as he pushed the bolt back into place, seating a new round. He fired again as the boy disappeared behind a massive pine tree. It was a hasty, desperate shot that went wide and took out the trunk of a smaller tree nearby, exploding into thousands of splinters as the .50-caliber round tore through its soft wood. There was a brief hesitation as the tree struggled to stay upright before it slowly tilted to the side, built up momentum and crashed to the forest floor.

The boy was safe. The mines were gone.

Now, all Collin was left with, was a furious Major Logan.

Chapter Twenty

Rock music boomed from a small stereo while Gary Kobyashi started to repair the broken handheld radio. Collin had seen it a while ago and asked him to repair it if he could, as if that was a serious question.

Of course he could fix it, Koby thought.

After a few quick spins of the Phillips screwdriver, the first of several screws that held together the plastic shell, slid out. The shell encased the damaged components. On the outside, the radio was in decent enough shape, just a few scrapes and scratches from normal use. Inside the radio, Koby wasn't sure what he'd find wrong with it. All he knew was that it had gotten wet and stopped working.

Having radios in town, even it was only two of them would certainly help communication for the Eagles. Koby knew he should have worked on the radios before. Every time he thought about it, he was too busy just keeping the town running. It hadn't seemed like such a pressing need. Given the recent circumstances, it felt like a critical project and he was happy to work on it.

At one point, Koby hoped to run an electronics and repair class for the young residents. Passing on his knowledge would help the town in the future and would give him a pool of trained technicians to pull from. Koby didn't like feeling that he was the only one who could repair and maintain their systems. Again, things were always too crazy.

Between the hydroelectric dam and the gardening systems, Koby worked harder than a farm horse. Not to mention the greenhouses. Of course, he had help but it still wasn't enough. Quite simply there were too many jobs around town and not enough people to do them all.

More so now that they'd lost so many Eagles.

With a heavy sigh at the thought, Koby continued his work examining the radio system.

Koby flexed his hand after unscrewing the case, then split the plastic shell open and looked over the components. Initial inspection just showed a lot of rust. That was to be expected. The radio hadn't been touched in who knew how long, at least since it broke.

Overall, the radio wasn't in bad shape. They were rugged little radios.

Koby took a drink of his coffee. Nursing the coffee trees to produce black gold had been one of his finest personal achievements. He smiled to himself. The satisfying, earthy taste warmed his body and fueled his mind while he bobbed his head to the music and began to remove rust, carefully brushing it away and wiping off the circuit board.

If he polished the contacts and re-soldered the board, it should make the frequency selector work. Even if it couldn't send out signals, Koby was certain he could make it receive signals. On the other hand, the pickup was in poor shape and would require extra tender loving care to repair.

Even one-way communication was better than what they had right now, which wasn't much. Their communication system was hardly better than two soup cans and a string. All they had were some colored flags in the church bell tower. Koby scoffed at the thought.

Using a cloth dampened with an alcohol-based cleaning solution, Koby wiped off the board, polishing the contacts. It was a small circuit board, so cleaning it was quick as a snap. He plugged in his soldering iron and while he waited for it to heat up, he grabbed the working handset.

The night before Koby had charged the radio batteries. So he turned on the other radio and set it on the workbench beside the stereo. Its red led light cast a cool glow on the side of the stereo. Then he went back to work on the busted handset.

When the soldering iron was ready, he touched up the board. Little curls of smoke rose up around Koby's face as he hunched over his workbench. He felt a little like a mad scientist. A small part of him wished he had more time to experiment and invent things; Koby loved tinkering.

He sighed and sat back. He examined the circuit board with a critical eye and nodded with satisfaction.

Not bad, if I do say so myself, he thought.

Koby double-checked the rest of the radio - the battery case, the antennae, and the various switches and buttons. Everything looked fine, so he began to put the radio back together.

Once it on, he began manually switching frequencies, hoping to see the LED light on the working handset to turn green. That would let him know they were connected. He set the channel and frequency on the working radio, then worked on getting the damaged one to the same settings.

On the bad handset, he reached channel nineteen at five-point-five megahertz and glanced up at the other handset. To his amazement, the walkie talkie's led turned from red to green, meaning that a connection had been made. Koby checked both radios to confirm the settings. He'd seen that the diode for the light and the wire was well insulated and working on the bad radio so if they'd matched frequencies then it should have turned green but it still glowed red.

Koby set the good radio on the workbench, turned off the music, and carried the repaired radio a few steps away. He pressed the button and spoke into the radio but nothing happened, instead of hearing his voice, all he heard was silence.

Back to the drawing board, Koby thought. He frowned at the radio in his hand.

He opened it back up and went back over the components. He quickly touched up a few connections with the soldiering iron. A big puff of smoke got into his eyes.

"Sonofabitch," Koby said. He blinked his stinging, watering eyes and set the tool down.

He walked into the kitchen to rinse his eyes out.

Koby bumped into the corner of his counter top, jamming the corner into his hip bone. He grunted in pain and stumbled over to the sink. With practiced hands, he turned on cold water. He let it run until it was frigid and then he leaned into the sink and splashed his face with the cool water.

Koby sighed in relief as the water cleared his vision and eased the stinging sensation. He stood up and toweled off his face with the dishtowel. It wasn't much better once he stopped using the water so he turned it back on and rinsed out his eyes again.

While Koby was rinsing his eyes, Anna's voice called out to him. "Are you there?"

He flinched and bumped his forehead on the sink faucet. Cursing his bad luck, he reached for the towel to wipe his face off again. He hadn't expected anyone to come over. "I'm in the kitchen," he said. "I'll be right there."

My luck's turned around, he thought. Now that he had a nurse in his house, Anna could check his eyes.

Through squinted eyes, he grabbed a tray, two glasses, and a pitcher of lemonade from the refrigerator, careful not to drop them or bump into anything else.

"Are you okay?" Anna said.

"Just some smoke in my eyes from soldering. Burns like hell," Koby said. "Great timing though, I could use a break. I hope you're thirsty. I mixed up some lemonade earlier. God, I'd kill for a real lemon, but the powdered stuff will have to make do."

"Is Hunter okay?" Anna sounded concerned.

Koby frowned to himself. He didn't know anyone named Hunter. With his hands full, Koby turned around and pushed open the door to the hall with his back. He turned around and smiled…to no one. The room was empty and the front door was closed.

She must have gone into the living room, Koby thought.

Watching the floor to make sure he didn't trip, he entered the living room.

"Hey sorry, I-" Koby looked up only to find another empty room. Well, empty of visitors, and more specifically Anna. He looked around confused. "Anna?"

"Hunter is fine, baby," a man's voice said from beside Koby.

Koby squeaked and jumped, tripping on an old desktop computer case. The pitcher of lemonade toppled from the tray, hit an old flat screen TV, and smashed against the floor. The cups slid wildly off the tray and broke on the floor.

"He got the mines and made it back thanks to you."

"Thank the Lord," Anna said.

Koby cursed the broken dishes but left them, scrambling up, he rushed over to the workbench. Then he understood, the green light on the good walkie talkie wasn't because it'd synced with its partner. It had picked up on another conversation entirely, one between his friend Anna and a male voice that was completely unfamiliar to him.

"Does he know?" the man said.

"No."

"Are you sure?" he said.

"Yes, Brady. As far as I can tell, he doesn't know who he is," Anna said, her voice firm but full of affection for this unknown man.

Koby leaned closer to the radio, enthralled. His heart thumped in his chest.

"Brady?" Koby whispered to himself. Whoever Brady was, he wasn't a resident of Goshen, Koby thought.

"Good and Logan?" the man said.

"No, hun. As far as I can tell, Logan hasn't told him anything. They don't, uh, get along too well." There was a smile in Anna's voice, almost as if she was trying not to laugh. "Collin beat the hell out of him yesterday. I heard that Logan wanted to shoot him but Pastor Pendell stopped him."

Anna sighed into the radio. "No telling how true that is. It's just what's going around the rumor mill."

Hun? Koby thought. This wasn't just an acquaintance. This man was a love interest.

Koby frowned again, his brow furrowed. He heard about the fight that morning directly from Collin, when they met for lunch. He knew that a boy had sneaked up and stolen the two land mines. Whoever this Hunter boy was, he was important to Brady and Anna. And if the boy was stealing weapons from the Eagles then he had to be a Viper, which meant that the man was a Viper too.

"Shit," Koby said. His stomach clenched and he looked around the room nervously. "Shit."

Anna was with them. She was a spy working for the enemy. How could she be? It didn't make sense to Koby.

He thought back to his conversation with Collin at lunch. Koby vaguely remembered that Collin mentioned he was going to the hospital to give more blood to the doctor.

If he was at the med unit, that meant Dr. Horner, Anna's mother, was there too. Did she know about her daughter? Was she with the Vipers as well?

Koby cursed again.

He had to tell Collin. For whatever reason, Koby knew he could trust the man. He had that way about him. Plus he'd been asleep since the beginning, which kept him removed for all the town politics and bullshit they'd gone through. He hadn't been corrupted by the pain of loss and hard choices.

Survival did that to people, Koby thought. Survival was a strangling vine that wrung the humanity from people until they were cold, heartless shells of their former selves.

With a plan in mind, Koby carried the radios with him over to the closet and pulled out a light jacket. He slipped into the jacket, shouldered a small messenger bag where he placed the two radios and left the house.

He had to talk with Collin about what he heard.

Chapter Twenty-One

Kobyashi clenched his fist.

Damn it.

The very person Koby hoped to avoid sat behind the desk in the outpatient clinic. Dr. Julie Horner looked up from a stack of papers and smiled at him.

"Hi, how are you?"

"I'm fine, doctor. Actually, I'm looking for Collin," he said. "He still here?"

"Are you feeling okay? It looks like you bumped your head," Dr. Horner said, standing and pointing.

"Nothing major," Koby said. He self-consciously rubbed the big, red welt that had formed after hitting his head on the sink faucet earlier. "Collin?"

"He's in the back, room four. We took a rather large donation of blood, so he's resting and drinking juice," Dr. Horner said. She looked him up and down with suspicion in her eyes.

Koby didn't want to expose Anna by having the "hey your daughter's a traitor" conversation yet. Especially if Dr. Horner knew her daughter might be in love with a Viper named Brady. There was no telling what she might do to him to protect Anna.

He had seen her mad before, which was scary. He preferred to avoid seeing her direct that aggressive mother bear attitude toward him.

"Thanks, doc." Koby was glad he had the information he needed. *Cue exit*, he thought as he walked toward the door to the back rooms.

Dr. Horner pulled the door open before he could get to it. He flinched a little with wide eyes before he regained his composure. Koby missed seeing her walk away from her desk. Now she was right in front of him looking suspicious as hell.

"Where do you think you're going?" she said, glowering at him.

Koby stuttered for a moment. "Um, room four?"

Dr. Horner continued looking at him.

Koby put his hands on his hips and copied her pose.

"I'm going back to see Collin," he said, after a moment of silent mockery. "It's important."

"This is a hospital, not a cafe for your idle chit chat." Dr. Horner held her serious pose for a moment then lowered her hands from her hips and grinned at Koby. "You should have seen your face. Hilarious."

She laughed at him and stepped aside, waving him in.

Koby let out a breath of relief.

"Good one, doc," he said. He wiped his forehead, wincing at the welt, beyond ready for this encounter to be over. The information he was withholding wanted to burn its way out but he swallowed the words down and politely edged past the doctor.

She laughed again and patted his shoulder as he passed by. "You two behave. Collin's weak right now."

After a few steps, Koby slowed. He looked back at the doctor.

"Yes?" She smiled at him.

"Where are all the nurses?" Koby said. What if Julie had thrown in with the Vipers? Nervous chills ran down his spine. He heard what happened the last time the Vipers were in the hospital.

"Katya is out on a break and Anna is home with a migraine." Dr. Horner closed the door and started back around to her desk. "Did you need help?"

"No, no, I'm fine. Just curious is all. It seems so quiet here," he said before continuing down the hall. When Koby reached room four, he looked up and down the hall. No one was around.

"Migraine, huh?" he muttered to himself. "Likely story."

He knew he wasn't imagining things. Anna was definitely speaking with a Viper and she didn't sound like she was uncomfortable or in pain. He imagined such an excuse was effective cover for secret rendezvous with this Brady guy.

As he pushed open the door, he briefly wondered where they found their radios.

Chapter Twenty-Two

Collin rested on the hospital bed with his head propped up by several pillows, sipping orange juice from a juice box like a little kid.

The door clicked as the handle turned. Collin looked away from the zombie novel he was reading to see his friend Koby enter the room, looking nervous.

"Hey buddy," Collin said with a grin. He was a little surprised to see Koby again since they just had lunch together. "Just couldn't stay away from me, huh? Too bad I like women."

"Bitch please. Don't flatter yourself big guy." Koby dug through his messenger bag. He tossed it to Collin who caught it one-handed.

"Does it work?" Collin looked at him hopefully.

Koby pulled up the rolling chair meant for the doctor and sat down. He looked at Collin with a serious look in his dark brown eyes.

Collin put his juice down and sat up a little straighter.

"I was at home working on these things," Koby said. He pulled another walkie talkie out and held it up. "It required a little soldering work so I was doing that when some smoke got in my eyes."

Collin wasn't sure if Koby was leading into a joke or what, but he wasn't acting quite normal. Collin sat still and waited patiently for him to get to the point.

"I went into the kitchen to wash the smoke out of my eyes because it stung like a bitch," Koby said. He paused and licked his lips, his eyes went to the door and he lowered his voice. "Then Anna started talking to me. At least that's what I thought. But she wasn't, man. She was really talking on that radio to some guy named Brady."

When Collin didn't say anything, Koby continued. "This Brady guy is definitely not from Goshen. It was a brief conversation, mostly about a kid named Hunter."

Collin wasn't sure what to make of Koby's story.

"Are you sure it was Anna," he said.

Koby nodded. "Without a doubt, man. She was asking if Hunter was okay. Apparently he was the kid you described that stole those claymores from us."

"No shit?" Collin straightened up on the bed.

"No shit, man. The thing is, she wasn't just checking in on the kid. The Brady guy called her babe and she called him hun, so they must be romantically involved. I don't know if it's possible, but what if Anna is that kid's mother?" Koby asked, wide-eyed. "She must have been feeding them information, because Brady told her that Hunter only recovered the mines safely because of her."

Collin grunted.

"That explains why they didn't even bother with the case. Why send a kid to get the mines though? Hell, why send anyone at all? They don't use modern weapons." Collin frowned and reached for his juice. He drank until the straw made a slurping noise. He still felt slightly lightheaded from the blood loss, so he fell back against the pillows stacked behind him to contemplate the situation.

Risking a young boy for a couple of mines seemed like a poor trade if it went bad. Did they care that little for Hunter? What was Anna thinking?

What did they plan to do now that they had two claymores? They could do serious damage if used properly.

Frustrated, he gave a little shrug. Anna was working with the Vipers to subvert Goshen. Collin had a hard time wrapping his mind around that one.

"I never would have fingered Anna as a mole," Collin said, scowling.

Koby giggled a little, but Collin ignored it.

After getting control of himself, Koby asked, "How could she have known about the mines? It's not common knowledge that I have them."

"Any number of ways, I suppose. Anna could have seen you and the soldiers, or she watched Alpha team and Raiford head out to the field," Collin said. "Or worse, an Eagle tipped her off, although I doubt that."

"And then she radioed Brady?" Koby sounded skeptical. "What a cluster fuck."

Collin stared at the wall for a moment. Koby had trusted him with this major revelation, so Collin decided to share a secret in return.

"It's weird because just yesterday, Anna and I were talking in the hallway, and she told me not to trust 'them,' whoever that is," Collin said. "I got the distinct feeling she meant Logan and Pendell. She may have included her mother in that because she looked nervous when Julie walked in on us talking."

Koby looked surprised by that.

"I think it'd be best if we kept this stuff to ourselves." Collin knew that instinctively. He watched his friend closely.

Koby nodded without hesitation.

"Seriously, Koby. This is dangerous information for a lot of people."

"I thought that too." Koby laughed nervously, then swallowed hard and nodded. "We need to keep this quiet."

"Good."

"It was so uncomfortable running into Julie out there." Koby jerked his thumb in the direction of the receptionist's desk.

Collin nodded absently; he was busy thinking about what their next move should be.

"And uh, they also said some stuff about you," Koby said.

"Me?" Collin looked up, curious.

"The guy on the radio asked Anna if you knew who you were. She told him that you didn't know anything. Weird, huh? Because why would anyone other than you be concerned about that, right?" Koby shrugged and lounged in his chair. "What could they possibly know about you?"

Collin frowned again at this unexpected twist.

"Do you remember anything about your past?" Koby asked.

Collin met his friend's gaze and slowly shook his head. "Not much. But the kid that stole the claymores, Hunter, looked exactly like a kid in my dreams. Just like my son."

Koby's eyebrows shot up.

"We have to talk with Anna," Collin said. He slid his legs over the side of the bed and tried to stand up. His head seemed to float off his shoulders, unleashing a wave of nausea. His stomach clenched hard. "Oh man, it'll be a while before I can walk out of here."

Collin slumped back onto the bed and put a hand on his forehead. It was damp with fresh sweat.

"Can you hand me another juice box, please," he said and pointed at the cupboard.

"They stock this place with drinks?" Koby said, slowly standing up and stretching.

"Yeah, the doctor knows how weak I get when she, or the nurses, drains me." Collin took a few deep breaths and relaxed. "I told her they're like vampires. It feels like they barely left with me any blood." He smirked. "It's okay though. I just hope the treatment works."

"Jesus! Look at this," Koby said, holding the cupboard door open and pointing at the dozen or so juice boxes. Koby pulled one out and smiled at the little cartoon orange on the front. "Kids all across Goshen will go thirsty if the doc keeps taking all your blood."

Collin chuckled. He pulled the straw off of the box, tearing it out of the cellophane with a practiced move and poked it through the hole in the top of the box.

He took a long drink then asked Koby, "Were you here when Anna was kidnapped and tortured by the Vipers?"

Koby shook his head. "No. That was before I arrived in Goshen." His face twisted in confusion. "How could she love someone that did that to her? Is it a victim syndrome thing?"

"Stockholm syndrome?" Collin grunted. "I doubt it. My theory is that she wasn't kidnapped or tortured."

"Really?"

"I'd bet money that she simply ran away to be with the Vipers and when Logan showed up at their camp she had no choice but to return."

"The Vipers are thugs. How can she be one of them?" Koby said, exasperated.

"Everyone has their reasons. I'm sure she has hers." Collin knew she was a smart woman. If she sided with the Vipers, then there had to be a compelling reason for it. He thought about his first encounter with her. "Why do you think she was in the hospital the night I woke up?"

Koby's head cocked to the side, tossing his black hair across his forehead. "It was her shift?"

"I mean why her? On that specific night? The Vipers were cutting up nurses left and right but when I came across her, she was unhurt and quite ready to help me escape both the Vipers and the Eagles, until we were stopped in the alleyway," Collin said.

"Who knows? I guess it's possible that she let them in the building or helped them somehow," Koby said.

"They must have been after BT76. So, why swing into the room on ropes? If she was helping them that was totally unnecessary." Collin chuckled. "And of all nights to break in they did it when I was awake to kick their ass. Who fucked up?"

"They fucked up," Koby replied.

Collin tried to stand up again. He still wanted to talk to Anna and they needed to do it before anything bad happened. He got to his feet without feeling light headed but his legs felt wobbly. His muscle fibers twitched, making his whole body tremble. He put a hand on the nightstand to steady himself.

"You okay?" Koby said.

"Yeah, just give me a second," Collin said. "Do you know where Anna is?"

"Not here. Dr. Horner said she was at home with a migraine," Koby said.

"A migraine?"

"Yup."

"Convenient cover, I guess," Collin said as he stretched. He felt weak and slow, almost exactly how he felt when he woken up in the hospital all those weeks ago. Thankfully, he would be able to exit the hospital without a fight this time. "And now we know where to find her."

"Only if you hurry up, grandpa." Koby hopped out of his chair and smirked at him.

Collin playfully pushed Koby aside and reached into the cupboard for another juice box. "I'm taking one for the road."

He shoved it in his pocket and slowly followed Koby's lead out of the room.

Dr. Horner wasn't at the reception desk and no one else was around. They left the hospital without a problem.

The air outside was crisp and smelled like sunshine and flowers. Collin couldn't help smiling.

"Have you been to their house before?" Collin asked.

"Man, I've been in everyone's house. If it's not one thing, it's another. Gardening systems, electrical systems, et cetera."

"No one else can do that stuff?"

"Sure, we have a few guys, but they're assigned to other work duties so they don't have much time. I've become the go-to guy for a lot of the odd jobs," Koby said. "I started out working on the hydro dam by myself, which was insane. Then Pastor Pendell reassigned a couple of guys that worked there before the fever to help me keep it running. Easy work for them and it freed me up to take care of other stuff."

Collin nodded while he prepped his juice box. If orange juice was addictive, he was on the brink of acquiring of a serious habit.

"Do you know what you're going to say to Anna?" Koby asked.

Collin shrugged. "We'll have to play it by ear. Let's try our best to not make her defensive, there's no telling what she might do if she feels cornered."

Julie and Anna lived in a large white house, surrounded by a ranch-style fence, with a massive oak tree towering over the front yard. Without even seeing the inside, Collin guessed it was at least double the size of his house. He wasn't interested in competing, he was just shocked only two people lived in such a big space. It must feel so lonely in there.

When they reached the porch, Koby motioned for Collin to do the honors.

"Don't be scared," Collin said with a smirk.

He stepped up and knocked on the door. To their surprise, the door slowly swung open.

Collin put a hand out as Koby leaned forward to peer in, so he would stay back. Then Collin stepped closer and looked inside for any immediate threats. He leaned forward and turned his head, listening carefully for any sounds. After a few seconds of silence, he felt comfortable enough to step inside the house.

He couldn't sense anyone.

Koby crept silently behind Collin.

Under different circumstances, Collin could have appreciated the beauty of the house. Large, elegant paintings adorned the walls and a wide staircase curved up to the second level, with a chandelier hanging down into the foyer.

The hall opened to the living room, which looked ransacked. Slashed couch cushions had their stuff flung everywhere. A vase of flowers was scattered on the floor. Near the coffee table, in front of the couch, was a pool of blood and streaks leading deeper into the house.

Robbery or murder? Or both? It was a mixed scene.

There wasn't much of value in the house, that wasn't provided for by the community so theft seemed unlikely. Stealing a TV or jewelry was pointless. Therefore, Collin decided it must have been a fight.

Collin glanced at Koby and saw the same type of questions running through his friend's mind that had popped into his.

Did someone else know about her connection to the Vipers? Had Anna attacked someone? Or had she been attacked? Were there other Vipers in town?

"Anna?" Collin said loud enough to carry beyond the living room. No response. "Anna, it's Collin. Are you okay?"

Still no response. No creaking floorboards, no footsteps, nothing. Other than Koby behind him, the house was completely silent.

Collin motioned for Koby to follow.

The blood trail led back toward the kitchen. Instead of following the trail into a possible trap, Collin led Koby back into the hallway and around the other way. Collin knew there had to be more than one way to enter the kitchen. There always was.

He was right.

Other than the blood on the floor, which continued toward the back door, the kitchen looked to be in order. Collin checked the hallway and stepped back into the room. The kitchen itself was large and clean looking with matching appliances, a bare table, and no dirty dishes. Nothing looked out of place on the counters.

"Hey," Koby said, snapping his finger at Collin. When he looked over, Koby pointed at the wall.

Collin turned to see a message written on a chalkboard on a small section of the wall next to the refrigerator. A wonderful place to leave a message for the family.

On the chalkboard was a note that said, "Anna and the BT76 belong to the Vipers now." Definitely not the type of message Collin had in mind.

He looked at Koby with his eyebrow cocked. "Thoughts?"

"Definitely not a woman's handwriting."

Collin smiled. "They want us to think she was taken against her will."

"And you think otherwise?"

"How close did you look at the living room?"

"I saw the blood," Koby said.

"We saw blood streaks. But where was the pool of blood from the victim? There wasn't one," Collin said as he looked around the room for more clues.

"Oh, right." Koby looked around. "I don't know. This looks pretty legit."

"You just finished telling me how she was talking to a Viper about a Viper boy. Why would they actually attack her?"

"Who knows what she was actually doing? Think about what they did at the Eagle's Bar - how many people they killed. If they felt she was a liability, they could have killed her."

"Fair point. For all we know, Ann may have helped with the Eagle's Bar attack. It could have been an inside job, especially if she helped," Collin said. He felt confident the blood was staged. Collin chalked it up to Koby struggling to accept that his longtime friend was a double agent of sorts. "She wasn't kidnapped before, and she wasn't taken this time either."

"You're so quick to judge her," Koby said, his face reddened and he scowled at Collin. "I think something else is going on. She was tricked or double-crossed by the Vipers. You know you can't trust a snake in the grass."

"It's possible, but not probable."

They heard a voice. Anna's voice.

Collin looked at Koby, who looked down at his bag. The radio.

Pulling the radio out of the bag, Koby set it on the table in the breakfast nook and the two men sat, staring at the radio.

"I say again: I am at the meeting point. I have the BT76. Send your Vipers for me. I love you," Anna's voice said over the radio.

Koby groaned and slammed his fist on the table. "I'm sorry, man."

"Shhh. Wait."

A few seconds passed without a response.

Collin looked at the radio to see if the thing crapped out. The light was on, so it was still working. Then Collin heard breathing, followed by the voice of the Viper.

"I love you too, babe."

Chapter Twenty-Three

"Oh, God! Not the BT76!" Koby snarled. A vein bulged out on his temple and Collin could see the carotid artery pulsing in his neck.

"C'mon, we have to go check for ourselves." Collin stood up, taking the radio with him as he did.

The air stunk of blood and he was ready to leave Dr. Horner's house. Anna was gone. Apparently so was the last of the medicine that Goshen needed to survive.

Collin strode through the house with Koby, hot on his heels. His short friend was fired up. He'd just argued that maybe his long-time friend was a victim only to have that theory explode in his face.

Now, they had to go back to the hospital and see if any BT76 was left. As Collin walked down the front steps, the front door slammed shut.

Not ideal, Collin thought.

He looked up and down the street and quickly scanned the windows he could see. It didn't look like anyone noticed. In a small town, you can never be too safe. Collin didn't want someone else to get curious about what they were up to, find the blood, and then report seeing him and Koby exit the house.

"Who has access to the meds?" Collin said.

"Dr. Horner of course, Pastor Pendell, and apparently the nurses," Koby said. "Or at least Anna. She's the doctor's daughter, after all."

Walking between the house and the hospital took half the time it had earlier. Suddenly the building loomed before them.

Collin reached for Koby to slow him down. "Hey, wait."

Koby stopped and turned.

"We need to keep the radios and everything we heard to ourselves."

Koby looked surprised. "We have to let Julie know her daughter's safe. I mean, I understand not talking about the rest. I have no problem with that. How can we let Julie think Anna's been stabbed and kidnapped?"

"How could we possibly come to the conclusion that she's safe if we don't talk about everything we heard? Don't worry, we'll tell her in due time," Collin said, reassuring his friend. "But right now, we need to keep that knowledge to ourselves. We don't know who, if anyone, is also a mole. We can't tip our hand to the Vipers or the rest of the council. There's a reason Anna told me not to trust them."

Koby's surprise turned into something resembling a grimace, like he was forced to eat a whole bag of lemons. Pain was evident in Koby's eyes, along with his internal struggle about Anna. They kept walking toward the hospital but Collin slowed the pace. Before Collin could say anything else he saw Koby's posture shift, then he nodded.

"Okay, fine. For now, we keep the details to ourselves; the radio, the conversation, and the fake blood. As soon as we can, we have to tell Julie that Anna is okay. She's going to be terrified until then and I don't think I could live with not telling her. Worrying about her daughter, won't bode well for her research either," Koby said. "And that's super important right now, especially if Anna really did take the BT76."

"If she doesn't already know about it. We don't know where Julie stands in all this," Collin said. Koby glared at him. He realized that if the Doc was also involved, Koby might just die from a broken heart. He held his hands up in defense. It was strange seeing his friend get angry. Koby was generally the funny guy, taking things in stride. "All I'm saying is that we don't know. But I agree, we should tell the doctor as soon as we can."

"I'm glad we agree," Koby said. "Now, how do we explain being at the doctors house?"

"Dr. Horner told you Anna was home with a migraine right? So maybe you just wanted to check on her to make sure she was okay. I came along for the fresh air and exercise and we stumbled upon the smashed open door, which is true," Collin said.

"To a point."

"Close enough that it's probable." Collin sped back up as they covered the last hundred meters to the hospital.

They raced up the steps and rushed inside. They went directly to the outpatient clinic, where both of them had last seen Dr. Horner. To their relief, she sat behind the receptionist's desk, sorting through paperwork. She looked calm as she worked.

Collin and Koby stepped up to the window and both started speaking. After a second of chaos where Dr. Horner stared at them in confusion, they both quieted down. Koby motioned for Collin to speak.

"Doc, can we please see the BT76 supply?" he asked, as he caught his breath. He was breathing harder than normal from rushing to the hospital. "We need to see that it's all there."

"What?" Dr. Horner said, narrowing her eyes at him. "Of course it's all there."

"Please, Julie. We need to see it. Just for a second," Koby said. His voice was urgent.

She seemed to relent a little, mentally. "Okay but you guys are acting weird. And you sir…" She jabbed her finger in the air at Collin. "…did not have permission to get up and leave. You need to rest and it's best if you do it here."

Collin nodded. "Sorry, Doc. Seriously, can you show us the medicine?"

"Why?"

"We heard that it may have been stolen," Collin said in a rush. "Hurry, there's no time to explain."

Dr. Horner's brow furrowed as she stood. She walked away and a moment later appeared in the doorway. Dr. Horner led them out into the main hallway.

"You don't keep it in there?" Collin said, glancing over his shoulder at the outpatient clinic.

"No, it's not safe enough," Julie said. Her white doctor's coat flapped around her legs as she walked.

She led them through a door, into the stairwell. Koby seemed to know where she was heading. Collin was confused about where they were heading. He had only been in the stairwell after he'd awoken from the fever. That night, it was Anna who tried to lead him out of the hospital.

"Where are we going then?" Collin asked.

"You'll see in a moment," she said. "Have some patience."

Collin shot Koby a look. His friend shook his head.

Dr. Julie Horner stopped at the bottom of the stairs and unlocked a door that was marked "Basement — Authorized Personnel Only." It was dark inside. She flipped a switch and the overhead lights buzzed with energy and flickered on. The hallway wasn't long, but it was wide like a typical hospital hallway, with enough room to move gurneys around.

"The morgue?" Collin said. Strange place to keep medicine, he thought.

Dr. Horner turned and smiled at him.

"Ugh, that's sick," Koby said, scrunching up his face.

"I figured it would prove to be a deterrent in itself," Dr. Horner said, smirking. She turned down an intersecting hallway and then stopped at the first door on the left. She fumbled for a moment searching for the correct key in the giant cluster in her hand. It made her hands look tiny.

"Here we go," she muttered to herself. She slid the key in, unlocked the door, and led them inside.

At least two locks between the thief, or thieves, and the BT76, Collin thought. This was quite the secret little raid. One he didn't believe Anna did on her own.

Once inside the morgue, Dr. Horner led them toward a medium sized office that, once upon a time, must have been for the mortician. The air still smelled faintly of formaldehyde and other chemicals. Koby held a hand over his mouth.

Nowadays, the mortician's office just held a simple looking desk and tall brown, metal cabinets for paperwork. The office featured large windows on three sides, which had opened blinds, and gave whoever sat at the desk a complete 360-degree view of the morgue.

Dr. Horner sat behind the desk and spun in the chair. She pulled open one of the cabinet doors and fiddled with something. Collin could hear it, even if he couldn't see over her shoulder very well.

A safe? he wondered.

There was a soft click. The doctor pulled open a squeaky door as she slid her chair back.

Dr. Horner gasped. Then she shrieked.

"Wha- What's going on?" she said, spinning in the chair to look at Collin and Koby. Her eyes narrowed and her face glowed red. "The medicine is gone."

The two men stared at the opened cabinet. It had to be six feet tall, three feet wide and just as deep. A lot of space for a lot of medicine.

What they heard on the radio was true though. Every box of BT76 was gone.

Koby leaned on the desk and whispered to himself, "No, no, no, no…"

The knot that had been growing in Collin's stomach dropped into a black hole. He felt nauseated, just for a moment, as if he had just given another round of blood. She'd done it. The radio call hadn't been a bluff. Anna had indeed stolen the BT76 from Goshen.

"Is anything left?" Collin breathed.

Dr. Horner turned around and opened the door wider and slid away. "Look for yourself," she said.

Koby stepped around the desk to look at the lower shelves. He turned to Collin and shook his head.

"What's the meaning of all this? Why did you want to see it?" Dr. Horner was standing with her hands on her hips.

"We need to convene the Council, doctor," Collin said ominously. He turned and walked out of the office.

Koby rushed out after him, leaving the doctor confused.

They were able to exit the doors that were locked from the other side. Collin didn't wait for the doctor, he didn't want to have to brush off her questions. It would be better to say everything in front of the full Council.

Collin and Koby were almost in the street before Dr. Horner came running up behind them, breathing hard.

"We'll explain everything when the council is formed up," Collin told her.

Dr. Horner looked hard at him then shot a look at Koby. He blushed and turned away, conspicuously avoiding her gaze.

His discomfort made Collin want to laugh. He fought valiantly to keep from smiling. A blushing Koby was a rare sight; Collin would put money on that.

All three of them strode across town. A sense of urgency radiated from them, repelling residents passing by who gave them a wide berth and didn't bother to interrupt them.

Seemingly moments later, they arrived at the large white church at the other end of town. When they entered Pastor Pendell's office after a quick knock, they found Major Logan already seated inside.

Collin had the same feeling as when HAGS had announced the medical shipment reduction and learned that dozens of people would die. He hoped with every cell in his body that it wouldn't come to that again.

"Excuse me, pastor," Collin said, nodding at the major because he needed to hear it too.

"By all means, barge into my office," Pastor Pendell said, with barely contained indignation. He closed his eyes for a half-second and then gestured at the chairs. Major Logan took his customary place to the side of the desk.

"We have critical information to tell you," Collin shot back.

"All of the BT76 is gone," blurted Dr. Horner.

Pastor Pendell gaped at her.

"Excuse me?" Major Logan said.

"All of the BT76 has been stolen," Collin said. "Anna is also gone."

He turned to look at Dr. Horner. It was now her turn to gape at him in shock. The doctor's cheeks turned bright red. She sputtered but couldn't get out any words.

"Koby and I went outside after my blood draw," Collin said. "We decided to go check on how Anna was doing. You know, see if there was anything we could get for her since she was feeling ill."

Everyone stared at Collin. He looked at each person, meeting their eyes, and saw mixed emotions.

"When we got to the doctor's house, the front door was already open." He gestured briefly at the doctor. "Inside there was…"

Collin's voice trailed off. He looked at the doctor again, with the most convincing apology face he could muster.

"Inside there was blood in the living room and a trail through the kitchen to the back door," he said.

"It's true," Koby said. "I'm so sorry, Julie."

"There was a message too. On the chalk board by the fridge, it said 'Anna and the BT76 belong to the Vipers now,'" Collin said. The looks on everyone's face sent a chill down his spine.

Dr. Horner raised a hand to her mouth. She looked like she wanted to vomit, and there was no mistaking the terror in her eyes. She looked up at Collin and then her eyes flicked away. "Not again," she whispered.

"Those bastards," Major Logan said through clenched teeth. He leaned forward on the desk and gripped the edge so hard his knuckles turned white.

Collin was worried about the BT76, but not about Anna's safety. He didn't believe she was hurt. The strength of Julie's emotions struck him like a palm strike to the solar plexus.

"We need that BT76," Pastor Pendell said. He raised his gnarled hands in front of his face, made a steeple out of his fingers, and tapped them against his pursed lips. "Goshen can't survive without it."

"Even though the town is blessed?" Collin asked. He hadn't meant it to sound so sarcastic. It was one of Pastor Pendell's favorite sayings and he'd heard it many times since waking up.

Pastor Pendell narrowed his eyes at him, but didn't respond.

"Major, you know what you have to do."

"Yes, sir. Get the BT76 and save the girl," Major Logan said.

Doctor Horner looked at him, appalled by his prioritizing of the tasks. "Excuse me. Anna's my daughter, Major."

"You think I don't know that, doctor? I've known Anna for years. This is bigger than our friendship, it's bigger than the life of your daughter. It's one life versus a whole town," Major Logan said with a sneer, waving his hand to indicate all of Goshen. "Our supply of BT76 affects the most lives. We'll save her, if she's still alive, but the medicine must be the priority."

He didn't need to be so harsh, Collin thought. Surely Julie understood that in the back of her mind. Under the circumstances, a mother's instinct is going to trump logic every time.

Dr. Horner looked at the pastor. He stared at his desk, not speaking. He stayed quiet for a long moment.

"Pastor?" Dr. Horner said.

He met her pleading eyes. Pastor Pendell lowered his hands with a heavy sigh and looked at Major Logan.

"Major, you will accomplish both missions — secure the medicine and rescue Anna," he said. "Whatever it takes."

"Yes, sir. Our Eagles can do it. If we hit any snags though, the BT76 comes first," Major Logan said, rock solid.

"Since we're on the topic of running a raid on the Vipers. I'd like to volunteer to lead a team specifically to go after Anna," Collin said. "Leaving Major Logan free to secure the BT76."

Dr. Horner looked at him with such affection; he thought she might kiss him. Thankfully, she opted for patting his arm.

Pastor Pendell shook his head though. "We need you here in town. Major Logan will deal with the Vipers. He's good at that. I'd like you to stay and lead our defenses in case they attack us again. Make no mistake, this was an attack on Goshen. They will pay for harming Anna."

Collin started to protest. "Pastor, I really think-"

"I agree with Pastor Pendell. You are the only one qualified to secure the town while I lead the team against the Vipers. It's beyond time we take the fight to them," Major Logan said.

Before Collin could protest further, Dr. Horner interjected.

"Collin, I appreciate your bravery, truly I do. We need you here though," she said. "I know we just took a blood draw but we'll need to do another one in the morning. Your blood is more important than the BT76 in my opinion. It's essential that you remain safe, and in good health."

"Very well. It's settled then," Pastor Pendell said. He stood up to address them and end the meeting. "Major Logan will lead the attack on the Vipers, and Collin will be in charge of defense. Koby, you will be Collin's second-in-command since he will be out of commission for a period of time to assist the doctor."

Koby looked like he'd been bitch slapped.

"You all know how to proceed, so I'll leave you to your work. May the Lord be with you."

Major Logan and Collin, followed by Koby, exited the church a few minutes later. Dr. Horner stayed behind in the church to pray for her daughter. Collin agreed to meet her first thing in the morning so she could take however much blood that she needed.

Koby nudged him with his elbow.

"I've never done this kind of thing before. I don't know jack squat about military stuff," Koby said. He was breathing noticeably louder than usual. Their pace was quick. Koby was also quite short, so his legs had to work twice as hard as Collin's did. "Other than technical stuff about some of their equipment."

"Don't worry buddy, I'll talk you through it. You're a sharp guy and we all trust your judgment," Collin said.

The high school came into view at the end of the block.

Collin smirked. Goshen High School barely looked like a place of education anymore. Since the Eagle's Nest explosion, the Eagles had been operating out of the high school.

In subtle and not so subtle ways, the look of the building had transformed. Sandbags piled into defensive fighting positions, with soldiers standing guard, flanked the entrance. They removed the shrubs and trees closest to the school and windows were either covered with wood planks or filled in with sandbags.

Collin had already toured the newly reused space. Seeing it again was impressive though. If he had been asked to imagine what a town would look like after the collapse of civil society, Goshen High School was currently what he'd have come up with.

The school functioned perfectly as a headquarters for the Eagles. Perhaps better than the old location. Although it lacked a bar, it had men's and women's locker rooms and the gym was the perfect area for formations and training. All of the salvaged equipment was stored inside one of the classrooms with guards posted. Across the hall from the equipment room was Major Logan's new planning room.

The Eagles had made even more improvements since the last time he saw it. There were maps and drawings of the area surrounding Goshen hanging on the walls. Several old students' desks held a military-style sandbox for plotting out offensive or defensive operations.

Major Logan yelled for the Combat Action Wing to form up as they entered the room. A runner passed by them on her way to pass along the message to the Eagle's on patrol, that a CAW meeting was taking place.

The Combat Action Wing was Goshen's special operations unit and had a membership of twenty Eagles that were handpicked and trained by Major Logan and Collin, following the last Viper attack. Collin knew they were still green but they were better trained than the rest. If they kept their cool and worked together, the CAW could put a serious hurt on the undisciplined and under-equipped Vipers.

Major Logan and Collin discussed the strategy in the planning room. Neither of them noticed how bored Koby looked until they called him over to show them where he'd seen the second crate drop.

They laid out a map on an empty table. Koby used a protractor to gauge the distance and a pencil to mark out the area where he witnessed the crate drop.

Surprisingly, the drop wasn't as close to the suspected Viper camp as they originally thought.

"How sure are we about the camp's location?" Collin asked.

"Better than eighty-five percent," Major Logan said.

Koby nodded. "HAGS wouldn't have dropped it off target. The Vipers are nearby for sure."

"How far away is that?" Major Logan asked.

Koby looked closely at the map and measured out the distance. "Looks like it's close to seven miles."

"I know that meadow," Major Logan said quietly. He pursed his lips and stared hard at the map.

"Will the Vipers even know the second drop was made?" Collin said. "You said their camp site was way over there." He gestured to a spot on the map that would be miles away.

"That was years ago," Major Logan said. "I doubt they stayed in the same place. There's no telling what direction they moved, but I am willing to work off Koby's assumption that HAGS has a decent idea of where they are. If they dropped the medicine there, then I'm sure there's a good reason."

Collin nodded in agreement. "How long will it take for the team to get there and secure the crate?"

"There aren't any worn trails or roads heading that way. Just rough, untended forest with the constant threat of attack the whole way," Major Logan said. "I'd say it'll take at least four to six hours, probably closer to six hours."

Koby whistled. "That's a long day's work."

An Eagle walked into the office to inform Major Logan that every member of the Combat Action Wing had assembled.

"Thank you. I'll be right out," Major Logan said. He sighed then looked at Koby. "Don't worry. Our team can handle it."

Major Logan slid the pencil and protractor off of the map. He rolled it up carefully and then slid it into a plastic tube. He tucked the tube under his arm and walked out to meet the Eagles in the gymnasium. Collin and Koby stood in the doorway to listen.

"The place they have to go is dangerous," Koby said in a low voice. "It's a large, open meadow with a river on one side and mountains on the other sides. We call it Devil's Meadow."

"Ominous sounding," Collin said. He watched the Eagles.

"The mountainsides are more like cliffs, similar to the ones along our dam. Some of the cliffs in Devil's Meadow have cave systems. It'd be just the kind of place snakes would love to hide," Koby said. "Back in the day, the town had adventurous spelunkers go missing there every year. An occasional survivor was recovered. Most of them died. Sometimes they couldn't even find the bodies."

Collin looked at Koby, surprised.

"There are hot springs up there, too. So it used to draw all kinds of people," Koby said. He watched the Eagles standing around chatting and sighed. "I hope they make it back okay."

Caves were no place for a soldier, Collin thought. There should be no reason for the Eagles to enter the caves though. If the Vipers were there, they could just collapse the entrances.

The major walked among the soldiers, a mix of men and women, young and old. Most of them were experienced Eagles, a few were survivors of the explosion. All of them were motivated, in great shape, and well-trained. This would be their first offensive action against the Vipers. Strain was evident on their faces, but they looked eager as well. Collin understood the feeling. He had a vague sense that he'd been in the same situation many times during his service, even though he couldn't recall specific missions.

Major Logan approached the formation and looked them over for a long moment.

"Eagles, we are about to embark upon your first offensive action. None of you has been on a raid before. Fear not. We have trained you up to a proficient level, in a short period of time," Major Logan said, pacing back and forth in front of them. "This time, we will have the element of surprise on our side and we will take full advantage of it. Eagles hunt Vipers."

The group cheered.

Major Logan walked to the front of the formation and faced the soldiers. He stood tall and called out, "Attention."

Everyone snapped to attention. Then he said, "Group, fall out."

The soldiers dispersed and went to their respective locker rooms to gear up.

Collin followed some of the soldiers. He trained each and every Eagle in the CAW.

"Hey boss," one man said. Collin nodded at him.

"You going with us?" asked a young man.

"Unfortunately not. I got stuck babysitting the town," Collin said.

A hand landed on his shoulder and gave it a quick squeeze. Collin fought the urge to grab the hand and crush it, before throwing the wielder into the lockers. Collin turned to see who the hand belonged to. He was surprised to find it was an older guy named Joe.

"There's no shame in protecting our families," Joe said.

"Thanks," Collin said.

"Koby, what are you doing here?" Joe asked him.

"Pastor made me Collin's number two." Koby scoffed. "You believe that shit?"

"Hey, it could be worse," Joe said with a hearty laugh. "Don't worry, man. If you're learning from Collin, you'll be good to go."

Koby didn't look reassured, which made Collin smile.

Several soldiers were sitting on wood benches loading magazines. The air smelled of gun oil and ammunition.

As each round clicked into the magazines, Collin started to recall another memory.

He was standing on a rifle range next to his battle buddy, a fellow trainee, while the two of them were being chewed out by the drill instructor for some minor infraction. Collin knew he did well on the range, but his battle buddy was going up for the third and final time to try to qualify on his weapon. If he failed, he'd be discharged. Of course, Collin remembered the drill instructor using different words to describe what would happen.

An Eagle bumped Collin. "Excuse me, sir," the soldier said with a nod.

Collin was pulled out of the memory, and realized he was standing in the way, as the Eagles prepared for their mission. Eagles were checking their rifles, sorting through their rucksacks, putting on their field gear, lacing up their boots, and painting their faces with camouflage.

"No worries soldier. I'm the one in the way here," Collin said. He caught Koby's attention and motioned for him to follow, then turned and walked out of the room.

Collin made his way back toward the planning room. He wanted to look over some of the maps he'd seen hanging on the walls. One in particular caught his attention. It showed Goshen and the surrounding area. He needed to know the lay of the land because he had his own operation to plan. With the remaining Eagles, he would have to defend the town against any potential attacks.

He removed the small plastic thumbtacks holding up the map and carried it over to a table. Collin laid it out flat and examined the area, starting in the center of town and working his way out in a spiral pattern.

Footsteps in the hallway vaguely registered as he studied the contour lines and land features.

"There you are," Koby said leaning against the door frame and letting out a heavy sigh. "I was looking all over for you. You just took off, man."

Collin grunted but didn't look up from the map.

"What's up?" Koby said.

"Nothing." Collin could feel Koby staring at him, but he found something curious. He traced his finger over a road he was told was overgrown and essentially ceased to exist. Likely the same road he spotted from the top of the dam.

"You were distracted in there."

Collin sighed and turned to face his friend. "Yeah, I was. The sounds and smells triggered a memory."

"That's good, right?" Koby looked hopeful.

"It was fine. At some point I must have served in the military, probably the Marine Corps." Collin shrugged.

Koby grunted. "That explains your moves at the hospital that night. From what I heard, you did quite a number on those Vipers." Koby lowered his voice and grinned. "Not to mention the ass-whooping you served up to Logan."

Collin smiled to himself and returned to the map.

"Come look at this," he said waving his friend over. "If you had to infiltrate Goshen, how would you do it?"

"I wouldn't. Not if I only had a bow."

"I'm being serious. It's up to us to defend the town while Logan and the CAW are on their mission," Collin said. "That puts us at a major disadvantage as far as personnel. If the Vipers are observing the town, which I assume they do full-time now, especially since Anna is out there with them. They'll see the CAW leave and know that we're down twenty Eagles and Major Logan."

Koby walked over and stood next to Collin. He folded his arms over his chest and leaned toward the map.

The noise outside the office picked up. Collin glanced back but couldn't see anything. He walked over to the door and looked down the hallway. He saw about half of the Eagles had finished prepping their gear. Almost everything was laid it out in formation.

Collin was just about to turn away when the gym door creaked open and Pastor Pendell entered the gym.

"Pendell is here," Collin said, looking over at Koby.

One of the Eagles saw the pastor and ran off.

Probably to fetch Major Logan, Collin thought.

The hum of conversation quickly subsided and everyone turned to face Pastor Pendell.

Pastor Pendell saw Collin and Koby and raised his hand in a brief wave. Collin waved back but didn't walk out to meet him. Out of the corner of his eye, he saw Major Logan striding out to the middle of the gym where Pastor Pendell stood with soldiers around him on one knee.

Within a minute, all twenty of the Combat Action Wing soldiers knelt around Pastor Pendell in a semi-circle.

He raised his hands out, as if he was channeling the power of the Lord into the room, and asked them all to bow their heads in prayer.

Beside Collin, Koby clasped his hands at his waist and bowed his head. Collin simply watched as the holy man commanded the attention of everyone in the room.

"Our brave Eagles, our protectors, and our family. May you find the honor in your mission for it is undertaken for a just cause. May your leaders have clear vision to meet victory head on. May you have the bravery to carry out the mission to the best of your ability. May you find the courage to face your enemy and defeat them. Crush your foes with no mercy in your mind, but with love in your heart, for only the Lord has the wisdom to sort the wheat from the chaff," Pastor Pendell said. His deep voice was rich and resonated well in the gym. "Go forth with pure hearts, strong minds, and the blessing of the Lord upon you. May you be triumphant. May you earn us a lasting peace, for without the enemy, we may worship and live in peace. Should you be injured, may your wounds fully heal. Should you perish in the struggle, may God embrace you and find a place for you in His kingdom. Amen."

As one, the Eagles said, "Amen."

Then they stood up and looked to their leaders for direction.

Major Logan rose from kneeling and said, "SSGT Raiford, form them up at the bridge and we'll move out from there. I'll be a few minutes."

The Eagles began picking up their gear and filing out of the gym. Major Logan walked toward Collin.

"Do you need anything before we head out?" Major Logan said.

Collin shook his head. "We're golden, Major. Good luck downrange. Keep your head on a swivel."

"Copy that. You too." Major Logan nodded at Collin and Koby.

Pastor Pendell walked up and tapped the major on the shoulder. "Can I have a word?"

"Of course."

The two men turned and walked away. Collin overheard Pastor Pendell say, "Remember, you have two goals — get the BT76 and kill Vipers. All of them. I'm sick of them harassing us."

Major Logan glanced over his shoulder at Collin. He nodded at the pastor and said something, but at that point, they were too far for Collin to hear anything else.

Chapter Twenty-Four

Major Logan watched as his soldiers began to filter water to top off their water supply from a stream coming down off the side of the mountain.

New leaves adorning the aspen trees along the banks of the stream rustled in a light breeze. The air smelled of fresh wild grass and damp earth.

"Get your fill," Major Logan said. "This may be the only time we can stop for water."

They left Goshen with one water filter for every two Eagles. Major Logan had his own. More than half of them consisted of a variety of pump water filters, so one Eagle would pump while the other would fill their canteens or hydration pack, depending on what they had. The others had squeeze-style water filters, which took a bit longer. What they lacked in speed, they made up in simplicity and durability. The water itself was cool, clear, and refreshing.

While the Eagles refilled, he laid out his map and used his compass to double check their location. He compared the terrain on his topographic map to what he saw around him and was satisfied. He knew where they were. The Eagles were making great progress.

Logan knew that many of the Eagles had never left the safety of Goshen's fields since the fever outbreak. Some of the younger members of the CAW had never left Goshen at all. This was their first foray out into the wider world.

Earlier on their trek, he'd seen the wonder light up their faces when they'd crested a ridge and could look back on Goshen from a distance. That's when the vast scale of the valley and their relatively small place in it, hit them.

Major Logan had a hard time imagining what it must feel like to leave the only safe and familiar place known to you. He'd been out in the forest before. Many times, in fact.

Where he knelt along the stream's bank, leaning on a large rock, deep in the valley south of Goshen, the forest looked so peaceful and normal that it was hard to tell that any problems existed.

They had a couple more miles until they reached the Devil's Meadow, a place that Major Logan knew would put them at a tactical disadvantage. According to Koby it was approximately where the crate had dropped, so it was where they had to go.

SSGT Raiford approached Major Logan and said, "Everyone's good to go, sir."

"Good. Form 'em up."

"Yes, sir." SSGT Raiford walked far enough away that there would be room for the formation and called for everyone to fall in.

Major Logan stood up, folded his map and held it in the same hand as the compass. He walked to the front of the formation. "We are close to our target. Just a couple of miles separate us from our BT76 shipment."

A few eyebrows twitched, eyes blinked, but no one said anything. Their discipline was good for now, but Major Logan wondered how they would hold up under fire.

Who will survive? He wondered.

"Keep your eyes and ears open. The Vipers are sure to know about the case, if they don't have it already. This means we can expect an ambush at some point. We can only deny them the privilege of an ambush by staying away of our surroundings. So be mindful," Major Logan said. "I am confident we will recover the crate. Don't kid yourself though. We will not recover it without a fight. You get me?"

"We get you, sir," they chanted.

"We are Eagles and we hunt Vipers. Remember that," Major Logan said. He looked at Raiford and said, "Sergeant, they're all yours."

Major Logan returned SSGT Raiford's salute, did an about face, and walked away from the formation.

Refilled and rested, the Eagles continued their journey through the mountain valley toward the Devil's Meadow. A short distance from the stream the ground began to slope down. In the valley, to their left, was a river glistening like a trail of precious gems in the morning sunlight. The river stretched into the distance until it had wound its way out of view behind the mountains.

Major Logan noticed the ground was soft and uneven so he glanced over his shoulder at the Eagle behind him, a woman named Maryann, and said, "Watch your step. Pass it along."

Maryann turned to the soldier behind her and passed along the major's message. Before long, everyone would know to be careful. The last thing they needed to deal with was a sprained ankle or broken leg if someone fell.

Behind Logan to his left, SSGT Raiford breathed out a sigh of contentment. "At least now I can say I've seen more than one river in my lifetime."

Shocked, Major Logan turned to look at Raiford. "Seriously?"

Raiford smiled wide, showing off his bright white teeth, and nodded. "Yes, sir."

"Sorry to burst your bubble then, sergeant," Major Logan said with a smirk. "That is the same river that runs through Goshen."

"Are you sure, sir?" SSGT Raiford said.

Major Logan shot him a look.

"Sorry, sir. This river just looks so much different than ours."

"Ours looks darker because of the silt churned up by the dam's waterfall," Major Logan said.

SSGT Raiford grunted. "That's too bad."

Trees grew thicker as they descended the mountainside along the edge of a deep draw. A tiny creek trickled down from the stream above to the river below. Major Logan began to weave the formation in a series of slow switchbacks. This made the descent easier on their knees and reduced the chance of someone tumbling downhill.

"This slope is going to be a bitch on the way home," Maryann said.

It was true, when they retrieved the medicine and began the journey home, it would prove quite challenging with the heavy crate. Major Logan was fully aware of the challenges. Every obstacle they came to would compound in difficulty and their progress would slow dramatically.

Major Logan raised his hand in a fist to call a silent halt. Everyone stopped walking and waited for the next command.

Turning to the larger than average SSGT Raiford, Major Logan waved him over. He didn't want to shout out commands this close to the enemy.

"Move the CAW into a file formation," Major Logan said quietly when Raiford reached him. They would need the flanking elements for security, since visibility in this part of the forest was even more limited.

"We're headed in the right direction, sir?" SSGT Raiford asked.

Major Logan stepped close, stared hard at Raiford and said, "Yes, I've been here before."

The two men just looked at each other for a couple of awkward seconds before Major Logan chuckled.

SSGT Raiford chuckled nervously, unsure why the major reacted that way.

"File formation, sergeant. Make it happen."

"Yes, sir."

While the Eagles repositioned themselves, Major Logan took a knee and double checked his map.

We're on target, he thought.

Major Logan stood up and looked around. The forest was thicker than he remembered. There was more underbrush and it smelled differently but that could be due to the season. The leaves and pine needles overhead in the trees rustled in a breeze that Major Logan couldn't feel down on the forest floor. He took a big breath in and savored the fresh air. He didn't know how everything would work out, but he was confident that no matter what, he would succeed.

"We good, sergeant?" he asked SSGT Raiford.

"Yes, sir."

"Okay, move out."

Two flanking security teams, made up of four soldiers, peeled off and took up their positions on either side of the formation. The point security team moved out at a steady pace, staying about ten meters ahead of the remainder of the platoon. Every one of the Eagles lined up and spaced out five meters apart behind the point team.

Not even ten meters had passed before the right flank team hit the deck after hearing a screaming sound and causing the rest of the formation to come to a halt. After a minute and no enemy contact, Major Logan rushed out to the flank team to see what was happening. He ran hunched over, in short bursts. He hid behind trees and changed directions every couple of seconds. It took him about eight seconds to cross the space between them.

When Major Logan arrived, the team leader apologized. They spotted the source of the noise.

"It was a red squirrel, sir," the team leader, Sergeant Benson said. He stared at the ground, frowning, waiting to be berated by his commander.

Major Logan smirked. "Better safe than sorry, right? But let's dial back the caution just a bit, eh?"

"Yes, sir. Sorry, sir," SGT Benson said.

"Everybody up, let's move out," Major Logan said. "We're almost there."

Then, he jogged back to his position at the head of the formation, just behind the point security team and motioned for everyone to move out. The Eagles stood, weapons at the ready, and continued their journey. Devil's Meadow was no more than five hundred meters away.

The Combat Action Wing made it fifty meters before several more squirrels began screaming like maniacs, exposing the platoon's presence to the whole forest. Major Logan thought it odd though, because the squirrels didn't sound like they were moving. Usually they would alert the area and run away, scampering up a tree or jumping across branches to move deeper into the forest.

Major Logan raised his hand in a fist, indicating the platoon halt. He scanned the trees for the squirrels. They still hadn't moved. He couldn't see them through the foliage either. It wasn't until he walked up to a tree with a screaming squirrel that he saw something disturbing.

The squirrel was in a cage made out of bent wire and sticks.

"Damn it," he said, looking around quickly, scanning the trees. The squirrels were being used as an early warning system; an alarm provided by nature and they had just lost the element of surprise.

In a normal voice, not shouting, he said, "Let's go. We have to double-time it. The damn squirrels are an alarm system."

He heard a few shocked whispers of surprise, which he ignored. There was no time to answer questions; they had to move.

"Corporal Wicks, bring the flank teams to within ten meters and tell them we have to double time it," Major Logan said, pointing at Wicks. The young man nodded nervously and ran off to relay the order. Then he pointed at Private Jones, she was young but tough and motivated. "Private

Jones, tell the point team to be on high alert. The Vipers know we're here."
She ran forward to relay that order. Both were back in formation before the
platoon was ready to carry on.

Major Logan motioned them forward and everyone began to jog at a
slow pace. Considering the racket the squirrels made, there was no point
worrying about noise discipline.

Running through the forest was tiring. Soft soil wasn't as bad as sand,
but it was close. Brush tugged at their feet slowing them down. They
plowed through a patch of bushes adorned with thorns, which inevitably
found their way through the fabric of their pants and the top layers of their
skin.

Dozens of squirrels were squeaking now. He grit his teeth against the
terrible racket that made Major Logan want to strangle each and every one
of the little bastards.

An overgrown path curved in from the left and led in the direction that
the Combat Action Wing was traveling. The point team leader looked back
at Major Logan. He motioned for them to slow to a walk and then waved
them forward.

Logan remembered the rough-cut logging road. These days, it was wild,
overgrown, and barely recognizable. He quickly realized that there was a
small path down the middle devoid of weeds and grasses, worn down by
constant use. Therefore, the road was in use by the Vipers.

They followed the old road for a couple hundred meters until the point
security team stopped and took cover. Major Logan slowed down,
crouched, and rushed up to the point team leader to see what prompted the
stop. SSGT Raiford showed up a half-second behind him.

Before any of them spoke, Logan saw what had stopped the formation.
A tall rock wall blocked the path that led to the meadow. It looked like
something straight out of the pages of a medieval tale. The wall caught
Major Logan off guard. The last time he was there, there had been no man-
made structures. His hand clenched into a fist at his side.

Adapt and overcome was the old motto, so Logan adjusted his plans to
account for the new obstacles. He'd been correct when he told Collin that
HAGS knew where to drop the medication. They knew exactly where to
drop it.

Major Logan estimated that the wall was roughly one hundred meters
long, connecting a rocky spire that rose out of the river that ran to the west
and the steep mountain cliff to the east.

With the wall in place, infiltrating the meadow by land would be
difficult. A water insertion may be possible, but they didn't have time for
that and bringing the crate around the wall via the river would require
extraordinary effort.

Centered in the rough wall, was a large wooden double-door. If they could open it, there would be plenty of space to get the crate through. The door itself was beautiful. The hinges were wrought iron and featured a curved and decorative pattern that complimented the carved wood, which featured a haunting scene that looked like a view of purgatory.

Major Logan figured the Vipers must have stolen it from an old church. He doubted they had the ability to craft something so breathtaking.

"That's an unexpected problem," Raiford grumbled. A grin slowly spread on his face. "Good thing we came prepared."

"Yes, it's manageable," Major Logan said. He hated the idea of destroying the beautiful doors. What choice did he have though? "Get Corporal Wicks to solve that problem with a quarter block. And have the flank teams stack nearby ready to breach the opening. Remind them we're here for the meds. So, if they make contact, kill'em all."

"Roger that, sir." SSGT Raiford's smile grew to a child-like grin as he hustled away.

Major Logan could almost feel the excitement radiating off of Raiford. The man loved a few things: God, his wife, a good home-brewed ale, and killing Vipers.

There will be enough killing for everyone, he thought. His stomach flipped, making him fidgety, so he got up and moved east along the tree line. Shit was about to hit the fan.

He moved carefully and kept an eye open for traps. When he stopped again to inspect the wall, he slowly realized that it looked like a curtain wall. If the Vipers kept up the medieval theme they had going, the wall before them was just the first perimeter wall.

Beyond the door there may be another one, which would explain why this wall was unmanned. Whatever surprises the Vipers had wouldn't be sprung until the CAW was penned in behind this wall.

Cursing his luck, Major Logan went back to the point team. He gathered the team leaders and gave everyone a sector to watch, while the flank teams went up to breach the wall. After issuing the orders, Major Logan dismissed them. The Eagles dispersed to organize their soldiers.

Corporal Wicks was already attaching the quarter block of C4 to the doors with two riflemen covering him. Major Logan lay down behind a large tree and watched as Wicks slid the blasting cap into the end of the block and pressed a button on the timed detonator that Kobyashi had made for the Eagles. Koby was often a thorn in Logan's side, with his stupid jokes and snarky attitude, but his technical prowess made him an invaluable citizen of Goshen.

Two teams of four Eagles stood by; stacked up and ready to go. They stood along the wall, out of the blast area and waited for Corporal Wicks' bomb to explode.

Corporal Wicks and his two riflemen ran back into the tree line and took cover. The wait stretched out as though time itself had slowed by a factor of ten. In reality, it was only a sixty-second timer.

Major Logan became aware of his heavy breathing as he lay behind the tree, ducked down behind the truck to avoid shrapnel. He wasn't dumb enough to peek out and look. He knew that if you could see the blast, it could hit you. He took a deep breath and let it out slowly.

A thundering explosion rattled the ground, vibrated through his chest, and echoed off of the mountains surrounding the valley. Rocks and wood splinters fell around him and a cloud of dust filled the air. Now Major Logan peeked around the tree and saw the two teams moving along the wall and into the space beyond, whatever lay in wait for them.

No shots.

Bounding over watch, Major Logan thought, recalling his training from his Army days.

He rose up on one knee, gave the signal, and waved the point team forward while his Eagles observed. Eight Eagles already through the door, another four heading through, and his eight soldiers covering.

Once the point team was through the door, Major Logan stood up and led the remaining Eagles through the settling dust. As he approached the wall, he saw the bomb had blown a sizable chunk out of the wall. Pieces of stone and wood littered the ground. A small crater marked the area where the door used to stand.

Still no sounds. The forest had gone still following the explosion and it was eerily quiet.

Through the crumbling wall, Major Logan saw what appeared to be a courtyard just as he'd suspected. It was empty save for several small, smoldering fire pits. Some of them had cooking spits set up over them. Debris was scattered everywhere from the explosion.

He felt like he stepped out of a time machine after being transported back in time. The scene was odd, a contrast of the modern-looking Eagles and the ancient-looking rock walls, fire pits, and the remnants of the carved wooden doors. Multiple boulders rose out of the ground, some twisted and shaped by the river when it had covered this part of land a millennia ago.

Major Logan grimaced when he saw exactly what he suspected. There was a second wall and another ornately carved door. He continued into the area and took cover behind one of the boulders. The CAW cleared the area. The two flank teams were already stacked up on the new door ready to breach it. Unlike the first door, this one was cracked open. Whether it was accidentally left open by fleeing Vipers or part of a trap, he couldn't tell.

SSGT Raiford jogged over to him. "We're ready to breach the door, sir."

"I see that."

"I'd like to pop smoke if you don't mind, sir."

"Make it so, Sergeant," Major Logan said, waving his hand. "Toss some frags too. Maybe we'll get lucky."

SSGT Raiford grinned and nodded. He glanced over his shoulder and nodded to the other team leader. He also motioned for the fragmentation grenades that Major Logan wanted thrown. SSGT Raiford pulled a frag grenade from his own vest and walked closer to the second wall.

The team to the left of the door took a few steps back from the wall, so they could safely throw their grenades over. Four Eagles held frag grenades, while the other four Eagles to the right of the door held smoke canisters. Raiford held his grenade up to his chest and pulled the pin out. He continued holding the metal tab, called the spoon, so the grenade was safe.

"Smoke first," Staff Sergeant Raiford said. "Three, two, one."

When he said, "one," the Eagles tossed their canisters. One went through the door and three went over the wall in slightly different directions to give them good coverage.

"Frag, out," SSGT Raiford said, as he threw his grenade high and far over the wall. The four Eagles followed suit, throwing their grenades just like the others had thrown the smoke — one through the door and three over the wall. As soon as they released their grenades, they lined up on the wall to wait for the explosions before breaching.

Major Logan smirked, hoping they'd get lucky and tag a few Vipers with some shrapnel just for fun. He could hear the smoke grenades hissing. Thick, gray smoke rose in the air. A series of loud bangs signaled the detonation of the grenades.

The team on the right rushed forward and filed through the door. As soon as the last man entered, the team on the left followed suit with their rifles raised and ready.

Still no shots, no shouts, and no screams of pain.

Major Logan counted in his head, giving the two teams enough time to clear the immediate area. Two soldiers would stay behind to secure their rear while the other six would accompany Major Logan into the Devil's Meadow, which was now more like the Devil's Lair.

Running forward, he led his team through the door into the next space, entirely unsure what to expect. A breeze blew through, making the smoke swirl and rush over more of the same type of boulders as the previous courtyard.

Still no shots. No Vipers in sight.

One of the flank teams moved up on the right side. All he saw were the dark shapes of his Eagles moving through the smoke. They rushed around a boulder with their rifles raised, that much was clear.

A sudden blast lit up the area, flashing orange against the smoke. Major Logan threw himself onto the ground. The blast wave crashed over him, nearly knocking the wind out of him. He could feel fragments of debris kicked up from the explosion ricocheting off of the boulder next to him, stinging his arms and shoulders.

Then, he heard another blast to the left. Major Logan flinched and rolled against the rock. He wished the rough stone would envelop and protect him. Instead, flecks of dirt and stone struck his hands and peppered his uniform, stinging his legs and arms again. Several shots cracked through the air.

"Help," a man yelled. He made a whimpering sound. The air filled with a chorus of cries from injured Eagles.

Major Logan rolled away from the rock. He rose up into a crouch and peered around the rock, searching for the man. Most of the smoke cleared so it didn't take long to spot him.

Before Logan could say or do anything, he heard the whoosh of bowstrings and arrows seemingly sprung from the man's chest. He made a gurgling sound as his head slumped back against the ground.

A breath caught in Major Logan's throat and a pang of guilt tore at him. He realized he couldn't even remember the man's name. He pounded his fist against the rock in anger and searched desperately for the enemy. Another whoosh and the rest of the injured soldiers were silenced like the man that Major Logan had witnessed.

A growl rumbled in Major Logan's chest and he stood up, leaning against the boulder. He gasped as he saw what he vaguely remembered from his previous visit there. Tall cliffs and rocky outcroppings surrounded the meadow.

Caves, large and small, dotted the rocky terrain. Each cave had at least one Viper aiming a bow right at him. The Eagles outgunned the Vipers, but they were grossly outnumbered. Few Eagles remained. It was pointless to continue the fight.

Sure, he could take out one or two, but it would do nothing to bring back the dead.

He felt defeated but he didn't budge. It would hurt his pride too much to let it show so quickly.

"You came in with twenty-one. Now you only have eight," a man said. His voice was even, authoritative, and matter-of-fact. He was not boasting, but in a way that infuriated Major Logan even more. Through the lingering haze from the smoke grenades, Logan could make out the form of a young man standing atop a large boulder. A man he'd seen several times before.

"Drop your weapon, no one else needs to die here today," the young man said.

Major Logan became aware of the remaining Eagles around him. Angela, a new Eagle, to his right raised her rifle toward the man on the boulder.

Four arrows struck her so fast it was as if they were fired from the same bow. Three sank deep into her chest and the final arrow nearly passed through her skull. Had the shaft been two inches shorter, it would have flown through her head and into the rock wall behind them that was boxing them in.

Angela slumped to the ground with a stunned look frozen on her face.

The man's head bowed, as he released a heavy sigh. "Now you only have seven," he said sadly. Then he spoke in the same calm, authoritative voice. "Put down your weapons. No one else needs to die today."

All eyes turned toward Major Logan. His remaining soldiers wanted to know what their commander had in store for them. For a split-second, Major Logan wasn't sure what to do. Then he grimaced and stood up. Several Eagles gasped in surprise. Logan knew they were done for. Like the man said, there was no reason for anyone else to die.

He held his rifle by the barrel raised away from his body. "I am Major Logan, commander of the Goshen Eagles. Let your leader step forward so we can come to terms."

"If your soldiers drop their weapons, then they are welcome here. Peace with Goshen has been a long time coming." The man jumped down off the boulder and approached slowly with his hands held out from his sides, with his palms facing them. He stopped forty meters away. "Drop your weapons. Until then there will be no terms."

Major Logan glowered at him, thinking through the options.

"Look around Major Logan, commander of the Goshen Eagles. You are surrounded and covered from an elevated position," he said. He looked thoughtfully at Major Logan.

Feeling like he was under evaluation, Major Logan shifted slightly under the young man's gaze.

Behind the Eagles, the old wooden door slammed shut. They could hear metal sliding against metal. Major Logan risked a glance over his shoulder and saw the bolts pushed into place, locking them inside. There was no room left for choice in the equation. It was either fight and die, or comply and hope for mercy.

Major Logan looked at the few remaining Eagles: SSGT Raiford, Corporal Wicks, PVT Pyle, PVT Brown, and couple of others he didn't know quite as well. He motioned for all of them to lower their weapons. He lowered his own and defiantly met the gaze of Vipers' leader.

"Major, sir. We can take these fools," PVT Brown said. He held onto his rifle.

"Lower the weapon, private," Major Logan said. "That's an order."

PVT Brown glanced at SSGT Raiford, who was glaring at him.

"You heard the Major, Private." SSGT Raiford leaned his own rifle against a boulder beside him.

"With all due respect, this is bullshit, sir," the young man said. He hesitated, but eventually complied with the order.

Major Logan made a mental note to deal with PVT Brown later. If there was a later. He stared with a level gaze at the Viper's apparent leader.

"Good choice. Now you, Major," the man said. His brown curls waved in the breeze as the last of the smoke cleared. A smirk was evident beneath his trimmed beard.

Major Logan leaned his rifle against the rock and clenched his fists at his sides.

"Now, please come in Major. You and I have a lot to discuss," the man said, gesturing to the cave behind him. "But your dogs must stay in the yard until we come to terms."

"Fine," Major Logan said through clenched teeth. He narrowed his eyes. "What's your name? I'd like to know who I'm coming to terms with."

The smirk grew into a wide grin and the man raised a hand to stroke the point of his beard. "You can call me Brady."

"My soldiers will remain unharmed, I trust."

"We'll be fine, sir. We can handle ourselves," SSGT Raiford said in a gruff tone.

Major Logan raised his hand to silence Raiford.

"Sir-"

Logan shot him a look that cut his words off.

Brady looked around at the bodies of the dead Eagles with a shocked and slightly bemused look on his face. Then he looked at the remaining soldiers, lingering on PVT Brown and SSGT Raiford. Finally, he met Logan's gaze. "What remains of your meager force will remain unharmed, so long as they behave."

Brady motioned for Major Logan to follow him.

The major glanced at his men, wondering if it would be his last time to see them. With a silent nod, he started after Brady.

"Stop!" a Viper shouted.

Major Logan glared at the Viper, thinking the idiot hadn't realized his leader motioned for him to follow.

Brady whipped around then held up a hand at Major Logan. "Stop walking, Major. You need to back up, and go the other way around the boulder." He pointed at the ground in front of Major Logan.

Stopping and glancing down, Major Logan noticed a trip wire less than six inches away. Then he searched the area in front of him. About twenty meters away was another claymore, roughly camouflaged against one of the many boulders that were strewn about the meadow. His eyes grew and he slowly backed up until he was well away from the tripwire.

The mines they stole, he thought.

He went around the far side of the boulder, skirted the claymore, and followed Brady toward one of the largest cave entrances.

Set back into the mouth of the cave, less than ten feet by Logan's estimation, was a stonewall built of carved blocks, similar to the walls that hid the meadow. Another wooden door, carved like the one they blew up, served as the entrance to their lair. On either side of the door were crude, empty sconces for holding torches, made out of what looked like wire clothes hangers.

Brady looked over his shoulder to see if he was following. The man smiled at the look on Logan's face. He reached out and pushed his thumb down on the large latch to open the door. This door didn't squeak at all as it swung open. Major Logan stepped through the door and was completely unprepared for what he saw.

Inside, the cave was well lit and bustling with activity. He felt like he was watching ancient history, because the scene in front of him looked just like something pulled from a history textbook about 11th century Europe.

"My God, man. This is incredible," Major Logan said.

A Cheshire cat-like smile spread across Brady's face and he waved for him to follow, beckoning him inside. "Welcome to the Viper's Den."

Chapter Twenty-Five

Collin War strode down the hallway, feeling numb and hollow inside.

He received word that he was needed in Doris' room.

She'd fallen victim to the fever when the supply of BT76 ran short following the Viper bombing of the Eagle's Club. Like dozens of others, the fever quickly took hold of Doris. She was bed ridden as her body fought desperately against the disease that would eventually consume her.

Shafts of light kindled motes of dust drifting through the air. White tile passed beneath Collin's feet, but he barely noticed any of it. He was lost in thought about his friend and wished that if there was a God, that He would do something to help her. She didn't deserve this.

Collin turned down another hallway and continued toward Doris' room.

One more turn, past an abandoned nurse's station brought him within thirty feet of her room. It was immediately obvious which room was hers, even if he hadn't already known.

Several families stood outside her door, glowing white candles in their hands. Flower blooms and twigs twisted into hearts decorated the doorway. Collin slowed his walk as he fought back a flood of emotion.

Doris had managed the kitchen and the women's auxiliary at the church. At some point or another, she had touched everyone's life in Goshen. Her outgoing personality and caring demeanor made her the unofficial grandmother of all of Goshen. Losing her would leave a hole in many people's lives.

Collin approached the door slowly, cautiously, as if his presence or any quick movements would disturb the peaceful vibe emanating from the room. A small crowd of people stood around Doris' bed, murmuring softly in conversation.

Koby sat in a chair beside her bed, rubbing an ice cube on Doris' lips. It was the only way she could take in fluids orally. It helped to keep her mouth from getting too parched.

Koby turned his head, spotted Collin, and nodded at him. Collin could see his friend's eyes were red rimmed. The two of them had been close.

An I.V. stand on the far side of her bed dripped steadily. Pastor Pendell stood next to it with a bible clutched lovingly to his chest.

Goshen's love for their friend was on display. Friends had decorated her otherwise plain hospital room with early spring flowers in makeshift vases and a lovely collection of handmade cards. All of the curtains were open, exposing the beauty of the river and the valley.

If I have half as good of a view when I die, I will be a happy man, he thought. The depth of compassion Goshen showed was surprising to Collin. Even with all the years of death and the constant struggle, people still respected those who stood on death's doorstep.

In the middle of it all, Doris lay on her bed. The heart monitor beeped slowly, but steadily. Her cheeks were flush, but she looked peaceful. Collin was happy for that; he didn't want his friend to suffer.

Collin looked around at the people standing in the room, nodding and smiling, chatting and mourning. Then he spotted Dr. Horner standing back behind Koby.

Spot lit from above, in her white lab coat, Dr. Horner had an angelic glow about her. An exhausted, sad angel. She leaned against the wall the way a wilting flower does in a vase. At that precise moment, she looked much older than she was.

Collin understood more acutely than most that Julie carried a great weight on her shoulders. The survival of the entire town, fear for her daughter's well-being, not to mention the inevitable loss of a dear friend were atrocious burdens to bear. He respected her tremendous composure and bravery. Few could forge ahead the way she did.

Collin walked right over to Julie and gave her a hug.

"We'll get her back," he whispered.

Dr. Horner tilted her head to look at him, realized that he meant they would get Anna back from the Vipers, and nodded her thanks as tears welled up in her golden brown eyes. Collin hugged her again as tears began to run down her cheeks.

"Thank you," she said.

After a brief embrace, they pulled apart and she dabbed her eyes on the sleeve of her lab coat. She sniffed and composed herself, slipping back into doctor mode with practiced ease.

Walking over to Doris, she checked her vitals and made a few quick notes on a chart that hung at the foot of the bed.

"How long does she have, doctor?" Pastor Pendell asked.

"She's putting up quite a fight, the tough old gal," Dr. Horner said. "Not much longer though. Her oxygen levels are dropping."

"Isn't there anything you can do?" asked Betty, one of the ladies from the women's auxiliary.

Dr. Horner's posture drooped slightly. "No. Not yet," she said, with a slow shake of her head.

Yet? That sounds hopeful.

He went over to stand next to the bed. Doris lay still. Her chest rose and fell slightly with each breath she drew in. Collin leaned over and whispered in her ear.

"I'm sorry I failed, my friend. I couldn't help you like I promised," he said. He brushed a piece of her curly white hair behind her ear and kissed her forehead. "Please forgive me."

Collin took her hand in his. It felt light and fragile as a feather. A tear slid down his cheek. He rubbed his chin, wiping it away before anyone could see. With one final reassuring squeeze, Collin released her hand and stepped back.

He looked up and saw that Dr. Horner was watching Pastor Pendell. Pendell in turn looked at everyone in the room and smiled.

"Ladies and gentlemen, let's clear the room for a few moments to give them some privacy. Please accompany me down the hall," Pastor Pendell said. "We have delicious, fresh brewed coffee available, thanks to Kobyashi."

The townsfolk looked agreeable to the suggestion and many of them looked relieved. It wasn't a stretch to think that spending time with the pastor was preferable to spending it in the company of a dying friend. People gathered their things and began to shuffle out of the room.

Pastor Pendell waited for the crowd to leave before he followed them out. He paused in the doorway, with his hand on doorknob, and fixed Dr. Horner with a stern look and said, "Do it."

His voice was firm and commanding.

Collin looked away from Pastor Pendell confused, and suspicious, then glanced at the doctor. The door swung shut before he'd gathered his wits enough to ask the obvious question.

"Do what?" Collin asked.

Dr. Horner ignored him and turned to Koby. He was still sitting beside Doris, holding her hand.

"Do you want to stay for the procedure?" she asked him.

"What procedure?" Collin asked, growing agitated.

Koby looked up at her with bloodshot eyes and said, "I'm not leaving her side."

"Very well."

"Goddamnit! What is going on here?" Collin looked between Koby and Julie. "One of you tell me."

Neither one answered him.

"Doctor, what the hell are you going to do?" Collin stepped forward and grabbed the edge of Doris' bed, defensively.

She continued to ignore him, which infuriated Collin. His pulse forced blood racing through his body. It hummed in his ears. His breaths came fast and his hands began to jitter.

"Koby. C'mon, man. What's going on?"

Koby just leaned over and kissed Doris' pale hand.

Dr. Horner reached into a pocket in her lab coat and pulled out a small, white box. She held it in the air for Collin to see. He instantly recognized it as the type of box that held BT76. When Julie pulled out the vial, the liquid inside was green, rather than blue.

Collin took a deep breath, trying to calm himself.

"What's that?" he asked, realizing as he said it, they would probably continue to ignore him. Collin clapped his hands together as a thought struck him. Excitedly, he said, "The treatment. You did it?"

She finally looked up at him, a slight smile played on her lips.

"You completed the treatment," Collin said, letting out a breath.

"I wouldn't go that far. Success rates have increased from the paltry seventeen percent we saw before, to just over seventy-seven percent," Dr. Horner said. She tilted her head slightly to the side. "That was on live cells that had been exposed to the pollen, not on people who had already succumbed to the fever."

Collin understood that it was a different situation but still felt hopeful. "That's still good news."

"Who knows? It's extraordinarily unlikely the treatment will revive her," Julie said. "However, it could stabilize her condition, giving us time to continue to develop the treatment. Either way, what we really need right now is a miracle."

She walked over to the I.V. stand with the medicine in her hand. She raised the vial of green fluid and looked at it in the light. Dr. Horner paused and looked at them both in turn.

"Pray for her. She needs all the help she can get."

Collin nodded solemnly.

"It's not going to hurt her, is it?" Koby said. He was now cradling her hand in both of his. His thumb ran over her wrinkled hands with a tenderness Collin never expected to see from him.

"No. She shouldn't feel anything." Julie carefully uncapped the needle, inserted the point into the vial to draw out the medication. Then she flicked the syringe a couple of times and squeezed until a small squirt of green fluid sprayed out. Julie nodded in satisfaction, eased the tip into the main I.V. line, which ran into Doris' arm, and slowly depressed the plunger on the syringe.

The serum swirled as it mixed with the I.V. fluid, diluting as it slowly crept toward Doris' arm. Dr. Horner emptied the syringe into the line, then pulled the needle out, and walked over to toss it into the garbage can. It landed in the can with a loud thump that set Collin's teeth on edge.

She cringed and looked at them with an apology written on her face.

At that point, it became a waiting game.

Dr. Horner sat down in a guest chair and Collin sat sideways on the window sill, alternately watching Doris and enjoying the view of the valley. Everything outside looked peaceful, relaxing, and safe. There was nothing to indicate that the air was filled with death, pollen carried on the wind swirling, seeking a victim, uncaring when it found one, and stole away their life.

Doris began to breathe slightly heavier. Both Collin and Koby looked at the doctor. She nodded her head.

"That's to be expected. Her body is having a boost of adrenalin," she said.

Dr. Horner stood up, looking exhausted, and checked her patient's vitals. "Everything is normal so far."

She slumped back into her chair, seemingly melting into the chair like butter on fresh toast.

Collin turned back to the view. His eyes followed the jagged line of the mountain peaks to the West. He wondered what things looked like from up there. Collin still hadn't been outside of the town. The most expansive view he had was from the top of the dam as Major Logan's spotter.

He wondered what Major Logan was doing at that moment. Had he found the medication? Were the Eagles fighting the Vipers? Had they found Anna? Was Logan dead?

Nothing was certain. That was the worst feeling of all - uncertainty.

Doris began breathing ragged and heavy. Panting as though she'd run up a mountain, Doris was also moving on the bed, something between a twitch and a hard shiver. He stood up and stepped closer to the bed. Dr. Horner was already out of her chair and standing with her hands on the edge of the bed.

"What's happening to her?" Collin asked.

"There's a war raging inside her," Dr. Horner said. "Her cells are fighting the new cells and whichever side wins will determine her fate."

"Goddamn it, Julie. You said she wouldn't even feel it," Koby said, his brow furrowed deeply in concern.

"She shouldn't be able to. This is mostly her body reacting to the treatment. It doesn't mean she's in pain," she said. Her tone wasn't as confident as the words she spoke.

Sweat beaded on Doris' forehead. Koby stood and patted her forehead with a cloth. "Is there anything we can do for her?"

Dr. Horner shrugged. "Keep her comfortable? That's about all we can do."

Doris was twitching and jerking on the bed. Her movement was unnatural and disturbing. Collin was unsettled by the sight of her suffering. He wished he could help her.

If only they had one more vial of BT76. None of this would be happening.

A groan escaped Doris' lips and her back began to arch. Her head leaned back, pressing into the pillow. Then she bolted upright, an ear-piercing scream forcing them all to cringe and cover their ears. Her eyes snapped wide open. They bulged as though they were going to pop out. Her mouth contorted and stretched wide open as she wailed like a horribly injured animal. Her body jerked back and she flopped up and down on the bed.

Collin and Julie both cursed.

Koby fought to help Doris as tears streamed down his face.

Dr. Horner was scrambling to find something in one of the cupboards.

Collin rushed to the side of the bed opposite Koby. He tried to keep Doris from striking something as she flailed and jerked on the bed.

"Doc, you better hurry up," Collin shouted.

The door to the room flung open and Pastor Pendell rushed in. When he saw Doris jerking around, he froze. He winced at her cries then proceeded forward slowly like a frightened child.

Dr. Horner rushed over to the bed and jabbed a small needle into Doris' shoulder. Her twitching and screams didn't ease up.

Pastor Pendell begin to mutter something, but Collin couldn't hear what it was above the awful din.

Doris bolted up again. Her face twisted into a crimson mask of rage.

Pastor Pedell stepped forward and held out his hand with his palm facing her head. "Go with God, in peace."

The scream warbled and changed to a deep growling, "NOOOOOOOOO!"

Doris' eyes rolled back in her head and her body slumped back in the bed. She was still and silent.

In the sudden silence, Collin realized how hard he was breathing. Koby was sobbing. Dr. Horner was cursing and muttering to herself.

Koby leaned forward, looking closely at his friend. Collin placed two fingers on her throat to feel for a pulse. No steady thump coming from her carotid artery. No pulse at all. Doris was gone.

Collin raised his hand across the bed and placed it on Koby's shoulder. He choked up and tears filled his eyes.

Koby shook with grief, but reached up carefully and closed her eyes. He leaned forward and tenderly kissed her forehead.

Collin remembered what Pastor Pendell said before he left the room earlier. Do it, he told Julie. It had been his choice to give Doris the serum.

Collin turned his head and glared at Pastor Pendell. "How dare you."

Pastor Pendell fixed his dark brown eyes on Collin and stared.

"This is your fault." Collin stood back and pointed at the body of his friend.

The pastor shrugged.

"All she wanted to do was die peacefully in her sleep. She told me so. She said given the circumstances, it wasn't such a bad way to go," Collin said, his voice rising to an angry bark. He jabbed his finger at the pastor. "You stole that from her. You! You forced her into this situation and then took away the last comfort she had. You are not a man of God, you are a monster."

Pastor Pendell leveled his gaze at Collin. "That is regrettable, Mr. War. However, I want you to remember one thing."

He shifted his stance and pulled the Bible out from under his arm. With both hands, he held it in front of him like lion tamer holds a chair. He glanced down at the book then back at Collin.

"Only the saved will be saved."

Chapter Twenty-Six

Brady led Major Logan past interior defensive positions. They turned down a hall, which opened up into an expansive chamber with a tall curved ceiling. Sunlight filled the cavern from a roughhewn hole cut in the center of the ceiling.

Major Logan looked around in awe. He'd never seen anything like it before.

Brady stopped in the middle of the chamber, directly underneath the skylight. A ring of light glowed around him.

Unsure, how things were about to go down, Major Logan stopped a few feet away and looked around the room for anything suspicious. Everything appeared to be copacetic.

Across from him, Brady smiled. Then he stepped out of the light to approach Major Logan.

He threw his hands wide and wrapped the major in an embrace.

"Good to see you again," Brady said, giving Logan a hearty slap on the back.

"Yes, it's good to see you too," Major Logan said, returning the embrace with a nervous chuckle. He hadn't been sure if Brady would still honor their deal but it seemed so. "Quite a place you have here."

Brady pulled back and smiled at him. He nodded and turned, gesturing forward. "Let's walk and talk. You can see how much things have changed since the last time we met."

Major Logan followed Brady. They walked side-by-side across the room, heading for one of the three tunnels that led away from the chamber at a leisurely pace. The rock walls were bare except in some places, little ledges had been carved out for small lights. It was strange because they weren't torches or candles, they were actual lights. Upon closer inspection, he could make out a tiny wire that ran along the wall.

"Yes, we have electricity and real lights, thanks to a particularly talented Viper named Jones. The guy's a whiz with electronics and whatnot. He setup solar panels on the mountain." Brady looked proud.

Major Logan grunted in approval. "Very impressive."

He didn't know a lot about such things, but guessed it actually wasn't too difficult. Back in Goshen, Kobyashi could easily setup something similar if they had access to solar panels. He made a mental note to look into acquiring some of their own.

The tunnel they walked through was long and winding. Undoubtedly, Brady chose it for those exact qualities.

"Tell me. How is Anna?" Major Logan glanced sideways at Brady. "You understand that I must see to her safety and well-being before we proceed."

Brady snorted.

"Major, this is the safest place for her," Brady said. "Not to mention the happiest place."

"You didn't answer my question."

"Yes, of course she's fine and well taken care of," Brady said, with a heavy sigh. "I would never harm or mistreat her."

"Perhaps we should go check on her now, so we can move on to other topics?" Major Logan eyed Brady, assessing the level of persuasion this topic may require.

Brady chuckled and patted him on the back. It was an overly familiar move, considering how little they actually knew each other. He took it because it was less important than securing Anna's release and assessing the Viper's strengths.

"You are too suspicious, my friend. You should probably take a vacation, the stress of your work may be affecting your judgment," Brady said with a chuckle.

"How I wish I could."

The tunnel curved to the left and then opened up into another chamber, albeit much smaller than the first one. No sunlight streamed in here. Light came from the bulbs installed along the walls, it was sufficient. The ceiling was lost in darkness.

In the chamber, a pair of women sat on small stools knitting something that had yet to take a recognizable shape. Major Logan nodded at the women with a slight smile but they just stared and didn't react.

"You have sheep?" he asked.

"Very perceptive, Major," Brady said. "We have a number of sheep that we raise and care for."

"Smart. We do as well," Major Logan said.

"We know. Where do you think we got them from?" Brady winked at him.

The bastard is cocky, Major Logan thought. He slowed his pace and when they reached the next chamber, he stopped walking and leaned against the wall.

"Feeling tired, Major? We can stop at the next chamber to enjoy some hot tea, if you'd like?"

"There's no point leading me around your tunnels, wasting both of our time. Especially, when we haven't dealt with the primary issue yet," said Major Logan.

"What's the primary issue?"

Major Logan scoffed. "Obviously, Anna's well-being and release."

"All in due time." Brady walked toward a tunnel on the opposite side of the chamber with his hands clasped behind his back.

"No."

Brady stopped and slowly turned his head. He took on the look of a predator, prepared to pounce at any movement. "Say again?"

"No. Not in due time. I demand we discuss and resolve this issue now," Major Logan said. "There is no valid reason to withhold Anna from me. We already have a deal and discussing terms is a part of it."

A smile curled the corners of Brady's mouth. He let out a barking laugh. Turning on his heel, Brady strode back and stopped right in front of Major Logan, nearly toe to toe. The smile was gone. Brady was several inches taller than Major Logan and used that to his advantage, but Logan was a tough, stubborn man and he wasn't budging on this issue.

"You are in no position to be demanding anything," Brady said, his hands still behind his back. "We have no reason to harm Anna, especially when her mother is so close to finding a cure for the fever."

Major Logan's eyebrows rose slightly at that.

"Yes, we know about that little project."

"How?" Major Logan asked. He planned to keep that to himself, it would have been a huge bargaining chip. Now it seemed like Brady was going to use it against him.

"We can be persuasive when we need information," he said, smirking. He reached up slowly and adjusted Major Logan's uniform and patted him on the chest. "Some are more willing to share than others."

"If you hurt her at all-"

"No!" Brady growled.

"If she's hurt, Collin will ensure that she's a rallying cry for the town of Goshen, and if the citizens want action, there will be little I can do to stop them," Major Logan said.

"She will not be hurt by our hands, unless you force the subject." Red faced, Brady turned away from him and said, "Follow me."

Brady began to walk slowly. Major Logan waited for him to take a few steps before he started walking. He didn't rush to walk beside Brady, he waited for the other man to match his pace. It was a small victory, but it brought a brief smile to his face.

"This Collin guy is quite annoying," Brady said, chuckling.

"You have no idea," Logan said in agreement.

"I have a question for you." Brady clasped his hands behind his back again and leaned forward slightly.

The move made him look older and tired, belying his youthfulness. Logan hoped he would be able to contain this wily Viper so that he could carry out his plans.

"What's your question?"

"Why didn't you warn us about the claymores being placed by the medical crate that was dropped the other morning?" Brady turned his head and watched intently for a reaction.

Major Logan met his gaze and held it steady.

"I had Pastor Pendell and Collin on my ass the whole time. It wasn't possible," he said.

Brady grunted and nodded his head in understanding.

"Well, when we take over Goshen, whoever shot at my son is going to be drawn and quartered in the public square," Brady said, watching him intently again.

Major Logan wasn't intimidated. "That's understandable. It may interest you to know that Collin shot at the boy. I had to disrupt his shot as the boy ran away with the mines. I wasn't about to let him murder a child."

"Sounds like Collin and I have a lot to discuss then," Brady said.

"Indeed." Major Logan smiled in his mind but didn't let it show. If Brady killed Collin, it would make it that much easier to wrestle control of the town away from the Vipers when it came time.

"These are turbulent times, Major. We're making moves and HAGS is making moves, on top of all the usual shit we have to deal with to keep our respective groups alive," Brady said.

"HAGS is certainly throwing a wrench in things. You obviously received the drop of BT76 but did you receive any notifications from them?"

"About the supply reduction?" Brady nodded. "We sure did. It sent a wave of panic through the ranks."

"Same with us." Major Logan looked farther down the tunnel and saw another chamber glowing in the distance. He was stunned at how extensive the cave system was.

"Thankfully, Dr. Horner is close to a cure, or at least some sort of treatment for the fever."

"I'm actually surprised HAGS knows your location. Do you have a contact with them?" Major Logan scratched his cheek.

"No. We've never had contact with them," Brady said. "Maybe a month ago, we noticed an airplane flying relatively low. It went in slow circles overhead. My guess was it was a surveillance mission and so far that seems to have been true."

"Doesn't it concern you that HAGS apparently knows so much about your whereabouts? And who knows what else?"

"Logan, why would that concern me?"

His eye twitched at the sound of this Viper using his name so casually. He bit his tongue to hold back a rebuke, for the time being he needed to play nice with Brady.

"It's simply a variable that cannot be fully accounted for," he said. "They can be a meddlesome bunch and like you said these are turbulent times."

"True enough." Brady pointed out their path since they'd reached a split in the tunnel.

"Thankfully, you, Anna, and I will be walking back into Goshen soon," Major Logan said. He nodded to himself and grunted. "It'll be nice to return to Goshen, especially with Vipers by my side."

"We look forward to that moment as well, Major." Brady slowed down and pushed open a door that Major Logan nearly missed. Brady motioned for him to enter and have a seat. "Speaking of, how do you plan to execute this coup of yours?"

Inside the small room were more lights embedded in the walls. Atop a small, square table in the middle of the room were several large candles burning brightly. The seats left something to be desired. They were bare, carved wood.

Major Logan inspected the room, suddenly doubting his personal safety for a split second. Brady walked over to a wooden bookshelf, picked up a silver tray. On the tray were two cups and a large glass bottle with a cork in it. He couldn't tell what was inside.

Whatever it was, he wouldn't drink until he saw Brady do so first. Major Logan hadn't survived the fever and the chaos left in its wake by being careless.

Brady sat down like he didn't have a care in the world. He set the cups down, motioned for Major Logan to sit since he was still standing, and began to fill the cups.

"Please, sit and enjoy a beer. I'm sure it's been a while since the Eagle's Bar went boom." He made a fist, spread his fingers, and imitated the sound of an explosion.

Major Logan just stared at him.

"Too soon?"

Logan narrowed his eyes, but took the seat opposite Brady. The decision to allow that attack go forward still haunted him. He'd lost some good soldiers in that blast, so it was hard to hear Brady joke about it.

He cleared his throat, and then began to explain. "You have already dealt with the Eagles of questionable loyalty, plus a few vocal residents I was able to pull into service following your attack on the bar. Their bodies now litter your courtyard. The ones left back in Goshen are loyal to me and won't hesitate to support me."

Major Logan shifted in his chair. His butt was already falling asleep, sitting on the hard wood. Brady took a long drink from his cup and refilled the cup.

"You will present me and Anna to the town, and demand Goshen's next drop of BT76 along with a few dozen vials up front, to seal the deal. Pastor Pendell will be the one to negotiate with you at which time you kill him."

"And then?"

"Naturally, I am next in line. I will succeed Pendell. We will fake our escape from capture, and after a brief cooling off period, I will invite you and the Vipers into Goshen as brothers and sisters," Major Logan said, raising his glass. He chugged the beer.

Logan enjoyed the tantalizingly hearty amber ale. It had a crisp finish that shocked his palate.

So god damned refreshing, he thought and nearly moaned in pleasure. He couldn't remember the last time he'd had beer. It wasn't cold but it was roughly the same cool temperature as the tunnels.

"What about non-compliants? Every group has them. Not everyone will be thrilled when you invite us in. Are you prepared to deal with them?" Brady asked. He took another swig of beer and topped off their cups.

"I don't imagine that will be a big problem. The pastor has them well-conditioned to accept almost anything without question. Ultimately, I think their will to live will trump any anger they have about you guys offing the pastor."

There was a light knock on the door and then it swung open. A pair of armed young men carrying trays of food walked in and set them on the table. Major Logan eyed them but they didn't do anything untoward. The boys walked out and disappeared without a word.

On the tray before Major Logan were pieces of dried fruit, a few strips of jerky, and a thick wedge of bread. It looked fresh and delicious. Since Doris had fallen ill, the kitchen had yet to produce any fresh bread. Major Logan briefly wondered if the woman was even still alive. His stomach wrestled his attention back to the food before him. He reached for a few dried berries that sat among apple slices and dried strawberries.

"Resistance is futile, huh?" Brady remarked.

"Basically. Then I will run the town, and you'll be head of security and the combined Eagle and Viper army. Combining our resources, we will have enough BT76 until Dr. Horner figures out this treatment she's developing, and we all live in peace," Major Logan said.

"I look forward to the day," Brady said, raising his glass and leaning forward to cheers with him.

Major Logan raised his cup and bumped it against Brady's cup. They made dull clicks since they were plastic. He felt giddy and the sound of the plastic cups made him chuckle.

In the small room, underground, sitting by candlelight, he felt like a spy from the Revolutionary War. Drinking ale and shooting guns in time honored American fashion.

Logan smacked his lips as he emptied his cup and slammed it down on the table, gesturing for more. Brady obliged him and topped up his cup.

"And I'll finally have Anna," he said. A burp escaped his lips, which he found hilarious.

Brady set his cup down carefully and leaned his forearms against the edge of the table.

"You'll have Anna?" Brady asked in a dark tone.

"Yes, she'll finally by mine. To the victor go the spoils, right?" Major Logan smiled proudly and chugged his beer. He reached for the bottle. When Brady didn't stop him, Logan happily poured himself another round. "And I intend to spoil her. Fact is, that little bitch is sexy as hell, and I deserve something sexy."

Brady coughed in his beer. He lowered his cup and wiped his chin off on his sleeve.

"She's been through a lot," he said. "I'm sure she'll be more than happy to be 'yours.'" He stood up and stretched.

A devious smile curled Major Logan's lips.

"Between you and me, that cherry's already been picked by yours truly. Right after you snatched her up the first time." Major Logan quaffed his beer and settled back in his chair like they were old friends hanging out in a bar. He put his hands behind his head. "I had some of that pie on the way back to town."

Brady looked surprised, which gave Major Logan a shot of satisfaction. He thought he spotted rage flare in his eyes, but it passed too quickly to know for sure. It made him feel good, rubbing it in Brady's face.

Brady wants some of that too, Major Logan thought. Soon, she would be his, and no one else would be able to touch her.

Major Logan leaned forward to reach for the bottle of beer, but it was empty.

"Any chance we could get some more of this?" he asked. "It's fantastic."

Brady shook his head and stood up. "That's all for now. Come on, I want to show you something."

Major Logan stood up to follow Brady into the tunnel. He felt good. Relaxed and just a little buzzed. He smiled to himself. All of his plans were going perfectly.

"Where are we going?" He put a hand on the wall to steady himself. Then gritted his teeth, stood tall, and matched his pace with Brady.

He never received an answer from Brady, they just walked in silence for several minutes. The tunnel began to glow around a corner.

When they turned, Logan saw the tunnel opened up to the outside. The mouth of the cave framed the glory of God's creation. He could see the birds soaring through blue sky, tall pine and spruce trees rising toward the heavens. All set against the gray-blue canvas of distant mountains.

Doors appeared along the wall set into the stone at regular intervals. All of them were closed. Which was fine, Major Logan wasn't as interested in them despite their beauty. They were carved with the same intricate designs that they'd seen on the door that was blown up earlier. Instead, he focused on the view and the obvious lack of a railing along the ledge.

What is he playing at?

Brady led the way to the ledge. He stood within feet of the edge and looked down into the valley and meadow below. Major Logan was shocked at how high they were above the meadow where he could see that Vipers were still moving the bodies of his former soldiers. He hadn't climbed any steep inclines, but he had to admit they had walked quite a distance.

Major Logan realized what a great defensive position this cave complex was. The view from where they stood was amazing, they could see for miles. He wondered how long the Vipers had watched them. There was no doubt that they had watched as the Combat Action Wing moved past the squirrel cages, setup the explosives on the first gate and then enter the courtyard.

"Incredible place you have here," he said.

"We like it," Brady said.

"Soon, you won't have to live in caves though. You'll have houses with electricity, running water and a great food supply," Major Logan said.

"Have you spotted any deficiencies here, Major?"

He looked at Brady, confused. "Not exactly."

"So what's wrong with the way we live?"

Major Logan smiled. "I guess you just don't remember what it was like to live before the fever hit. Goshen is a gem. Our town serves as an example, as hope for the future of America, or what's left of it, and the rest of the world."

Brady made a face. "Ambitious words."

"I'm an ambitious man. You should have figured that out already."

Brady raised his eyebrows briefly and made an affirmative sound.

"What exactly did you bring me up here for?" Major Logan asked. He took a step forward so that he stood even with Brady. He fought against the churning sensation and tension he felt being so close to the edge. To prove he was as brave as Brady, he took a small step forward and leaned over to look down on the meadow with what he hoped was an appraising look.

The fresh air had a sobering effect, because Major Logan suddenly felt acutely aware of everything.

"I brought you here so you could see what we see. And perhaps to bid farewell to your soldiers. Even though you turned on them, they didn't turn on you."

Logan balled his hands into fists and clenched his jaw. He knew that he'd done what was necessary to ensure the future of Goshen and, most importantly, himself. Swallowing his anger, Major Logan forced a tight smile and said, "I appreciate your consideration."

"My pleasure." Brady clamped a hand down on Logan's shoulder, which pushed him forward just enough to give him a start.

Major Logan shot Brady a dark look to which he smiled and nodded back toward the tunnel.

"We should go," Brady said. "There's some stuff you need see."

They both stepped away from the edge before turning to retreat deeper into the mountain.

"I'm rather tired of walking around, as you know it's been a long day. I hope you're bringing this meeting to its conclusion."

"I figured you for a patient man, Major," Brady said, clasping his hands behind his back again.

It quickly became apparent that Brady was leading him in a new direction and this time he was aware of the downward slope as they came down from their vantage point above the meadow.

Humidity levels rose slightly. It felt good, but Major Logan wondered what could be causing it. He had never spent much time in caves before. As they descended to the lower levels of the cave complex, turns and intersections came up with growing frequency until the tunnel dead ended at a door.

Two armed Vipers stood near the door behind a low wall of neatly stacked sand bags. Both men nodded at Brady and then turned their attention to Major Logan, looking him up and down. Logan returned the visual assessment, and found that the only remarkable thing about them were the weapons. Both men held rifles, which had almost certainly originated in Goshen.

"Open up, guys." Brady gestured toward the door.

"Yes, sir," said one of the guards. He turned to open the door while the other man stood, eying Major Logan.

Major Logan ignored him. A guard was below his interest.

The other guard fumbled for his keys, after an awkward moment, he plunged a large key into a large, industrial-looking padlock. It clicked open. After removing the lock and lifting the metal bar that helped to secure the door, the guard stepped back to allow the men to enter. He used a different key to unlock the door handle and then he swung it open and stepped aside for them to pass.

Major Logan looked inside for a moment but there was nothing much to see. Only one small light glowed in a distant corner and it failed to cast enough light to be useful. He stepped forward to get a better look inside. As he did so, Brady snapped his fingers and several large overhead lights flickered and snapped on.

Surprised at the sight before him, Major Logan took an involuntary half-step back. Stacked on the floor were several HAGS medical crates. He had only expected to see one.

Anna lay atop one of the crates with her eyes closed. She looked good - clean, unhurt, and fed. Her hands were handcuffed together and a chain ran toward the back wall. It was at least four feet long, a reasonable length given that the room was rather large and mostly empty.

"Anna, are you okay?" Major Logan asked.

She opened her eyes and sat up. When she saw Logan, she stopped and leaned back against one of the other crates. It looked terribly uncomfortable.

Major Logan looked at Brady. "You couldn't give her better accommodations?"

"I'm fine," Anna said in a dull voice. It was enough to send a tingle down Major Logan's spine that warmed his desire for her.

He walked closer and sat on the crate next to her.

"Do you need water or anything?" Major Logan asked.

Anna sat up and inched away so there was space between them. She glanced at Brady again.

Brady smiled and shrugged at him.

Anna shook her head, flipping her hair back and forth. "I'm fine, really."

"Unlock her, Brady." Major Logan stood and pointed at the handcuffs encircling Anna's thin wrists. The metal cuffs glinted in contrast to her pale skin.

"No. I don't think I'm going to," Brady said. He held a hand up to stave off a rebuttal. "At least not yet. First things first, Major. We need you to open the crates."

Major Logan stood for a moment and looked from Brady to the crates and back at him. Then he broke out into a hearty chuckle.

"You mean to tell me that you've been stealing crates from us and you can't even open them?" Major Logan burst into laughter. He wiped the corner of his eye and grinned openly at Brady. "Dumbasses."

With the clank and spine-chilling grind of chain against stone, Anna stood up and looked at Logan with pleading eyes.

"We have to open these for the Vipers," she said with a gesture at the crates. "Or they're going to kill us."

Major Logan whirled and jabbed his finger at the smug bastard behind him. "That is not a part of the deal."

"We need the crates opened. You know how to open them. Consider it a demonstration of our cooperation. We killed your soldiers; you open our crates. It's a very simple request," Brady said. He raised his hand and mimicked turning a dial. "Just a few quick turns on the lock and we will all be happy."

"Do I look happy to you?" Major Logan glared at Brady.

"You look like a man that will do what he needs to do to survive. I trust you'll make the right choice."

"Please, Logan. Just unlock the cases," Anna said. The chain grated against the floor as she moved closer to him. Her big doe eyes gazed at him, stirring his ego and spurring him to action. She jerked to a stop as the chain went taut. She squeaked a little in surprise.

"Why haven't you opened them?" Major Logan asked. "Even if you don't know the code, they would be easy enough to open with the right tools."

Brady crossed his arms over his chest and tapped a finger against his chin.

"We've had…issues. Some of the cases are not what they seem." He looked pointedly at Major Logan, who looked confused.

"What the hell does that mean?"

"Ever since our attack on the Eagle's Bar, we've received a retaliatory crate…or two," Brady said. "We lost a lot of good men."

Major Logan's eyes went wide.

"You look surprised, Major."

"Well aren't you a fucking genius?" he growled sarcastically. He frowned and rubbed the back of his neck.

"So, now you understand why you are in here. You will open the crates. I will wait outside with the guards just around the corner. Once the crates are safely opened, then our previous agreement is back in full effect," Brady said.

"I'm your canary in the mine, so to speak," Logan said. He brushed past Anna and inspected the crates carefully.

Brady wore another of his devious smiles.

"Major, please open the crates so we can go home," Anna said.

He ignored her and continued his inspection of the crates. He needed a moment to think. Major Logan looked over each crate, and then stood up.

"There are no explosives in these crates," he said to himself, louder than he intended. He was confident of that fact even though he still felt nervous at the prospect of opening them. If HAGS had booby-trapped a crate before, it was possible these were too. Possible, but not probable.

"You can't possibly know that," Brady said.

"I know for a fact and I don't need to open them to know."

Brady just looked at him.

Major Logan gestured at the three crates. "HAGS didn't put explosives in any of these crates."

Anna tilted her head at him. She looked from Logan to Brady and back.

"How do you figure that, Major?"

"Because I'm with HAGS." Major Logan sat on the crate, where Anna had been earlier. "I didn't tell them about the plan to blow up the Eagle's Bar. So, they must have returned the favor of their own volition."

"You work for HAGS?" Brady said, cocking an eyebrow at him.

"You think Goshen would survive without me?" Major Logan threw his hands up and gaped at him. "You think they would provide a small, insignificant town military grade weapons and medication without a man on the ground? Don't be so naive, Brady. I am HAGS. We are building a better future. A future that you can be a part of."

Anna rushed at him, chain clanking, and swung her hands at his face.

Major Logan blocked her strike and stood up, stepping out of her range.

"You knew about the attack?" Her face turned red. "How could you?"

Major Logan nodded. "It forced Pastor Pendell to authorize a retaliatory strike, which is why I'm here now."

"But you knew HAGS would bomb the Vipers too?" Anna looked furious.

He didn't answer right away. Reluctantly, he nodded again.

"Population control was part of it. Another part was to diminish the Viper's defenses enough that both sides would be forced to negotiate and merge for survival. The orders came from the top." He shrugged. "Right or wrong, management saw it as the only way."

"That's idiotic," Brady said, frowning.

"You killed my friends!" Anna screeched at him.

Her anger tore at his heart. He did the right thing. The only thing he could do.

She lunged for him again with her fingers curled like claws. When she came to the end of the chain, she twisted and lashed out with a kick at his head.

Major Logan threw his forearm up to block the blow. Otherwise, it would have caught him in the cheek. The impact sent a sharp pain shooting up his arm. He stepped back and cradled his arm to his chest.

She glared at him through the tears that streamed down her face. "You bastard."

Major Logan looked at her curiously, thankful she was chained up and that the medical crates were now between them.

"Are you upset about Goshen or the Vipers?" he asked. Women had always seemed so emotional to him.

Couldn't she see the logic behind my actions?

"Both. You monster," she said, wiping tears from her cheeks.

Major Logan shook his head and bent down to unlock one of the crates. The dial spun easily as he twisted it to the three numbers that would release the shackle. With a click, the lock opened, and he opened the crate and held up a shrink-wrapped pack of BT76. Brady and Anna stared at it.

"See. No bomb," he said with a satisfied look on his face. "Combined this with the supply you borrowed from the hospital, thanks to little miss ransom here, and we should have enough BT76 to last us until Christmas."

"Us?" Brady said with a doubtful look. He walked toward Anna.

"Us - Goshen and all of your Vipers," he said.

Brady stopped beside Anna and pulled a key out of his pocket. He unlocked her handcuffs and she threw herself at him. She wrapped her arms around his neck and pulled him close. They kissed passionately, unconcerned that Major Logan stood mere feet away, with betrayal burning in his gut.

Major Logan slammed the lid of the crate and pounded his fist against it.

"You dirty little whore," he screamed at Anna. Veins bulged in his neck. Rage tinted his skin fire engine red.

"You never needed to kill Eagles or Vipers. You never needed to listen to HAGS. You never needed to listen to Pastor Pendell's foolish raving," Anna said. "You only needed to open your heart and your mind to other possibilities. Now you reap what you sow, you creepy bastard."

He glared at both of them while they continued to hold each other in a tight embrace.

"No, no, no," Major Logan said. "You're mine. That's part of the deal."

"I will never be yours."

Brady pulled out of her embrace and led her to the door.

Major Logan just stared after them. It'd all been a ruse he realized.

Anna walked through the door.

"No! You're mine." Spittle flecked his lips as he threw the box of BT76 at Brady and Anna. His aim was terrible. It flew wildly off target and smashed into the wall. They all heard the glass vials break inside the packaging.

Brady stopped in the doorway, turned sideways, grabbed the doorknob, and looked over his shoulder at the major. "You know, I never understood why you let that crazy, old bastard run the show. It would have been so easy for you to make him go away."

Major Logan glared at Brady. Breaths came in short, quick puffs. His brow had grown damp with sweat. In a low voice, he said, "HAGS considered removing him, as did I. He was always a memo away from elimination. I don't make policy, I just carry it out. If only toppling him was as simple as it sounded. But there are bigger things at work here and it's not so simple. It's a big game of chess and sometimes a king must sacrifice a few pawns."

Brady scoffed at him.

"Then consider this checkmate," Brady said as he backed out of the doorway and pulled the door closed behind him.

Panic seized Major Logan. He rushed for the door, hoping to catch it so they couldn't lock him in the room. He was still feet away when the door slammed shut and the lock clicked into place.

Chapter Twenty-Seven

Water ran over Collin, washing away the sweat, dirt and grime from gardening. Helping his neighbor, Rick, tend to his greenhouse garden had been dirtier and more tiring than he expected. Collin never considered himself a green thumb, but out of necessity, he began to pick up the skills.

After moving a couple of wheelbarrows full of compost nearly halfway across town and then spreading it among the plants, he was almost thankful for the scheduled trip to the hospital. Dr. Horner told him it may be his final blood donation. Oh, how he wished that turned out to be true. He smiled to himself at the thought.

He finished washing up and stepped out to dry off. He dressed quickly and rushed out of his house. Despite all of the work he'd done with Rick, Collin felt refreshed and ready to tackle the rest of his day.

With Major Logan still out on a big raid, he was left in charge of security. He could delegate most of the work. He would spread it around to a few extraordinarily capable sergeants. Despite their lack of formal military training, the sergeants still managed to live up to the reputation that came with their rank.

He recalled the old saying, "We've done so much for so long with so little that we can do anything with nothing."

Several things still required his personal attention such as details regarding the construction of the wall along the river and personnel issues. None of those was critical though. Whatever cropped up since the last round of status reports could wait until after his appointment with Dr. Horner.

He passed a security patrol on his way to the hospital. The Eagles saluted him as they would with Major Logan. He felt awkward, but he returned the salute, and then picked up his pace. The faster he got to the hospital, the faster he could get out and back to the kind of work he could understand.

Dr. Horner's ramblings about vaccines, genetics, and other medical sciences were entirely beyond his base of knowledge and understanding. He always smiled and nodded like he understood but in truth, he was clueless. Still, he went along with it because he enjoyed Julie's company.

Collin entered the hospital and strode into the outpatient clinic to meet Dr. Horner. She already knew his preference that she be ready to draw blood as soon as he got there. No small talk in the lobby beforehand. It was all business.

He sighed as he neared his room. Dr. Horner and the nurses had even taken to calling it "his room" because he was there so often. They joked with him that he should bring a blanket and pillow from home. Settle in a little and make it comfortable but quickly shot down that idea.

Blood donation wasn't a cakewalk for him the way it was for others. It made him lightheaded and sweaty. Recently the draws seemed to wear him out for hours afterward.

Seeing blood, didn't bother him. He could get hurt and bleed without adverse side effects. But take a vial or a pint and he was out of action. He complained about it to Julie. All she said was, "It's normal." Luckily, it didn't normally hamper his ability to do his job as a member of the Eagles.

He opened the door to the room and saw Dr. Horner leaning against the sink with her head resting against the cupboards, which held supplies and other goodies like his juice. She straightened up and ran her hands down her white doctor's coat. She looked at him and he could see that she cried recently.

Collin pushed the door closed behind him and approached her. He looked into her golden brown eyes and put his hands on her shoulders.

"We'll get her back," he said.

She silently nodded her head. Julie leaned forward, slid her arms around him, and rested her head against his chest. They embraced for several long seconds.

When she pulled away, she sniffed, and looked up at him sheepishly, embarrassed by the show of emotion. Collin reached for the box of tissue that sat beside the sink. He held it out for her and she smiled in thanks.

"So, you ready to sink your fangs in for some more juice, doc?" he said with a grin, trying to lighten the mood.

"You know the drill," she said, gesturing toward the examination table. She began to pull the stuff she needed out of the cupboards. In her distress over Anna, she hadn't setup, but Collin didn't mind.

Even though Collin knew the real reason Anna was with the Vipers, he couldn't tell the doctor. Not yet.

"How's the research going?" he said.

She smiled at him. It was a genuine smile filled with hope and true joy. "Very well. We're close."

"Excellent news, Julie. Truly amazing work you're doing on this," he said. "When the history books are written, yours will be the name that lives on. Everyone will know who Dr. Julie Horner was."

She chuckled a little. "Don't be absurd."

"When Goshen is cured of the fever, we won't have to fight the Vipers for BT76 anymore. There won't be much use for me. I'm not a skilled technician nor a farmer. And I'm certainly no Kobyashi."

"Thank the Lord for that," Dr. Horner said with a hearty laugh.

From tears to cheer, he thought. *Score one for me.*

Once her hands steadied after laughing, she stuck him with the needle. Collin barely even noticed the slight prick in his arm anymore. He'd become so accustomed to it that he didn't give it a second thought. Then it was a matter of waiting for his blood to fill up the bag that she attached to the end of a small rubber tube that attached to the needle.

He eyed the cupboard, knowing there was a stash of juice waiting for him. Julie must have noticed because a few moments later, Collin was lying on the bed sipping orange juice and thinking over the rest of his day. After he checked on the construction of the wall, he was going to go to Koby's house for dinner.

"Would you like to join Koby and I for dinner?" He was sure Koby wouldn't mind.

"Thank you but no. I have too much work to do."

"Too much work to eat? Come on now, doc. You have to take care of yourself," he said.

"The kitchen staff are kind enough to deliver food to me," Dr. Horner said. "They've been great about supporting me during my research."

"That's good to hear," he said skeptically. "I guess I don't have to worry about coming upon your desiccated corpse next time I come in. Seriously though, make sure you take at least a few, short breaks to give your brain a rest."

"How's Koby holding up?"

He sighed at her redirection. "He took Doris' passing harder than I would have imagined. I think they were much closer than he let on."

She didn't say anything.

"Like I said, I'll be joining him for dinner tonight. We'll see how that goes. I think it helps him to have something to focus on, keep his mind busy. Maybe we should come up with a big electronics project for him?"

"That would be nice," Dr. Horner said. She cleared her throat and glanced at him, then turned toward the cabinets and rummaged around. "Any word...from..."

"Nothing yet," Collin said softly. "But I'll be going over a plan with Pastor Pendell if we don't receive word soon."

With the Eagles still missing, it meant they ran into significant problems. They might just be evading the Vipers, but if that was the case, he figured they could just book it home. It's not like the Vipers didn't already know where they lived. He worried about the new Eagles they trained. They were so fresh and untested in actual battle that it was hard to know how they would react. He just hoped Major Logan could hold them together against whatever obstacles they faced.

Minutes passed without any conversation. So he closed his eyes and just enjoyed his juice.

If he was lucky, another memory would come to him.

Lost in thought, Collin wasn't expecting the doctor to rip the tape holding the needle in place in his vein. Little hairs in the crook of his arm were yanked from their follicles sending a small jolt up his arm.

"Done already?" he asked, not bothering to open his eyes. He rubbed his skin to dull the pain.

"All done. Thank you again for agreeing to help me and for being such a great patient…"

"Patient?"

"And friend," Julie said, her smile apparent in her tone.

Collin smiled and sat up just a little. Julie handed him a cotton ball that he pressed to the needle hole in his arm. He bent his arm to hold it in place and leaned back. He noticed that she placed several boxes of juice on the nightstand beside his bed.

He helped himself to another one.

He adjusted his position on the bed. Dr. Horner patted him on the shoulder and smiled.

"I wish it had been you leading the raid. I'd feel more comfortable with you in charge," Dr. Horner said.

"Everything will work out, Julie. We'll get Anna back unharmed. I'm sure of it," he said.

She gave him another quick pat and turned away. When she reached the door, she looked back and said, "Rest easy. You'll need a few minutes for the sugar to kick in. And I'm quite certain that I won't need to draw any more blood."

"Great news then," Collin said, grinning.

"Thank you," she said. "For everything."

"Come on, doc. You're the one doing all the hard work."

"Seriously. Thank you." Then she walked out of the room. The door clicked closed behind her.

Collin leaned back onto the bed and relaxed. He got the feeling that Julie Horner was probably one of the people in town that he could actually trust. Despite what Anna told him in the hallway, he trusted Dr. Horner.

He sighed and closed his eyes. The hospital was quiet, he was probably the only patient in the entire building at that point. There were no more infected citizens still alive.

Lying on the bed, Collin's thoughts wandered to his family. He'd pretty much figured out that Pastor Pendell was full of crap. He knew nothing about his family. He still wanted to find them, if they were alive.

He almost nodded off and realized that he was lying in bed for almost an hour. He sat up, grabbed another juice box, jammed the straw in for a long drink that quickly drained it. Testing his condition, Collin stood up carefully and picked up the last juice box.

For the road.

Satisfied that he could walk without fainting from blood loss, he made his way out of the hospital. There was no sign of Dr. Horner but he figured that was a good thing. She was probably hard at work, tweaking the treatment.

Chapter Twenty-Eight

The sky overhead was a tangle of orange and blue as the setting sun passed behind the mountains. Long shadows crossed Collin's path as he hurried along the gravel road to Kobyashi's house.

His stomach growled. Before it registered with his brain, his belly noticed the scent of food on the air. Collin pulled in a deep breath.

Grilled meat.

"Oh that's good," he said as he walked up the path from the sidewalk to the front door. Collin rapped his knuckles against the door several times and stood there waiting for Koby to answer.

"Come in," said Koby's muffled voice through the closed door.

Collin entered the house. "Hey buddy, you need a hand?"

"Don't try to get fresh with me buddy," Koby said from the kitchen. "We're going outside to eat. I grilled up some steak."

"I could smell it on my way over," Collin walked into the kitchen where Koby was busy prepping some vegetables for a salad.

His friend looked up and smiled briefly. "Go on out, I'll be right there."

"Okay."

"How'd the hospital visit go?"

"You know how it is. She took a lot of blood and I sipped my juice. So, the usual," Collin said, standing in the sliding doorway leading to the backyard porch. "The good news is that I probably won't have to go back again."

He left the door open and sat down in his usual spot.

"We can only hope," Koby said.

Collin nodded and poured himself a jar full of beer to go with his meal. Unlike the coffee, Koby kept his beer brewing private. Collin felt lucky that he'd been let in on the secret because it was going to pair nicely with the steak. His mouth watered in anticipation.

A bowl of mashed potatoes, dinner rolls, and cobs of corn, sat on the table next to the bottle of homebrewed beer.

"It smells so good out here, man."

"Go ahead and dish up," Koby said. "I'm just finishing up the salad."

Collin didn't need to be told twice. He dished up mashed potatoes, a roll to help soak up the delicious brown gravy, and a cob of corn. By the time Koby emerged with the salad, Collin had already cleaned off his plate and was piling on more.

"Steaks still on the grill?" Collin asked.

"Are you kidding me?" he shot back. Koby set down the bowl of salad and went back into the kitchen without a word. He came out with a covered platter. He set it down and removed the curved lid, with a flourish like a cartoon waiter. Inside were two giant steaks atop a bed of potatoes, carrots, celery, and onions. "The meat has to rest before you cut into it."

"Wow, you really outdid yourself," Collin said, staring at the food with wide eyes. "I bet no one would imagine you could eat this good in the end times."

Koby smiled. "Thanks."

They ate and caught up on news and the minor issues of daily life.

"Progress on the wall is coming along nicely. I think it should be finished soon. I'll be happy when it is," Koby said.

"Everyone is looking forward to the completion of the wall. Especially since it'll free the guys up to get back to their work assignments."

Koby looked at him skeptically.

"And the town will have another layer of protection against the Vipers," he quickly added.

Koby nodded and took a bite of salad.

"Any other plans tonight?" Koby asked.

"Just a meeting with Pastor Pendell and I'll probably do another round to check on the Eagles," he said. "I should probably go see the wall too. I didn't pay attention on the walk over. My mind was on Logan and the CAW."

"Any word?"

"Nothing."

"Jesus," Koby said with a low whistle. "It's been too long."

"I agree and that's what I'm going to discuss with Pendell."

"Have fun with that." Koby smirked. "I'm glad I'm just the assistant."

"Yup, it frees you up to fix things like those power bumps."

Koby groaned. "That's old news. Done and done, man. Get with the times."

Collin laughed then dug into another mound of mashed potatoes with a piece of steak skewered on his fork.

Before long the two of them had cleaned off their plates and all the food on the table.

"That was a great meal," Collin said, leaning back in his chair. He threw a quick two-finger salute and reached for his drink.

"Thanks. You're always welcome to come over," Koby said. He raised his glass to cheers with Collin.

With a clink of their pints, they drank. Collin emptied his but didn't pour another. Pastor Pendell wouldn't be pleased if Collin showed up buzzed.

"Let me help you clean up before I jet off to my meeting with the old man," he said.

"No need to help. I find cleaning up to be almost as relaxing as cooking," Koby said. "Seriously. Go to your meeting."

"Someday you'll make a good wife," Collin joked.

Koby looked at him briefly and took another drink.

"Are you sure?" Collin felt odd leaving like that, but Koby looked serious.

"Yeah, man. Don't worry about it. I appreciate the busy work." Koby stared into his glass as he swirled the beer around.

Collin knew what he meant. "Okay. How about I cook tomorrow?"

Koby drank his beer and nodded at Collin, with a little wave. "Tomorrow then."

Collin looked at his friend for a moment longer unsure what to say or do. Then he turned and left.

Collin eased the door closed as he left before he jogged down the stairs and walked quickly across the yard toward the church where he was meant to meet Pastor Pendell.

On his way to the church, Collin detoured toward the bridge. Even in the fading light, people were working on the wall. The logs were massively thick and at least twelve feet tall. The lumber mill Koby directed them too had paid off big time. Next time the Vipers tried to slither into town, they would have a big problem.

Above the bridge, the craftsmen were securing a beam, connecting the section of wall that went downstream to the section of wall that was upstream. The plan was to have a small Eagle's nest above the bridge for defense.

Collin smiled and shouted, "Great work everyone." He spread his arms, gesturing at the wall. "This is fantastic."

One of the carpenters approached Collin. "We're making good progress, sir."

"Looks like it. The main work is nearly complete from what I've heard."

"That's right. We have about three hundred feet to go on the East bank before we can return some of the workers to their respective duties. Then our group will outfit the wall with a walkway and a few more Eagle's Nests," he said, pointing to either side of the bridge and finally up at the first log spanning the bridge, indicating the locations of the planned guard towers.

"Excellent. Keep up the great work and let me know if you need anything," Collin said. He patted the man on the back and looked back at the wall.

The structure was a formidable barrier against the Vipers. It was important to Collin, to Goshen's defense, but more importantly, it was soothing to the townsfolk.

One thing he had learned and understood from all of the great military minds, from Sherman to Sun Tzu, Alexander to Patton, or Machiavelli to Hannibal was that they had to make the townsfolk feel as though they were safe, and protected.

With the recent attacks, especially the bombing of the Eagle's Bar, the enemy sowed doubt among the citizens about the Council's ability to keep them safe. That was a slippery slope and one that all military leaders understood they had to defend against. Constructing a wall was as much a physical defense as it was a mental defense.

Satisfied with the work, Collin bid farewell to the crew and continued along the main street toward the church. The houses still practiced the same light discipline they had during his first night in Goshen, but outside people walked around and a few of them carried either torches or flashlights. Seeing the clash of old and modern, not to mention the construction of a defensive wall made of logs, made him realize just how odd his life was now.

People took notice of him as he walked down the street. Collin greeted and waved at them. Most smiled and waved back. Word had reached Collin that some people were grumbling about him, saying that he had something to do with the current state of affairs in Goshen. He hoped there would be an opportunity to allay those unfounded fears.

Pastor Pendell told him to meet in front of the church, but Collin didn't see him anywhere. He walked up the stairs and sat down, leaning against the carved stone railing. He looked down at his watch and pressed the button for the light. Luminescent blue digits glowed in the dark as he watched lights move around the town. The pastor should be there any minute.

The last rays of light glowed behind the mountains in the west, silhouetting them. Down in the valley, it was already quite dark. The one exception was the area where the construction team worked. Several small torches cast a glow against the tall logs that made up the wall.

Collin heard footsteps and saw a dark form moving through the darkness toward him. The shape of the shadow and the cadence of his footsteps suggested it was Pastor Pendell.

"I'm glad you made it, Collin," the pastor said, his voice sounding loud in the darkness though it was at a normal conversational volume.

"You too, pastor," he said.

"Any word on our boys?"

Collin didn't mention the fact that the Eagles weren't all men, there were several women among the Combat Action Wing. He simply said, "No."

Pastor Pendell grunted. He stopped at the bottom of the steps and leaned against the railing.

"The wall is coming along nicely. Hank says it should be finished soon," Collin said. He gestured at the bridge even though the pastor probably couldn't see him in the darkness. "They're finishing up the section above the bridge. Later on they'll build it out to be another Eagle's Nest."

"Your idea?"

"Actually, no. I think one of the carpenters came up with it."

"How is security?"

"Well, we've had no contact with Vipers. Nothing else noteworthy has happened," Collin said. "We are vulnerable while the wall is under construction because we have so few Eagles left. But, nothing new there."

"Very well. I trust God will watch over us."

Collin snickered.

"Do not doubt the Lord, Collin," Pastor Pendell said in a serious tone.

He cleared his throat and changed the subject. "When the wall is complete, if we still haven't heard from Major Logan, I am going to put together a small strike force to go look for them."

Pastor Pendell slapped his hand against the stone railing. "Absolutely not. I will not have this town's defense weakened even more."

"Pastor-"

"We will be attacked again. It's not a matter of if, but when, and we will not be caught off guard," Pastor Pendell said.

"That won't happen. If need be, we can arm more of the citizens. Our town has two massive advantages: technology and defenses. Just the snipers alone will keep the majority of the Vipers at bay. With the river and the addition of the wall, the Vipers would be hard pressed to do much to us. Even with explosives."

"You are right about our strengths," Pastor Pendell said. "But if you take out a strike force, then both of those will be weakened. If the larger Combat Action Wing was overpowered, what makes you think you can do more with less? If you don't come back, who would lead the remaining Eagles? You're not thinking clearly."

"I have built you a fortress and I can build more defenses to bolster what we already have."

"You have built nothing." Pastor Pendell swept an arm, showcasing the town. "None of this. You simply woke up in a kingdom that's been provided to you."

Collin sighed and his shoulders slumped just a little. "But we can't just hide behind the wall," he said. "Fear will not save us."

"No, God will."

Collin rolled his eyes so hard, he was thankful it was dark outside.

Pastor Pendell activated the light on his watch and grunted. "It's nearly time for Bible study, so that concludes our meeting. You will not take a strike force, or any Eagles, outside of Goshen without my express permission. Are we clear on that point?"

"Sure."

"You sound unclear," Pastor Pendell said as he slowly climbed the steps. He stopped beside Collin and looked at him. He was close enough that they could see each other in the dark. "Are you clear?"

Collin held his gaze steady, clenched his jaw briefly then gave a curt nod and said, "Yes."

"If you would like to join our Bible study, you're more than welcome. Your knowledge of the good book doesn't seem to be where it should be," he said.

His barely veiled condescension made Collin clench his fist. He knew he couldn't hit the man regardless of how powerful the urge was.

"Unfortunately, I'll be helping cover a guard shift near the bridge. Gotta keep your kingdom safe, right?" he shot back.

"Indeed."

Pastor Pendell glanced back over his shoulder as something caught his eye. Collin noticed and looked in the same direction.

There was a shout and some loud talking, but it was much too far away for them to make out the words.

Through the gap in the wall where the bridge crossed the river, they could see two bright lights shining out in the fields. He saw at least two figures in the glow of the light.

They looked at each other briefly.

"Then God said, 'Let there be light.'" Pastor Pendell started back down the stairs.

"First Genesis," Collin said, following.

"Good. Maybe you don't need to attend tonight after all."

Collin shook his head and began to jog toward the bridge to meet the torchbearers. The steady crunch of the pastor's shoes could be heard behind Collin, but the older man couldn't keep up.

Chapter Twenty-Nine

As soon as Collin reached the bridge, he took a rifle from one of the citizens filling in on guard duty.

He could clearly see two hooded figures crossing the field, heading toward the bridge. The glow of their torches lit up the field with a bright orange glow.

Two Eagles stopped working, grabbed their rifles, and flanked Collin as he crossed the bridge. He motioned for the two soldiers to fan out.

"Keep your eyes peeled. This may be a diversion," Collin said. He held his Bushmaster AR-15 at the ready and scanned the darkness, but he couldn't see beyond the glow of the torches.

The light from the workers on the wall was enough to illuminate the immediate area but it didn't light up the fields, which were hundreds of yards wide, by Collin's quick estimation.

When the cloaked figures were within fifty yards of where he stood, he took two steps to the right and took a kneeling firing position, in case anyone had taken aim on him. Kneeling made him a smaller target in case the two people foolishly decided to attack.

"Halt!" Collin shouted. "Stop right there and remove your hoods. I want to see your faces."

Both figures stopped where they were. The taller of the two lowered a sack about the size of a backpack from their shoulder.

Collin immediately thought it might be a bomb and regretted letting them get so close.

Too late now.

When the taller of the two pushed back their hood, he was shocked to see Anna. He stood up slowly, but didn't lower his rifle, instead he shifted his aim to the smaller figure.

"Christ, Anna? What the hell?"

"It's me. I'm fine," she said. Her nose was scrunched up like she was sick or disgusted. He couldn't tell which it was.

She turned to look at the shorter figure and gave them a quick nudge with her elbow. "Take off your hood, it's okay."

A small hand came up slowly and pulled down the hood, exposing the face of a young boy.

Collin gasped and nearly tumbled over.

It was the boy from the other day. The same one who had crawled out into the field and stolen the two claymores. The boy that looked like his son.

He looked from Anna to the boy. After a moment, he lowered his aim to the ground. He wouldn't shoot either of them, but it made him suspicious of an ambush.

"Is anyone else out there, Anna?"

She shook her head. "Not that I know of."

The boy stood quietly and stared at him. Collin stared back. He wasn't sure what to say so he turned his attention back to Anna.

"What's going on?"

"Brady, the leader of the Vipers, sent me to retrieve some of the cure," Anna said.

"How do the Vipers know about that?"

"Major Logan," she said simply. "Apparently, he squealed like a pig."

Collin looked past Anna and the boy, scanning for any movement, but he saw nothing.

"Where is Major Logan?" he asked.

Anna shifted in place, looking awkward. Her eyes flicked over to the boy, then back at Collin.

"Actually, I'd rather not say in front of my escort," Anna said with an apologetic look and a quick gesture toward the boy.

"The child? He's your escort?" Collin was curious about that.

"Yes. It's not like I had a choice. The Vipers assigned him to escort me. Plus, he knows the way between the Viper's camp and Goshen." She shrugged. "I don't."

Collin shot her a curious look.

"He's a very impressive young man," she said.

"We've seen what he can do," Collin said with a grunt. He looked the boy up and down, expecting some kind of trick. "How did you survive those barbarians?"

The question was mostly for Anna, but he wanted to see if it would stir the boy's anger. The kid was watching him, carefully. Weary, but also appraising. He didn't react to the slight against his group. Collin was impressed. He showed great restraint and control over his emotions.

Collin caught the end of her rolling her eyes at him.

"They kept me alive because I promised them a share of the cure."

"Is that yours to bargain with?"

Anna opened her mouth to answer, but he cut her off.

"That's on top of what you've already stolen? You delivered every drop of BT76 that we have to them," Collin said.

Her mouth dropped open at the accusation. She sputtered and crossed her arms over her chest. "You…"

"I know what you did."

"You know nothing," she said defiantly.

Collin reached into his cargo pocket and pulled out the radio that he and Koby heard her talk to the Vipers on. He dangled it between them, swinging it by the antennae.

Her eyes grew wide, she gasped and covered her mouth. Her cheeks blazed noticeably red even in the glow of the torches.

Anna turned to the boy and shoved him. "Run, Hunter. Run!"

They both took off like frightened deer, bounding through the fields.

"Damn it," Collin said, dropping his rifle and taking off after her.

Behind him, Collin heard shouts and before he'd closed half the distance to Anna, he heard and then saw a flare overhead. It cast odd, shifting shadows over the area as the flare drifted down slowly from its parachute.

Before they reached the midpoint of the field, Collin caught up and kicked her foot. Anna grunted as she slammed into the ground. A cloud of dust billowed around her.

Collin looked unsuccessfully for the boy. It was too late, he melted into the inky darkness.

Collin turned and jogged back to Anna. She had rolled onto her back and was panting. He stopped next to her and put his hands on his knees, breathing hard. They sprinted more than one hundred yards.

"Goddamnit, Anna," he said between big breaths.

He stood up and looked toward the bridge. Pastor Pendell stood at the apex of the bridge, with his hands on his hips. Even from a distance, Collin could tell the pastor was furious.

"Come on," Collin said, holding out his hand to help her up. "Don't run again, please."

Anna sat up and looked down at herself. She shook her head and bits of dirt and pieces of vegetation fell out of her hair. Another flare popped and burst into light. The two beacons made shadows dance behind Anna as she stood up, shook her head again and dusted herself off.

She looked right at Collin. "Don't trust the pastor. He's not a good man, Collin."

He gave her a knowing smile and nod.

"And Logan was with HAGS this whole time. Did you know that?"

Collin grabbed her arm to dissuade her from running again. They began to walk toward the bridge.

"You know your mom has been worried sick about you."

"She'll be fine. This is more important. You can't trust them," Anna insisted. "Major Logan wanted to start a coup against the pastor. He was going to kill him and take over Goshen."

Collin looked at her. He sensed the truth. "I always knew there was something off about him, but I can't pass any judgment until he's here to defend himself. Besides, the pastor will be sure to have his say as well."

She smiled weakly when he mentioned Logan. "Just don't let them kill me."

"I doubt it will come to that, Anna."

"You don't know him like I do." She gestured toward the bridge.

The pastor started walking toward them, which confused Collin. He should wait on the bridge where there's more light and safer if the Vipers still intended to spring a trap. The Pastor stopped when he reached the bag Anna had dropped.

Pastor Pendell tilted his head like a curious dog as he looked at the bag. Then he picked it up and began to tug at the zipper, it must have been stuck because it took him a few tries.

"Pastor, no!" Collin shouted. They still didn't know what was inside and he didn't want the pastor to set off a booby trap. "Drop the bag."

He was too late. Pastor Pendell held the bag by the handles and spread it open.

Collin gripped Anna's arm and hustled her along. By the time they had closed to within twenty yards of the pastor, his face contorted, whether in pain or rage Collin couldn't tell.

"Secure Anna," Collin said, motioning to the Eagles that had escorted the pastor from the bridge. Two of the men jogged over to comply with his order.

Pendell's eyes widened wildly and he squealed. A strange piercing sound that made everyone nearby wince. The bag dropped from the Pastor's hands. He cringed away from it like whatever was inside might strike out at him. The Eagles hesitated and turned back toward the pastor.

Collin pushed Anna toward one of the men. The soldier took her arm. Collin jogged over to Pastor Pendell and took his arm. The holy man looked like he might topple over. He was as pale as Collin had ever seen a black man get.

"What's in the bag?" Collin asked. He gave Pendell a light shake to get his attention, but the pastor just stared at the bag with a look of utter disgust on his face. He look at Anna and said, "What's in the bag, Anna?"

She just shook her head.

Collin got the impression she knew, but didn't want to say. He let go of Pastor Pendell, walked over to the bag and picked it up. A strange, sickening smell wafted up at him. The last flare was nearly to the ground and it's light was waning but he could see something dark and twisting in the bag. It looked like string or rope but when he pulled the bag's handles apart and took a closer look under the dim light he realized it was hair.

Hair? Twisted, damp, and sweaty looking hair.

Collin's gut twisted itself into a knot as his body reacted to the sight. He still wasn't fully conscious of what exactly he was looking at. He looked up at Anna. She had a sad look on her face, her hand was covering her mouth and tears glimmered in her big, beautiful eyes.

Collin looked at Pastor Pendell, who knelt, muttering something, likely a prayer.

He released one of the bag handles and slowly reached into the bag. His knuckles brushed against the inside of the bag, the rough heavy-duty nylon soon giving way to a wet, sticky texture. Collin grasped the stuff he saw inside and slowly pulled whatever it was out of the bag.

As he pulled his hand out of the bag, holding its contents between his fingers, he hand to pull the bag down with his other hand because it became stuck. He could see that it was hair.

Then an ear emerged from behind the edge of the bag. Collin's eyes sprung wide at the realization. His skin suddenly felt a chill and he had the urge to drop whatever it was he was holding. With massive effort, he freed the contents from the bag and held it high.

Everyone gasped at the sight.

Twisting in Collin's grasp was the severed head of Major Logan. Torn skin, veins and connective tissue dangled from the portion of neck that was supposed to be attached to his torso. The knot in his stomach cinched itself tightly and Collin had to fight the urge to hurl right there. Amazingly, he retained his grip on the man's hair.

Pastor Pendell yelled in anguish. The sound snapped Collin out of his daze. He became hyper-aware of the others and their reactions.

Rather than holding it aloft like a morbid lantern, he picked up the bag and shoved it back inside.

Pendell yelled again, angrier this time.

Even with the head covered, the image of Major Logan's eyes rolled up in his head, his mouth frozen in a scream, and the flecks of blood splatter around his mouth and across his cheeks, would be burned into his memory forever. One of the Eagles stepped forward to take the bag, but Collin raised his hand to stop him. As unsettling as it was, he would handle it himself.

"No. Nooooo," Pastor Pendell bellowed. Then he sprung up, quick as a rabbit, pointed at Anna and yelled, "Shoot her."

Every stared at him.

"Whoa, wh-" Collin started to say.

"No. I want her dead. Now!" Pastor Pendell jabbed his finger in her direction. "Davies, I order you to shoot this traitorous bitch right now. If you find that little rat she slunk back here with, shoot him too."

"I had nothing to do with this," Anna said, pleading with the pastor. "Please, you have to believe me."

"We will not be swayed by your evil words, witch woman," the pastor raved.

Davies stepped forward and unsnapped the holster that held his silver Colt 1911. He racked the slide as he raised it and aimed it right at Anna's head.

Collin held his hand up and stepped in-between Davies and Anna. "Stand down, Davies. This isn't how things are going down."

Davies looked at Collin briefly then refocused on Anna. His gun was still raised although Collin was pushing it away. He gritted his teeth and said, "I don't take orders from you, Collin."

"Shoot her. Damnit, Davies. Shoot her," Pastor Pendell said. His face contorted in rage.

"Without Major Logan, you take your orders from me, Davies," Collin said. "Listen to me. We will put her in detainment and hold a hearing. We don't know what happened and we don't execute our own."

"Davies, we are Holy warriors. We must punish the wicked," Pastor Pendell said, spittle flecked his chin. His eyes were wide and wild. "Do your duty."

"Nathan, look at me," Anna said softly. "You know me. You've known me all my life. You know I would never consent to this barbaric behavior. I didn't kill Logan, I didn't steal anything."

Nathan Davies shifted slightly, but continued to point the gun at Anna.

"Nathan, please don't kill me. Don't help this man who has caused so much unnecessary pain and strife for all of us." She pointed at the pastor. "Pastor Pendell is just trying to protect himself and all of the lies he's built his position on."

"Lies! Don't let her heathen tongue confuse you, Davies. Shoot her now," Pastor Pendell screamed at him. "Shoot her! The Lord demands it."

Collin saw Nathan blink a few times and glance at Pastor Pendell and Anna. Then he flicked the safety off with his thumb.

"Don't do this, Davies. If you pull that trigger you will be put on trial alongside Pastor Pendell," Collin said.

Pastor Pendell stalked closer to them, sidling up to Davies. He stretched out his arm, parallel the Nathan's gun arm and pointed at Anna. "Shoot the whore," he said softly. His voice sounded snake-like and sinister, it sent a chill down Collin's neck and made his shoulders shiver.

"The last person to call me that ended up with his head in a bag," Anna said through clenched teeth.

Davies looked at Collin and it was plain he was struggling with the decision.

"Put down the gun, Davies. Put it down and save yourself a lifetime of regret," Collin said evenly.

Pastor Pendell glared at Collin. Then he dropped his arm and leaned in close to Davies' ear. The pastor's breath made Davies tilt his head to avoid the awkward closeness.

"You will shoot her or you and your family will be banished from Goshen and fed to the Vipers," Pendell hissed. "Only the saved will be saved."

Anna pleaded with him softly in the background.

Collin shook his head. "Lower the gun, man. Don't do this." He stood ready to knock the gun away if he thought Davies was going to shoot.

With a heavy sigh, his arm dropped and Davies pointed the gun at the ground. "I can't do it," he said, starting to sob. His gun thumped into the dirt.

Collin stepped forward onto the gun so he couldn't change his mind.

"Arrest Pastor Pendell," he said to the other Eagles.

Anna dropped down to her knees, crying.

Two men immediately stepped forward and grabbed the pastor.

"You did the right thing, Davies," Collin said, patting the man on the shoulder.

Pastor Pendell roared like a wild beast and twisted out of their grasp. Collin barely had a chance to react before Pendell slammed into him. Collin staggered back a few steps and tripped in a shallow furrow. Davies splayed out in the dirt next to him.

Collin glanced back just in time to see the Eagles diving for Pastor Pendell as his gnarled hands wrapped around the pistol.

A shot rang out just before they tumbled to the dirt, wrestling for control of the gun.

Chapter Thirty

Anna's body jerked slightly as the bullet penetrated her breastbone and tore through her vital organs.

In a split second, her eyes rolled back and she slumped to the ground. Blood trickled out of the small hole in her chest, while the rest poured out of her into the dusky earth below her.

Collin couldn't hear the anguished growl that he could feel rumbling in his throat. The blast of the gun was still ringing in his ears. He scrambled up, making it to his feet at the same time as Davies. Collin went after Pendell who was thrashing wildly trying to fight off two Eagles.

He walked over to where Pendell's head was poking out from the pile. Without a word, Collin pressed his boot onto the throat of the pretender lying on the ground. Pastor Pendell tensed up, his eyes swiveling to look at Collin while his head was pinned in place.

"You fucked up, pastor." Collin pulled his Colt M45 from his thigh holster and pointed it down the pastor's head. "Pick him up."

When the two Eagles had his hands and arms bound and secured, Collin moved his foot and the two men forced Pastor Pendell to stand.

The pastor must have felt a new wave of defiance come over him because he started screaming about how they were all heathens and they'd face judgment. He kept repeating, "Only the saved will be saved."

Collin just stared at him like the idiot he was. Pendell must have felt the disgust in Collin's gaze. He spit in Collin's face.

Bad move.

Collin punched the pastor in the face with two quick jabs. Then he clubbed him over the head with the butt of his Colt. Pastor Pendell crumpled and the two men had to adjust their grip to keep him standing.

"Get him out of here," he said, wiping the saliva from his face. "Lock him up and keep two guards on him at all times."

"You," he said, pointing to a young woman, an Eagle. She stood on the bridge among the carpenters and others that had been working on the wall, all of them witnesses to what happened in the field. "Go get help for Anna. Hurry!"

She blinked a couple of times in surprise at being called out. She quickly turned and pushed her way through the crowd to carry out the order.

Collin walked over and knelt beside Anna. He felt her neck for a pulse. Nothing.

Her chest wasn't moving with breath and he couldn't feel any air escaping her nose or opened mouth. He closed her eyes and stood up. Collin stayed behind with Anna's body and the bag that contained Major Logan's head. An Eagle stayed with him while they waited for others to arrive and help them move her body.

"Keep an eye out for that kid," Collin said. "Or any other Vipers."

The man nodded at him, took position on the far side of Anna's body, as if shielding her from the darkness and turned to face the field.

Several Eagles emerged from the crowd and ran over. They carried a large green cloth stretcher, essentially a heavy-duty green canvas rectangle with thick handle straps sewn onto the corners and the midpoint.

"Come on. Let's go," Collin said waving them over.

The single gunshot must have drawn the crowd. He could see light emanating from beyond the bridge which suggested dozens and dozens of people. From the last few battles with the Vipers, Goshenites had fled to the safety of their homes. He wondered if the wall emboldened people to gather around the bridge.

Two of them spread the carrier on the ground. The rest of them gently lifted Anna and placed her body on the cloth. Then each of them grabbed a handle, with Collin in the middle.

"Three, two, one, lift," he said. They stood up in unison and began to carry Anna toward the bridge.

Before they reached the bridge, Collin spotted Dr. Julie Horner and Kobyashi standing together, watching them approach. Their presence wasn't a surprise. Julie was always the go-to person for medical assistance. But this was for Anna and Anna was already gone from this life. Dr. Horner wasn't needed for that.

Koby looked around at the group, down at the stretcher and then fixed his gaze on Collin, concern apparent in his eyes. Gritting his teeth, Collin met Koby's gaze, then looked quickly at Julie, confirming Koby's fears. Koby gave a slight nod and slowly raised his arm to her shoulders. This way he was prepared to offer her support if she fell, or comfort if she began to sob. She must not have thought it was odd because it looked like she shifted slightly to lean into his embrace.

Collin's chest felt hollow. He only knew Anna for a short time, but he'd liked her. He also liked her mom, quite a bit. They were strong, smart and kind women. Wonderful people to know.

"Group, halt," Collin said. He wanted to give Dr. Horner some warning before she saw her daughter's bloody corpse being carried up to her. The Eagles slowed to a halt and Collin released his hold and jogged the last twenty meters or so to the bridge.

He was suddenly overcome by emotion, which he fought back with great effort. His eyes stung and his throat felt thick. He cleared his throat and scowled to hold off the tide of emotion that threatened to burst through his armor.

"Dr. Horner…Julie." Collin took a deep breath and looked up at her. She turned her head, looking at him sideways, not sure what to expect but obviously unsettled by his behavior.

She must have passed the runner he sent to get help for Anna. Had the soldier thought it best not to be the one to inform her mother? He let out the breath and the words just tumbled out. "I'm so sorry, Julie. I regret-um…Anna was shot. She died instantly. My Eagles are bringing her back into Goshen."

Dr. Horner gasped and slumped, but Koby held her up. "No, no. It can't be…My baby, my poor baby," she moaned. She looked shocked as tears slipped from her eyes, down her slender features and dripped off her chin.

The crowd began to murmur and stare at Collin with a mix of anger and mistrust. They must have seen Pastor Pendell being taken to jail, or if he'd woken up, maybe they'd heard his demented raving.

Sensing the need to regain the initiative from the crowd before it turned into a mob, he climbed up on the railing of the bridge, and laid a hand on the wall for support. He raised his gun in the air and when the crowd failed to quiet down, he fired a shot into the air. Silence fell upon them so quickly that Collin could hear the shell casing clatter on the wood below him.

From his perch above the crowd, he could see Dr. Horner and Koby following the Eagles that carried Anna's body toward the hospital. He hoped that Dr. Horner had enough strength, because the town would need her and her skills in the coming days.

"Citizens of Goshen, tonight has been a tragic one for us. Two of our citizens, each one a leader in their own right, are dead," Collin said. Murmurs rippled through the crowd. "Major Logan is dead, viciously murdered by the Vipers. They sent Anna back to us with proof. She was sent to negotiate with us for medicine and a special medication that her mother, Dr. Horner, has been working on."

Collin met the curious gazes of the onlookers with his own sorrow plain on his face. "She was shot dead before our very eyes."

Confusion swept through the crowd. "Who would want to kill Anna?" a woman asked.

"Who shot her?" a man yelled.

Collin held his hands up to stave off the torrent of questions. "Pastor Pendell," he said, pausing for a beat to let it sink in. "Pastor Pendell shot and killed Anna Horner."

"It's true. I saw it happen and so did all of the work crew. We were all here when Anna returned to us," a man said.

It was the carpenter that he spoke to earlier; Collin nodded his thanks to the man.

A stunned silence fell upon the crowd again, so he took the opportunity to plow on. "As acting Commander of the Eagles, I have ordered Pastor Pendell to be arrested and detained for the crime of murder. Anna returned with news about Major Logan, the pastor accused her of terrible things and tried to have an Eagle execute her. When he was stymied, he took it into his hands to punish her on his own without a trial. This is not behavior that we can tolerate in Goshen. We may be the last fragment of humanity left over from our great nation. Justice by trial is one tradition we should carry on."

Collin took a breath and bowed his head for a moment. There was more bad news, bad because it wasn't good. "As for the Eagles that accompanied Major Logan, we don't have any definitive information regarding their whereabouts. We will consider them as missing in action. They will not be forgotten."

He looked at the citizens gathered around him. All of them looked back at him, expectantly.

"We have turmoil here that needs to be settled, no doubt about it. But don't forget for one second that the real enemy is out there," he said, pointing out beyond the fields. "The Vipers want each and every one of us dead. They want what is rightfully ours. We cannot let that happen just because we have some house cleaning to do. Make no mistake, Goshen is at war."

"We are at war: not about land, food, or medication, but our very existence. The Vipers will be coming for us and we must prepare. Steel your mind against fear, for there's a very real possibility that each and every one of you will be needed to defend our homes. We must crush their assault. We will end the Vipers once and for all."

Heads nodded in agreement.

"I recommend we all pray for each other. Hell, while you're at it, pray for the Vipers as well. Pray that if there is a God, he forgives us," Collin said. He looked around at the Eagles, pointed to a few of them, and shouted, "Eagles strike!"

"Vipers die!"

He felt proud of their strength and resolve. "Eagles strike," he shouted again.

"Vipers die!" The town shouted back. Their rallying cry echoed through the valley.

Collin looked at the church. He knew he had to go confront Pastor Pendell about his actions. He began to climb down from the railing. Sensing that the action was over, the crowd began to disperse.

He walked over to the bag that held Major Logan's head and lifted it up. He felt tense, not worried, but anxious at the coming battle that he could feel brewing. Collin handed the sack to Davies and told him to deliver it to the morgue and under no circumstances should he allow anyone other than medical staff open the bag.

"You understand, Davies?"

Davies blinked a few times and accepted the bag. His face looked pale.

"Yes, sir."

"Just don't look at it okay. Get it to the hospital and then get back to your duties," he said. "Stay alert."

"Stay alive, sir." Davies nodded and started walking toward the hospital.

Collin watched him go and then turned to stare into the darkness beyond the wall.

He couldn't deny the seed of fear that roiled in his gut.

"Whatever the future holds," he muttered to himself. "We will prevail."

Chapter Thirty-One

Collin approached the church and walked around to the side door that lead down to the basement.

The old detention center in the police station had been destroyed at some point before Collin's awakening. The one the town had built to replace it had been destroyed in the Eagle's Bar attack. Lacking any other suitable locations, the pastor insisted on an improvised detention cell in the basement of the church.

Collin felt it was a strange location. Pastor Pendell had told him a story about an archbishop in medieval England, who also had his own prisons. He was certain that Pastor Pendell never imagined himself in one of the cells.

Lighting was dim in the basement, it wasn't a modern space, that was for sure. A cord ran along the upper corner where the ceiling and wall met. A pair of work lights lit up the hallway. On one side of the hall were two detention cells with crude bars welded together. Over the bars, they welded sheet metal that looked like it was salvaged from old cars and trucks.

One small slot about two feet off the floor, was left open to pass food through. A square was left open at eye level. Unlike the slot, the square had bars on the inside and outside. That way whoever stood in the hallway could easily communicate with the person in the cell. The two cells were well built, even if they looked like a patchwork.

On either side of the door stood an Eagle, armed with a pistol and baton. Given the tight confines of the hallway, it wasn't practical to carry rifles.

It was virtually silent inside, save for the swish of Collin's clothing and the slosh of the small bottle of water he brought with him. His gun thumped slightly against his thigh. He took a few moments to gather his thoughts and formulated a plan for confronting the pastor.

Collin smirked at the savage appearance of the space, but quickly composed himself before the Eagles could notice. He didn't want them to get the wrong impression about his intentions. This was not a power play on his part; he never intended to take a leadership role. It just happened.

A strong sense of justice ran through Collin's veins. He did intend to make sure that justice was served. Detaining the pastor also presented a unique opportunity to get to the root of the corruption problem in Goshen. With the revelation that Major Logan was a part of HAGS, there was no telling what other secrets and conspiracies had festered over the years.

"Wait in the room for me. Stay alert in case a mob forms," Collin said, holding out his hand for the key to the cell.

"Yes, sir," they said in unison. The woman handed him the key to the cell. They walked away.

Collin stepped up to the door and looked inside. A small amount of light came from inside the cell. Koby installed strips of LED lights on the ceiling, high above where most detainees could reach. Roughhewn rock walls cast jagged shadows on the bare concrete floor. The cell featured a short plastic chair that would look more at home in a daycare center, and a thin sleeping pad with one military blanket. A metal toilet and sink combo unit, from the police station was bolted to the wall. Given the state of post-fever life, it was a rather impressive cell.

"You awake yet?" Collin said, eyeing the man who lay on the floor.

No response.

Collin didn't worry about being overpowered by the pastor. In the unlikely event he was, there were two guards in the hallway. So, he unlocked the door, lifted the large bar that reinforced the door, and pulled it open. He stood in the doorway, waiting to see if the pastor would move. He didn't.

Collin stepped in and nudged him with the toe of his boot. Still nothing.

He didn't have time for this shit. He grabbed Pendell and rolled him over. Kneeling beside Pendell, he gave him a quick pat down to see what, if anything, the man had on him. Collin found a set of keys, a silver crucifix on a silver chain, and a small pocketknife, all of which he removed and pocketed.

He stood up, flipped open the mouthpiece on the small sports bottle and splashed water on Pendell's face.

No response.

Collin splashed more water on his face and gave him a slap on the cheek. The pastor's eyes fluttered, he groaned and turned his head sputtering as water dribbled off his swollen face.

"Wake up," Collin said, pouring the rest of the water on Pendell.

Spluttering and holding up a hand to block the water, Pendell rolled onto his side and sat up. When he got comfortable, Pendell looked around the room through squinted eyes. He looked up at Collin.

"Is it true?" he mumbled. Collin noticed that one of his teeth was missing and wondered if that was from him or one of the Eagles, not that he cared either way.

"What's that?"

"Is it true?" he asked again. "About the cure. Is it true?"

"Yes, apparently it is. Anna seemed quite sure although I have yet to hear it from Dr. Horner. I trust what Anna told me," he said.

Pastor Pendell held out his hands, palms up and looked up at the lights. "Praise to Jesus. Thank you, Lord."

"Shut your mouth, Pendell." Collin scowled at him and his fake piety. "The time for your charades has passed."

Pastor Pendell scrambled to his feet. Collin stepped back to block the door, just in case.

"We must inoculate everyone. Right now. Get out of my way and follow me to the hospital," Pendell said.

"You're not going anywhere," Collin said, holding out his hand to stop him.

Pastor Pendell looked at him confused. "I order you to move. We must inoculate everyone now. There's no more BT76 coming."

"What do you mean, no more is coming?"

"They're never going to deliver more BT76." Pastor Pendell rushed toward Collin.

Stepping forward quickly, Collin shoved him back. He didn't use a lot of force, but the man practically flew into the wall.

Pendell growled and leapt forward. "Move, heathen!" he screamed.

Collin landed an uppercut. He enjoyed the clacking sound as the Pastor's teeth collided.

"This is for Anna," he said, punching Pendell in the stomach. Then he shoved him back again. Pendell hit the wall and slide down into a seated position, gasping for breath. A trickle of blood streamed down his chin.

"You'll burn in hell for this," Pendell said. He leaned over, glaring at Collin as he did so and spit a glob of blood onto the floor.

"Perhaps," he said. "By the way, what is a 'pastor' doing with a pocket knife?" He held it up so it was clearly visible.

"That's mine. I'll have your hand for stealing from me."

Collin cocked an eyebrow at that. He couldn't help the smirk that spread on his face as he looked down at Pendell.

Pendell stood up. Once he was up, he leaned back against the sink and glowered at Collin. His shoulders hunched forward and his arms hung limp at his sides.

Collin leaned against the frame of the door and just watched Pendell.

"You know, considering the revelation that Major Logan was working for HAGS, I have to wonder if you're doing the same."

Pastor Pendell didn't say a word.

"What do you say to that?" Collin asked. "Is that why you killed Anna? To hide the truth?"

"Only the saved will be saved," he replied.

"What exactly do you mean by that? I get the feeling it has less to do with God and a whole lot more to do with who you decide to keep around." Collin crossed his arms and watched his detainee closely.

Pendell smiled. It was a sinister smile. The look in his eye chilled Collin to his core.

"Like that foolish, old woman?"

Collin snapped up, moving away from the doorframe. "What did you say?"

"Doris was not one of the saved."

"You're not really a pastor are you?" Collin tried to change the subject; he didn't want to beat the man to death. "Did you pick up that title during the fevered time?"

"Wouldn't it burn you up to know she didn't have to die? But you left me no choice."

"What?" Collin stepped forward; his hands were already balled into fists. "If you have something to say, say it."

"Only the saved," Pastor Pendell said, leaning back, spreading his arms and smiling at the ceiling. "Will be saved."

Pendell reached down suddenly and flung the plastic chair at Collin. He blocked the chair with his forearm. He connected with a hook on Pendell's cheek before he threw an elbow into his chest, emptying his lungs. Pendell punched at Collin, but it was a slow swing. Collin caught his arm, moved his hips to the side, and threw Pendell over his back. He slammed into the wall with a dull thump and crumpled to the floor, again.

"What did you say," Collin said. He straddled the man and punched him again in the chest.

Pendell groaned and winced.

"What?"

"She was worthless. She was expendable. I couldn't waste anything on her," Pendell said. He began to cackle. "She couldn't be saved. I wouldn't allow it," he shouted.

Collin punched him twice in the face. Hate burned in his chest like a furnace, but a voice in his head told him to stop. With all of his strength, Collin stopped and stood up. He wiped sweat off his face and spit on the ground next to Pendell.

"That's for Doris, you monster." He pulled the keys out of his pocket and jingled them. "You think on your sins while I go take a look around."

Pendell saw the keys and scrambled on the floor. "No! Those are mine. Give them back, heathen."

He clawed at Collin, and got his hands kicked away in return.

Collin backed out of the room and slammed the door shut. He locked it and lowered the bar.

"Hey," Pendell shouted. "Hey! The righteous will overpower the heathens."

"Whatever." Collin shook his head and turned away. He looked back when he heard Pendell slam into the door. It held firm. There was no reason to think the pastor could escape by ramming his way out.

"Remember, heathen," Pendell said, pressing his face against the bars in the window. "Only the saved will be saved."

Collin slammed his palm against the door, causing the prisoner to erupt in a wild-eyed cackle.

"You're all doomed," Pendell shouted in glee. "Only the saved will be saved."

Something about that phrase always rubbed Collin wrong. Now he wondered if it was in fact some kind of secret message. A tickle in the back of his mind made him think it had something to do with the selection process, and who was and wasn't administered BT76 when supplies ran low. Doris had practically told him that the process was more of a popularity contest, than any sort of objective selection.

Major Logan was HAGS. Did it have something to do with them? Collin shook his head. He hoped that with the keys, he could find some sort of evidence one way or another.

Anna said Logan planned to overthrow Pendell. So maybe he wasn't HAGS, but there was something fishy going on. The two men had seemed close and he was curious to find out why.

He thought about the church and realized that there wasn't much to inspect. The church had always been open and people came and went whenever they wanted to. Pastor Pendell's office seemed like the first place to search but he'd been in there many times.

Within the office were a pair of file cabinets and he'd seen the contents. They held church records and various copies of paperwork from before the fever. The desk had small drawers that Collin had never seen. However, Pendell never acted secretive about them.

From where he stood in the hallway, he thought through each section. Upstairs was Pendell's residence, then there was the office, and the main church area filled with pews, and then the basement. In the basement were two detention rooms, the hallway, a storage closet, and the room that had served as a medic unit following the blast at the Eagle's Bar.

He looked around. There were two doors at the end of the hall. Ones he never opened, or seen open, before.

Collin walked down the hall to the doors. Neither door had a sign or markings of any kind. He tried the first door handle but it was locked and wouldn't budge. The second door was just like the first.

He bent down to look at the locks on the door. A manufacturer's logo pressed into the metal above the keyhole, so he began to search through Pendell's sizeable key ring for a matching key. Buried roughly halfway through the keys was one that looked promising.

He glanced down the hallway, feeling almost like he was doing something naughty. Then took a breath and pushed the key into the keyhole.

Only the tip made it in before it stopped. Collin walked to the door closest to the detention cells and tried it there.

With a satisfying grind of metal on metal, the key sank in. He turned it and was rewarded with the click of the deadbolt sliding open. The door handle still didn't turn. Collin looked at the key ring. He found the correct key to unlock the handle was right next to the one he just used.

Finally, he pushed open the door. It was dark inside and the light from the hall wasn't sufficient to light up anything other than the blank space where the door swung inward. He felt along the wall for a light switch. After a moment of sliding his hand along the wall, he found it. He clicked it on and was disappointed to find it only contained supplies. Shelves lined the walls inside. They held cleaning supplies, like bleach and rubber gloves, a few large stacks of bibles, some folded cloth, a box labeled "candles, white" and various other church stuff.

He turned off the light and went back to the door at the end of the hall.

Finding the key took another minute of flipping through the keys. Sliding it into the lock, he twisted it and the door unlocked. He repeated the steps with the door handle lock and opened the door. Same thing as before, he had to feel around for a light switch. He found it.

When the lights came on, he saw boxes and boxes of BT76.

Collin gasped and cursed. "That bastard," he muttered through clenched teeth.

He looked down the hallway but it was still clear, so he stepped inside. A quick count of the boxes that he could see suggested roughly four hundred doses of the medication.

He leaned against the wall for support. He couldn't believe it. All of those people, fifty something souls who died recently because of the supply issue that HAGS claimed in their note. Yet Pastor Pendell had hundreds of doses of medication the entire time.

Collin's heart thumped in his chest, faster and faster. Fury filled him from head to toe. He wanted to smash Pastor Pendell's head into the wall of his cell until there was nothing left but mush. Instead, he pounded his fist against the wall as he thought of Doris needlessly dying and the others who were suffering and dying.

Pastor Pendell was no man of God. He was no true pastor at all. He would face justice from a furious town, Collin knew that deep down to his core. He make sure of that.

Collin turned off the light and closed the door. He locked both locks.

He took a deep breath and stood there, staring at the door. Sickness burned the back of his throat. It was here the whole time. He leaned his head against the cool door and sucked in more deep breaths to calm down.

After a few minutes of composing himself, he walked back to the cell and looked inside. Pendell was sitting on the floor, leaning his head back against the wall. He had a satisfied grin plastered on his face.

"You sick sonofabitch," Collin said, slamming his hand against the door. "Why?" he asked through clenched teeth. His jaw muscles flexed and his voice was low, yet menacing.

Pendell's head slowly turned in Collin's direction. His eyes popped open, followed by a wicked sneer.

"You still don't get it, do you?" he said in a venomous tone. "How many times do I have to tell you?"

His voice was rose quickly as Pendell questioned his captor, booming off the walls, and echoing down the hall.

"Only the saved," he screamed at Collin, pumping his arms for emphasis. "Will be saved."

"You let people die. People that didn't need to die," Collin said evenly. "You can repeat that bullshit as much as you want, but there is nothing that will save you."

Collin turned and walked away, ignoring the furious rantings behind him. When he reached the large room that had once served as a hospital, he looked at the two Eagles and shook his head.

"Guard the door and under no circumstance are you to release the prisoner to anyone," Collin said. "I will hold onto the key, so you don't fall prey to the silver tongued snake in that room. Stay here until you receive further orders."

"Yes, sir." They spoke in unison and walked down the hall to take up station on either side of the door.

He let out a huge sigh, releasing the tension that was building up, and threatening to explode. He carefully rolled his neck, stretching the muscles, while he refocused his attention. Collin should go check on Dr. Horner, check the guard rotation and make sure the snipers were fresh and alert.

Not wanting to waste any more time, Collin strode up the stairs and exited into the night air. He realized just how musty smelling the basement was and was thankful he didn't have to spend much time down there.

Even from the front of the church, he could tell that work had already resumed on the wall. Hammers banged against wood, saws ground away at tree fibers and torches glowed in the dark of the early evening.

Collin felt a sudden surge of pride in the men and women of Goshen. Their will to survive, their work ethic and resilience was incredible. He didn't know if they were backing him or just afraid for their lives, but either way, they understood the wall was important and they were doing whatever it took to get it up right away.

Collin shoved his hands in his pockets and stared down at the ground while he thought through the problems the town would face in the coming days. Gravel crunched under his feet as he walked along the road toward the hospital.

Light flicked across the path in front of him. He looked up and watched as the light approached him at a slow and easy pace. Collin didn't carry a flashlight, he liked being enveloped in the darkness. His night vision was sufficient most nights for him to navigate the town without any problem.

Collin stopped walking when it became obvious that the person walked toward him. The light swung lazily across the road in time with their gait. Before he could tell who it was, he heard Koby's voice.

"Collin, is that you?" he asked.

"Yeah, it's me," Collin said. "I'm headed to the hospital to see Dr. Horner."

"No need," Koby said.

"I'm right here," she said.

He strode toward her and pulled her into a hug. Dr. Horner buried her face in his shoulder. Her hair tickled his chin but he didn't move, he just held her.

"I'm so sorry, Julie." He stroked her hair. "I'm sorry I couldn't protect her."

She shook her head against his shoulder, and then looked up at him. Their eyes met. Tears trickled down her face.

"It's not your fault," Julie said. "I…I heard what you did."

It was his turn to shake his head.

"I didn't do anything. I had no idea the crazy bastard would try something so stupid." Collin felt the anger rushing back, heat crawled up his neck. He fought it back. There would be a time to release it, but right now was not the time.

He beat down the demon inside him but he couldn't hide his own tears. One slid off his jaw and landed on Julie's hand. She looked at him and held his face. She kissed him lightly on the cheek. After another embrace, she pulled away, wiping her face with her hands.

Collin saw that Koby was also wiping away tears. He gave Koby a questioning look.

Koby shook his head, no. He hadn't told Julie about her daughter's actions.

No point in it now, he figured. Better to let her memory be a proud one, rather than belittled as foolish love and clouded by controversy.

Julie finished wiping her nose with tissue. She balled it up and shoved it in her pants pocket. She tucked hair behind her ear and straightened up.

"My daughter's death will not be meaningless," she said confidently. "She will not be just another one lost to this cruel new world. With her help, we developed the treatment to eradicate the fever."

"That's fantastic, Julie." Collin tried to smile.

"I brought one with me for you to see." Julie pulled out a syringe filled with bright red fluid.

Collin held it carefully. Koby shined the flashlight on it so he could see. He wasn't sure what he should do with it because he was already immune. It was impressive that she was able to create this given the limited supplies the town had.

"How effective is it?" Collin asked. He was skeptical give the results of the previous version.

"The new treatment protocol has a ninety-eight percent success rate. The remaining two percent will still require BT76," Julie said. She added softly, "But the treatment will not be fatal."

No one else would suffer the fate of Doris. A fate that came at Pendell's order. Collin just nodded. He felt a sense of relief though; poor Doris had suffered terribly in her last moments. A fact that would likely haunt him for the rest of his life.

"Well, if only two percent will continue to need BT76 that won't be a problem for a long time," he said with a weak smile.

Julie and Koby glanced at each other then back at Collin.

He turned and motioned for them to follow. "Come on. There's something I have to show you."

They followed Collin back to the church. He led them around to the side of the church to the basement door. Just as they started down the steps leading into the basement, someone near the front of the church yelled for him.

"Collin, er, General War, sir!" yelled a young man. "General War."

Koby gave him a funny look.

"Look at what you started," Collin said to Koby.

Koby held his hands up in defense. The grin on his face gave him away though.

"You gotta admit, General War does have a nice ring to it," Koby said.

Collin shook his head in exasperation. "Wait downstairs for me. I'll be right back."

"Okay," Dr. Horner said.

"See ya soon, General." Koby winked at him.

Collin rolled his eyes and raced back up the steps.

The Private who was yelling for him nearly bumped into him at the top of the staircase.

"Oh, General, sir. We need you at the bridge," PVT Gibbs said nervously. "Sir."

"Right. Okay, lead the way Private."

"Sir, yes, sir." PVT Gibbs turned to run back toward the bridge. He glanced back to make sure Collin was following.

"Double-time, Private."

As the came around the edge of the church, Collin could see what had stirred up the guards. Huge fires, like a bonfire celebration, burned in the fields. Their glow reached above the wall, casting jagged shadows across the road.

"Wait," Collin shouted. He ran back to the stairwell to the basement.

"Koby, get up here."

He saw his friend peek his head up the staircase. "What?"

"Get up here."

Koby ran up the stairs.

"Go ring the bell, then meet me on the bridge," Collin said.

"Huh?"

"Ring the fucking church bell," Collin shouted. Without waiting for a response from Koby, he ran back to the front and met up with PVT Gibbs. "Let's go."

Halfway to the bridge, the alarm bell began to ring, alerting everyone in Goshen of a pending attack. A few moments later, they arrived at the bridge.

Collin was breathing heavy; PVT Gibbs was fast.

"Good pace, Gibbs."

"Thank you, sir. SGT Dale is over there," he said pointing across the bridge.

"Thanks. Carry on, Private."

"Yes, sir." PVT Gibbs saluted, then spun on his heel and jogged away.

Collin walked over to SGT Dale, watching as hundreds of torches blazed in the darkness. They moved back and forth in the forest at the edge of the farmland.

"What's the situation, Sergeant?"

SGT Dale turned and saw that it was Collin. He started to snap to attention but Collin said, "At ease. What's the situation?"

"A few minutes ago these huge fires erupted in the fields and then the torches started to light up as well," SGT Dale said, gesturing at the Vipers in the tree line. "It looks like they're ready for that fight you mentioned, sir."

"Looks like it," Collin said. He knew the wall was only at seventy-five percent completion, but the section of river that had yet to be walled up was rapid. An unlikely point of attack. They would likely go for the bridge.

Torch after torch lit up. Hundreds of torches, held by hundreds of Vipers. The forest glowed orange from all of the torches casting light, almost as if it was consumed by a wildfire. He could make out the shadows of the Vipers holding torches and wondered how many it would take to overrun the bridge.

Slowly the line of torches began to move forward into the fields.

"Christ, they're moving in," Collin muttered to himself. He turned to SGT Dale. "Get everyone in position and put out the word for the residents to arm up and man the designated choke points."

"Roger that, sir." SGT Dale jogged off to make it happen.

Collin walked over the guard station on the town side of the bridge. "Weapon, please."

"Yes, sir." The guard reached behind the fortified position and raised a rifle. He handed it over to Collin.

Collin immediately did a function check on the rifle and then took up a position on the bridge. He knelt down, adjusted his location and then flattened himself out into a prone firing position.

The torches began an odd and fast pattern. It took a few moments to realize what was happening. The Vipers were not running, they were mounted.

"Cavalry," Collin said to himself. "They have a damn cavalry."

Chapter Thirty-Two

Doctor Julie Horner stood at the bottom of the stairs when Collin yelled for Koby. She knew what was happening.

Some sort of attack was happening, which is why the soldier came looking for Collin. For her, the timing worked out perfectly. She was the only council member in the basement. Collin was busy at the bridge and Koby was upstairs, making for the church bell to alert the town.

Julie ran in place for a moment, and then bolted into the hallway.

"Get up there, now!" she shouted at the two guards. Julie raised her hands above her head to catch her breath. "Come on, go! We're under attack."

The guards exchanged glances. They shifted a little, but didn't move.

"Ma'am-"

"Don't ma'am me. I work for a living."

"Um, right. Dr. Horner, we're on orders from General War to guard the prisoner and make sure he doesn't escape," the shorter one said.

For a second, Julie couldn't remember his name. Then it came to her in a flash. She put on her "mom face" and called them out by name.

"Richard Allen Cruz, Paul Oliver Edwards, I have known you both since you were six years old. Do you really think I would free this man? Don't be foolish. Goshen needs you. General War needs you. Go help your fellow Eagles," she said, the urgency in her voice seemed to stir them both. But they hadn't quite decided to move yet. She needed them to leave.

"General War asked me to come down here and tell you his orders. He wants you up there to help him." She jerked her thumb over her shoulders and scowled at them. "He's probably waiting for you at the bridge, right now. Move your ass!"

"Okay. Are you sure?" the short one called Richard asked. They both still seemed reluctant.

"Look, I'm not the one doing any fighting. And I'm not your direct commander, but he asked me to relay the order to you," she said with a shrug. "Goshen needs your help. Don't let us down. Hurry."

"Are you sure you'll be okay?"

"He's in a cell. I'm out here. No one is going to come to the church because you guys will be out there fighting off the enemy," she said, sliding over an empty chair. "I'll just sit here and wait for you two to come back."

The taller one looked at his partner and nodded. "Let's go. Be careful, Dr. Horner."

"Eagles strike."

"Vipers die," the two Eagles said with smiles. They dashed down the hallway and jogged up the stairs.

Julie turned to face the cell door. She hadn't seen the pastor for some time now. This would be the first time since finding out that he was the one who murdered her baby.

She took a deep breath and pulled out the bunch of keys from her pocket that she'd lifted from Collin when they hugged outside. Julie felt a rush of excitement at her ruse. She felt like a rebellious teenager again. Except she wasn't. This was life: real, hard, and unforgiving.

Julie unlocked the door and pulled it open. She put the keys back in her pocket and palmed a small object.

Pastor Pendell was kneeling on the ground, praying. His back was to her.

"Forgive me, Father, for I have sinned," he said.

It was the last thing she heard him say before three small bangs cracked in the air. She lowered her small .22 caliber pistol and stepped inside the cell.

Julie shot Pastor Pendell in the back, three times. She was happy that all of her shots hit him. She stole a look down the hallway, worried that someone may have entered the basement. But it was all clear.

Blood welled up from the holes and he toppled onto his side. He groaned in pain, clutching his chest and curled into a ball. Underneath him, blood pooled up and spread out on the smooth concrete.

Julie walked up to him and looked down at her handiwork. He turned his head and looked at her. His face contorted in pain and a ribbon of blood leaked out of the side of his mouth. She noticed he didn't have exit wounds and smiled.

"Good," she said softly. "The bullets stayed inside. You know .22 caliber rounds just tumble around inside, ripping through tissue and organs. Just the kind of suffering you deserve."

Pendell's mouth opened slowly. A blood bubble filled his mouth, but no words came out. When his mouth started to close, the bubble popped and left a splatter of blood on his lips. Their eyes met, his filled with pain, hers filled with a mother's fury. Julie felt no compassion for him or regret for her actions.

"I'm…I'm…s-" he sputtered and specks of blood covered his face and neck.

"Don't even say it," she said, with a wave of her hand. "I have no patience for your lies anymore."

She pulled a syringe from another pocket. Instead of the red serum that she'd shown to Collin, this one was the green serum that Pendell had ordered her to give to Doris. The treatment that had caused her so much pain and torment in her final moments in this world.

Pendell saw what it was. When realization dawned on his face, he tried to pull himself away from her, but he was too weak.

Julie held up the syringe and slowly uncapped it.

"Do you remember her screams? The way her body convulsed?" she asked, rage dripped from her words like venom.

"I'm...sorry..." he gasped. His eyes were wide, panicked.

"Not as sorry as you'll be when you're burning in hell," Julie said. With that, she stuck him in the shoulder with the needle and emptied the contents into his body.

She dropped the syringe and crouched on the ground to watch him suffer. Her observation was very clinical. As a doctor, she was familiar with pain, suffering, and death. Especially since the fever outbreak all those years ago, she became almost numb to death.

Doris had cracked her armor and the death of Anna had disintegrated it. The pain she felt now ached in the marrow of her bones. It was a visceral pain, emanating from the center of her soul and burning through every cell of her body.

Pendell arched his back and began to shake in far less time than it took Doris. Julie wondered if it had to do with the loss of blood. If there was less blood volume to deal with, did that mean the effects hit faster? She wasn't sure.

His spasms grew in strength, forcing Julie to stand up and move back. She walked backward to the door. Her eyes never left Pendell's body; she didn't want to miss a single moment of his suffering. For her, his actions would cause a lifetime of pain. It felt unfair that his suffering would be over so quick.

Pendell groaned and spasmed, twitching on the floor. Even through the battle raging inside him, Pendell spotted Julie and crawled toward her as best as he could. Amazingly, he made it to one knee, which made Julie think she may have to shoot him again. Convulsions struck and he vomited blood onto the floor.

He tipped over sideways, slow motion almost. When he hit the floor, he was gone.

Pastor Pendell was no more.

Chapter Thirty-Three

Personnel ran in every direction as Collin issued orders for the defense of Goshen.

One of the sergeants was rallying the civilians and putting them into some semblance of a formation so he could address them. Collin had seriously underestimated the firepower that the civilians had in their personal arsenals. As a group, they were nearly as well armed as the Eagles and some of them were better equipped.

God bless the Second Amendment, he thought.

The Vipers halted their advance out in the fields. They were presumably setting up some kind of fighting positions. Collin dispatched the remaining sniper teams and told them to watch for his signal, but that if they saw any kind of armored contraptions like last time, they were free to fire as they saw fit. All of the Eagle's Nests were full; a team lay atop the wall that crossed over the bridge. They didn't have any cover but lying down they made a small target and the two Eagles had asked to be stationed there. Collin reluctantly agreed. He already had three sniper teams on the dam. That was more than enough.

Hunters and the outdoorsmen augmented the Eagles on the front lines. There were two large sandbagged fighting positions on the far side of the bridge. They also had sandbagged and fortified fighting positions in town, just in case the wall or the bridge was breached.

His plan called for half of the civilians to be split into groups to secure choke points in town and slow any Viper advance. The other half would wait in the woods, to be called down in a flanking maneuver if things got real tough. Collin hoped, and almost prayed, that it wouldn't come to that.

The church bell stopped ringing anew although its echoes could be heard rebounding through the valley.

"Sir, all of the fixed fighting positions are manned and ready," SGT O'Bannon said. He was a short, serious man with a sharp nose and a quick wit.

"Thank you, Sergeant. Carry on."

What the Eagles of Goshen lacked in manpower, they more than made up for in firepower, training, and defenses. If the Vipers had suddenly upgraded to firearms instead of attacking with bows and arrows, Goshen wouldn't stand a chance. As things stood, Collin was confident of their ability to defend themselves and in fact, crush the Vipers. It was as close to a fair fight as they could hope for.

Collin stood in front of the bridge, on the town side of the river. He watched the Vipers and tried to decode their movements. He didn't want to be overly focused on this display in case it was a diversion. So, he'd ordered hunters to take up watch along the flanks. He sent a pair of woodsmen to the dam to watch the mountainsides in case the Vipers had morphed into mountain goats. He gave the woodsmen instructions to also keep an eye on the lake behind the dam for anyone crossing.

Koby appeared beside Collin, pulling him from his thoughts.

"This looks bad," Koby said, obviously impressed by the display before them.

"Honestly, it's shit tactics. Why would you announce your presence so far in advance of an attack?" Collin said, crossing his arms. "It makes me wonder what they're really up to. They seem smart enough, but this is not smart." He pointed at the hundreds of torches lighting up the forest.

He sighed.

"Is it rigged?" he asked, waving at the bridge.

"You know it. I placed the C4 myself," Koby said with a grin. He pulled out a radio and held it out before him, admiring it. "It's all wired up. All you have to do when you're ready is turn to channel sixty-nine, press call button and boom shakalaka."

Collin shot his friend a look. "Shaka- what?"

"Boom. It goes boom," Koby said, shaking his head in exasperation. "Channel 69, press the button, and boom. Has no one in this town ever watched basketball?"

Collin chuckled and accepted the radio. He slid it into a pouch on his MOLLE vest, which he retrieved from his house, along with his personal rifle.

"It had to be channel sixty-nine, didn't it?" Collin smiled.

"You know it," Koby said again.

The Vipers began to chant. It started low, nearly inaudible like the murmur of a peaceful stream. Their chant began to build up in volume, slowly, steadily like a storm.

"That sounds ominous," Collin said, frowning. He put a hand on Koby's elbow and led him over to the fighting position near the right-hand corner of the bridge. They stood behind it and slightly to the side, still in the street that led to the bridge, but at least they weren't smack dab in the middle of the bridge. No sense in making themselves easy targets if this was the launch of the attack.

"You're right," Koby said. "But at least they don't have drums."

Collin wasn't entirely sure that drums would make it worse, but he couldn't say for sure. Instead he continued watching the Vipers' movement.

The chant rose in volume and then peaked. It sounded like they said, "Make way" but it was hard to hear clearly. Whether it was or not, was irrelevant, because the torches parted neatly. Each side parted and widened, a seam ran through the crowd, until a dark, torch free path cut straight through their formation.

"A rider," Koby said.

"I see it." Collin brought his rifle up to the ready position and flicked the off the safety.

Everyone waited to see what Collin would do. He hadn't given the order to attack yet and it was clear that many of the Eagles wanted to strike hard at the enemy before they had a chance to hit first. It was tempting to unleash them on the Vipers, but he was concerned about the boy that looked so much like his son and what role he played in all this.

Collin looked up at the Eagle's Nest above the bridge. A soldier looked back at him, apparently waiting to see what he was going to do.

"Three flares with an even spread," he said.

The soldier nodded and turned away. Mere seconds later, flares hissed through the air and popped open high above the farmland. Suddenly blanketed with light, the formation of Vipers looked slightly less disturbing. But it also brought into focus just how many Vipers there were.

Atop a fine looking horse, sat a young man in his late twenties or early thirties. He had a beard, long curly hair and a white flag clenched in his hand, which he waved every few steps.

He seemed to be looking directly at Collin. It was unnerving because Collin had never seen this man before so the stranger shouldn't be able to pick him out of a crowd.

"I think he's here for you," Koby said, nudging his arm.

Collin moved his arm. "I can see that." He stepped away from the fighting position.

"Wait! Don't go out there," Koby said quickly. "I wasn't suggesting that."

"I have to," he said.

"We've got you covered, sir," said one of the Eagles.

"I know you do. Thanks." Collin took a deep breath and walked toward the bridge.

He made his way to the center, and stood with his rifle at the ready, watching the horse rider approach. As the man neared, Collin noticed that he had a bow slung over his arm, a quiver of arrows over his shoulder, another quiver on the side of his saddle, and a sword, of all things, swaying with the movement of the horse.

"Like Goddamned, Robin Hood over here. What're we in the seventeenth century?" he muttered to himself. It was as if medieval times made a comeback. He shook his head in disbelief.

Collin decided to move up to at least level with the other two fighting positions. Power projection was key here and he didn't want to make Goshen look weak by staying back away from the action. He would face the horse rider on his own terms.

When he reached the other side of the bridge, he checked out the two fighting positions and nodded at the men. They returned the gesture and looked back at the approaching rider.

"We got your back, sir," one of them said.

"And I have yours, soldier." He felt another surge of pride as he walked out to meet the rider. He was a little nervous, not for his safety but for the well-being of the town and the only friends he had left in this world.

Keeping his rifle ready, Collin walked as casually as he could for another twenty yards into the field. The rider was maybe fifty yards from him. Shadows traversed his face under the shifting light of the flares floating toward the ground. It was inadequate light but it was all they had. He took in the sight of the man before him.

"Halt right there," Collin said, shouting to ensure the man heard him above the growl of the bonfires that still burned in the background. "Dismount and approach on foot."

The man on the horse pulled back on the reins and slid off the saddle. He thumped onto the ground and Collin half expected him to be wearing pieces of armor, but he wore a normal battle dress uniform, like the Army. He stood by his horse for a long moment. His eyes were darting over the scene behind Collin.

He looked wild to Collin. If they sailed the open seas and came upon an uncharted island and this guy emerged from the jungle, it would be less surprising than it was now. He didn't appear to be carrying anything other than the bow and sword. Neither weapon was especially quick to draw and use. He slung his rifle over his shoulder and placed his hands over his belt buckle, close enough to his pistol to draw it at a moment's notice.

"Impressive defenses that you've built here," the man said. His voice was low but still sounded young.

Collin just stared at him.

The man stepped forward, closing the distance between them. He didn't look scared but like any smart predator, he was weary of a new adversary. They were both vulnerable, alone, and facing dozens of weapons aimed at them. The young man walked toward Collin with confidence.

Collin didn't move. He'd already made his move.

The man was only ten yards away. Collin figured he would stop but the man kept walking, slowly. He narrowed his eyes at the man, but allowed him to continue.

Five yards. Three yards. One yard.

The man stopped just beyond arms reach.

They watched each other for several long moments. Neither man moved or spoke.

Collin searched the eyes of the man across from him for clues about his intentions, but they revealed nothing sinister. In fact, his eyes seemed to twinkle with curiosity, understanding and…joy? It didn't fit. None of the pieces matched up at that moment.

Out of his peripheral vision, Collin saw the torches the Vipers held. Behind him were the Eagles and citizens of Goshen. Yet before him stood a man that conflicted with the setting.

"My name is General Collin War," he said, his gaze never wavering. It felt funny to use the new title, one that the town had apparently bestowed upon him. "You are trespassing on the lands of Goshen. Turn back, leave this area, and never come back."

A wide grin spread underneath his beard and the man chuckled.

"You are outgunned and as you said, our defenses are impressive."

"You mistake my laughter…General War," said the man, wiping the corner of his eye. "There is no need to introduce yourself. I know you better than you could ever imagine."

Collin was skeptical about that claim. "And who might you be?"

"I am Brady, leader of the Vipers."

"Brady," Collin repeated softly. The name sounded familiar. He looked hard at the man. He couldn't recall his face, yet something was familiar. With a grunt, he said, "Brady, I advise you to take your men and leave this valley. Forever. If you attack Goshen again, I will end you."

Brady tilted his head and narrowed his eyes at Collin. "Attack Goshen?"

"We will destroy you if you attack Goshen again."

"My, my, general. We wouldn't need to attack Goshen, even if we wanted to. I could have my Vipers control these fields and the entire valley. You wouldn't have grain to feed your livestock. Without the livestock you'd lose a large portion of your food supply. Don't think that I don't know about your greenhouses and indoor gardens either." He folded his arms over his chest. "If we wanted to cripple Goshen, we could destroy the dam, and sit back while everything those people have worked to build is washed away."

"Of course we could raid your town, kill the men, capture the women and wrest away the small amount of control the Council has, but despite what that pastor of yours has told you, we are not the monsters," he continued. "We haven't attacked Goshen in years. In the short time span since you awoke from your coma, we haven't attacked a single time."

"You must take me for a fool then because I woke up to your snakes trying to attack me," Collin said.

Brady lowered his hands and clasped them behind his back. His head drooped, tossing his hear down over his face. It waved back and forth as he shook it. "No, no, no. I'm afraid you have it all wrong, General. We did not attack the hospital," he said, looking up at Collin. "We were on a rescue mission."

"Horseshit, Anna could sneak out anytime she wanted to. There was no reason for a rescue mission."

"That mission was never about saving Anna," Brady said. He spread his hands out wide.

Collin frowned. "Who were you trying to rescue then?"

"The mission was to save you...dad." Brady pointed at him and smiled.

He was sure he hadn't heard Brady clearly. Collin tried to speak but his mouth was suddenly dry and the words didn't come to him.

Brady took a step forward, looking at him intently. "The mission was to rescue you, dad."

Collin looked him over; it was hard to see with the long hair and beard, the grime on his face and his wardrobe. But he would be about the same age as his son, if...

Can it be? He thought. It hardly seemed real. Yet the words rang with truth. Warmth spread through him, tingling down his limbs and heightening his senses. Was this his son? Every day since he'd awoken, Collin had wanted to find his family but he'd been redirected and used as a weapon against his own flesh and blood.

The boy from his dreams had grown into the man before him.

His son. Brady War.

Collin gasped and leaned forward. "My son."

Brady leaned forward and enveloped his father in an embrace.

"I've been waiting so long for this moment, dad," Brady said, squeezing tightly.

"Me too. I thought I'd lost you forever," Collin said to Brady. Then he remembered something. "But the boy...the boy in the field."

"He's my son, Hunter. Your grandson," Brady said, pulling back. Tears of joy streamed down the small window of skin above his beard, and wet his whiskers. He held his father by the shoulders and smiled at him. "Now, do we battle or would you like to stand down your men and meet your grandson?"

Collin burst out laughing and a tear fell into his mouth but the bitter salt was nothing compared to the rush of emotion that he felt.

Chapter Thirty-Four

Under the golden light of sunrise, Collin walked slowly toward the bridge over the Goshen River. Kobyashi and Dr. Horner walked beside him as they approached the crowd gathered near the crossing.

Collin looked at the bridge, a symbol of what they were about to do.

The crowd parted to let the three of them through. The remainder of the council had met after the revelations the night before and decided to call a town meeting at the bridge first thing in the morning. Word had spread quickly.

Collin looked over his shoulder and looked at the faces in the crowd on the Goshen side of the river. He smiled and nodded at them, knowing that he was doing the right thing for their future, for everyone's future. For the survival of the town, the country, and the human race.

As he started to walk up the arched bridge, he took a deep breath and despite himself, said a small prayer.

When he reached the apex of the bridge over the Goshen River, he climbed up onto the railing so everyone could see him. He looked upon his people with the stern but loving gaze of a father. On one side sat the town, with its residents crowded around the bridge. On the other side, were the Vipers, led by his son, Brady. They were so numerous that they had filled the rows between the sprouting crops so that others began to ring the edge of the forest and line the river's edge.

Collin felt a deep sense of calm as he stood atop the railing. Below him on the bridge, stood Kobyashi and Dr. Horner. They were united in their cause and in their plan for the future of the two factions.

Brady led hundreds of Vipers, warriors and civilians alike, to the doorstep of Goshen. It was a stunning sight to see how many people could have come against them. Collin turned to look at the town's residents. Most of them watched the Vipers, people that, for nearly two decades, had been their mortal enemies. Their faces reflected their internal struggle: fear, hope, distrust, anger, and curiosity.

The two sides were present and accounted for; each side staring at the other. So, Collin raised his arms for their attention.

In one hand, Collin held a radio. Koby had disconnected the other radio from the explosives rigged to blow up the very bridge they stood on. Instead, Koby connected it to a speaker system, effectively turning it into a makeshift PA system. He pressed and held the button on the radio. He was about to talk, but stopped.

He smiled and released the button.

He took a deep breath to steady his nerves and started over. He held the button and said, "Welcome everyone. Thank you for coming out for this vital and historic moment."

Many of the people surrounding the bridge found the strength to break their stares and focus on Collin.

"Over the years, our two groups have grown apart. We were, and still are Americans, yet people in power have needlessly separated us. We have survived the terrible tragedy of the fever and in the process; we've been pitted against each other. Vipers versus Eagles. Goshen versus outsiders. And because of this, many terrible tragedies have transpired. Many precious lives have been lost."

"Goshen was full of secrets before I awoke. Since then, many of the secrets have been revealed." Collin held the radio before him in both hands, as if he was at a candlelight vigil. "But I believe there are more to come. Things have not always been as the way they seemed. In fact, many of the things that we thought we knew about Goshen, the Vipers, HAGS, and even the fever were lies. That much is painfully, tragically clear."

He paused for a breath, and to let it all sink in.

"Since I've woken up, I've learned to adjust to a new way of life. Many things have changed but some are still the same. One of the most surprising developments has been the fracturing of our society."

Heads nodded in agreement. Collin had overheard conversations in the cafeteria and he knew how they felt. No one liked the way things had turned out. Yet they allowed themselves to be steered in a direction that chalked up the abhorrent behavior to survival.

"Now we have an opportunity to unite our two sides."

Murmurs spread through the Goshen side.

Collin eyed the crowd with a sympathetic look on his face. Then he keyed the radio and raised his voice.

"I'd like to call Brady War to the bridge," Collin said, looking across the bridge at the man who had turned out to be his son. Their eyes met and they both smiled.

He climbed down to meet Brady.

The leader of the Vipers, Goshen's enemy for more than a decade was now about to shake hands with the presumptive leader of the town.

Brady smiled and extended his hand to Collin. Their hands clasped firmly and both men shook heartily.

"We welcome you to Goshen," Collin said to his son. It broadcast from the speakers and the crowd stirred, but no one protested.

Kobyashi and Dr. Horner started clapping. Slowly, more and more people joined in. Collin looked around and most people on each side looked hopeful. On the Goshen side, he noticed a few backs as several residents walked away from the bridge.

Collin climbed back up onto the railing so everyone could see him clearly. With a bright smile, Collin looked at the people on both sides of the bridge. His people.

He raised his hand above his head to calm the clapping.

"We are on the brink of a great leap forward. Uniting against HAGS, with a common cause of survival, we will race into a more secure future for our families. But make no mistake…" Collin's voice trailed off as the steady whoomp-whoomp-whoomp of helicopter blades reverberated through the valley. He found his voice and finished his sentence, "Everything is about to change."

Just then, three helicopters, flying in formation, crested the mountain peaks backlit by the sun.

Even without seeing the markings on the choppers, Collin knew who it was.

"HAGS." Koby muttered.

Collin nodded slowly as the choppers approached.

Thank You

Thank you for reading Praying for War. Find out what happens next in **Living for War**, book two of The Collin War Chronicles, coming January 2017.

Become A Warrior

Claim two FREE audiobooks now by becoming a Warrior. Receive new release updates and subscriber only exclusives at: HathawayAGS.com

What now?

Please take a moment to write an honest review of Praying for War on your favorite review platform (Amazon, Goodreads, etc). It doesn't have to be long. For today's authors, every bit of exposure helps, and when you leave a review it helps the right readers find our work.

About the Authors

Tim Moon is a writer and avid hiker from Washington State. Tim was an editor for the Salmon Creek Journal at Washington State University, where he graduated with a BA degree in political science and a minor in psychology. Tim is a lifelong fan of science fiction and fantasy and primarily writes in those genres. He loves to travel, go backpacking, play with his dog, and watch movies. After five years working airport security, Tim moved to South Korea to teach English and wrote Dead Apocalypse. Tim currently lives in China with his beautiful wife. For more information about Tim Moon and his books, visit his website http://www.timdmoon.com

W.C. Hoffman is a lifelong resident of Michigan. If you took a guy who loves to hunt and fish and then made him a professional magician with a decade long career in law enforcement who also enjoys his work as an ordained wedding officiant you would have W.C. Hoffman. A loving husband and father of two, his writing utilizes the outdoors knowledge he has gained over the years he has spent chasing game in the wildest areas of North America. Hoffman's unique life skills are often evident in his novels. For more information about W.C. Hoffman and his books, visit his website http://www.wchoffman.com

Made in the USA
Middletown, DE
13 August 2016